CHARLOTTE BINGHAM

The Nightingale Sings

'A racy tale of love and heartbreak . . . This is a novel
rich in dramatic surprises, with a large cast of vivid
characters whose antics will have you frantically turning
the pages'
Daily Mail

To Hear A Nightingale

'A lovely sprawling saga with a heroine you can't fail
to love'
Prima

The Business

'Probably more sun-tan lotion will be spilled on the
pages of Charlotte Bingham's *The Business* than any
other book this summer . . . the ideal beach read'
Homes and Gardens

In Sunshine Or In Shadow

'Superbly written . . . a romantic novel that is romantic in
the true sense of the word'
Daily Mail

Stardust

'Charlotte Bingham has produced a long, absorbing read,
perfect for holidays, which I found hard to lay aside as
the plot twisted and turned with intriguing results'
Sunday Express

Change Of Heart

'Her imagination is thoroughly original. This book has a
fairy-tale cover containing a fairy tale, which is all the
more delightful as it is not something one expects from a
modern novel . . . It's heady stuff'
Daily Mail

'A l

D0992725

NANNY

Charlotte Bingham

BANTAM BOOKS
TORONTO · NEW YORK · LONDON · SYDNEY · AUCKLAND

NANNY

All of the characters in this book are fictitious,
and any resemblance to actual persons, living or dead,
is purely coincidental

A BANTAM BOOK : 0 553 40496 2

Originally published in Great Britain by Doubleday,
a division of Transworld Publishers Ltd

PRINTING HISTORY
Doubleday edition published 1993
Bantam Books edition published 1994

Set in 10/11pt Linotype Plantin by
Falcon Graphic Art Ltd,
Wallington, Surrey.

Bantam Books are published by Transworld Publishers Ltd,
61–63 Uxbridge Road, Ealing, London W5 5SA,
in Australia by Transworld Publishers (Australia) Pty Ltd,
15–25 Helles Avenue, Moorebank, NSW 2170,
and in New Zealand by Transworld Publishers (NZ) Ltd,
3 William Pickering Drive, Albany, Auckland.

Reproduced, printed and bound in Great Britain by
Cox & Wyman Ltd, Reading, Berks.

For my beloved partner Terence Brady, in memory of one particularly perfect morning of creation which this book commemorates, but most of all for the hundreds of joyous hours spent together giving birth through the fingers.

THE NANNY

First exhibited in the Royal Academy 1954

The painting is of a young woman in a large straw hat banded by a broad white ribbon. She kneels on the fresh green grass. Beside her is a large wheeled navy blue perambulator, covered by a white lace coverlet. Nothing can be seen of the baby, and little of the young woman's face which is bent over her needlework.

We must presume that the baby was fast asleep when the painter set up his easel, because the scene is so peaceful. Perhaps the two of them, the baby and his guardian, are unaware even that the artist is painting them. Perhaps that is why the young woman seems so happily unselfconscious, her feet tucked decorously under her long skirts, her head bent towards her sewing, a finely threaded needle between her thumb and her index finger, her left hand holding the blue ribboned baby garment that she is making.

The outline of the face is not clear and yet somehow the onlooker senses that the girl in her pale blue uniform with its crisp white collar and cuffs, stiff white belt, and long decorative skirts, is lovely. She may even be beautiful. But what we can be certain of is that she is a nanny, and that however much she loves the baby in the pram, he does not belong to her.

O N E

Keston, Buckinghamshire. 1907.

It was a bitterly cold December morning, still and crystal clear. A deep frost lay on the ground, icing the dark brown furrows of the ploughed fields and whitening the dull green of the winter grass, while above the dawn sky turned slowly from a faint pink to a light and cloudless winter blue. Grace pulled the eiderdown she had taken from her bed tighter before huddling even lower into the cane armchair by the window, pulling her knees under her chin, and tucking her bare feet further under the end of the cover. As she wiped the window glass with the sleeve of her flannel nightgown she suddenly shivered all over, this time not from the cold but from excitement as she watched the landscape being slowly illuminated before her. It was so cold there was even a frost on the inside of the window, but as long as Grace kept breathing on the pane of glass nearest her, and rubbing it constantly with her sleeve, she could see the day awakening and study the colour and the perspective of the scene outside her window.

'Grey,' she whispered to herself. 'The trees aren't brown, you chump, they're grey. They're ash, and mole, and silver. They're anything but just brown. They're greeny-grey, and mouse. And in the shadow, in this light, the back of the big oak is almost black.'

Again she wiped the pane of glass clear and pressed

her face almost to it, frowning as she tried to make sense of all the colours she could now see in the picture. She stared and then sat back with a sigh.

'Oh blow,' she muttered, reconsigning the camel-haired brush to a clay beaker in front of her on the window-sill, and tearing the page from the pad on her knee. 'Blow it – why can't I get it *right*?'

The sound of paper being crumpled or perhaps Grace's whispered admonitions were enough to wake the small fair-haired figure in the other bed.

'Grace?' Lottie said, sitting up and rubbing the sleep from her eyes. 'Grace, what are you doing?'

'Sssshhh,' Grace replied. 'Nothing. Go back to sleep.'

'I can't,' Lottie said after barely a minute. 'I'm too excited.'

Grace smiled but said nothing. She was too involved with her sketch, tracing a barely visible outline of the landscape on to a fresh sheet of cartridge paper with her softest pencil. She knew why her younger sister was so excited. Today was Prize-giving Day at the school, and Lottie's heart was set on getting the English Prize, something which Grace happened to know her sister had won because Mrs Jenkins, their teacher, had already told Grace, having of course asked her to keep it a secret.

'What do you think, Grace?'

Lottie was now behind her, whispering in her ear and looking over her shoulder, wrapped up in her blue quilt and kneeling on all fours.

'Do you think I really will get a prize?'

'You must have a good chance,' Grace whispered. 'Look what good marks you've had all term for your essays.'

'You're going to get the Scripture Prize,' Lottie said, reaching down into the wastepaper-basket to retrieve Grace's crumpled discard. 'Everyone says so. Why did you throw this away? It's so good, I'll have it.'

'I can't get the light right.' Grace glanced at the unfinished watercolour her sister had straightened back

10

out and laid on the bed beside her. 'The trouble with the dawn is that it happens so fast. I watch it every day, but I still can't get it right. This morning, for instance, with this frost.' She looked longingly out of the window at all the magnificence of the still whitened landscape in front of them. 'If only I could have got it right. The frost on the branches was so heavy it looked like snow. And as the sun started to come up the trees looked as though they were on fire.'

Lottie straightened the last of the creases out from the rejected painting and sat back admiringly.

'It's a pity there isn't a prize for art,' she said. 'You'd win it easily, Grace, really you would.'

She leaned forward and kissed Grace on the cheek, before crawling back up her bed and diving in under the covers.

Dawn had broken now, and the deeply frozen countryside lay still under a slowly changing light. Distantly the church clock struck seven while below them in the house came the clatter of iron and the rattle of coal as the maid stoked up the kitchen range. Grace painted in silence for the next half-hour while Lottie fell back into a new sleep. She painted without once looking up, she painted entirely from memory for the very first time, as an experiment, and by the time Mary knocked first on her mother's door and then on theirs she was so absorbed she barely noticed the call.

'Miss Grace? Miss Lottie? It's nearly half past seven, Miss Grace!'

Another five minutes and it was done. It was there. A faint imprint of an early December dawn in a mallow pink wash, shadows of dark grey and grey-green trees fingered in rose frost, the plough burnt umber by the still unseen sun, the spikes of the frozen grass the colour of skin.

'Gosh, Grace,' Lottie said, sitting and pulling on her woollen stockings. 'That is excellent! You must show that to Mrs Jenkins!'

'Sssshhh, Lottie,' Grace warned her sister as she hid the painting away. 'You never know who might hear.'

'It's so silly,' Lottie protested. 'When you can paint as well as you can.'

Grace didn't reply, even though she knew it to be true; it was pretty silly that her drawing and painting had always to be kept a secret from their parents, but there it was, the subject was taboo since both their parents were of the confirmed opinion that an interest in art was not just bad, it was positively unhealthy, and certainly something to be actively discouraged in respectable families. Even the very mention of the subject was forbidden ever since Grace's twelfth birthday when she had shown her parents a pastel drawing she had done of Lottie in her night things.

One look at Grace's depiction of Lottie in a sweetly rumpled state had Father declaring art and painting to be a dangerous and wasteful vanity, since it gave objects that people normally ignored a totally unworthy significance, most particularly the human frame. So as usual Grace put her latest painting carefully away in the folder with all her other artwork, first securing it with strong red ribbon, then wrapping it between several sheets of newspaper before hiding it away in her usual secret place under the floorboards. She was longing to show Mrs Jenkins her latest watercolour, but knew she must be patient and wait for an afternoon when her mother was out visiting.

Since it was Prize-giving, there was no school that morning, so once Grace and Lottie were dressed all they themselves were required to do was to help their mother prepare herself for the ceremony. Privately Grace enjoyed the ritual, sitting on the velvet-covered button-back chair in her mother's bedroom while Mary their maid fussed and fluttered round her employer, smoothing and straightening imagined crinkles out of each of the proposed dresses, and then carefully adjusting the set and angle of a seemingly endless supply of hats. As each ensemble was paraded Mother would demand a verdict of Grace, which would then be promptly ignored, while Lottie sat on the dressing-table stool with her hands under the backs of her knees, fidgeting constantly and swinging her ever growing legs backwards

12

and forwards, much to her mother's very evident irritation.

Finally, after over an hour of parading herself in front of her two children, Millicent Merrill chose, although with no great certainty, a day dress in cream serge, with a fifteen-pleated skirt, double buttoned front, chin-high collar and the newly fashionable narrowed sleeves puffed only at the shoulder.

'That's very smart, Mother,' Grace volunteered as her mother turned herself one hundred and eighty degrees in front of her full length dressing mirror. 'I don't think we've seen you in that before.'

'Yes we have,' Lottie began before catching a warning look from her sister. 'No we haven't,' she amended hurriedly. 'I'm sorry, I thought that was the dress you wore to church Sunday before last.'

'I like the bands of blue on the skirt, Mother,' Grace said, hoping Lottie's muddled remarks had gone unnoticed. 'And on the bodice. And those panels at the wrist. It makes the dress look so graceful.'

Their mother stood staring at herself in silence, and then put her hands either side of her tiny tightly corseted waist.

'When I first married your father, he could touch finger and thumb around me,' she sighed. 'Now will you look at me.'

Grace looked while Lottie busied herself trying to make her hands meet around her own unbound waist. Millicent Merrill's figure was quite remarkable, a fact of which Grace knew her mother was well aware, otherwise she would never have spent so much time drawing attention to it. Unrestricted by stays her waist measured less than twenty-three inches, while her hips were a slender thirty-four. Among the rest of the matrons assembled for the Prize-giving ceremony, Grace knew her mother would look more like a daughter than a wife.

'I'm not at all sure about this hat.'

Grace snapped out of her reverie as her mother turned round to face her. She was wearing a lozenge-shaped hat made of satin which parted her dark curling hair in the middle.

'What do you think, Grace?'

'I think it's perfect, Mother,' Grace replied. 'It's exceedingly smart.'

'Perhaps. But it gives the entirely wrong emphasis,' her mother insisted. 'See?' She turned back to the mirror. 'It's almost too military. I think after all, no matter what you all say, I think my first choice was the right one. With the ostrich feathers. A wide brim does have the effect of making the hips look just that much slimmer.'

'Anyone would think she was going to meet the king,' Lottie moaned when they were finally dismissed and sent off to get their overcoats. 'Everyone will stare. As usual.'

Which everyone did when the three of them arrived and made their way to the seats reserved for them in one of the front rows. There was no one else in the whole parish hall dressed like Millicent Merrill, in her cream dress and her sealskin cape topped off with a dark blue hat emblazoned with yellow-dyed ostrich feathers, nor was there anyone to match her delicate looks and her perfect figure. As a matter of fact the rest of the women seemed to be of a different sex altogether, most of them with younger children than Millicent Merrill but looking ten, twenty years her senior, their charms long lost, their vitality sapped by years of almost continuous pregnancy. Of course Grace knew that Mother realized that she was the object of everyone's attention as she led her children up the aisle, and that being so, now and then she would graciously bestow a smile on one of the other mothers, carefully choosing those of the plainer sort, a queen among her subjects.

Grace felt so sorry for poor Mother, busy imagining that the women were staring at her because they admired her, because they wondered at her elegance and admired her refinement, for that was how Millicent Merrill thought of herself, as an object of these women's reverence. It never occurred to her, because it could never occur to her, because it would be quite outside her comprehension,

14

that the reason why the other mothers stared at her was because they all hated her.

Unfortunately Grace knew why her mother was always the object of such intense attention. She'd known it from the first day she had started at the National School to which her mother had delivered her in their carriage. It had taken a year for Grace to be accepted by the other children, and even now in this her last term she knew there were still one or two girls who resented her presence, thinking that with such a very rich-looking mother, Lottie and she were out of place at the little National School, and who could blame them? It had been sadly obvious from the very start, if only from their mother's clothes and the smartness of their pony and trap, that Grace and Lottie should really be at a private school.

'You're different, you're not one of us, you're more like one of the gentry,' had been a pretty frequent accusation in the early days. 'What'ud you want to be one of us for?'

Eventually, very eventually, Grace had managed somehow or another to overcome most, if not all, of the prejudice her mother's rich appearance caused, but it had taken a long, long time. Occasionally, when she had wound up at the end of yet another term, unhappy and friendless, she had longed to tell one of her tormentors the truth, which was that if Mother did not insist on spending so very much money on so very many clothes for herself, well, Lottie and herself might well have been able to go to a private school with the so-called 'gentry', but Mother preferred her clothes to their education, and Grace knew this because she heard it over and over again, from Mary, indeed from everyone who called at the back door. In the town the tradesmen mocked Mother, calling her 'jumped up' behind her back, but Grace noticed they never turned her money away.

'The School Prize for English, for pupils twelve years and under,' Canon Cooper announced, bringing Lottie to the edge of her seat, 'goes to Lottie Merrill, Form IV.'

Grace watched with pride as her young sister tossed

15

her fair hair back from her lightly freckled face and in her excitement all but ran up to the green baize-clothed table to collect her award, applauding her ceaselessly all the way up and all the way back. It was remarked by everyone that Mrs Merrill did not applaud her younger daughter, but merely glanced around waiting to receive the appreciative smiles of her neighbours as her own. Her smile soon faded as, having waited until Lottie had returned to her seat, everyone pointedly ignored her and congratulated Lottie.

Five minutes later it was Grace's turn to collect the School Prize for Scripture. Canon Cooper, red-faced and bulbous-nosed, held her slim hand in both of his hot and fleshy ones while he lengthily extolled Grace's diligence, his rheumy eyes meanwhile straying from her fresh pretty face to her lustrous dark hair and then unashamedly to the outline of her breasts under the cotton of her blouse, and finally to her slender and as yet unconstrained waist. As the canon finished his murmured felicitations, Mrs Jenkins took Grace's hand with an almost audible sigh and whispered enigmatically to Grace as the applause restarted that there was another prize awaiting her, a secret one.

Afterwards, during the traditional buffet lunch of sandwiches, iced cakes and lemonade, Canon Cooper attached himself to their party accompanied by his son Everett who was studying for the ministry. Everett, who at five feet three inches tall was a good two inches shorter than Grace, had particularly small eyes, a slack mouth and far too much to say for himself, not one word of which, most unfortunately, was interesting. Grace disliked him for his pompous snobbery even more than for his slack mouth. When in his company, for however short a time, to compose herself and, more importantly, to control Lottie from succumbing to one of her notorious attacks of giggles, Grace had developed the habit of saying 'fancy-that-fancy-that-fancy-that' to his every utterance, while leaving Lottie to count how many she could get through before Everett was called away by his mama.

On the other hand, their mother saw Canon Cooper's

16

eldest son as the perfect match for Grace, a view which, to judge by the enthusiasm with which the canon agreed to certain social arrangements proposed by Millicent Merrill, was warmly reciprocated.

'If I'm forced to marry that loathsome little toad,' Grace whispered as the two girls hung back while their mother wished Mrs Jenkins goodbye, 'I shall kill myself.'

'That would be terrible,' Lottie whispered back. 'For one thing it would be such a waste. Much less of a waste to kill him. Actually, it would be a positive kindness.'

On the way home their mother fortunately was so busy quizzing Grace as to the general success of her outfit, and seeking reassurance that her wide-brimmed ostrich feather-trimmed hat was in fact the right choice, she quite failed to notice the paroxysms of laughter which were silently convulsing her younger daughter.

Lottie's attack of the giggles got even worse when their mother stopped off for a fitting at Mrs Collins'. For as long as the family had lived in Keston, Mrs Collins had been making Millicent Merrill's clothes, but despite the length of their mutual acquaintance, and the regularity of the visits to each other's houses, neither Grace and particularly not Lottie had become in any way immune to the dressmaker's idiosyncrasies.

Mrs Collins in person was a remarkably large woman, which nature had most unfortunately teamed with a very tiny and totally unsuitable high-pitched voice that had the habit of whistling sharply on every sibilant, added to which she had the habit of saying the last part of any sentence more or less at the same time as it was being said to her. This led to a lot of confusion whenever she guessed the end of the other person's sentence wrong, an all too frequent occurrence which when it happened led to Lottie's making a garbled excuse and leaving the room. Whenever Grace visited Mrs Collins by herself or just in the company of her mother she coped perfectly well thanks to her trick of saying poems in her head at moments of *extremis*. Lottie had learned no such safety device, with the result that joint visits invariably ended up with a purple-faced young sister standing outside in the garden with Grace's hankie stuffed in her mouth.

This particular visit proved to be one of the most difficult. Because of their prizes, and for Grace the promise of another secret one, and with Christmas only a week away, the girls were already in high spirits which even their mother with her constant litany of small woes failed to damp. In fact they were so busy chattering about the holiday ahead as they sat in Mrs Collins' parlour they quite failed to notice the unusually sombre atmosphere. So too did their mother, but then there was nothing unusual in that because Millicent Merrill was always wrapped up with her own affairs, so much so that one day Lottie had persuaded Grace to take home her friend Joyce from school instead of her, the bet being that with their father away as usual on business their mother wouldn't even notice, which indeed she hadn't until well past teatime when Lottie had triumphantly emerged from the bushes in the front garden to reveal her real self to her mother. Mother had not been amused, but at least she had had the grace to give Joyce tea until her own mother, unaware of the practical joke, had arrived to pick up her daughter and hurry her home from the house of the gentrified Merrills.

So it was less than surprising that Millicent Merrill noticed nothing in the least untoward in her dressmaker's parlour. Neither in all fairness initially did Grace, who was far too busy working out if and how she could get to Mrs Jenkins and pick up her secret prize before having to go on to tea at the Rectory. Her only chance was to prolong her mother's appointment with Mrs Collins, and there was only one way she could do that, namely to give her wholehearted approval to the dressmaker's latest creation.

'So. What do you think, Grace? Lottie?' their mother enquired, appearing from behind the screen in the corner of the room in a violet visiting dress. 'This is the very latest material, Mrs Collins assures me. A Flemish silk.'

'Flemish silk, that's right, Mrs Merrill,' the dressmaker repeated through a mouthful of pins. 'Known as *fail*.'

'*Faille*,' Millicent Merrill corrected with a small sigh and a smile. '*Faille*.'

'*Fey*, yes that's right,' Mrs Collins echoed, down on her knees now, adjusting the hem. 'Perfect for the new shape. For this new tighter fashion. Clings, you see. Clings so much better than brocade. And glassy taffetas, of course.'

'*Glacé*, Dorothy,' Millicent Merrill once more corrected. '*Glacé* taffetas. My dear husband brought the material back from his last continental visit. It's already very much in vogue on the continent, I gather.'

'Vogue on the continent you hear you gather, yes that's right,' Mrs Collins parroted, letting the back of the hem down a fraction of an inch. 'Just right for all this new tighter fashion.'

'I think it's quite perfect, Mother,' Grace said. 'It makes you look even younger.'

'Really, Grace? Not too young, you don't think?'

'Very young, Mother.' Grace rose and walked all the way round their mother, appraising the cut of the gown. 'And it's so shapely. Particularly across the front. I just love the way this material clings. Don't you, Lottie?'

But Lottie was too busy staring at the cat in front of the fire to reply. Grace walked round behind her mother.

'Oh, you should see it at the back, Mother,' she exclaimed. 'It's wonderful. It looks as though it's moulded to you.'

'Moulded to you that's it, Miss Grace,' Mrs Collins echoed. 'Just as if it's moulded to you, Mrs Merrill.'

'Moulded to me,' Millicent Merrill wondered doubtfully, turning herself halfway round to the dressing mirror. 'I'm not altogether sure we want that, Dorothy. Not moulded.'

'Not moulded no, that's it,' Mrs Collins repeated.

'Is this cat all right?' Lottie suddenly asked, getting to her feet. 'It hasn't moved all the time we've been here.'

'All the time you've been here, well no it wouldn't,' Mrs Collins said in a low tone. 'Because poor pussy's dead.'

'I'm really not at all sure I want the dress this tight,' Millicent Merrill announced obliviously. 'I'm not at all sure Mr Merrill would altogether approve.'

'How long's it been dead?' Lottie asked, coming and taking Grace's hand. 'And why is it dead in here?'

'Dead in here dear, that's right,' Mrs Collins agreed. 'I always lay my cats out in here when they leave, so as their spirits are at peace, you see.'

'No no,' Millicent Merrill decided, after one last sweeping turn in front of the mirror. 'No, I fear the whole look is far too young, and a little too adventurous for Mr Merrill's taste. I think we must unpick and start again, Mrs Collins.'

'Start again, I see,' Mrs Collins agreed, turning her attention away from her dead cat and back to the now rejected visiting dress. 'You want me to start again from the beginning, do you, Mrs Merrill?'

Lottie drew Grace aside as their mother turned sideways to the mirror to regard herself in profile.

'I wonder how long it's been dead,' Lottie whispered. 'It's awfully stiff.'

'No,' their mother announced suddenly. 'I don't think you need to start again from the beginning.'

'The beginning, I see,' Mrs Collins nodded, sticking pins from her mouth into the mushroom attached to her wrist.

'I think what you need do is to unpick the main seams and simply generally loosen the garment. I may have the figure of a girl, but I am in all fairness no longer one.'

'Fairness no longer one no,' Mrs Collins concurred. 'No I know, Mrs Merrill. These things come to us all.'

At this last Lottie's shoulders started to shake.

'Lottie?' Grace whispered. 'Lottie, if you start one of your laughing fits, and Mother notices the cat, she'll leave in disgust and I shall never get to Mrs Jenkins!'

Fortunately their mother was still far too deeply involved with the proper cut and style of her new dress to notice the growing crisis.

'I can't help it!' Lottie gasped, as Grace pinched her

20

arm. 'What would Mother say if she knew she was trying on her new dress with Mrs Collins' cat lying here dead in front of the fire—!'

Once again the very idea proved too much for Lottie and she began to gasp with helpless laughter. Grace quickly turned her towards the door and stifled her sister's moans with her handkerchief.

'Lottie's feeling faint, Mother,' she said, opening the parlour door. 'It's very hot in here, and after the excitement of Prize-giving, I think perhaps a walk would be advisable. May we meet you at the Rectory in time for tea?'

'Yes, yes. But just mind you are not late.'

Their mother waved her consent with one carefully manicured white hand, while keeping the other held to her mouth in a heightened expression of concern as she continued to stand on in the mirror. Grace got her sister outside the house just in time, before Lottie finally succumbed to a real explosion of laughter.

'You know how Mother *hates* anything dead!' Lottie cried, holding her sides, as Grace walked her smartly away up the street. 'The thought of her trying on her new dress with that cat just behind her!'

Grace stared at her and then she too began to laugh, and the two girls linked arms for support as they turned and made their way along the lane that led to Mrs Jenkins' cottage.

The prize was a book called *The Art of Watercolouring*, by Samuel Goodfellow RA. It wasn't a new book, it was one of Mrs Jenkins' own, and bore the inscription *To my dearest H, with my love, Mary. Christmas 1898.*

'This was your husband's,' Grace said with a frown as she closed the already faded crimson cover. 'Are you sure you want me to have it?'

'I would not have given it to you, Grace,' Mrs Jenkins said, with one of her tiny sighs, 'had I not wanted you to have it. Don't you want to know what it's for?'

'I'll bet it's for art,' Lottie volunteered with her

usual cheerful confidence. 'I'll bet you anything.'

'Lottie's quite right,' Mrs Jenkins said. 'I've always argued we should have a prize for art, but Canon Cooper thinks of painting only as a pastime, and a wasteful one at that.'

'Just like Father,' Lottie groaned. 'And Mother.'

'However,' Mrs Jenkins leaned over the hearth to turn the muffins roasting on their forks, 'you know my feelings on the matter, and you know how I feel about your talent, Grace. So since this is your last term, I wanted you to have a prize. And because I believe that you have a special talent, I wanted you to have a very special prize. To show that you have not gone unappreciated.'

Mrs Jenkins, her cheeks suddenly red from the fire, sat back in her chair and smiled gravely at her pupil.

'Thank you, Mrs Jenkins,' Grace said, reopening the book on her knee. 'I'm not at all sure that I deserve it, but I do know that I have never been given anything that has meant so much to me, nor something which I shall treasure so dearly.'

She smoothed the page of tissue protecting the frontis-piece and gazed at the illustration. She knew how much this book meant because it was the last present Mrs Jenkins had given her husband, the Christmas before he was sent out to Africa where only a few months later he was killed at the siege of Ladysmith.

Again she carefully smoothed the protective page of tissue down with the back of her fingers before showing the reproduced watercolour to her sister.

'Look, Lottie. Isn't that beautiful?'

'Yes,' Lottie agreed. 'But it's not nearly as good as the one you've just done.'

Having summarily dismissed the work of one of England's leading watercolourists, Lottie set herself to rescuing her smoking muffin from the roaring fire and sitting crosslegged began buttering it, while Mrs Jenkins enquired after Grace's latest painting. Grace began to explain why she had been unable to bring it, but then stopped as she saw she did not have the teacher's attention.

'How would you like to meet Samuel Goodfellow?' Mrs Jenkins asked Grace. 'He teaches at the London Academy, you know.'

'I wouldn't know what to say to him, Mrs Jenkins,' Grace replied. 'I so love his paintings. I always remember them from the first time you showed them to me.'

'You have until next Tuesday to think of something,' Mrs Jenkins said, quite straight-faced. 'Knowing you, I'm sure you'll have come up with something by then.'

'Is he to visit Keston?' Grace asked her, puzzled. 'Does he have relatives here perhaps?'

'No to both those questions, Grace. The school treat for prizewinners this year is a trip to London to visit the Science Museum.'

'Do you think Mother will allow us to go up to London on the treat?' Lottie asked as she and Grace hurried on to the Rectory.

'I don't know really, Lottie,' Grace replied. 'Actually I do. No, of course she won't.'

Lottie stopped in her tracks and stared up at her sister. 'No she won't, will she? That's just what I thought.'

'I know.' Grace smiled. 'That's why I asked Mrs Jenkins to ask her. Mother won't be able to refuse Mrs J, because she won't want to look mean in front of all the other mothers. All the other mothers who really can't afford it.'

'Yippee! You're just brilliant, Grace!' Lottie cried, and then ran ahead of Grace up Church Hill. 'Yippee! Hurray!'

When they got to the Rectory, Grace left *The Art of Watercolouring* with her other prize and Lottie's on a settle in the hall. She knew it would go unnoticed because their mother's only interest was in her appearance. She had never been known to sit down willingly and read anything except the family Bible of a Sunday, and even then she always seemed to stay glued to the same page.

*　*　*

Although Grace remained outwardly confident that her mother could be talked round, inwardly she feared that she and Lottie would never really reach London and see the famous Science Museum for themselves. Her fear was based on sound experience, and in particular Mother's sudden incapacitating headaches which always arrived just in time either to enable her to get out of doing something she didn't want to do, or to prevent her daughters from doing something which they did want to do. You didn't have to be a genius to guess that one of her famous headaches would almost certainly be used to thwart their outing. Grace had often noticed that they had a habit of intensifying during the school holidays, and were at their very worst approaching and over Christmas, when they would leave their victim so stricken she could barely lift a glass of water to her lips. Since the household staff consisted of just Mary and Cook, inevitably this would mean Grace and Lottie were called upon to organize and run the house at such moments of crisis.

This year the writing was already on the wall as early as Prize-giving Day, when on her return from tea at the Rectory, as soon as she was back through her own front door, Millicent Merrill was overcome by a sudden dizzy spell and a bout of nausea, forcing her to retire to her darkened room while her daughters held the fort and helped prepare the house and dinner for her eight invited guests, who when they all arrived at half past six found their hostess in the very best of spirits, leaving them all with not the slightest suspicion that only one hour before Millicent Merrill had earnestly and quite loudly been considering cancelling dinner and summoning Dr Granger to her bedside.

'How are we to stop her stopping us going to London?' Lottie whispered when Grace finally came to bed. 'Because she will, Grace. She'll want us to do all the shopping. And put up the decorations.'

'I've already thought of that,' Grace whispered back as she sat on her sister's bed and began to unroll her stockings. 'I told Mrs Jenkins, and Mrs Jenkins told

Mother the outing wasn't till Wednesday. What she's going to do is call by on Monday night after Mother has gone to bed and leave a message with Mary that she got the day wrong. Of course it will be too late to tell Mother, because you know how she hates to be disturbed after she's retired, so Mary will explain what happened at breakfast the next day, by which time we shall be on the way to London.'

'You're brilliant,' Lottie gasped. 'Truly brilliant, Grace. Thanks to you, nothing can go wrong now.'

'Nothing was ever going to go wrong, Lottie,' Grace whispered, leaning over to kiss her sister good night. 'Now go to sleep.'

TWO

The London Academy of Art was housed in a handsome stone building in Bloomsbury. By the double front doors an ornamental tablet set in a garland of carved stone leaves announced the school to have been founded in Anno Domini 1865, while inside the polished marble hall echoed with the footfalls of the staff as they went about the business of shutting the Academy down for the Christmas holidays.

Grace sat on a mahogany bench to one side of the hall, dressed in a grey cloak over one of her mother's cast-offs, a dark blue woollen dress which, even though it was now a good five or six years out of fashion, looked marvellous on Grace with her lustrous black hair, her dark blue eyes and pale skin. But even the knowledge that she looked her best failed to calm her nerves. She sat as still as she could, her gloved hands folded in her lap, and her head tipped demurely forward as she waited to be called in for her appointment, but not even the repeated mental recitation of as much as she could remember of *Intimations of Immortality* could quell the butterflies in her stomach.

It had all seemed so easy back at Keston. At least it hadn't, it had seemed quite difficult, to get permission to go to London, to get Mrs Jenkins to help them by calling by and saying she had the wrong day, but what

Grace hadn't catered for was her dear friend, her teacher, taking her aside, and having given her the money for a hackney cab instructing her to leave herself and Lottie to the delights of the Science Museum while Grace found her way to the Academy steps all on her own. Grace had stared at Mrs Jenkins hoping at first that she was teasing her, but when she realized that she wasn't she found herself pleading with her. She had never been to London before let alone travelled anywhere by herself, she reminded Mrs Jenkins, but Mrs Jenkins just gave her usual sweet, graceful laugh and assured Grace that she would be perfectly safe, adding that anyone as intent as she was on being a New Woman must learn to travel alone in hackney carriages.

'Miss Merrill?'

An extremely tall, bearded and bespectacled man wearing a rough tweed suit and a badly tied cravat towered over her, hands clasped behind his back.

'You do realize that you're talking to yourself?' he enquired.

Grace blushed and put a hand up to adjust her hat.

'No, forgive me, I didn't,' she replied. 'I was saying a poem in my head, you see. And I must have started saying it aloud.'

'Might I enquire who the poet was?' the man asked as Grace rose. 'Or may I hazard a guess? Tennyson, no doubt. Maddening. Sometimes you'd imagine no one else had ever written any blessed poetry. You'd think Browning had never existed. What were you reciting? Don't tell me. *The Lady of Shalott. The Lady of Shalott*, what else? Eh? Yes of course, what else.'

'I was reciting Wordsworth as a matter of fact,' Grace said, trying to keep up with the stranger who was now striding ahead of her with massive steps down the echoing corridor. 'His *Intimations of Immortality*. I don't happen to like Tennyson.'

The man stopped as suddenly as he had started walking and turned to stare at the small figure behind him.

'They say his poem *Maud* has one too many vowels

27

in its title,' he announced. 'And it would make sense no matter which was deleted.'

Then he turned and strode off once more ahead of her away down the corridor.

By the time Grace had caught up with him, he had disappeared into an office at the head of the corridor, through a door which was marked *Principal. Professor Goodfellow RA.* Grace stopped and stared at the name of the man she had come to meet, the man whose delicate watercolours and pen and washes had entranced her ever since Mrs Jenkins had first shown her copies of his work five years ago, when she was twelve years old. Now she knew who the man who had summoned her was, Grace hesitated outside the half-open door, unsure whether or not she had the courage to enter. At which point a great bearded face suddenly materialized from behind the highly polished panels and frowned at her.

'There's really very little point in you standing out there,' the professor said. 'Come in, come in.'

In contrast to the orderliness of the halls and corridors through which they had just come, Professor Goodfellow's office was a mass of clutter, a room which smelt over-poweringly and intoxicatingly of a mixture of paint gum, ink, lead pencils and rough paper and which was dominated by a huge oak desk awash with a flotsam of letters and notes on top of which were piled untidy mountains of books on top of which were balanced jam jars crammed full of drawing pens, pencil stubs and water-colour brushes. Another table under one window was barely visible beneath a litter of drawings and sketches, boxes of paints, enamel palettes and large jars of differently and faintly coloured brush-water, while around the room a variety of easels supported a series of watercolours, some finished, some almost so, and all of them of naked women. Grace looked away from them at once, not because she was embarrassed, but in case she was embarrassed to be seen looking at them.

'I can't seem to find them,' Professor Goodfellow said, opening and closing the drawers of his desk one after the other. 'I know I had them because I was showing them to somebody only this very morning, so I know I haven't lost them. Just because I can't find them doesn't mean I have lost them, you know. And why don't you sit down, Miss Merrill. You remind me of someone waiting for a train.'

Grace took a pile of books off a nearby wooden chair and sat while the professor began to ransack the cupboards at the bottom of a large and overstocked bookcase.

'This will never do of course,' he muttered, 'but there you are. These things happen. But while I'm looking and in case I fail to unearth them before it's time for you to go, I feel obliged to tell you that they're brilliant, you know. Quite, quite brilliant.'

Imagining him to be extolling the merits of his own work, Grace smiled and undid her bonnet, just as the professor straightened up and turned in her direction.

'What remarkable hair,' he said after a moment's contemplation. 'In that light – hmmm.' He stroked his thick moustache with thumb and forefinger four or five times, smoothing it away from his Roman nose to the corners of his mouth. 'Alizarin cyanine, perhaps. Or immedial. Black's never black, you know. Well of course you know. No it's never simply black. There's always some blue. Or green. Yes. Immedial. Immedial. Immedial.'

He repeated the word as he reached for a small tray of paints and a sketch pad. Licking the end of a brush which he'd carefully selected from one of the jam jars, he sat on the edge of his desk, knocking over a tall pile of books in the process, and screwing up his face as he stared at Grace until one eye was all but closed and his mouth protruded in a crooked pout between his beard and moustache, he began to paint.

'I must just catch that light on your hair,' he murmured. 'Don't worry if you move. It's perfectly all right. Or you can talk if you want to. Tell me how and why you began to paint.'

Grace stared at him in astonishment. As it was she hadn't an idea of what she was going to say to the famous

29

painter when she met him, but now she was totally at a loss for words.

'How do you know I paint?'

'How do I know you paint.' Professor Goodfellow looked up at her for a seemingly endless moment, then resumed painting. 'How do I know you paint,' he repeated, leaving the question unanswered as he dipped the fine brush in water and then carefully drew it across a tablet of black paint. 'Because.'

'That is. I didn't know you knew I painted,' Grace said rather helplessly after a long silence.

'Indeed?' It was less of a question and more of a statement Grace realized, as once again she found the famous artist squinting at her all but one-eyed through his round brass-rimmed spectacles. 'Indeed,' he said again. 'Do you know. Do you know you have eyes the colour of smalt. You know what smalt is of course, but I shall tell you even so. It's glass. Glass coloured deep blue. Coloured deep blue with oxide of cobalt. A very exciting colour. Thrilling really. Pulverized by artists, as a pigment. Smalt. That's what smalt is. So remember, if you're going to be a painter, the first thing to learn is to look for the truth of a colour. Never let it be said that the sky is blue or that the grass is green.'

'At the risk of sounding foolish,' Grace persisted after a moment, 'I'm afraid I don't understand how you knew that I painted.'

'You don't, don't you?' Professor Goodfellow sucked the end of his paintbrush, turning his lips blue-black. 'Unless my senses have left me, you are the girl whose teacher sent me examples of her work, and quite remarkable they are, too. Altogether quite exceptional. I was looking at them again only this morning. Showing them to a student. Wanted him to see an object lesson in line and naturally correct emphasis.'

'Mrs Jenkins sent you some of my paintings?'

'No don't do that, if you wouldn't mind. Please don't frown that way.'

'I'm sorry, but I couldn't help it. I had no idea anyone

had sent you any of my paintings. Mrs Jenkins just said she knew you, and asked me if I'd like to meet you. And just – well – talk about your paintings, I suppose. Not mine. I mean the last thing I imagined was that I would end up here, with you. With you painting me. And talking about *my* paintings.'

'You don't think they're worth talking about.'

'Not compared with yours, Professor Goodfellow, no.'

'I assure you, young lady,' the professor said after a good minute's silence, 'that they are. Which is the reason you are here.' He got up off the desk and handed Grace the completed sketch while he pulled a briar pipe from his jacket pocket and began to fill it with tobacco. 'Mrs Jenkins? Yes. Mrs Jenkins I don't know from Adam. At least I didn't until she began badgering me about you by letter, saying I should see you because you were the most naturally gifted young painter she had ever met. Do you see what I mean about there being no such thing as black?'

He leaned across and pushed the painting down with the end of his pipe so that he could study it upside down.

'Your hair has six, seven different colours. Where the sun falls on it, it's almost indigo. I must paint you properly some time. You have a Florentine quality. Very interesting.'

He stared at Grace quite dispassionately while he sat back on the desk and lit his pipe.

'I get hundreds of letters,' he suddenly continued, in a cloud of blue-white smoke. 'Letters from all sorts of Mrs Jenkinses. Then they send me examples of their pupils' work, and I am afraid to say I send most of it straight back. But your work. Hmmm. I wish I could find it.'

'I think you might be sitting on it,' Grace offered, having suddenly caught a glimpse of what looked like part of a pencil sketch she'd done of Lottie on their swing. 'In fact I'm almost sure you are.'

The professor stood up at once and retrieved the package which did indeed contain the examples of Grace's work from beneath him without a word of either gratitude or apology. Instead, and much to Grace's private amusement, he admonished whoever it was who had put something so important in such a ridiculous place, oblivious of the fact that to most people a desk would be the obvious and safest of choices. Then having sorted and straightened out the contents of the package he instructed Grace to come over and examine her own work as if it was something done by a total stranger.

'Good graduated tone here, do you see. Good strong irregular outline. Shows a precocious confidence.' Professor Goodfellow bent even more closely over the series of small landscapes before him and removed his spectacles. 'The washes used have just the right consistency. Just the right amount of luminosity, achieved, do you see, by building layer upon layer. And here.' From underneath the pile he pulled a painting whose corner he had dog-eared for reference. 'Look at this and study it well because it's an excellent example of how to capture a sense of distance. The artist has done this, young lady, by using these two trees here as a central focus. And then by placing strong, warm colours in the foreground and less intense ones in the distance it gives us this sense of the land receding. A sense which is greatly enhanced by the way he has carefully lightened the sky, do you see? And let it just fade away, fade away completely into this strip of white at the top. Which is just bare paper. No paint. He's allowed the sky simply to evaporate into the paper.'

Looping the ends of his spectacles one by one back over each ear, Professor Goodfellow straightened up and tapped the pile of paintings.

'This is the sort of thing you will learn here, young lady,' he concluded. 'If you are fortunate enough to gain admission as a pupil.'

'And how would I do that, Professor Goodfellow?' Grace enquired, having decided that the only way to handle the interview was to do as Alice had done in Wonderland, and treat everything illogical as perfectly logical.

'How would you do that?' the professor wondered, and taking his spectacles off again this time he held them up to the light and then put them back on again. 'How would you do what precisely?' he enquired, seemingly of himself with a frown.

'How would I gain admission as a pupil?'

'I would have thought that was perfectly obvious,' the professor replied, tapping the pile of Grace's paintings. 'You would have to submit work as good as this.'

In the hackney cab which was returning her to the Science Museum, Grace did her best to order her thoughts. On the strength of the paintings Mrs Jenkins had submitted and which Professor Goodfellow had finally recalled were indeed Grace's, she had not only been offered a place at the Academy but the promise of a major scholarship as well, an award which although it had first to be ratified by the Board of Governors, on the evidence of her talent the professor was completely confident would be a mere formality.

The problem was what to do, if indeed she could do anything. Because of her parents' strongly disapproving attitude to art, Grace had never once considered studying painting seriously. She loved it, and she knew she had a certain ability, but she had resigned herself to accepting that her painting could only be a recreation, and one which must be kept secret until such time as she left home to be married or until her parents were no more.

But now, it was literally unbelievable, now she had been given the chance to study free under one of England's greatest watercolourists the whole complexion of the matter had quite suddenly changed. The first thing she had to do was to earnestly and honestly apply herself to a rigorous self-examination, and if the result of her findings was the discovery that she had a vocation, then she would move heaven and earth to take up the scholarship and make the very best of her gift.

'There simply is no argument, Grace,' Mrs Jenkins told her on the train journey home. To Grace's astonishment she had shown absolutely no surprise when Grace had broken the news, although she had been demonstrably delighted, embracing Grace fondly and kissing her on both cheeks. 'You cannot even consider you have a choice in the matter,' she continued, raising her voice a little as the train entered a tunnel. 'Never cast away the gifts of the gods. To you, at your age, it might not seem much, to be able to paint and draw the way you can. But I do assure you, Grace, if you had never been given the joy of these gifts, you could never get them by wanting them.'

Another shrill whistle signalled their exit from the last of the Chiltern tunnels and the train slowly gathered speed for the run to Aylesbury. Grace watched the dark winter landscape passing by through a veil of smoke while once more she tried to order her thoughts.

'It's no good, Mrs Jenkins,' she sighed, turning back to her teacher beside her. 'You know and I know my parents will never allow it.'

'That, dear Grace, is just an assumption,' Mrs Jenkins replied, taking Grace's hand in hers. 'Of course they will say no, initially, but your family are good Christians. So then you will remind them of what the Bible teaches us about what we must do with the talents God gives us. No man lights a candle, remember, and places it under a bushel.'

'My father doesn't consider art a subject suitable for young ladies.'

'Then you must prove to him that it is.' Mrs Jenkins placed a slim, gloved hand on Grace's arm and pressed it lightly to make sure of her complete attention. 'The world is changing, Grace, and most particularly for women. It isn't the fact that women now ride bicycles, as the popular papers would have us believe; that is not the reason. The world is changing because women are determined to be heard. We've known for a long time how important it is for us to be educated, fully educated, irrespective of whether we are pretty or whether we're plain, we know there is a world outside the home, and we know we have the right to make the most of our lives. Women are beginning to leave behind the foolishness of the Nineties, thank heavens, and we're determined to become involved in the running of the country, because it is our country as well. So you see, Grace, you must fight for your right to take up this scholarship, you must fight and you must win. It's your right to follow your star, it's your right to become if you have the chance not just somebody's wife, but someone who counts.'

By the time they had arrived back at the branch line station of Keston, having changed trains at Aylesbury, Grace had been given plenty of time to think about what Mrs Jenkins had said on the journey and how she might best approach her parents.

'But whatever you do,' Grace warned her younger sister as they walked the last part of the journey back alone, 'don't mention anything about me going to meet Professor Goodfellow. Mother probably wouldn't even take any notice, I'm sure. But I don't want it mentioned in front of Father when he returns. You know how that can be?'

Lottie nodded, already looking overburdened from knowing Grace's secret, and she pursed her lips in a way that she always did when she was trying to look and be more grown-up than she felt.

But as it turned out, there were matters of far greater gravity than keeping the secret of Grace's art to which the two girls had to attend after their father had come home for the Christmas holiday.

T H R E E

All Grace and Lottie knew about their father's occupation was that he was a businessman. Occasionally Grace had sought amplification from her mother, but as ever her mother was vague and non-committal.

'Your father is a very successful *entrepreneur*,' she would say with a sigh, as if such a thing was obvious from the comfortable way they lived. 'And why he is successful,' she once added, 'is because he is not a man to sell wood in a forest, nor fish on a lake.'

Since no other information was ever forthcoming, Grace never pursued the matter further. By custom she knew their father travelled, and that his travels often took him abroad, whence he would sometimes return armed with gifts of material for his wife, and very occasionally *bon-bons* for his two daughters. He was always generous to his wife, but rarely so to his children, even at Christmastime when the most they could expect was one small gift each, usually a second-hand book for Grace from the time she had entered her teenage, and some small gee-gaw for Lottie, such as yet another wooden animal for her toy farm which she was fast outgrowing. On the other hand their mother was presented with sometimes as many as half a dozen gifts, hats, gloves, shoes, scent, lace, always something feminine and never anything cheap, and George

Merrill would stand in front of the fire in his best dark suit nodding his great handsome head with its thick dark curls, a cigar in his mouth and his thumbs in his waistcoat pockets, while his wife sighed and exclaimed her delight as she opened her succession of expensively wrapped gifts.

'Oh George you shouldn't!' she would ritualistically gasp as she examined each offering. 'George I simply do not deserve all this!' While at her feet Lottie would push her latest wooden cow or horse across the carpet and Grace would feign interest in the illustrations of a book she had already been loaned by Mrs Jenkins.

As for the rest of Christmas, the two girls were rarely out of the kitchen where they were expected to act as auxiliary staff, helping Cook and Mary prepare and serve a seemingly unending succession of huge meals for the houseful of friends and relatives which their parents insisted on inviting every year. By the time the New Year had been seen in the two girls were completely exhausted from their extra duties.

'There seems no end to pots and pans at Christmas,' Lottie would remark dolefully every year to Grace.

'Soon be done,' was Grace's automatic reply.

This year, however, Christmas at Oak Lee House was different.

'Do you think he's mad?' Lottie wondered as they prepared themselves for bed. 'Or do you think he's ill?'

'I don't know what to make of it,' Grace replied, helping Lottie out of her best velvet dress before turning her own back to be unhooked. 'Mother has looked astonished ever since he arrived home half-buried in presents for us.'

After she had undone the back of Grace's dress and helped her out of it, Lottie sat on her bed in her chemise and petticoat and picked up the objects which she had laid so carefully beside her.

'A fox-fur hat and muff for me,' she wondered. 'And that lovely French manicure set for you.'

'And what about that wonderful necklace he gave Mother?' Grace asked as she undid her mane of black hair, and it fell to below her waist. 'Have you ever seen anything so beautiful?'

'Only in pictures,' Lottie sighed. 'Do you think it's real, Grace?'

'Mother said it was. She said you can tell by biting the pearls, if they scratch against your teeth they're real, and if they don't they're not.'

Lottie slipped both her hands into her fox-fur muff and getting up off her bed pirouetted round the room.

'I still don't know how he could afford it all,' Lottie said, once she had come to a standstill.

'It must have been this last business trip,' Grace said, combing her hair out at the dressing table. 'Father must have had a very successful time in Paris.'

'That wouldn't explain all this,' Lottie argued. 'He always comes home and says how well his trips have gone. I really do think he's gone mad, Grace.'

Lottie looked so serious Grace had to laugh. While she couldn't actually agree with her sister's conclusion, even so, his change of attitude was strange. Something wonderful must indeed have happened to his life for him to have become so different. These last days he had been as much fun with them as he was normally with the rest of the world. No leaving his smile at the gate, no laughter and merriment which ended the moment Mary shut the door behind the last visitor, only to be replaced with carping and criticism. It could only mean that he had had some big success in business, and since the change was obviously so much for the good, and since it had been far and away the best Christmas they had ever had together as a family, it was surely ridiculous to examine the reason too closely? Besides, since he never discussed his business with anyone, least of all Mother, they would never know.

'This is the best Christmas we've had, isn't it, Grace?' Lottie's voice rang out in the darkness. 'It's been like one of your paintings, right the way through.'

Only minutes before their father had been in to kiss them good night, something which he hadn't done since

38

they were quite small. Smelling not disagreeably of port and cigars he had looked round their bedroom with affection.

'I remember the two of you in here with your nurse as if it was yesterday, sitting up in bed all ribbons and lace, like something on a biscuit tin the two of you were.'

He looked taller and less portly standing by the door, and powerful and masculine too, Grace thought proudly. His thick head of hair swept back, his eyes sparkling, his cheeks slightly flushed, she could see why their beautiful mother had fallen for him all those years before.

'You used to say your prayers so sweetly for me,' he sighed happily. 'What a little pair of angels you were. How we loved you both, your mother and I and Nurse.'

He smiled across at them.

'Oh yes, you were angels all right.'

He went out on a sigh of nostalgia, quietly shutting the door behind him, and Grace closed her eyes as she heard his retreating footsteps down the wooden stairs. Father loving them like that, Mother without a headache, Lottie was right it was the best Christmas. Never mind the cooking and the washing, they had had the best time yet this year.

When Grace and Lottie were woken by the sound of anguished howling from below them somewhere in the house naturally they both thought that someone had died in the night. Pulling on their robes over their nightgowns, and hurrying from their bedroom, they rushed downstairs to find the maid in a state of near hysteria. She was sitting by the unlit kitchen range, howling uncontrollably into the folds of her apron which she had raised to cover her face.

'What is it, Mary?' Grace asked, taking the girl by her shoulders. 'What are you crying like that for? Have you hurt yourself? Have you burned yourself or something? What on earth has happened?'

The maid took no notice of her, only continuing to howl and grabbing even more of her apron to hold to her face.

'Perhaps it's Cook,' Lottie ventured, standing back fearfully. 'Perhaps Cook's died, Grace? Do you think Cook has died?'

'Is it Cook, Mary?' Grace took hold of the maid by her shoulders once more and tried to pull her to her senses. 'Has something happened to Cook? Try to stop crying just for long enough to tell us, will you?'

By now the girl's anguished cries had turned to breathless gasps as she started to rock herself to and fro, her face still buried in her apron.

'Let's go and find Mother,' Lottie said quickly, backing towards the kitchen door. 'Perhaps she will be able to tell us what has upset Mary so much?'

'No wait, Lottie—' Grace caught her sister by one wrist, drawing her back to her side. 'Mary's trying to say something.'

From behind the folds of her apron, the girl was howling out some words, including two words of which Grace finally was able to make sense.

'It's Father,' she said to Lottie. 'Something's happened to Father.'

Both the girls turned and rushed out of the kitchen back upstairs, where they saw the door to their father's room was ajar. Lottie held back, trying to tug herself free of Grace's hand which had her held fast by one wrist.

'No, Grace, no!' she cried. 'No don't, please! Suppose he's dead!'

'He's not dead,' said a voice from behind them. 'But it would be better for us all if he were.'

Grace turned and saw their mother on the landing outside her own bedroom, dressed in a half-fastened *peignoir*, with her long hair unpinned and a handkerchief held to her mouth.

'What's happened, Mother?' she asked.

Lottie was already crying and clinging now with both hands to Grace where only a moment ago she had been trying to shake herself free.

'Mother – what has happened?'

Without replying, their mother crossed the corridor,

pushed open their father's bedroom door and then stood aside for her daughters to see inside. The bed was empty and unmade, the doors of his wardrobe were wide open, and all the drawers pulled out of his tallboy. Grace and Lottie stood looking at the chaos and then at each other. Their mother had left, gone back to her own room.

'He said he didn't have to go away again until after the New Year,' Lottie said, holding Grace's hand even more tightly.

'I know,' Grace agreed quietly. 'So in that case where has he gone?'

She led her sister back across the corridor and into their mother's room, where they found her lying on her side, her face turned away from them, her handkerchief still held to her mouth.

'What is it?' Grace asked, coming round and standing awkwardly beside the bed, her younger sister half a step behind her. 'What has happened to Father?'

In the silence which ensued, Mary could still be heard crying below them in the kitchen.

'Mother?'

Finally Millicent Merrill pointed to a folded letter on her bedside table.

'See for yourself,' she whispered. 'It was on the carpet, under the door.'

Grace picked up the letter and unfolded it. It was three pages long, written in her father's careful, even, forward-sloping hand. '*My dear Millicent,*' it began. '*When you read this I shall be gone.*'

'He's run off,' her mother announced suddenly, making Grace look up from the letter. 'He's left me for another woman. And do you know who he's left me for, Grace? Of all people? That dumpy little schoolteacher of yours and Lottie's.'

Millicent Merrill turned on to her back, taking the handkerchief from her face, but there were no tears on her cheeks, just a look of utter disbelief. 'He has left me,' she whispered, staring up at the ceiling. 'He has run off, would you believe, and left me. Of all people.'

'Don't be silly, Mother,' Grace told her, and she took her hand as if she was a child and patted it as Mrs Jenkins would do if you fell over in the school grounds. 'You must have one of your migraines.'

'It's true, Grace,' her mother groaned, the blank look in her eyes being replaced by one of agonized reality.

Grace stared at her. Father. Father who was so upright, so moral, who disapproved of art, of her drawing of Lottie because it showed half an inch of petticoat, Father with his brogue shoes for walks, and his polished black ones for Sunday, Father who was as stiff as the leather that made up his footwear of which he was so inordinately proud, their father had run off with Mrs Jenkins, the saint of the village, the person whose face lit up at the very sight of Grace and Lottie, and who had taken them to London that day despite Father, who had organized their lives to thwart his puritanism, they had run off together?

'You're wrong, Mother, really you are. It's just one of your migraines coming on. The flashes and the lightning in your head, that's what it is.'

She said this over and over to her mother, over the sound of Lottie's sobs. As Millicent Merrill lay there in the half dark of her bedroom, quite still and utterly silent, Grace had insisted to their mother.

You're wrong, she had told her, *terribly, terribly wrong. Mrs Jenkins would never do such a thing, never, ever, ever. Mrs Jenkins still loves her dead husband. Every time I go and see her*, Grace had continued, ignoring the evidence of the letter in her hand, *all she ever does is talk about her dead husband, and tell how he used to read poetry to her, how on every anniversary of their wedding he laid a red rose on her pillow, how they walked the hills high above Keston on the long summer evenings before he left for Africa, planning what they would do on his return. How her heart was broken when he was killed, how she wept when they brought his body home, how still she mourns him. There has to be a mistake. It has to be another Mrs Jenkins. Mrs Jenkins would never ever ever do such a terrible thing, above all not with Father.*

Her mother was silent through Grace's protests. She

just lay in the bed staring at the ceiling as if she was alone, as if she was waiting for something, for Grace to go away, for Lottie to stop crying, it didn't really matter, she just lay there, as if she was already laid out.

'Read the letter,' was all she finally said. 'Read the letter and see for yourself.'

But Grace preferred to run to Mrs Jenkins' house in order to see for herself.

Leaving Lottie in the care of Cook, Grace ran all the way through the small town and out the other side, up the hill, left down the lane and in through the small wooden gate. Mrs Jenkins would be there, she knew she would be. The dear kind look in her eyes, waiting for Grace to show her the newest drawing, the way she had tried to capture that frosty morning the week before.

Grace knocked and knocked on the door but no one came to open it. Shading the light from her eyes with her hands, she leaned over the carefully tended flower-beds at the front and side of the house and looked into the windows. Every room she could see was dark and uninhabited. Finally, feeling very much as though she was trespassing, she dared to walk around to the back door, where she had never been before. One push of her hand and the old, thick, carved oak door opened.

A little awestruck by her own impudence she called into the dark of the cottage.

'Mrs Jenkins!'

Her voice echoed dully through the red-tiled kitchen whence she could smell the homely fragrances of wood smoke, herbs drying, and baking done and turned out of tins a little rusty on the outside. On her fifth call of 'Mrs Jenkins!' she became bolder and stepped into the kitchen, and from there into the silent house.

Inside everything was as tidy and orderly as it ever was, with reference and text books piled high on the floor by the chair where Mrs Jenkins always sat, and the usual pile of exercise books waiting to be corrected neatly stacked on the desk opposite the bow window. But there was no fire laid, only the remains of one which had burned the night before, and most probably all over Christmas. The cottage in fact was very cold and completely silent, except for the ticking of the clock on the mantelpiece.

Upstairs in Mrs Jenkins' bedroom, which Grace had never before seen nor would have ever dared to enter, it was a different scene altogether.

There were clothes and bedclothes everywhere, and just as in her father's bedroom, there were signs of flight. The doors and drawers of all the cupboards and chests were open, with unwanted garments left either hanging half spilled from them or scattered strewn on the floor. Just like her father's room, it was as if there had been a burglary, as if someone had rushed into the room and in a desperate hurry ransacked it for what they wanted before anyone should discover them. The sight was undeniable. It was as if a crime had been committed.

But too there was something else that lingered in the room, another and different atmosphere which made Grace uneasy, which caused her to shiver and pull her coat around her, as if a door behind her had suddenly been flung open by a bitterly cold wind, and she knew what it was before she even turned round. It was the bed.

Nothing could explain how in that one moment Grace knew she was wrong, that her father and Mrs Jenkins were indeed lovers, and that they had slept together and made love together in the brass-framed bedstead from which she was now recoiling in horror. To anyone else it was just a pile of dishevelled bedclothes, a bed from which someone had got up in too great a hurry to make. There was nothing visibly incriminating about it, no carelessly forgotten articles of clothing, nothing that could evidence illicit behaviour, nothing physical. Yet something lingered, something potent had been left behind by whoever had fled, some sense of iniquity and deceit. It hung over the rumpled bed and filled the corners of the room, making Grace retreat until her back was pressed against the wall by the door.

For fully a minute she stayed there, one hand to her face, until unable to bear what the room was telling her

44

she ran out and down the stairs, almost knocking over Mrs Jenkins' daily maid Bertha who had just let herself into the house.

'Why, Miss Merrill!' Bertha said when she had recovered herself and seen who her assailant was. 'And what might you be doing here this time of day, dear? Poor Mrs Jenkins not been taken bad, 'as she?'

Bertha looked up the stairs past Grace, as if she too suddenly sensed that something was wrong.

'Mrs Jenkins has gone,' Grace said in a voice that was little more than a whisper, while she edged her way to the front door.

'Gone?' Bertha echoed. 'Gone – but that's impossible, dear. Mrs Jenkins never goes nowhere without telling old Bertha.'

'She has this time,' Grace said, fumbling to get the door open. 'This time she's gone and she hasn't told anybody!'

Except my father! the voice shouted in her head as she ran back down the lane and into the town. *She told my father all right – or rather he told her! We're going away, Susan! he must have said. Hurry! Quick! We'll run away tonight! And we won't tell anybody! Not a soul! We'll just take the things we need and we'll run far, far away! And we won't tell anybody at all! Not one single soul!*

The voice then became several voices, voices which laughed and mocked as she ran hot-faced back through the town, past people who first greeted her then wheeled in astonishment as Grace flew past them without a word. *They'll know soon enough!* one of the voices laughed. *Why bother to stop and tell them now? Very soon the whole town will know! The whole town will be laughing soon!*

There was a horse and trap outside Oak Lee House which Grace recognized at once as that belonging to Dr Granger. A small crowd had already gathered on the pavement which was busy gossiping as Grace arrived and which now fell silent and stared at Grace as she slowed from her breakneck pace to a more sedate walk. Once she was past them, Grace again broke into a run, dashing up the path and in through the front door.

Dr Granger was in the hall with Cook. As soon as he saw Grace he took her into the morning room.

'Miss Grace, there is no real cause for alarm,' he stated, for no reason, it seemed to Grace, taking out his pocket watch and fiddling with it without looking at the time, before replacing it in his waistcoat.

Grace was old enough to know that when grown-ups told you that there wasn't something it meant there was. She stared up at Dr Granger and a strange sort of stillness settled around her as if they were both in church and waiting for the blessing of the rector.

'Your mother has had a little accident. Her wrists, you know, the shock, the moment of shock caused her to have an accident, but she is now all right. She will not die, Miss Grace, she will be all right.'

How could she be all right? Grace wondered at the stupidity of the man, and then realizing what he was telling her, and how he was telling her, her despite quickly turned to gratitude, for if it was proved that her mother had tried to take her life she could be removed from them and thrown into prison, or at best a madhouse.

'Just a little accident,' the doctor repeated smoothly.

Staring into the kind expression in his eyes Grace became numb. Supposing it had not been Dr Granger who had been called? Supposing it had been one of his partners, someone not sympathetic to Mother and her migraines and her trials and tribulations, how much worse it could have been!

'Thank you, Dr Granger,' she whispered, turning away.

The lovers had flown to France. News of their exodus came in the shape of a letter sent care of Mr Bragge, the family solicitor, who called with the letter and instructions for Grace herself to read it and convey its import to her mother who lay upstairs in silence in her bedroom, from where she had not moved since the morning she learned of her husband's infidelity.

46

'Dr Granger informs me your mother is still in the deepest shock,' Mr Bragge said to Grace as he handed her the letter. 'That she neither speaks to anyone, nor seems to take notice of anything that is said to her.'

'That is perfectly true, I'm afraid,' Grace replied, beckoning the lawyer to a chair by the fire then sitting down opposite him. 'For a week she ate nothing at all, and it's only now that we've managed to get her to take some broth, and occasionally a little white fish or chicken meat.'

'There's worse to come, alas Miss Merrill,' Mr Bragge sighed after Grace had finished reading her father's letter. 'Besides his avowed intention never to return to England, I have to say that if he ever did, he would most probably be arrested.'

The letter which she still held began to flutter in Grace's hand, as if it was a trapped butterfly, so she laid it aside on the table by her chair and folded her hands carefully in her lap.

'Why should he be arrested?' she asked. 'Surely my father has done nothing wrong?'

'It seems that it never rains but it pours, Miss Merrill,' Mr Bragge replied gravely. 'From my understanding of matters, it appears your father may well have misappropriated various funds which were lodged with him for investment. He was also considerably in debt.'

'This can't be so,' Grace stated, trying to keep the rising note of panic from her voice. 'My father was most successful at his business. Why only this Christmas he returned from his travels laden with the most expensive gifts imaginable for us all! Surely he would hardly be in a position to be so extravagant if what you say were true! If he was in debt! Or if he had taken money belonging to other people!'

Grace was on her feet, although she couldn't remember the precise moment when she rose. She also realized the futility of her argument even as she was expounding it. If her father had been misappropriating funds entrusted to him, then he would be even more able than usual to

47

return with expensive presents. Or if he was just simply in debt, then anyone reckless enough to get himself in such a position would hardly think twice before increasing his liabilities. When she had finished, she stood uncertainly for a moment while Mr Bragge smiled kindly at her, before sitting back down and staring dismally at the floor. She knew what the lawyer was telling her was the truth, just as she had known by standing in Mrs Jenkins' bedroom that her father and Mrs Jenkins were lovers.

And while she sat and stared at the pattern on the carpet, the words of Canon Cooper came back to her, words she had overheard one night after dinner when the door of the dining room had been left half open after the ladies had retired. Never trust an adulterer, she had heard him warning his fellow diners. An adulterer lives by deceit, and if he has lied about another man's wife, he will think nothing of lying to you in business. No, never trust an adulterer gentlemen, an adulterer is not and never could be a gentleman.

Besides, Grace thought, as she smoothed her skirts and raised her eyes from the floor, she had no reason to defend her father. She barely knew him. He showed her no affection, and just as one swallow doesn't make a summer, so one happy Christmas doesn't make a happy family. No, the person who she simply could not believe had betrayed her was Mrs Jenkins, someone she had not only admired but had loved like a mother, and more, much, much more than her own.

The debts her father had amassed were not yet fully assessable, but from what Mr Bragge was saying it appeared that unless some monies could be found and found quickly, his creditors, many of whom it seemed had been trying to get their accounts paid for over a year, were threatening to take remedial action.

'What did Mother say?' a wide-eyed Lottie asked at bedtime when Grace told her the news.

'I didn't tell Mother,' Grace replied. 'I couldn't. There's no point, and even if there was there's nothing she can do.'

'You said Mother had some money. You said when she and Father got married – what is it you call it?'

'Her *dot*.' Grace tucked her sister in, and then sat on the edge of her bed. 'Strictly speaking it's her dowry really, but nearly everyone uses the French, *dot*. It's what women bring to a marriage as their share, or their portion, and Mother actually brought quite a lot to hers.'

'Well then,' Lottie replied over the top of her sheet, as if that was that.

'Father spent it all, Lottie,' Grace said. 'Ages ago.'

'The beast.'

Lottie sunk lower into her bed until nothing but the top of her head could be seen above the bedclothes. Grace knew why, long before the bed began to shake with her sister's muffled sobs. Poor Lottie, it was so difficult for her to understand. Nowadays, in her confusion, she was oddly euphoric one moment, and then frightened and tearful the next.

'Don't worry, Lottie,' Grace said, sounding as calm as possible. 'We'll think of something, you'll see.'

'But what, Grace? What can we think of?'

Lottie's face surfaced, hot-cheeked with her dark blond curls clinging damply round her face. 'What can we ever do? We're only children. And even worse, we're girls.'

Grace sat down on the bed. She didn't mind at all when a small warm arm grabbed her round the neck and held her in a tight embrace.

'I heard Cook and Mary saying we'd have to move from here!' Lottie muttered. 'I didn't know what they meant, I just thought perhaps we might be moving to a different house, another house like this. But I think I understand now. What they meant was we can't afford to go on living here, not ever again!'

Lottie's statement became a truth which Grace discovered with alacrity as her father's creditors no longer bothered to write demanding settlement for their accounts, but began calling at the house in person.

At first Cook did her best to send them away with a

reprimand, or order them at least to call at the back door, but the dunners were well past such niceties and on being told off they merely stuck large and strongly shod feet in the door until Cook was forced to admit them.

Once they were inside, and finding that the lady of the house flatly refused to see or speak to them, if they had already issued a doorstep ultimatum the more ruthless of George Merrill's creditors simply helped themselves to furniture or artefacts which they considered to be roughly the value of their outstanding debts.

Every time it happened Grace, realizing that few if any of them would know the exact value of the articles they were purloining, protested vociferously, but in vain. The dunners were indifferent to her pleas or to the howls of Lottie, who would watch from the landing above them, holding the banisters as if they were prison bars while screaming childish abuse at the tradesfolk as they walked freely in and out of the house with the last of the silver, the paintings and the best of the furniture.

They even took the best of their mother's wardrobe, most particularly her silk evening gowns, her ermine-trimmed opera cloak, and her sealskin coat.

During all this Millicent Merrill just lay silently in her bed, her face turned away from the door as Mary trooped to and fro from her cupboards to her bedroom door bearing all her mistress's best articles while the tradesfolk waited outside in the corridor. Once there was nothing more of Mrs Merrill's to take, they turned their attention to the girls' room, and little though there was of value, they nevertheless took that, the coal merchant even taking Lottie's fox-fur hat and muff and the chandler Grace's silver-backed French manicure set. 'The wife will 'preciate this no end,' he kept muttering happily as he followed the blackened marks from the coal merchant's footfalls back down the primly carpeted staircase.

'No wonder no one lets them in the front door,' Lottie said, when the gate finally banged shut one Friday evening, leaving them in an all but empty house.

'It's not their fault,' Grace replied. 'It's Father who's to blame, leaving so many bills unpaid.'

'Cook said he can't have paid anything for *years*. Cook said Father's debts were worth hundreds and hundreds of pounds.'

'Maybe, Lottie, and maybe not,' Grace said, walking through into the drawing room, her feet echoing on the bare boards. 'I don't imagine poor Cook's been paid for weeks either.'

'She hasn't,' Lottie gasped, running after her sister. 'Neither has Mary. Father promised them both they would be paid in full come the first of the month—'

'While all the time he was planning to do a bunk long before,' Grace interrupted. 'You know, Lottie, I don't think our father was a very nice man.'

'No neither do I, Grace.'

'It's not a very nice feeling, is it? Knowing that one of your parents was a liar and a cheat. I wonder if either of us will turn out to be as bad?'

'Why should we, Grace? We're girls anyway, so if we're going to be like anyone, we'll be like Mother.'

'It's not necessarily anything to do with gender, Lottie. The tendency of like to produce like. Look at your friend Victoria Williams, who sings so beautifully, and plays the piano. Her mother can't sing or read a note. Her father's the one who's musical.'

'Gosh,' Lottie whispered, lighting the first candle of the evening carefully with one of the few remaining matches. 'That means you think either you or I might turn out to be thoroughly bad. But how simply *awful*. I would hate to be dishonest, and cause as much unhappiness as Father has caused all of us.'

'You won't be, Lottie,' Grace assured her. 'You're a very sweet and gentle girl. You'd never do anything to harm anyone. Now come with me and let's go to the kitchen where it's warm. I'm afraid there's not enough coal left to make a decent fire here or in the morning room, and I'm completely frozen.'

When they came into the warmth of the kitchen Cook

was in her coat and hat and there was no sign of Mary.

'Are you off already, Cook?' Grace enquired. 'Isn't it a little early? We were hoping perhaps we could have an early supper tonight, since we had to miss lunch.'

Cook continued to fasten her coat and refix her hat before she finally replied.

'I don't know how to say this, Miss Grace,' she said, clasping her hands and her large bag in front of her. 'I'm that fond of you and your sister, you know that, and I'd do anything for you, really I would. But I can't stay here without being paid. I could if I had been, if you see what I mean, but I'm weeks out now, I'm nearly eight weeks out of pocket and I just can't afford it no more. Mary's gone as it is—'

'Mary's gone?' Grace echoed. 'Without as much as – without even saying goodbye?'

Cook shook her head.

'She couldn't, Miss Grace. We had more of her terrible hysterics only this morning, because she's as fond of you both as I am. But she couldn't face you to say her goodbyes. Mary's not been paid these two months neither.'

'But why didn't you say, Cook?' Grace asked, taking Lottie who was beginning to look tearful again by the hand. 'I have nearly thirty shillings saved in the Post Office. In fact I could pay you that now, if you stay, and then somehow, somehow we'll earn some more. Or perhaps Mother still has some savings somewhere—'

'Bless you, Miss Grace, but no.' Cook interrupted her and put a hand on Grace's arm. 'I couldn't take your money, because God knows you're going to need it. I'd work for you for nothing, really I would if I could. But I can't, see? I have to live too, Miss Grace, and God knows it's been hard enough of late. I've had to eat into my own savings as it is.'

'You should have said, Cook,' Grace said, squeezing Lottie's hand more to prevent herself from crying than to comfort her sister. 'You really should have said.'

'Now you just mind you call in and see me when

you're passing,' Cook said, giving her feathered hat a final adjustment. 'Both of you, mind. Don't think we've seen the last of each other, because we haven't.'

She put a finger under Lottie's chin and lifted the little girl's face up so that she was looking at her.

'You'll be all right, Miss Lottie,' she said. 'You both will. Because you're good girls. And you're nice girls. You just take care of yourselves, and something will come up, you'll see.'

'Why does everyone keep saying something will come up?' Lottie asked Grace as they sat eating the last of the chicken broth and the remains of Cook's homemade pork pie. 'I mean really, Grace, why should it, really, it's as if they all still believe there are fairies at the bottom of the garden.'

'Aren't there?' asked Grace, straight-faced, essaying a little joke. But Lottie didn't smile, she was too busy eating her pork pie, practically cramming it into her mouth, which wasn't at all like Lottie, but who could blame her?

A bell sounded above them and automatically Grace looked up.

'I'd better see what Mother wants,' she said as she got up.

'I don't know how you know what she wants,' Lottie said, 'when she doesn't say anything.'

'I ask her if she'd like anything to eat, or drink, and she either nods, or shakes her head,' Grace replied. 'You know because you do the same.'

'Yes I know that,' Lottie sighed. 'What I meant was how can you know what she wants to *do* about anything if she won't speak?'

'If she really wants anything, she writes it down. Like when she wanted Dr Granger back the day before yesterday.'

The bell rang again, longer and more persistently.

'I'd better go.'

'Grace?' Lottie turned round in her chair so that she

could face her sister. 'What's going to happen? I mean when you go to London and take up your scholarship. What will happen then? To Mother and to me.'

'I'll talk to you about it when I come back down, Lottie,' Grace replied, opening the kitchen door. 'I've got an idea. But don't worry – ' she added quickly, seeing the look of apprehension on her sister's face. 'Nothing's going to happen to you. I'll make sure of that.'

'Grace?' Lottie called after her, but Grace was gone, hurrying away in answer to a third impatient ring on her mother's bell. She had been thinking all day about what she should do about the Academy, ever since a letter had arrived from Professor Goodfellow in that morning's post, confirming the award of the scholarship.

She climbed the darkened stairs up to her mother's candlelit bedroom. The door was half open, and inside the room Grace could see the shadow of her mother sitting up in bed, slowly brushing out her long hair, something she hadn't done since the day her husband had deserted her.

Her husband. Grace stopped on the stairs and frowned. She realized she had stopped thinking of the man who had partially created her as her father, and now saw him only as her mother's husband. Whenever someone sympathized with her plight, and told her how sorry they were to hear about her father, it was as if they were talking about a complete stranger. She didn't even hate him. It was simply as if as a parent, as her father, he had never really existed.

'Grace?' her mother's voice called. 'Grace, is that you?'

At once Grace ran, up the rest of the stairs and along the shadowy corridor, astonished by the sound of her mother calling which signalled the end of her silence. She hurried as fast as she could to the door of the bedroom, and opened it wide. Her mother was sitting up in bed, in a fresh gown with her best lace shawl, which she somehow or other must have managed to hide from the dunners, wrapped around her shoulders. She must have been brushing her hair for ages, because even in the faint light of the two candles Grace could see it spread about her shoulders in an orderly fashion.

'Come in, Grace. Come over here, please.'

Her mother turned to her briefly, as she would to her maid, and indicated with her hairbrush where Grace was to come and stand. Grace hurried forward to the end of the bed.

'I was so happy to hear you call, Mother,' she said. 'Lottie and I, we've been so worried about you. Are you feeling better? Is there anything I can fetch you?'

She stopped, and whatever the words were that she had been going to say she found she had forgotten them as she felt an odd chill overtake her. The eyes which now stared back at Grace were not the ones Grace was used to seeing. Her mother's eyes had always had a kind of softness about them, as if they were never quite focused on life, a little vague, just like her character. Now they were hard and bright, and seemed to stare right through her daughter, lit with a strange and vengeful light.

'I have been thinking as I have been lying here,' her mother said, over-precisely, 'and you will be glad to learn that I have reached a conclusion.'

Grace waited, unsure to which particular matter her mother was referring.

'Yes, Mother?'

'I understand it all now, Grace, and so too must you.'

Her mother picked a book from her bedside and placed it on her lap. Grace saw it was the Bible. 'I now understand why everything that has happened to me has happened. It has happened, Grace, because it was meant. And the reason why it was meant is because it is God's will.'

'It's God's will that Father ran off with Mrs Jenkins?'

Lottie's eyes were almost popping out of her head as she sat listening to Grace, huddled in a chair by the kitchen range wrapped up in a woollen carriage rug. 'How can that be God's will, Grace? To leave a family without money? And servants? And everything.'

'According to Mother it's a lesson in humility, Lottie.'

Grace raked the bottom of the dying fire with a poker and pulled her chair closer. Outside the kitchen windows an east wind was bringing the first snow of the year. 'She's been hearing voices, you see—'

Lottie giggled.

'No, it isn't funny, Lottie. At least it is, it may seem so to us, but it isn't funny because Mother *believes* it. She really believes the voices come from God.'

'And what we have to do is wait for His bidding.'

'That's what the voices keep telling her.' Grace stared into the fast fading glow of the fire. There was no more coal, and the wood they were burning now was the last of the cut and seasoned timber. 'Apparently we are God's vessels, and have been put here for a very specific purpose, a purpose which will be revealed to us very shortly.'

'By another voice.'

'Yes, Lottie. By another voice.'

Lottie moved her chair even closer to the fire and nearer her sister.

'You don't really believe this, do you, Grace?' she asked. 'Because I don't.'

'Of course I don't,' Grace agreed. 'But as I just said, Mother does. That's the whole problem. She's become convinced that she's been selected for some special task on this earth, that Father was taken away from her because he wasn't a good man and he would impede this work she has to do, and that we must live a life of humility and poverty in preparation for the work we have to do.'

There was a long silence during which the girls sat with their hands held out to the fire. The silence grew longer and longer because at that moment neither of them knew what more there was to say.

Conversely, Grace had found plenty to say to their mother on learning her conclusions, but it didn't take long for her to realize the pointlessness of trying to hold a sensible conversation with someone who had become convinced they were on a divine mission. At first Grace had made a brave effort to try to explain her plan, namely that while she knew they could no longer stay on at Oak Lee

House, it might be possible for them to move to a small house in London, a lodging whose rent Grace could pay for by working all the hours when she wasn't studying or sleeping. But her mother heard nothing of what she was saying, and after a while began to talk at the same time as Grace until Grace was forced into a helpless silence.

'You could always run away,' Lottie finally suggested. 'There's nothing to stop you going to London.'

'Only you,' Grace replied. 'And Mother.'

'I'd be all right,' Lottie argued bravely. 'I'm nearly thirteen, and I could do housework, or sewing or something. Until Mother's better. I don't see why you should have to give up such a wonderful chance. The chance of a lifetime.'

'I have no option, Lottie dear,' Grace said. 'I'd never leave you, and Mother is far too unwell.'

'Then let's call Dr Granger. He can give her something.'

'We can't afford Dr Granger, Lottie. We haven't any money. And even if we had, there's nothing he could do for Mother. What Mother's suffering from can't be cured by medicines.'

'You don't think that she's gone mad as *well*, Grace? Oh, with two mad parents, what chance is there for us?'

Lottie began to sob so deeply, Grace took her from her chair and sat her on her knee.

'Father's not mad, Lottie, whatever you think,' she said. 'He's just done something very foolish perhaps, or perhaps not. Who are we to say? And Mother isn't mad either. Really.'

'Even though she thinks God is talking to her?'

'Dr Granger said she's had a terrible shock. That it will take a long time for her nerves to recover. That's all it is, Lottie. It's just Mother's nerves.'

Of course Grace thought it was no such thing and that her sister was right. She had known it was nothing to do with nerves the moment she'd seen the different light in their mother's eyes. She had known it as she walked out of the bedroom and heard her mother still talking away, not to her but to herself. And she had known it for certain when her mother had told her what she, Grace, had to do, as decreed directly by God.

It seemed if she was not to be damned for ever for disobeying God's ordinance Grace must forget any fanciful notions she might have for herself and learn the meaning of true humility. To achieve that end she was to take herself at once up to Keston Hall where she was to seek employment, but only employment of the humblest kind. Grace was not to expect a job which befitted her social standing. Because it was God's will she must be employed in only the lowliest of positions in the Great House. In other words Grace was to go into service.

FOUR

That very same night, a few hours after Grace learned of her mother's divinely inspired wishes, unknown to Grace and unfortunately for her, a position suddenly did become free up at the Great House, due to the death of one of the between-maids, an Irish girl called Aggie who had been found hanging from a beam in her tiny bedroom.

Nothing was known of this tragedy outside the Great House, and even if it had been it would have been of no interest. The girl was Irish, an orphan. As no note was found, it was presumed to be a suicide. To prevent any embarrassments being caused for the owners of Keston Hall, Lord and Lady Lydiard, the death was certified as accidental. A broken neck sustained as the result of a fall downstairs, and within four hours of the body's being discovered it was discreetly removed to the local hospital for use by the students, after which it was taken for burial by the local Catholic community.

Grace passed the remains of the girl who was to be her predecessor as they were being taken by horse and covered cart from the house. She stepped aside as the vehicle trundled down the back drive, but as she had no knowledge of the contents of the gloomy-looking vehicle, she paid little attention to it, but quickly turned her attention back to the house that lay before her basking in the early morning light of an English January.

She had never seen it close to, even though she had lived all her life in the town dominated by the Great House. In fact few townsfolk had seen it, except for the tradesfolk, and even they were only ever allowed up the back drive when they were calling, a drive which as Grace was discovering gave no real sight or indication of the splendour of the house at all, since it was lined with tall dark-leaved conifers all the way from the back gate to the walls which surrounded the yards behind the house.

Through the vast main gates which hung on ornamented pillars the house could be seen as it was designed to be seen, at the top of a long drive which ran straight through manicured parkland. It was a single handsome block built of mellow stone, capped by a hipped roof along and around the top of which ran a promenade protected by a stone balustrade, in the centre of which was an octagonal cupola, which people said was used by the family and guests as a gazebo or occasional banqueting room.

The only times Grace had ever before seen this splendid vision were when she was a little girl and had stood at the main gates and stared up at the house, trying to imagine what it would be like to dine out on the roof of your own house, attended by liveried servants and uniformed maids.

Small as she was she had found herself wondering about the row of dormer windows in the roof, and trying to imagine what they housed. Perhaps a nursery floor, full of bright sunfilled rooms where children played under the watchful eyes of their crisply uniformed nanny and nursery maids, a caravan which could occasionally be seen promenading through the grounds. What a different world it had all seemed to the child who had stood staring through the gates, and what a different world it in fact was, as Grace discovered when a shirtsleeved footman opened a back door in the house in answer to her third ring on the bell and demanded with a nicely calculated show of impertinence what she might want.

'Could you please tell Mrs Quinn that Miss Merrill is here to see her?' Grace replied, as the footman stood eyeing her up and down.

'You've come about a position, that right? *Miss* Merrill?'

'Yes. That is perfectly correct.'

'Very good, *Miss* Merrill,' he smirked, before running a forefinger straight across the end of his nose. 'Please come in, won't you? Miss Merrill.'

Grace ignored the boy's impudent mockery and walked past him into the house. The footman waited till she'd passed him then kicked the back door shut with his booted foot.

'Oi!' he shouted as a maid scuttled by. 'Edith! Go and tell Mrs Quinn there's a girl 'ere to see 'er! And be quick about it!'

The maid stopped for a moment, her arms full of mops and brushes, and took a quick look at the caller.

Grace recognized her immediately, just as the maid recognized her. They had been contemporaries at Keston School until Edith Crane had left at fourteen to start earning her living sweeping the floors at the sawmill. Edith had hated Grace from the moment she had arrived at the school wearing one of Mother's cut down, but silk-lined, cloaks, and expensive velvet hair ribbons, but unlike the other children's her animosity had remained unabated throughout their joint schooldays.

Now she said nothing. She just looked at Grace, the flicker of recognition gone from her eyes and replaced with something close to triumph, before hurrying away into the dark of the passageway to do as the footman had bidden her.

'She's a right scut that one,' the footman said, wiping his nose with his finger once more. 'Close your eyes when she's around and there's no saying what you won't lose. This way. You'd better come and wait in the hall.'

The hall turned out to be a subterranean room where the servants obviously ate their meals and relaxed in whatever time they got off. There was a long wooden table down one wall, with benches either side and a wooden armchair at either end, and a selection of easy chairs in various states of disrepair arranged in a semi-circle round the hearth, where the remains of a small fire still smouldered.

The footman instructed Grace to sit down and wait before grabbing a plain black tail-coat off the back of a chair and hurrying away to answer a bell which had started to ring insistently on the wallboard by the door. Number eight bell. Grace wondered where it was. The library perhaps? Or her ladyship's drawing room?

Rather than sit, Grace stood and waited by a window, watching the activities in the yard outside. Two men were offloading barrels from a brewery dray into a cellar whose doors stood open to receive the contents of their arms. The doors waited for their burdens as if they were large wooden envelope flaps, while a seemingly endless line of variously shaped and sized boxes were being carried from the grocer's van into what Grace supposed must be store-rooms and pantries in the block directly opposite. Three stable lads were busy sweeping the yard clear of straw, horse dung, and the light scattering of snow which had begun to fall that morning. From another door four or five housemaids all in a line appeared, carrying before them what looked like chamber pots covered with cloths which they took across the yard to an outhouse in the far corner. As they disappeared inside, a man appeared at the gates making his way quickly across to the door where the groceries were being unloaded to knock on the window beside it, all the time looking over his shoulder as if he was being followed. Moments later a large red-faced woman in a long white apron whom Grace took to be the cook came to the door bearing a muslin-covered bowl which she handed the man in exchange for an empty bowl and a handful of coppers which he carefully doled out to her, after he had anxiously inspected the contents of the bowl Cook had given him. Cook obviously wasn't happy with the transaction because after she had received the money she poked the man in the chest with one sturdy finger and remonstrated with him, and kept on doing so until with a hangdog grin and a shake of his head he fished some more money out of his pocket and handed it over, before slipping out of the yard as quickly as he had come in.

'Grace Merrill?' a voice asked sharply from behind her. 'This way, please.'

The owner of the voice had turned and begun to leave the hall before Grace had time to glimpse what she looked like. All she could make out as she hurried to catch up was that the housekeeper was a tall woman in a black dress, with her hair hidden under a white frilled cap of lace and ribbons, and that she strode in a masculine way down the dimly lit corridors, accompanied by a jangle from the keys which hung from a *chatelaine* at her waist.

The woman finally stopped by a dark green-painted door, opening it and then standing aside, but saying nothing. Grace walked past her into a warm and comfortably furnished room, surprisingly so, after the austerity of the servants' hall.

'You may sit down,' the housekeeper said, closing the door and indicating a straight-backed wooden chair for Grace before taking her own place at a small desk facing the wall, where she sat silently sorting through some papers before paying Grace any further attention.

'You're from Oak Lee House, isn't that right?' Mrs Quinn said, still with her back to Grace. 'The other side of the town. On the Kingswood Road. A very pleasant spot. A relative of mine lives out that way. I often walk past your house.'

Taking her glasses off, the housekeeper turned round and faced Grace for the first time. Grace saw she was a surprisingly good-looking woman with a square jaw-line, an aquiline nose and thick dark eyebrows, but that when she smiled, as she was doing now while she looked at Grace, the smile was only on her thin-lipped mouth and not in her eyes.

'You're here to apply for a position in the house, I understand,' she continued, once she had finished her visual appraisal. 'Although for the life of me—'

Mrs Quinn paused and shook her head with a sigh.

'I think perhaps I ought to make it perfectly clear from the outset that there is no place here for any so-called "lady servants". This is a traditional household, run along traditional lines. What the fashion is in the cities is of no interest here. In my household a maid is a maid, not a lady servant. Is that clear?'

'Yes, Mrs Quinn,' Grace replied, as evenly as she could.

She had prepared herself for such instant provocation, resolving that she would not let herself be goaded into making any sort of reply which could jeopardize her chances of employment.

She had already fought and lost the battle as to why she should be placed in service. She was a girl, she was still legally in her mother's care, and most important, at least as far as her mother was concerned, it was God's will. God had spoken. It seemed that true humility was only to be learned by Grace's serving others. And by her bringing home a regular wage.

As if reading her mind, Mrs Quinn next expressed her surprise, an evidently enjoyable one, that a girl of Grace's background and breeding should wish to enter domestic service.

'I have to be scrupulously careful, you understand, as to whom I employ,' she told Grace. 'Working in a house such as this, for such a family, is a position of great trust, and one which I cannot have abused. You are not the usual sort of girl who applies for this sort of post. You must be aware of that, surely?'

'I have to find work,' Grace replied with perfect truth. 'My father has left home, and we have no money.'

'Have you no brothers?'

'Only a younger sister.'

'And your mother, she has no investments?'

Grace thought that must be perfectly obvious, otherwise she would not be there having to endure such humiliation. But, mindful of the fact that the final choice was either a job in service for her or the workhouse for them all, she merely nodded and continued.

'My father left my mother with no money when he went, Mrs Quinn,' she said, deciding on utter frankness, 'and the shock of it all has reduced our poor mother to frail health.'

Mrs Quinn narrowed her dark eyes and pursed her thin-lipped mouth.

'Your mother is not valetudinary, I trust?' she enquired. 'Worse, she isn't suffering from a mortal illness? I will not employ any more girls with mortally ill parents. Only last weekend, just when his lordship was entertaining a houseful of guests, one of the wretches wanted time off to visit her dying mother. I'll have none of such nonsenses, I must be frank with you, Merrill. I will not have my staff running hither and thither if and when they feel like it.'

Being called just by her surname was as if the woman had suddenly leaned forward and handcuffed Grace. Much more than the import of the housekeeper's tirade, that use of her surname 'Merrill' was as if Mrs Quinn had pushed a foot into her face and sent her hurtling down a ladder. Never before in her life had she ever been anything other than 'Miss Grace', or 'Miss Merrill', not once. Yet here she was now being called by her surname by someone greatly inferior to both her mother and to herself. Here she was being treated, Grace realized with a sickening shock, just like the servant she was, if she was very lucky, going to be.

She wanted to get up and go then, to take her leave of this odd-looking woman, who for reasons Grace couldn't understand frightened her. She wanted to stand up and confront her, and ask her how she dared speak to her like that. And then walk out of the house, not out of the servants' entrance through the back door, but the way she should rightfully have entered, through the front door.

But she knew she couldn't, just as she knew Mrs Quinn knew she couldn't, which was why the housekeeper was now staring at her in the way that she was, with an expression in her eyes that Grace didn't understand. Grace was there because she had to be there, and she had to take whatever crumb Mrs Quinn might decide to throw her, and they both knew it.

'You're quite a good-looking girl, Merrill,' the housekeeper suddenly said. 'Take your hat off so that I may see you better, please. Thank you.'

Grace did as she was bid, and sat with her hat on her knees, looking down at the floor.

'What remarkable hair you have, Merrill. It reminds me of my sister's hair; it was just that colour. I used to brush it for her every night. One hundred strokes. Every night I brushed it for her, little Annie. Alas, she was taken from us just past her tenth birthday. My little Annie.' Grace heard the scrape of the housekeeper's chair as she rose and came over to her. 'Just such hair as yours, long and silken.'

As soon as she felt Mrs Quinn to be near her, Grace sat bolt upright and stared ahead of her at the perfectly white wall opposite.

'Yes,' Mrs Quinn said finally as she returned to her chair. 'Yes, lovely hair, but I'm afraid you're far too pretty, Merrill. Far too pretty that is to be a housemaid. Far too pretty to be wasted on men. I don't imagine that first thing in the morning when they wake and see you with your pretty-pretty looks, with that shiny dark hair piled up under your lace and ribboned cap, I don't imagine any of the young *gentlemen* that stay here would be able to resist you for a moment. Nor any of the older ones, come to think of it. And while just like all the girls who come to work here you're probably thinking that could be an end to your troubles, having a flirtation with a handsome and *rich* young gentleman in the hope that he'll marry you, you can put such nonsensical ideas out of your head. Girls like you, Merrill, servant class, they're not for the likes of them. All you girls are for is a bit of their idle pleasure.'

'Are you not then able to offer me a position, Mrs Quinn?' Grace asked carefully, overcoming her almost uncontrollable desire to leave.

'I don't know quite what you can do, Merrill.' Mrs

Quinn sat back in her chair, folding her hands carefully in her lap. 'Girls from your background – you must have had everything done for you.'

'I have always helped in the house, for as long as I can remember,' Grace replied. 'We only ever had one maid, and Cook. My sister and I have always helped clear and wash up, and – and with the housework. And at Christmas and New Year, and any other big occasion, we help – or rather we helped, we always helped Cook.'

'Show me your hands.'

Grace held out her hands, palms up as instructed. Mrs Quinn took them in her own rough ones and examined them very carefully, without expression but most precisely, as if they were to perform surgical operations, not housework.

'I don't for a minute imagine they have ever blackened a range with Wellington lead,' she concluded. 'Nor cleaned out the flues. Nor scrubbed a stone floor.' She paused, waiting to look Grace straight in the eye. 'Which is what they'd have to do here,' she added, 'if I was to offer you a post.'

'Thank you,' Grace said, carefully withdrawing her hands, hoping the housekeeper hadn't noticed their involuntary tremble. 'I would only be grateful if such an occasion should arise.'

Mrs Quinn picked up her chair and placed it back facing her desk as she sorted through some papers. While her back was turned, Grace recomposed herself, breathing in deeply, and folding her hands on her lap. If she had to learn to endure humiliations such as this, then she must learn to do so with her pride somehow intact.

'A position for a "tweeny" has come free,' Mrs Quinn announced, turning back round. 'A "tweeny" being, as you might or might not know, a between-maid, a servant girl who helps both Cook and with the housework. As I said, I could not possibly allow you to work purely as a housemaid, were such a position free. Well?'

'Might I enquire as to the wages, Mrs Quinn?'

67

'Twelve pounds a year all found, you to supply the uniform.'

Two hundred and forty shillings. Twenty shillings a month. Grace realized that would barely cover the cost of the rent of number three, East Street, a furnished terraced house on the wrong side of Keston which was to be the family's new address as from next week.

'Is that the most I can expect?'

'No,' Mrs Quinn replied. 'If you work hard and gain promotion to parlour maid after two or three years, you could earn up to twenty-five pounds.'

Feeling suddenly that she was suffocating, Grace eased the collar of her blouse with one finger while trying to suppress the feeling of panic that was rising in her chest and now her throat. She felt as she imagined an innocent prisoner must feel when he hears the judge sentence him for a crime he never committed and faces an interminable sentence in gaol with hard labour.

'I must speak first to my mother.' Grace heard her own voice trying to say, distantly, as if from far away, down a long passage. Twelve pounds a year! That would hardly keep Mother and Lottie in firewood and bread.

'There is no question of my keeping the position open for you, Merrill,' Mrs Quinn's thin nasal voice echoed back. 'There are plenty of other girls needing the work.'

'Very well. I accept.'

Again Grace's voice seemed to her to come from someone else in some other place. The future perhaps, she wondered dully. The grim future.

All Millicent Merrill did when Grace told her how little she would be paid as a tweeny was nod, as if she had known the outcome of the interview all along.

'Twelve pounds a year. God's will, Grace dear. God's will that we should be poor and humble.'

'Poor and humble perhaps, Mother, but not cold and hungry too?' Grace said with sudden force.

'God will provide, Grace,' she explained, her eyes half closed with reverence. 'Work, and God will provide for us all.'

'What will you do, Grace?' Lottie wondered in a whisper after they had blown out their candles that night, and as they lay sharing the one bed left to them, glad of each other for the warmth as well as for the company.

'More important,' Grace countered, 'what will you do? Once I've bought my uniform, which I can only do by taking an advance from my wages, then I can give you all my earnings because I won't have to spend anything. But it won't be enough for you and Mother to live on, Lottie. Not nearly enough.'

'It might be when added to what I'm going to earn,' Lottie replied. 'Mrs Banks-Jones has asked me to read to her every afternoon after school, for sixpence a week, so has Miss Wardle, and so has Mrs Booker. So that's one shilling and sixpence a week, plus the money I make from the mending and sewing I'm going to take in.'

Grace hugged her sister to her and kissed her amongst her curly hair.

'You're wonderful, Lottie,' she whispered. 'And don't worry. We won't go down without a fight.'

'We won't go down at all,' said Lottie. 'Don't *you* worry.'

Grace did worry. While the wind blew stronger and stronger outside their bedroom window bringing more snow in from the east, she lay in the dark with her young sister asleep in her arms worrying about what was to become of them both. Even if Lottie did manage to earn an extra two or three shillings a week their joint weekly income would still be less than eight shillings; less than a farm labourer earned, less than sweat-shop workers in the east end of London were being paid. It was only six weeks since their father had walked out on his family, and in that short space of time they had been reduced from a comfortable genteel existence to near penury.

They had been forced to move since they could no longer afford the rent on their old home, and most of their possessions had been confiscated to help pay off the family debts. Grace wondered as she stared into the night what kind of man could do that to his family.

What kind of a man could spend money which he didn't have on expensive gifts and invite his relatives to share a Christmas dinner for which he hadn't paid and had no intention of paying? What kind of man could suddenly smile on his children and embrace them for the first time in their lives when all the time he was preparing to run away with their schoolteacher? What kind of a man could rob his wife of her *dot* and then run away with his *paramour*, leaving his family destitute? And his wife to go mad?

What kind of blood coursed in his veins?

And what kind of woman could take someone who loved and trusted her to the top of a mountain and promise her the world which suddenly lay at her feet, while all the time she was committing adultery with her father and planning to run away with him, in one cruel and fell swoop dashing all the magical hopes she had quite purposefully raised?

Was this what love was? Was it all a sham, a cheat, and a lie? Was this what men did to women and women did to men? Was this what would happen to her, and to the young girl who lay so fast asleep beside her? Were they both destined to have their hearts broken by men or be driven mad by their deceptions?

Would anyone ever love her now, now that she was to enter service; that is, anyone kind, or decent, or proper? Or was her life to be spent not only in domestic service, but also in the sort of service to which the strange and sinister Mrs Quinn had alluded in her interview, whereby the gentlemen guests at Keston, both young and old, might expect to take their pleasure with her? What was her life going to be like, the rest of her life, a life which only six weeks ago had suddenly promised so much but which now by force of circumstances had changed so dreadfully? Was it to be spent always in service or would there be a chance for escape, any chance at all?

There was no point in praying to God. If as her mother insisted this was God's will, then there was no point in beseeching Him to help her. If God had allowed all this to happen to a family which had always believed in Him and prayed to Him, then why should He pay any attention to prayers which sought to change His mind and His purpose? There was no comfort to be found anywhere, there was no hope left in the world, not in the world Grace was now being forced to enter.

She finally fell asleep just before from a leaden sky an uneasy dawn broke slowly over a snowswept landscape, and began to infuse Grace's last day of freedom with a cold grey light.

FIVE

Mrs Quinn showed her down a set of stairs at the end of a corridor which ran from the servants' hall and then led her along a dark passageway which from the cold and the lack of light Grace realized must be below ground level, until they came to an annexe with four plain black-painted doors and a stone staircase in one corner leading to another floor above.

'This is where you will sleep,' Mrs Quinn said. 'Kitchen maids and tweenies on this the lower floor, parlour maids above.' She placed a hand on the latch of one of the four black doors but didn't open it. 'You will rise at five-thirty in the morning to begin your duties. Crane will be your tutor for the first week. I understand you know each other, so that will be a help for you.' Now she opened the door and stood aside. 'Supper will be in half an hour in the hall, by which time you will be expected to be in uniform. Do not be late.'

Then she was gone, back into the gloomy shades of the passageway lit by only one sputtering oil lamp. There was no light in Grace's room, nor was there a window, just a grille high on the back wall, a couple of feet above head height. But before she could take in any more of her surroundings, the draught swung the door shut behind her, plunging the tiny room into pitch darkness. Propping the door back open with her suitcase, Grace saw a candle and a box of matches on a small table by the wall under the grille. She lit the candle, closed the door to stop the flame from dying and then looked round the room. Besides the table the only furniture was a large cupboard in one corner, a wooden chair and a cheap chest of drawers behind the door. There was no bed.

At least no bed was visible. It wasn't until Grace opened the large cupboard which she had assumed to be a wardrobe that she found an iron-framed truckle which folded back neatly into the cupboard when not in use. Several of its springs were broken, and the thin mattress curled up at the edges as soon as the rope which held it in place was undone. Two worn and rough woollen blankets lay folded on the cupboard floor, underneath a pair of patched and yellowing flannel sheets.

Pulling the chair away from the wall, Grace stood on it to look out of the grille. Even though it was dark she could see that the room was indeed below ground and that the only view in daytime would be of the pipes which she could vaguely make out in the murk. There was nothing else in the room besides an already fading photograph of the household staff posed in one of the courtyards outside and a strip of linoleum which stopped well short of the walls and the gap where the bed came down. With the heavy wooden door shut and no view of the world outside Grace considered she might as well be in prison.

She unpacked her uniform and laid the clothes of her service out on the bed, a spare chemise and pair of drawers, two flannel petticoats and one top petticoat, an extra pair of stays, two nightdresses, two print dresses, one stuff dress, four coarse aprons, four white aprons, two pairs of stockings, a pair of boots, a plain hat, a jacket and a pair of slippers, all of which she had purchased that morning in Aylesbury for five pounds, with the help of a charity which specialized in helping girls of good character who had fallen on bad times, the debt to be paid off by regular deductions from Grace's meagre wages.

Having laid out her duty clothes on the bed, Grace then

took off the dress in which she had arrived and her good petticoat and did as Mrs Quinn had instructed, changing into a plain flannel petticoat and pulling on a pair of thick wool stockings and ankle boots before dropping the thick stuff dress, which was fashioned out of a cheap and coarse woollen material, down over her head and tying on one of her white aprons.

Finally she fixed her plain white cap in place and then automatically looked round for a dressing mirror to check her appearance, only to find there was no such thing, just a scrap of broken glass nailed inside the cupboard door in which her predecessors could have done no more than arrange their hair.

While she might not know what she looked like, Grace knew at once what she felt, which was a sense of shame. The unusual weight and coarseness of the materials against her skin made her feel demeaned, as if the uniform was a symbol of her social debasement. She sat on the bed and slowly began to wring her hands as if she was grieving, so appalled was she by this powerful feeling of humiliation. As if having to apply for such a job and having to remain silent through Mrs Quinn's deliberately provocative interrogation and then being housed in such a tiny, dank and spartan cell hadn't been belittling enough, she now had to endure the indignity of donning and wearing this most menial of uniforms, a habit little different as far as Grace was concerned from that worn by criminals.

From the plain cap perched on her lustrous black hair and the coarseness of the cheap flannel and wool of her petticoat and stockings against her young skin, to the weight of her heavy thick-laced boots and the drabness of the rough wool dress, she felt utterly wretched. More than that, and even though she had done wrong to no one, she felt what she knew she was meant to feel: namely no better than she was. The simple process of stripping her of her clothes and subjecting her to a harsh regimentation had in a moment changed her from a free spirit into a vassal. She laced the fingers of both her hands tightly together to stop herself from crying, but it was no good, the lump in her throat would not go. Finally she pinched herself hard and long to give herself the strength to face what had happened to her, and the courage and fortitude to endure and survive what she now saw as her enslavement.

No one spoke to her at supper. She ate a meal of bread and cheese in the servants' hall along with all the other lower staff, Cook, the kitchen and the parlour maids, the footmen and the coachmen, while the senior servants, the house steward, the valet, the butler, and Mrs Quinn the housekeeper, took their supper separately in the steward's room. Among the lower servants all the talk concerned the behaviour of the weekend guests and how much the housemaids had made in tips.

One of the footmen who had acted as a valet for a gentleman guest who had arrived without a servant of his own boasted loudly that he had been given half a sovereign, which when challenged by the other footmen he was finally forced to admit was in fact only two shillings.

'I got five shillin's from my gentleman,' a snub-nosed maid called Dolly bragged. 'And here it is to prove it.'

She laid the silver coins before her on the table for all the other girls to see.

'That's because turning down his bed and emptying his po wasn't all you did,' Edith Crane told her. 'Maisie said she heard tell you left your cap down his bed while you was a-makin' of it.'

'That's enough of that,' said Cook, draining her glass of beer. 'We'll have no more of that sort of talk, thank you.'

'What I'd like to know is what your cap was a-doin' down the *bottom* of the bed, that's what I'd like to know.'

'You 'eard what I said, Edith Crane,' Cook bellowed. 'One more filthy word out of you, and I'll send you straight to Mrs Quinn for a larrapin'.'

Shortly after that Edith excused herself from the table and disappeared, slipping out of the room unnoticed by everyone except Grace.

Grace had seen the look in her eyes when she caught

Edith staring at her several times during supper, but whenever Grace tried to talk to her she immediately turned away as if she had no idea who she was, nor cared. Grace knew very well from school that Edith Crane was nothing if not unkind and malevolent, so she perhaps shouldn't have felt quite so hurt. Even so, she wondered miserably at the fact that she had quite obviously remained so unchanged. Even her shoes still had steel-capped tips to them, making her every movement across the flagstoned floor ring out with an importance that only matched the expression in her eyes. 'Got you!'

If only Grace had not been able to remember how she had once reported Edith to Mrs Jenkins for spiteful behaviour, but if only was just a little too late now.

Someone had been in her room. Grace knew it the moment she opened the door, just from the sense of it. Someone bad had been in the room, and of course it had to be Edith. But what she had wanted Grace didn't know as she stood by the table, the lit candle in her hand. Most probably she had been in to see if there was anything worth stealing, which there wasn't because Grace had brought no money, nor anything of the least value which still remained to her, for the very reason that she knew it would only be putting temptation in people's way. All she had brought to Keston were her uniform and a set of good clothes for wearing when she went home.

She checked through the chest of drawers in case it was clothes the intruder had wanted, but everything was just as Grace had left it, neatly folded and tidied away. The three books she had brought were still on the chair, by the photograph of Lottie and Grace Mrs Jenkins had taken one afternoon last summer in the garden of her cottage. The only thing that wasn't right was the smell, but it was hard to define because the room reeked anyway, of damp and rot, and of the drains which ran immediately outside the grille.

It wasn't until Grace slipped between the sheets that she realized what the smell was.

The one place she hadn't thought of checking was her bed. When she leaped off the truckle with the shock and turned the blankets back she found the whole mattress was soaking wet. The wretched girl must have turned back the blankets and walked up and down while she was relieving herself in order to make quite sure she didn't leave one dry patch.

Even Grace's nightdress was now soaked from where she had momentarily lain. Shivering from cold and from sheer misery Grace pulled off the ruined garment, rubbed herself as dry as she could with it and then changed into her spare nightdress. Next she turned the mattress, in the faint hope the urine hadn't yet soaked right through, but the mattress was so thin and worn by now it was nearly as wet on the underside as it was on the top. All Grace could do was to take the bare pillow and the top blanket, which mercifully were both bone dry, put on her jacket and her coat, and make herself up a nest on the worn thin lino floor.

Edith Crane was indefatigable.

She kept the torture up for the whole of the first week. Every night Grace went to bed, she found it soaking wet and stinking, and the troublemaker now made sure the pillow and both blankets were ruined too, so that by the weekend Grace was reduced to sleeping in a corner on the floor in just her working clothes and coat with her jacket rolled up as a pillow. The whole room stunk of stale urine. So much so, that once she was sure all the other maids were in bed, Grace had to sleep with her door open.

By the end of her first week at Keston she was running a streaming and feverish cold. And yet there was nothing she could say, and she knew it. It had to be borne.

There were other shocks in store for Grace that first week, from the sheer drudgery and hardness of the work to her revulsion at having to empty the full chamber pots she was instructed on her very first morning to help fetch from the bedrooms once the family were at breakfast.

Because, she discovered, the house did not have its full complement of water closets, it seemed that most of the older members of the household couldn't be bothered to make the short journey down the corridor during the night or even when they arose in the morning, so all their pots nearly always required emptying and then scouring clean and wiping. Everything needed cleaning, and every day as well. Each morning Grace was assigned to helping with the housework, never alone but always in the company of Edith, her shadow, who never addressed one word to her other than to instruct her what to do.

' 'Ere, Merrill,' she would say, 'open them windows wide! Mind the mirrors! Don't knock over the mirrors, you stupid gel! Or Mrs Quinn'll larrap you! Drape them bedclothes over the chair there! Pick up them clothes! Turn them mattresses and then clear out that grate!'

Sometimes, when she was sure no one else was about, Edith used to lie with her feet up on the unmade beds while Grace did the work of two, relaying the fires, dusting the rooms, making the beds and polishing the grates. Yet Grace endured it, thinking only of Mother and Lottie and the firewood stacked in the hearth, and that Lottie was well, despite everything. That was all that mattered. Not one word of complaint came from her, least of all about Edith's disgusting night-time routine.

At least not until it was brought to public attention. On the Monday morning of her second week, after she had finished her first set of household chores, and while she was tucking in thankfully to her breakfast in the hall, Mrs Quinn appeared at the doorway. At once the whole table fell silent, as everyone turned to see what the housekeeper wanted.

'Merrill,' she said. 'Stand up.'

Grace did as she was told, reluctantly putting the slice of meat pie back on her plate.

'Yes, Mrs Quinn?' she asked. 'Is something the matter?'

Mrs Quinn didn't answer. Instead she stepped back and snapped her fingers at an unseen servant. Edith

Crane appeared from the passageway with an armful of soiled sheets.

'I would have thought this was a habit we would have grown out of by now, Merrill,' said Mrs Quinn, nodding at Edith to hold up the stained linen for all to see. 'What is the matter? Afraid of the dark, are we?'

'No, Mrs Quinn,' Grace said, refusing to lower her eyes despite the terrible shame she felt.

'Then what is it, girl? Do you have something medically wrong with you? Because if that is the case — '

'There is nothing wrong with me,' Grace interrupted quickly, her voice ringing out clearly in the horrible silence around her. 'Nothing whatsoever.'

'Then how do you account for this, Merrill? This disgusting and utterly ruined sheeting?'

'I do not account for it, Mrs Quinn. I cannot account for it at all.'

There was a long silence, while all eyes switched from Mrs Quinn to Grace and then back to the housekeeper.

'Are you saying someone else did this, girl? Is that what you're saying?'

'All I am saying, Mrs Quinn, is that I cannot account for what happens to my mattress and my bedlinen every night.'

'Are you willing or indeed able to furnish me with another explanation?' the housekeeper enquired icily.

'No, Mrs Quinn,' Grace replied. 'That I'm afraid I cannot and will not do,' she added in quiet tones, suddenly only too aware of the difference between her voice and those of the people she was addressing.

'In that case I will need to see you in my room when your day's duties are over. In the meantime, you will take your mattress to the boiler room where it may be dried out.'

Mrs Quinn turned to go.

'I'm afraid I can't do that, Mrs Quinn,' Grace replied. 'That mattress is past redemption. You cannot possibly expect anyone to sleep on it any more.'

Mrs Quinn turned back. Across the table the snub-nosed Dolly winked at Grace while next to her one of the young footmen, the tousle-haired Tom, purloined her slice of meat pie, stuffing it into his mouth in one movement.

'I cannot have heard aright,' Mrs Quinn said. 'I gave you an order.'

'I know, Mrs Quinn. But I can't obey it. With the greatest respect you wouldn't even expect a dog to sleep on a mattress as soiled as you know that one is, Mrs Quinn.'

'Quite right too.'

Cook, who had been silently eating her way through a plate of cold meat and dumplings washed down with her first glass of ale, suddenly came to life, turning to face the housekeeper as she wiped her mouth on the back of her hand.

'This is no business of yours, Cook,' Mrs Quinn replied. 'This is a housekeeping matter.'

'Stuff,' said Cook, half-stifling a belch. 'Does she look like the sort of girl who'd bloomin' wet 'er bed? Course she don't. Don't be such an ass, Mrs Q. Merrill's a lady, more's the pity for her sake, and you know it. You're taking advantage cruelly.'

'Don't you call me names, Cook, or I'll be upstairs and with his lordship before you can say Jack,' Mrs Quinn hissed.

'Stuff,' Cook replied, with a wink to Grace. 'His lordship wouldn't dare get rid of me, 'cos I'm the only one who's ever made his soft breaded chicken cutlets exactly 'ow 'e likes 'em, like his old nanny made 'em. And you knows it. So just you leave this poor girl alone. If you asks me, which you never does, someone here's been playing a nasty little prank on Merrill, and wouldn't be the first time it's happened to a new tweeny.'

Cook's eye fell on Edith, and remained there until Edith was the colour of a tomato, then she wiped her mouth on her hand again and calmly poured herself another glass of ale which she drank down in one.

That night Grace slept in a dry and uncontaminated bed for the first time since she had joined the staff at

Keston Hall. Mrs Quinn also rescinded her demand for Grace to present herself for punishment after work, and for the first time at table in the servants' hall she was suddenly included wholeheartedly in the general conversation.

On the other hand no one addressed a single remark to Edith Crane.

Because she made no effort to ingratiate herself with the other maids, and because she went about her menial duties diligently and without complaint, Grace soon made friends of all the lower servants, bar of course Edith, who it appeared was radically disliked by all.

The other girls knew that Grace was different from them, coming as she did from what had been a respectable middle-class family, and that if her circumstances hadn't altered so dramatically instead of working as a servant at Keston Hall Grace might herself, even now, be employing a tweeny, if she had married. Grace was pleasantly surprised by the *camaraderie* she found below stairs, most particularly among the lower servants. She had been perfectly prepared to be ostracized initially, and in fact had mentally steeled herself for a long spell in Coventry since she thought the other maids must surely take against her the moment she opened her mouth. However, when she found how readily she was accepted once it was obvious she wasn't going to try to assert her superiority, and because she hadn't complained about or betrayed the wretched Edith Crane, Grace's misery greatly lessened. Although the work didn't become any less arduous or unpleasant as a result, the growing comradeship helped considerably to alleviate the rigour and monotony of their daily round.

The snub-nosed and bright-eyed Dolly became Grace's most immediate friend, and Cook her staunchest supporter. Dolly had been in service since she was eleven, starting as a scullery maid and earning promotion to full-time kitchen maid four years later. Unlike most of the other maids Dolly had no ambitions whatsoever to get married or save enough to set herself up in business.

She considered herself to be very lucky to have found a home in such a great house, and to be well fed and kept moderately warm and comfortable in return for doing the sort of work she'd been doing free for her drunken mother since she was six. Completely illiterate, as were several other members of the lower staff, she liked nothing more after supper than to have Grace read to her by the fire. By the end of Grace's first month this had become a moment to be treasured not only by Dolly, but by all the other maids, by Cook, and finally even by the male members of the lower staff.

In the beginning, when her audience was just her fellow maids, Grace read from the *Girls' Own Paper*, usually absurd tales of humble housemaids falling in love with the dashing sons of rich households and ending up as mistresses of vast estates to which Grace's audience would listen in rapt attention with shining eyes, some so familiar with the stories that they would often mouth the words as Grace read them, or join in the dialogue between maid and dashing, handsome son.

Sometimes for fun she would read from the *Servants' Magazine*, a journal which was designed to remind servants of their proper station, and which not unsurprisingly was met with hoots of mirth and a great deal of barracking whenever Grace read it out loud.

By the time Grace had graduated to the *Strand Magazine*, and was reading aloud everything from E. Nesbit's wonderful children's stories to serials by H. G. Wells and Conan Doyle, her audience had grown to the size of the entire complement of the servants' hall, Edith Crane included, who, although she never sat in the circle which now gathered around the story-teller, was always to be found sitting at the table pretending to read on her own when the time arrived for Grace to ask her fellow servants what they would like to hear that evening.

'You reads so well, Grace,' Cook would sigh, deeply settled in the best armchair, her feet up on the fender. 'I can just see it all happening. You reads like a teacher would.'

As for the family who employed her, Grace knew of them only what she heard at mealtimes in the hall, which would throb with the latest gossip.

At first Grace had been amazed at the inquisition which sat daily in judgement on the behaviour of the family and its acquaintances. She was also privately amused at how conservative and conventional the servants were compared to their employers as reported at the dinner table, and how shocked they were by any eccentricity or uncommon behaviour.

John, the senior footman, a dark-haired handsome boy of over average height, as was the general requirement for footmen, had won not criticism but approval from his peers when one day he reported making a gentleman caller wait for three quarters of an hour before announcing him, on no better grounds than that he had mistrusted his appearance.

'Why?' Grace had asked him, greatly intrigued. 'Was he inebriated? Or was it because he looked violent? What was it that made you suspicious, John?'

'For a start, Grace,' the young man had explained, 'he was clean shaven, which always arouses my suspicions. And secondly, his boots were fearful muddy and his clothes a sight. He was wearing a tweed suit to call, no less. And a cloth cap.'

'Tell Grace who your caller was, John,' Cook had urged. 'Go on, lad, tell 'er who 'e was.'

John hadn't found the incident in any way amusing, even in the retelling.

'He was none other than His Grace the Duke of Bruton,' he'd confessed, before adding an explanation which it seemed to Grace might be straight from *Alice in Wonderland* for what could have been a catastrophic lack of judgement. 'The whole point is that only a very few can afford to dress so poorly. Indeed, as my father would have it, it's perfectly possible to be too much of a gentleman to be a gentleman at all.'

Fortunately the Duke was apparently so eccentric himself that he wasn't in the slightest bit upset by his long wait and passed the time quite pleasantly by standing on his head. At least that was the position in which John had found him when he returned to announce him to Lord Lydiard.

From what she could gather it appeared to Grace that Lord Lydiard himself was hardly the most conventional of men. His two great pleasures, by all reports, were dining once a month with his six dogs, all of whom were made to wear specially fashioned tail-coats and bow ties, in the cupola on top of the roof, and playing plainchant on a church organ which he had ordered to be installed in the library.

'I was up there once,' Dolly told Grace, 'which I shouldn't oughta have been by rights, but I'd only left me cleaning things in the grate, see, that morning. Anyway I 'eard 'is lordship approachin', which you always can, mind, 'cos he trumpets like an elephant.'

George, another footman, cleared his throat loudly and slowly in imitation.

'So I runs behind the screen, don't I,' Dolly continued, ' 'cos like we said, 'is lordship cannot *stand* the sight of us. Of 'is servants. 'E catches sight of you and out you go, and no messin', like I said. Anyway, I'm behind this screen, see, in the corner of the library, when 'is lordship sits down at the organ, pumps it up like, then starts to play. And *abracadabra!*'

'*Cats' meat and mahogany gaslamp,*' Cook added.

'Out of one of the socking great pipes shoots a cat!' Dolly screamed. 'Flyin' through the air it was! Like a furry great cannonball!'

A few days later, Grace had first-hand experience of her employer's pathological dislike of seeing his servants. What was much worse was she also had her very first experience of the inherent dangers maids faced when setting a gentleman guest's early morning fire.

It was shortly after seven one morning, and she had already set and lit one of the fires in the guest bedrooms. She had then let herself into the next room through the

84

service door and was silently going about her work when behind her she heard the occupant stirring in his bed. By now Grace was well used to the sight and the sounds of gentlemen in the early morning so she simply continued with her work. She'd become so expert at laying and lighting fires in almost total silence that never once had she fully awoken any member of the household in all the weeks she'd been at Keston.

It wasn't until she saw the face looking at her in a mirror that Grace realized this morning was to be the exception.

The face was neither handsome nor prepossessing, nor young. It belonged to a bulbous-nosed middle-aged gentleman with slack wine-stained lips and red rheumy eyes. Grace knew who he was, she remembered from the gossip at last night's suppertime. The guest in number six bedroom was Sir George Parkin, member of Parliament for High Wycombe.

'Hello, my pretty,' he said in a thick unclear voice. 'I don't remember you at all.'

Grace dropped her eyes and continued with her task, only a little faster.

'Last time I stayed here, it was an Irish girl. Plain as a mule,' Sir George Parkin continued. 'This house is famous for the drabness of its skivvies. So you really are most refreshing.'

The bed creaked behind Grace as the man changed his position. A glance in the mirror showed him to be now lying on his side, staring at her.

'That's better.' He smiled back at Grace in the looking glass on the chest of drawers. 'Your backside's pretty enough, but your frontside's even prettier. Now hitch up your skirts and show me an ankle, there's a good girl. Just like they do in the Haymarket.'

Grace ignored him and leaned forward to put a match to the fire. She could hear her heart pounding in her chest.

'No need to,' Sir George said, lowering his voice. 'From here I can see two shapely little ankles well enough for meself.'

The fire wouldn't catch properly despite help from Grace's small pair of bellows, so she quickly lit another match. On top of the pounding of her heart she could now hear the man behind her breathing more heavily and slightly more rapidly.

'I can see your stockings, too,' he whispered. 'Just a bit of your stockings. Just enough.'

Grace pumped the bellows even faster and at last the fire caught. In a rush she threw her cleaning things back into her box with a clatter and got to her feet, resolutely avoiding any look at the man in the bed.

'I'm sorry for waking you, sir,' she muttered, starting towards the service door which was the other side of the room. But she had misjudged the distance between her and the bed, and even though she quickened her step it was too late. A hot, moist hand had her by one wrist.

'You light an excellent fire, child,' Sir George said, slowly breathing out. 'And not only in the grate. D'you see?'

Grace had her back to him, waiting for the moment he slackened his hold on her wrist. But not yet. He still held her tight, and now pulled on her arm.

'I said – d'you see?'

The second time it wasn't a request, it was an order, but one Grace refused to obey, deciding instead now to make a run for it, trying to free her slender wrist from her captor's thick strong hand.

'I said see, you little scut!' The voice was an angry animal growl, and the hand was too strong, pulling Grace back and turning her to the bed where Sir George Parkin now lay on his back, the bedclothes thrown back from his vast body, his nightgown hitched high up over a huge white stomach.

Grace knew nothing of this, nothing of what a man looked like naked, nor had anyone prepared her for such a moment. No one had warned her that in life this was what might actually happen to a girl. Words and images raced through her head as she tried to free her arm, as she shut her eyes against what she had seen, words and images from school, from the classroom, things she had been told – but they were nothing. *They were nothing like this.* The birds and their eggs, the flowers and pollen, bees and frogs – what had all that got to do with this? Yet her teacher must have known. Mrs Jenkins must have known what happened because *Mrs Jenkins must have seen this with her father.*

'Don't you scream,' she heard him command her. 'You scream, skivvy, and I'll make sure you're down that drive with your little bundle before I've taken me breakfast. Now come *here.*'

The hand pulled her roughly towards the bed, so brutally that Grace lost her footing and fell to her knees. But still Sir George Parkin didn't let her go.

'I want you to come here,' he whispered, bending down so his whiskered wet mouth pressed against Grace's ear. 'I want you to come here and make this happy. I want you to do just exactly what I tell you. And if you do, there'll be a shilling in it for you.'

Grace knew there was no refusal for her sort. You did as you were told. If you didn't, if you tried to refuse, if you made a scene and protested, if you screamed and called for help, no one believed you. No one would take your word against a member of Parliament's, against anyone come to that who was a house guest, a friend of the family, against anyone who was Upstairs.

'Yes, sir, of course, sir,' she heard herself whisper. 'Whatever you say, sir.'

'That's a good little girl. That's my pretty.'

He rolled once again on to his back and as he did so, just as Grace hoped and thought he would, he slackened the hold on her wrist. Grace was free in an instant, on her feet and flying headlong for the door, the wrong door, it wasn't the service door to the back steps, but it didn't matter. Not then, not just at that moment. It was a door, and it was the way out of the nightmare that the morning had turned into, and in another moment she was through it.

Through it and into the main corridor which mercifully at that moment was empty.

But Grace didn't know where or which way to go. The corridor ran straight along the first floor to the main landing and the stairs. Tiptoeing along it, past paintings of beautiful women and men on splendid horses, past sculptures of heads and torsos, and fine vases full of flowers, Grace's panic increased. She couldn't go down the main staircase. She could hear voices floating up from the hall below. Even if it were only the servants down there she knew she couldn't risk it because it wouldn't be any of the lower staff. It would be the butler, who was hand in glove with Mrs Quinn, or the parlour maids who by now would be up and about their duties, and there was nothing the parlour maids loved more than telling tales on their inferiors.

There just had to be another way out, another pass door somewhere.

A second corridor ran off at right angles to the main landing, at the end of which was a pair of large highly polished doors. If that was the main bedroom, Grace reasoned, then there had to be a service exit somewhere along the passageway. She made her way silently down it, and then suddenly stopped, rooted to the spot as she realized one of the bedroom doors in front of her was open.

There was someone asleep in the bed, and a maid on her knees at the fireplace. Grace waited to see who it was. It looked like Dolly, and if it was she could sneak into the bedroom and out with her through the service door at the back. But the maid didn't turn round. She was too busy trying to get her fire to light.

She was the right size for Dolly, small and with dark hair piled up under her cap. Unfortunately Grace couldn't get a clear enough sight of her because whoever it was now ducked down out of sight behind the bed as she struggled with her recalcitrant fire.

When she got up a moment later, Grace saw with a sinking heart that it wasn't Dolly at all. It was Edith Crane.

Edith didn't see her. Nor for some reason did she make for the service door in the bedroom. Instead she walked straight out of the main door and into the corridor.

'By all that's fancy what on earth — '

Edith stopped and stood staring at Grace who was doing her best to hide away in the shadows.

'I'm lost, Edith,' Grace whispered. 'The man in bedroom six. He tried to — ' Grace was at a loss for words. Not any more from the fright, but because she didn't know quite how to describe what had just happened to her. 'He tried to — '

'I'll bet,' Edith hissed back. 'They're all the bloomin' same. Filthy bastards, that's what they all are, Grace, and no mistake.'

Grace hadn't the time to be shocked at Edith's language. Besides, after what had just happened to her Grace thought she would never again be shocked by anything.

And anyway Edith now had her by the wrist.

'Just don't say nothin',' she whispered, beginning to lead Grace back along the corridor. 'And in case you're wonderin', we always come back this way, 'cos it's quicker. Rather'n all 'em back stairs. It's all right. None of them lazy aristocrats is ever up at this hour.'

But as luck would have it, just as they were in no man's land halfway along the corridor, to their horror they heard the main bedroom doors flung open behind them and a sound like a trumpeting elephant.

'Landsakes!' Edith hissed. 'Quick – up against the wall! No – not back to it – face it! Press your face to the wall, stupid!'

Grace did as she was told and as Edith was doing, pressing herself as hard as she could against the corridor wall, until her nose was so flattened her eyes began to water.

'Don't move!' Edith urged in a whisper. 'Don't even breathe, not even for a second!'

From the corner of one eye Grace could see a very tall and very stout man dressed in a quilted dressing robe rushing towards them, trumpeting just like George's imitation, with both his arms stuck out straight in front of him. The nearer he got to them the faster he went, until he passed them by, arms out like ramrods and his gaze now firmly fixed on the ceiling.

Neither girl moved until they were quite sure from his footsteps and his trumpetings that his lordship was safely out of sight. Then they bolted as fast as their legs would carry them back through the pass door which was only a matter of feet away and which took them straight down to the corridor outside the kitchens.

'Thank you, Edith,' Grace said as both girls stood straightening their dresses and aprons. 'You saved my neck.'

'No matter,' Edith replied before she walked away. 'Nothing to it. Anyway. You saved mine and all, and that's for sure.'

Otherwise nothing was said of either incident, not a word. The only repercussion was an order to the steward which he duly passed on to Mrs Quinn that the main corridor walls outside Lord Lydiard's bedroom were to be washed down thoroughly with carbolic soap. After all, with servants being as they were, you never could tell.

It was fully three months before Grace saw anything more of the Lydiard family. Her day was so long and the work so hard, she never had time to go outside the house at all. Up at quarter to six every day, she spent all morning in housework before returning to the kitchens to help Cook prepare lunch, after which she would help wash up, clean and scrub the kitchen until mid-afternoon by which hour and following a hastily snatched cup of tea it was time once more to start helping Cook prepare and make dinner, wash up again afterwards, then read to everyone by the fire until the household proper had retired for the night and everything else had been washed and put away. By that time everyone was too exhausted to think of anything except sleep.

In six weeks she had one day off, half of which she slept away, and the other half she spent at home with Lottie and her mother. Six weeks later she had a second day off which she spent alone with her mother so that poor Lottie could have some time visiting friends of her own age.

Her mother was no better and no worse. According to Lottie she spent the whole time in her room, either in bed, or up and piously reading the Bible, while Lottie cleaned the house, shopped, cooked and spent her evenings sewing and mending.

Between the two of them, they made just enough money to get by, to feed and house Mother and Lottie, with a little left over which was put aside for emergencies. Gone were the days of new clothes hand-made from expensive materials. Everything now Lottie patched or darned, nor was she too proud to turn away charity. Several of the local benevolent societies who had learned of Millicent Merrill's plight called on Lottie to find out the family's circumstances, and one in particular, the Aylesbury Association for Distressed Gentlewomen, finally undertook to rehouse Lottie and her mother in a small but much more comfortably furnished thatched cottage on the outskirts of Lower Pitchook, a hamlet three miles from Keston but on the same side as Keston Hall. This helped the family finances considerably, since they no longer had to worry about the rent, nor about fuel since sufficient wood and coal were supplied with the tenancy.

It was one warm April day when at the end of her day off she was walking back to work from Lower Pitchook that Grace caught her first sight of the entire Lydiard family as they drove slowly by in a scarlet and black four-in-hand, drawn by a team of superb skewbalds in shiny, gleaming black harness. Lord Lydiard, in a black topcoat with a grey top-hat, had the reins, with his wife beside him, a slender woman dressed in a green velvet coat trimmed at the collars with long white ostrich feathers and a large broad-brimmed hat beplumed in inky-dark green. Behind them on the third row of seats sat a handsome young man and a beautiful woman, whom Grace assumed to be their son and daughter-in-law, the Honourable John and Serena Rokeham, with their two small children Henry and Harriet placed in safety on the middle row. Finally, perched on the dicky seat behind the Rokehams sat two of the footmen, John and George, as smart as paint in their shiny black top-hats and leather gloves, double-breasted black livery, breeches and top-boots. It was a handsome sight, and for the first time Grace felt oddly proud that she was connected with the family, however spurious her connection might actually be. Not that anyone in the splendid vehicle paid her the slightest heed. It rolled by to the clatter of sixteen hooves with all on board staring silently ahead. Even the footmen ignored her, although once the carriage was past, both John and George waved a hand privately behind their backs.

That was the last Grace saw of the family until Lord Lydiard was found dead in his bed on midsummer morning and the entire household assembled for his funeral.

S I X

'Meg's poorly again,' Beth, the tallest and most handsome of the parlour maids announced at midday, just as Grace was finishing laying the table for their dinner in the hall.

Cook, who had just collapsed in a welter of sweat after preparing a six-course lunch for twelve, sighed and held up her empty beer glass. Edith took it and scuttled away to replenish it from the large earthenware jug which in an effort to keep it cool had been stood in a corner of the flagstoned floor. It was a baking hot June day, and even though the kitchens and the hall were below ground level the whole of the staff quarters was like a furnace. Even the walls of Grace's cell-like bedroom dripped with condensation, just as all the servants ran with sweat, despite the fact they were all in their summer uniforms and dresses. There was no way of getting cool, either. For the servants it was baking inside and outside.

'What is it this time?' Cook asked Beth, who had stretched herself out on one of the long wooden benches and was fanning herself with an old copy of the *Illustrated London News*. 'Not Meg's chest agin, surely not?'

'I really don't know, Cook,' Beth sighed. 'Just as I don't rightly know how to keep my cheeks from shining. Mrs Quinn had another word with me about it this morning. As well as complaining of my fragrance.'

'Lack of it more like,' Cook grunted, emptying her half glass of ale in one swallow. 'Smells like a farmyard in 'ere.'

Grace couldn't help but agree. In the winter the unaccustomed smell of so many people working in close quarters had become tolerable surprisingly quickly, as indeed had the all-pervasive and ever-present odour in the servants' quarters of linoleum and stale cabbage, but now that summer had arrived and with it a heatwave the fetid reek of so many perspiring bodies was suffocating, a situation aggravated by the fact that the house was full of guests who required constant feeding, which meant that the kitchen ranges were roaring from dawn until dusk. Grace set a meat plate at every place and envied the lot of Meg and the other nursery maids, high up under the roof of the house on the very top floor, with all the windows flung open to catch the breeze, far, far away from the murderous heat below in the kitchens. Whatever was wrong with poor Meg, and from the sound of her malaise it seemed to be nothing more than another summer cold, Grace would gladly have swapped places with her, rather than endure one moment longer in her subterranean hell.

She was to be given the chance less than a week later.

Mrs Quinn summoned her from her bed in the middle of one thundery night, ordering her to get dressed and to go up to the nurseries with scrubbing brushes, mops and a plentiful supply of carbolic, iodine and soap. Edith and Dolly were also roused from their beds and given the same orders.

As the three girls gathered in the gloom of the servants' hall with their buckets and disinfectants, Edith hissed at Grace and Dolly to come over to the window and see what was going on. Outside in the yard, lit by the constant sheets of white lightning, stood an ambulance, into which a stretcher was being loaded by two men, the lower portions of whose faces were hidden behind white masks.

'I'll bet 'tis Meg,' Edith whispered. 'Jahn said she were bad.'

' 'Ow'd John know?' Dolly retorted. 'John knows nothin' 'bout what happens up there.'

'Dick do,' Edith replied. 'Dick what looks after Master 'Enry's ponies. Dick told Jahn Meg were taken real bad this time.'

'What is it exactly that's wrong with her?' Grace asked. 'I thought she just had a weak chest.'

Edith looked at Grace for a long time before she replied.

'Jahn says 'tis the sepsis,' Edith whispered. 'They say 'tis TB.'

On Grace's insistence all three girls fashioned themselves protective masks before they set about scrubbing out and disinfecting Meg's now empty bedroom on the nursery floor, and then the whole of the nursery suite except the three bedrooms occupied by a fast-sleeping Nanny, Rose the other nursery maid, and their two young charges. Grace was worried about the danger to the children, but in the event Dolly turned out to be a mine of information on the subject of tuberculosis and put her mind at rest.

'It's only babies what are in real danger,' she whispered to Grace and Edith as they scrubbed their way on their knees across yards of lino flooring. 'I remember my sister tellin' me, when the baby next door died, and then its mother. Once they're about six month, babies get – what's it called?'

'Immunity?' Grace volunteered.

'Yeah,' Dolly agreed. 'They get this immuninity and you can't get the sepsis again till you start comin' on. You know what I mean, till you start gettin' your monthlies. Then you can get it till the day you die, like. That is if you don't die from it before.'

'But 'tis infectious, in'it though?' Edith asked nervously, holding her mask close to her mouth as she scrubbed. 'I'd 'eard some'un only 'ad to cough at 'ee.'

'Nah,' Dolly scoffed. 'That's old wives' palaver. What you got to watch is the damp, right? Damp dark rooms is what does it. That's what did for all 'em what got it down our street.'

Once they'd scrubbed and disinfected all the floors and flat surfaces, their last instructions, issued by Mrs Quinn from the bottom of the nursery stairs which was as far as she would go, were to take all Meg's bedding, linen and towels down to the boiler room and incinerate them.

'Do you really think the children are safe?' Grace asked Dolly again on their way downstairs. 'It seems so odd to wash everything down and take away all the bedding yet leave the children asleep up there.'

'They'd have got it by now, Grace,' Dolly assured her. 'You mark my words. Meg's had a chest ever since she come 'ere.'

'And what about Nanny?'

'Nanny's as tough as an old boot. Anyway, she keeps 'erself well and disinfected, know what I mean?'

Dolly grinned at her and kicked open the door of the boiler room. Grace didn't know what she meant, nor did she have time to ask because at that moment there was a brilliant flash of lightning, a crack of thunder and a hand took sudden hold of her elbow.

'Merrill,' Mrs Quinn's voice said in her ear. 'I want to see you in my room just before breakfast.'

At a quarter to eight when Grace knocked and entered Mrs Quinn's parlour she found the housekeeper in a very different mood from usual. She was obliging, interested in Grace's progress, and on several occasions even managed to smile. Far from being charmed, Grace found herself unaccountably even more disconcerted by the woman than ever. There simply was something in Mrs Quinn's aura which frightened her, so that the more the housekeeper tried to beguile her, the less at ease Grace felt.

'I'm very satisfied with the way you've settled down here,' she said, smiling kindly and fixing Grace directly with cold, black eyes. 'It isn't ever easy, joining a household such as this. And it must have been particularly difficult for a girl like you. A girl from your background. With your social graces. Blessed with your looks. I trust the gentlemen have been behaving themselves with you?'

'I've had no trouble whatsoever, Mrs Quinn,' Grace replied, lying without repentance.

'Downstairs as well, I trust?'

'Downstairs as well, Mrs Quinn.'

'At even their best men are poor sorts of creatures, Merrill, wouldn't you agree?'

'I find their company agreeable enough. Men like John and George — '

'Footmen,' Mrs Quinn interrupted contemptuously, before remembering to sugar her disparagement with another smile. 'A girl like you, Merrill. You can do a lot for yourself. You would hardly want to waste yourself on a humble Johnny or George.'

Grace was then offered some tea, but declined in the hope of truncating the interview.

'You won't get tea like this in the hall,' Mrs Quinn insisted, pouring her a cup. 'This is as good as you would get upstairs, I assure you.'

For a few minutes they sat and sipped their tea in silence. Mrs Quinn's boast hadn't been an idle one, Grace realized, as she enjoyed the kind of tea she remembered having with Mother, in what she now thought of as the old days.

'There are other advantages in preferment, you see,' Mrs Quinn continued, carefully replacing her cup and saucer on the table. 'Other than just the vulgarity of more money. The entire quality of one's life improves, the higher up the ladder one climbs. But then I don't have to remind you of that, Merrill. It is hardly as if you were unfamiliar with luxuries. Equally I am sure you look forward to the day when once more you will be able to enjoy shall we say, niceties?' Mrs Quinn paused. 'Or have you perhaps quite given up hope of ever seeing such a time again? I do sincerely trust this is not the case.'

'I have every hope that one day my life will be once again a little different.'

'Good,' Mrs Quinn murmured. 'Good. Good.'

She left her hand on Grace's knee for just a moment

more, and then sat back, folding her hands in her lap.

'It surely must have occurred to you that following the wretched Parker's removal to hospital there will be a vacancy on the nursery floor,' the housekeeper continued, with both her eyes now closed. 'The girl will not be returning here, whether she lives or whether she dies, the latter of which I understand to be the probability, and so naturally I shall be required to see that the now vacant position of nursery maid is filled, and as soon as possible.' The dark eyes flickered slightly, seeming suddenly opaque, and expressionless.

Grace said nothing, and her face said nothing. But against her will her heart leapt.

'I understand you more or less brought your sister up yourself, Merrill, as I did. We have a great deal in common.'

'Lottie and I are very close, but I wouldn't say I exactly brought her up — '

'Cook told me.' Mrs Quinn nodded briskly, while her eyes seemed to roam around Grace's face. 'Because we have so much in common, I thought I would put you forward as my first recommendation.'

'That's very kind of you, Mrs Quinn.'

'Her ladyship will approve of you,' Mrs Quinn continued. 'You're well spoken. Presentable. A most attractive girl.'

'Thank you, Mrs Quinn.'

Grace made as if to move, brushing her skirts out with her hands, before looking to the housekeeper to see if the interview was concluded. Whatever she did, Grace knew she mustn't betray the excitement she felt. Mrs Quinn was often the subject for muted discussion in the hall, and everyone spoke of her quite open sadism, and of how she relished setting up your hopes and then dashing them.

'You may go now, Merrill,' Mrs Quinn said. 'I shall keep you abreast of developments.'

Grace thanked the housekeeper and made for the door.

'There is just one other thing.'

A hand took one of hers, a cold, dry hand which caught Grace's warm and still soft one, holding her back.

Mrs Quinn turned Grace to her, taking both her hands.

'If I manage to procure this preferment for you, Merrill, I should very much like you to come and see me. We could take tea together, you and I. We have so much more in common than the rest of the herd in the servants' hall. Whatever you may think, I get lonely here in the evenings. There really isn't anyone on the staff who is of my disposition. Socially as well as otherwise. You're different from all the other girls. You're different from anyone else here; I mean anyone else employed here. I should so like you to come and visit me whenever you have the chance so that we can talk. You're a very intelligent girl. Good conversation is sadly lacking in a housekeeper's life, you understand. If you gain this preferment, my dear, you will have to promise to come and see me. Now I know you will at least promise me that, won't you?'

There was no good reason why Grace should not promise to do so, no good reason of which at that moment Grace could think. She couldn't refuse on the grounds of finding the woman's company awkward and uncomfortable. Perhaps she was strange, Grace thought, because she spent so much time alone. There were all sorts of *perhapses*, and none of them provided a good enough reason for Grace to refuse to come and see her.

More important, none of them provided Grace with a good enough reason to turn down the chance of this promotion. She would have done almost anything for the chance of getting out of the kitchens, to get out of emptying chamber pots, scrubbing bare boards and stone floors, washing up a never-ending stream of crockery, cutlery and glassware, and emptying, scrubbing and scouring filthy, sooty fireplaces. So how could she refuse? What was the odd slightly uncomfortable evening spent with an obviously lonely woman compared with an escape from drudgery? Life upstairs, way up there under the roof, far away from the heat and noise and smell of the kitchens, life had to be heaven compared to the hell of these months below ground. So yes of course, she would agree. She would come down and pay Mrs Quinn a visit whenever it was possible, whenever her work allowed it, whenever she was free to do so.

And whenever it wasn't possible, whenever her work was too much, or whenever she wasn't free to do so, she would send down her apologies and a promise to pay another visit at the earliest opportunity.

Mrs Quinn would understand. Mrs Quinn would see how hard she was working, and how well she was doing in her new post, and she would understand that Grace would be able only to pop in when she was passing and just exchange the time of day.

'I shall hold you to your promise, girl,' Mrs Quinn told Grace, smiling. 'Never fear.'

It was still hot up under the roof, even with all the protectively barred windows open. But Grace no longer felt she was in prison. Up under the roof where outside the house-martins had built their nests beneath the eaves the sun shone directly into all the south-facing main rooms, which overlooked nothing but the magnificent parkland. The rooms on the back and north side of the top floor were beyond the boundaries of the nurseries and used only as attics and boxrooms. After the rank and subterranean gloom of the kitchens and the servants' quarters, it seemed to Grace as if she had ascended into heaven. At least, that was her first impression as the other nursery maid, a tall morose and adenoidal girl called Dora, showed her around.

There were three main and good-sized rooms: the nursery playroom, the dining room, and a sitting room for Nanny; a small kitchen with washroom and pantry off, separate bedrooms for Nanny and the two children, a spare bedroom, and one which Grace was to share with Dora, a large bathroom and two water closets. The door of the nursery playroom was the main entrance into the suite of rooms, leading off the landing from the main staircase which in turn led one floor down to the schoolroom and rooms occupied by Miss Chambers the governess. From the small kitchen a dumb waiter dropped all the way down to the main kitchens, four floors below. But although the rooms were sunny and bright, all the furniture was old and well past its prime, most of it obviously having gradually worked its way up through the house. The nursery suite was also surprisingly untidy and disordered.

'It weren't always like this,' Dora sniffed when Grace remarked on the clutter. 'Not so long ago you could eat off the floor. The rule up here was – well, you can see for yourself.' Dora pointed to a hand-painted motto above the main nursery window. *Do as you would like to be done by*, Grace read. *And leave as you would most like to find*.

'So what happened?' Grace asked.

Dora shrugged and blew her nose.

'Don't ask me,' she replied. 'Ask Nanny.'

In all her months at Keston, Grace had seen Nanny only on a handful of occasions, and then always distantly, up at the front of the estate chapel at Lord Lydiard's funeral, or out walking her two small charges in the park. Neither was much said about her in the servants' hall, little beyond jokes about her fondness for the bottle and vague references to how long she'd been in service to the family, none of the estimates matching. As for the two children, nothing was said of them at all, because nothing whatsoever was known of them by the lower staff. As the days rolled on in the basement caverns of the great house in a changeless stream, to the staff those up under the roof in the nurseries were just yet more mouths to be fed.

'That'll do 'em,' Cook would say, piling a tray of lukewarm porridge and none too fresh bread into the dumb waiter at breakfast time, or a dish of overboiled fish and cold potatoes for nursery lunch. 'And I'll 'ave no more complaints that it ain't good enough. Law luv me, we're only feedin' bloomin' kids.'

Besides, as Grace gathered, it was deliberate policy on the part of families such as this to keep the children poorly fed because a simple plain diet was taken to teach them self-restraint.

'I think that's all eyewash meself,' Dolly once volunteered. 'We eats better 'n 'em down 'ere, and while I'm not sayin' that I knows all the ins and outs of 'avin' servants, I do knows that can't be right.'

But to her shame, because she was so hard pressed to find enough time to do her mountain of work, like all the other maids and lower servants very soon Grace gave little thought to what went on in the nursery and even less to what went up to the nursery in the way of food, food which all too often came down again untouched, to the undisguised disgust of Cook. Grace's attitude soon changed once she experienced nursery life at first hand.

Admittedly she had been expecting Nanny Lydiard to be old. After all, if it was true that she had been Nanny to the late Lord Lydiard, subsequently to his son, and now to his grandchildren, she would have at least to be in her early seventies since the late lord had been fifty-four when he had died so unexpectedly. But when Grace actually met Nanny Lydiard face to face for the first time she realized that the old nurse must be well into her eighties.

She was a tiny woman, grown even smaller with age, with a round brown-button-eyed face which was etched so deeply with lines it looked as though it had been crumpled like an old sheet of brown paper, while her back was permanently bent so that she could no longer quite straighten her neck, and her fingers were so crooked and stiffened she had great difficulty holding a teacup or cutting up food. Yet her mind seemed as bright as her button eyes as she sat that first morning at breakfast assessing Grace, although Grace noticed her head nodded slowly and uncontrollably as she talked.

'You're not the usual sort of gal they send me up at all, not in the slightest,' she said as the two children sat silently over their porridge, trying not to stare at the new arrival. 'You're not a bit like Dora here. Dora's greatest ambition in life is to marry a vicar, but somehow I feel that would be of little interest to you. Dora's a good girl and works very hard, but I think even Dora would agree you two are as chalk and cheese, wouldn't you, Dora?'

'Yes, Nanny,' Dora replied dutifully, cleaning the last lump of lukewarm porridge from her bowl.

'And take that horrible elbow off the table, Henry,' Nanny instructed, although she wasn't even looking at the boy. 'Joints are put on the table for carving only, as you well know.'

'Yes, Nanny,' Henry said, removing his elbow and putting his spoon to one side of his still full bowl.

'Isn't it a little hot for porridge, Nanny?' Grace ventured, noticing neither child had touched their gruel.

'The weather has nothing to do with what Cook sends us up, girl,' Nanny replied rather sharply. 'And it's certainly not your place to question it. Although I will allow that Cook seems to know how to cook little else for our breakfast other than porridge.'

'I could have a word with Cook if you like,' Grace volunteered. 'I'm sure it's just an oversight. She has so much to do this time of the morning I'm sure she'd be only too happy if she didn't have to make porridge as well.'

'Hmmmph,' Nanny snorted, the disapproving grimace squashing her old lined face up even more so that she bore an even closer resemblance to a hedgehog. 'The gal's been up here for all of an hour and already she's telling Nanny how to run her nursery. Now just you eat up all your breakfast, children, or there'll be no getting down from table until you do.'

A couple of minutes later Nanny had fallen fast asleep and begun to snore, still upright at the table. As soon as she did, Dora took both the children's bowls, scraped their uneaten porridge into her own plate and polished off the lot.

'Is this the rule, Dora?' Grace wanted to know in a whisper. 'Is this what happens every morning?'

'Only the mornings Nanny gets up,' Dora replied. 'Or rather remembers to get up.'

The pretty little blond girl giggled at Dora and then bit her lip to stop.

'It's all right, Harriet,' Grace said. 'You can laugh if you want to.'

'No we can't,' Harriet told her. 'We're not allowed to laugh at table.'

'We can do what we like when Nanny's asleep,' her brother said. 'And you don't have to worry about *her*, Harriet.' He pointed at Grace. '*She*'s only a maid.'

'Yes, that's right, Henry,' Grace began.

'Master Henry,' the nine-year-old boy corrected her.

'Master Henry,' Grace agreed. 'And as I was saying, Master Henry, I may indeed be only a maid. But it's still rude to point at someone, whoever they are. Now eat your bread and jam, and drink your milk.'

'I don't like bread and jam. And neither does Harriet.'

'Dora does,' Harriet said, pushing her plate towards the nursery maid. 'Dora eats anything.'

Henry followed suit, and then both the children drank their milk, folded their napkins and got down from the table.

'Don't you have to ask to do that?' Grace said.

'Nanny's asleep,' Henry replied scornfully. 'You can't ask someone if they're asleep.'

Since Dora was still stuffing herself with the extra rations of stale bread and jam, Grace cleared away and began to wash up.

'What you doin'?' Dora asked accusingly, appearing at the kitchen door.

'What do you think?' Grace replied, looking for some soap to wash the dishes.

'I 'aven't finished me breakfast yet. And what you lookin' for?'

'Some soap, Dora. To wash up our dishes.'

'Don't be daft. You don't wash them. Them go straight back down to the kitchen to be washed.'

'I know,' Grace said, at last finding a scrap of soap. 'For some poor overworked girl to wash up down there. Did you ever work in the kitchens?'

'No.' Dora frowned, wiping her mouth on her apron. 'I was employed as a nursery maid, first off.'

104

'That makes sense,' Grace replied. 'Now find a cloth and start drying these.'

'Hang on, whatever your name is.' Dora stayed where she was in the doorway, picking her teeth with the nail of a little finger. 'Don't you go telling me what to do and what not to do. You're a scullery, so don't you go cheeking me.'

'I was a scullery,' Grace corrected her. 'Now I'm a nursery maid. The same as you.'

She threw Dora a drying-up cloth, and with exceedingly bad grace the girl began to wipe the handful of dirty dishes.

When they were finished, they found Nanny still fast asleep where they'd left her at the table. The two children meanwhile were heading hand in hand for the main door.

Grace intercepted them.

'Just where do you think you're going, you two?'

'We do actually have names, you know,' Henry said loftily.

'So do I, Master Henry. Mine's Grace.'

'Then please let us out of the door, Grace,' Henry replied, 'or we shall be late for Miss Chambers.'

'Their governess,' Dora said with a sniff, *en passant*.

'Shouldn't someone take you to Miss Chambers?' Grace asked.

'It's only one floor down, Grace,' Harriet explained. 'You really don't need to bother.'

'Nanny sometimes takes us down,' her brother added. 'When she's awake.'

'You mean when she remembers,' Harriet added with an impish grin. 'We'll be perfectly all right, Grace.'

Nanny in fact didn't wake up until half an hour after the children had gone downstairs for their lessons. Grace was all for rousing her, but Dora indicated it would be more than her job was worth.

'You've 'eard of sleepin' dogs no doubt,' she said. 'Well sleepin' nannies is a whole sight worser.'

While the old lady slept, Grace organized Dora into

tidying the cluttered and chaotic nursery with her. They were almost through by the time Nanny awoke with a sudden start.

'What's all this?' she enquired, staring around her with a blank look. 'We've had our spring clean, Dora. And why aren't the children up for breakfast? And who – ' she added, with a sudden sharp look at Grace, 'who in heaven might you be, if you don't mind telling me?'

That evening, after Grace and Dora had put the children to bed and Grace had read to them, Nanny summoned Grace into her sitting room. Having ordered her to pour her half a tumbler of brandy, Nanny Lydiard then directed Grace to come over and sit in the seat by the window.

'In the light, girl,' she said, taking her first sip of brandy. 'Where I can see you. Now tell me. How long have you been at Keston?'

'I started in February, Nanny,' Grace replied.

'Yes, yes. But which year, girl? Which blessed year?'

'This year, Nanny Lydiard. Five months ago.'

'Gracious heavens.' The old lady snorted, as if she'd never heard of anything so preposterous. 'Do you know how long I've been here? I've been at Keston for sixty-five years.'

Grace's eyes widened. That was considerably longer than any of the estimates. It also meant that Grace had been right when she had reckoned Nanny to be in her eighties.

'No I'm not as old as that,' the old lady answered, her little brown buttons of eyes twinkling through her spectacles. 'You're guessing that I must be at least eighty-four, eighty-five perhaps. Because you think I couldn't possibly have become Nanny until I was nineteen or twenty. A little older than you are now, I should think. What are you, eighteen? Nineteen? No matter—' Nanny continued before Grace could confirm her age. 'The point is I was fourteen when I started here as a nursemaid. There were three of us then. Three nursemaids. Two under-nannies, and of course old Nanny Lydiard. Who was a right old

106

stickler. You'd have got by, I dare say. You're as neat as a pin. Not Dora. Dora would have never got over the threshold. Not with her ways. Messy pup. Eighteen forty-three I started here. The year those Siamese twins – the Bunkers. That was it. Chang and something or other Bunker. What was I telling you?'

Nanny Lydiard stared across at Grace, her whole face blank as her memory failed her.

'You were saying the year you started here was the same year as some Siamese twins called Bunker did something,' Grace prompted.

'Siamese twins,' Nanny Lydiard pondered. 'Why on earth should we be discussing Siamese twins? For the life of me . . . ' She petered out again and frowned out of the window. 'The only Siamese twins I remember were Chang and Eng. Who married two sisters. The Yates gals. They were still joined together, you know. Imagine. And one of the twins was always getting drunk, while the other was teetotal. Chang and Eng Bunker, that's right. Chang and Eng Bunker.'

Grace just caught the half-full glass of brandy as Nanny fell fast asleep. When she found Dora and asked her what they should do, Dora shrugged and said they'd have to do what they usually did. Put the old lady to bed if she forgot to do so herself.

Putting herself to bed wasn't the only thing old Nanny Lydiard forgot to do. She had to be reminded to do everything, including taking the children downstairs for their daily visit to their parents at teatime, and the people who did most of the reminding were the children.

'Now come along, Nanny,' Henry would announce in his oddly mature fashion. 'It's time for you to take us to see Mama and Papa.' Or – 'Nanny, don't you think it's time for us to go to bed?' Or – 'Nanny, go and fetch your hat and coat because you're taking us for a walk.'

But rather than finding such routines amusing, Grace worried. Henry might act with a precocious maturity, but he was only nine years old and his sister was only seven, neither of them yet of an age where they could be

107

considered anywhere near responsible. Nor could either of them swim, and besides a lake and a multitude of ponds where Henry always insisted on being taken fishing, the park also boasted a trout stream, a fast-flowing tributary of the River Ray, with several deep pools and slippery banks. Yet whenever Henry organized one of his afternoon fishing trips, despite all Grace's offers of company and help, Nanny insisted on taking her charges out single-handed.

'What do you think I am, girl?' she would snort. 'Some sort of Boetian? Think I've lost my marbles?'

Cook offered Grace no consolation on such afternoons when she slipped down to the kitchen for a cup of tea and a gossip.

'If it's working, my father used to say, then don't try and mend it,' she would advise Grace. 'Least said soonest mended.'

'If we're going to do battle with idioms,' Grace would counter, 'then I'm a firm believer in forewarned being forearmed. Just because nothing has happened so far — '

'It isn't your concern, Grace. One word out of place from you and you won't be back down 'ere, my girl. You'll be back out on the streets.'

But Grace wasn't prepared to let it run until something calamitous happened, as she believed given the circumstances it was bound to do. She'd already heard on the servants' grapevine that the atmosphere in the great house was considerably less formal under the new Lord Lydiard than it had been under his father, so she nursed the idea of approaching young Lady Lydiard directly with her worries. After all, Henry and Harriet were her children and to Grace's way of thinking it simply wasn't safe to have an old and forgetful woman in charge of the nursery. It was also very unfair on Nanny Lydiard herself.

Grace knew from the affectionate way the old lady spoke of her charges and of her life in the nursery that she would drop dead of shock if anything happened to either Henry or Harriet. They were her life, the stuff of her existence. All those years of care and devotion would mean nothing if in the twilight of her life anything happened to either of them. So day by day Grace began to summon up the courage to find an opportune moment to go downstairs and voice her anxieties to the children's mother.

Meanwhile day by day the situation on the nursery floor grew worse. It was almost as if, now that she had in Grace a safe pair of hands to help her, Nanny had more or less abdicated the nursery throne. She rarely now got up for breakfast, she slept through lunch, and she found the continuing heat too oppressive to go out in the afternoon so generally she stayed behind in the cool of her sitting room and dozed, while Grace was delegated to take the children out for their exercise.

On cooler afternoons she would still occasionally supervise Henry and Harriet by herself while they played in the parkland, and when she decided this was what she wanted to do, there was no point in opposing the idea. When Nanny was in full control of her senses, she was still a woman of considerable authority, and one who would tolerate no backchat or contradictions from her underlings.

'I am not senile,' she would insist, if Grace as much as dared suggest she might like some company while she walked the children. 'I may be old, and I may be a little frayed around the edges. But I am not yet extinct. If Lord and Lady Lydiard are still content to entrust their children to my care, then so be it. I most certainly do not need to be fussed over by a nursery maid who I should have thought would have better things to do than while away the afternoon ambling around the park.'

Much to Grace's relief, nothing untoward happened on these occasional exclusive jaunts, outings which she was also glad to note were becoming far less frequent. Nothing, that is, until the afternoon when Nanny returned to the nursery floor without either Henry or Harriet.

'I thought they were with you, Grace,' she said, as she sank slowly into an armchair. 'I thought you were taking them – or was that yesterday? I'm getting confused now. What day is it, Grace? Monday we go fishing. Tuesday. Tuesday.' The old lady closed her eyes and put a bent and smooth-skinned hand wearily to her forehead. 'What do we do on Tuesday, Meg? I thought you were taking them both riding.'

Another second and she was asleep. But Grace was already halfway to the door, giving Dora her instructions as to which part of the park to start searching.

'But I don't know the park, Grace!' Dora moaned as Grace hurried her through the door. 'I'll probably get lost meself!'

'No you won't, Dora,' Grace said grimly. 'Not if you use your head. Now come on.'

As the door was shutting and their footsteps were receding down the corridor, the girls imagined that old Nanny must have suddenly awakened for just as they flung themselves down the stairs two at a time they heard her murmuring.

'What do we do on Tuesday, Meg? I thought you were taking them both riding.'

An hour was spent fruitlessly searching the grounds, an hour during which Grace felt her mind was somehow on ice. She couldn't think of what might have happened, she couldn't even contemplate it.

She remet Dora by the old stone boathouse overlooking the main lake convinced that she must have had better luck than herself, but Dora had also drawn a blank.

'Didn't you even see anyone to ask?' Grace said. 'There must be someone about.'

'Only one of the grooms exercising the 'orses,' Dora replied. ' 'E said 'e 'a'n't seen no one in the park all afternoon. Least not from the 'ouse.'

'That's what I don't understand,' Grace replied, turning round to look back over the vast estate. 'Everyone I asked said the same. Normally they always see Nanny out somewhere with the children. But this afternoon — '

Grace shrugged and then started to hurry back towards the house.

'Come on, Dora!' she called. 'We're going to have to tell the family and organize a search party!'

She broke into a run, down the slope away from the lake and across the bridge towards the west end of the magnificent house where she could see people sitting out on a terrace.

'We can't go there!' Dora shouted back, already trailing Grace by a good twenty yards. 'We can't go down there unannounced!'

Grace paid no attention. All she could think of was the children and what might have happened to them. They could be anywhere. They could have fallen out of a tree, slipped into the stream, or drowned in the lake.

Except there they were, a hundred yards away, ninety yards, eighty, seventy, sixty yards from her, on the stone balustraded terrace directly outside the house, knocking a shuttlecock back and forth between them watched by their father and mother, and old Nanny Lydiard.

When the children caught sight of Grace and the red-faced Dora as they slithered to a stop at the far end of a beautifully manicured lawn, they stopped playing for a moment and then waved.

So did Nanny Lydiard.

'When did you remember where they were, Nanny?' Grace wanted to know.

'I get these blanks, Grace,' Nanny Lydiard replied. 'You'll be the same when you get to my age. You remember everything that happened all those years ago and not a thing you did that morning.'

Once again they were sitting in Nanny's sitting room, as another fine, hot summer's day began to draw to a close. The children were safely asleep in their beds, and Dora was doing a final tidy in the playroom.

'Do you often get these blanks, Nanny?' Grace enquired carefully, only to find her question greeted with a hoot of laughter.

'Don't you think I don't know what you're at, girl,' Nanny replied, still chuckling. 'You think I shouldn't be in charge. And you think you know who should be.'

Grace said nothing, taking the glass of brandy instead

from the old lady's hands as she tried to put it back down on the table.

'Well, I might not be as young as I was,' Nanny continued. 'Then which of us are? I mightn't have as much energy, or the stamina or whatever. But what I haven't lost is the *experience*. I still have all my experience, and you can put as much young wine into as many old bottles as you like, but it still comes out young wine. Imagine. You're thinking what everyone else is thinking, I know. And I don't blame you. But that's not the point. The point is what I've earned. And while I might not have earned all that much money, although I'm not complaining, I've done well enough, and I've been well looked after. The point is what else I've earned. Namely the right to do as I please. That's the point. This has been my home for over sixty-five years. And I'm not being turned out of it now I'm old like some worn-out carthorse. Imagine.'

'I think she's testing you,' Cook said, breaking a dozen eggs into a bowl and then automatically passing them to Grace to whisk as if she were still a kitchen maid. 'Same as she tests all 'er girls. Same as she done with poor Meg, God rest 'er soul, and with Matty the girl before 'er. And with little Rose. She won't stand any nonsense from 'er nursery maids old Nanny, and that's for sure. From what I 'eard you got to 'ave two pair of hands and eyes in the back of your bloomin' head.'

Grace sat at the enormous scrubbed kitchen table whisking the eggs and sipping her tea while Cook elaborated on her theory about Nanny Lydiard's behaviour. From what she was saying it appeared that the old lady was quite content to stay in position as long as her nursery maids were hardworking and capable. The children were both old enough not to require a nanny's full supervision, and spending half their day under the tutelage of Miss Chambers all they really needed when they weren't in class, at least according to Cook, was just organizing and superintendence. Evidently the nursery regime was in place and so well oiled it all but ran itself.

112

'Provided Nanny's got the right girls behind 'er,' Cook reminded Grace. 'Funny enough Meg was a real treasure, so I 'eard, but then of course there was the girl's 'ealth, God save the poor child. What a wretched business to be sure, 'cos she could cope all right could Meg. Whereas them other two, Matty and little Rose, well, they didn't know whether they was comin' or goin'.'

Poor little Meg had died within a week of being admitted to the infirmary from tuberculous meningitis, a complication which apparently she must have been developing for some weeks and for which there was no known cure.

Even though she hadn't known the girl Grace was deeply shocked by her death since she felt they were all part of the same body, the army of staff who ran Keston Hall. But no one else seemed anything more than momentarily disconcerted by Meg's demise, even though all the lower staff had known her since she had started out in the kitchens as a scullery maid. Cook had sensed Grace's bewilderment at the apparent lack of concern and had put her right, telling her that the household staff was indeed just like an army, and that no army she knew ever stopped to mourn the fall of one of its number.

'It's afterwards they're remembered, Grace,' she'd said. 'When the battle's over and the day is done. You can't stop in the middle of a battle, my girl, and you know as well as I do that that's what it is down here, one long battle and the enemy is chaos. We stops for a minute and we're done for, believe you me. No, it's when the day is done you sit and count the cost. I think of who's gone every night. I remembers Meg this year, and that poor Irish girl Aggie. I remembers them in my prayers. But down here in the midst of this bloomin' battle we're fighting, this poor old life of ours must go on.'

Grace understood then that it wasn't heartlessness which allowed her fellow servants to continue their daily round as if nothing had happened but courage, the courage to face their monotonous existence knowing that they had little hope of anything better from their lives, anything other

113

than years of facing the same tedious routine day in day out.

'If I sees another chicken gizzard, or another bloomin' fish 'ead,' Cook used to complain almost daily, 'then so help me I don't know what I'll do.'

Some escaped. Some seeing what the future held for them got out as soon as it was possible. Grace knew that from the incessant conversation on the subject at mealtimes. They saved up every penny they could and finally left to set themselves up in small businesses, which according to everyone they left behind generally ended in either failure or disaster, particularly since nine out of ten times the business they ended up running was a public house.

'Enough said,' Cook would pronounce. 'A public 'ouse indeed. Well, you can imagine.'

Others, younger female members of the staff, some of them escaped through marriage, only to find out and usually all too quickly that they had exchanged one form of slavery for another, since it seemed men deliberately sought out young women who were in service because they knew they'd be well versed in the skills of running a household. Other less fortunate girls, and less sensible ones, on the strength of the sort of life they heard visiting servants boasting of, ran away to London where invariably they ended up not in the chorus at the London Hippodrome but on the Haymarket, as prostitutes.

The rest of their number stayed put, prepared to spend their lives doing their jobs to the best of their abilities and biting their tongues when scolded, in return for which they were fed and housed, and in good households cared for when they were ill and looked after when they retired. So when one of their number died prematurely or accidentally, the army kept going forward, the prevailing philosophy being *there but for the grace of God go I*.

Every time she heard such talk, Grace felt the trap closing ever tighter. She knew that if she didn't take care she would be swept forward in the army's remorseless onward march, until either exhausted by her labours or hypnotized

114

by the monotony of her existence she too settled for what was rather than what might be. She knew that there was no chance of escape yet. Her mother and her sister were still dependent on her and there was no other employment for her in Keston, at least nothing which would pay her any more money. The most she could hope for would be to find a position as a lady's maid in an altogether smaller house, a position which would pay her slightly more money but which Grace doubted very much she would secure since as things stood she wasn't yet sufficiently experienced.

So she would watch and wait. In the meantime her promotion to the nursery floor was in terms of preferment a considerable step, and furthermore she knew that if she could win the trust of old Nanny Lydiard at least she would never have to return to the hell that was the kitchen floor. She might even sufficiently impress Mrs Quinn with her diligence that the housekeeper would put in a good word for her the next time a position for parlour maid became vacant, which could well be soon, judging from the rumours downstairs that Gwen, the prettiest of the parlour maids, was expecting a proposal of marriage from her soldier boyfriend before the end of the summer.

Meanwhile she still had to deal with the problem of old Nanny, and despite Cook's reassurances that the old lady was probably only testing her and that as far as she could gather the nursery ran itself, Grace continued to worry about the vexed question of the safety of the children, so much so that she finally announced to Cook that she was going to seek out Lady Lydiard and discuss the matter with her personally.

'You'll do no such thing, my girl!' Cook stormed, doing battle with a row of near boiling saucepans on the range. 'Who do you think you are?'

'I'm one of the people paid to look after her children, Cook,' Grace replied, obviously a little too primly for Cook's liking, judging from the subsequent contemptuous snort which came from the sweat-soaked woman. 'I'd be failing in my duty if I didn't express my concern to Lady Lydiard,' Grace continued, not one bit chastened. 'You've no idea what a worry it is, Cook. Why only last night when they were meant to be tucked up safely in bed and asleep I found them up on the roof. In one of the domes. Having a midnight feast.'

'They're only kids, Grace,' Cook retorted. 'Same as any other kids. They're bound to get up to mischief.'

'They said Nanny had given them permission. But when I asked Nanny she had no recollection of it whatsoever. I dread to think what they'll get up to next.'

'You just leave well alone, Grace. You take my word for it. Going to talk to 'er ladyship indeed. I'd like to see it. If 'is lordship's anything like 'is father, you'll be out of 'ere and into the work'ouse before you can say knife.'

'Someone's going to have to say something, Cook.'

'Be that as it may, Grace. But it ain't goin' to be you.'

It was, as it happened, although it was in no way as Grace had imagined it.

The day after Miss Chambers brought the summer term to a close dawned hot and cloudless, and no sooner had the children got to the breakfast table than they were making whispered plans. Nanny, who was up early for a change, clucked at them like an old hen from the head of the table but for once made no effort to correct the lapse in manners, an omission Grace attributed to its being the first day of the summer holidays, while Dora quietly and systematically set about eating up everyone's leftover porridge and bread and jam. Finally Henry announced that Harriet and he had decided what to do. They were all to take a picnic to the great lake where Grace could take them out fishing in the rowing boat while Nanny watched from the bank. There then followed a long bout of inexplicable giggling from the two children accompanied by a great deal of good-natured hushing from Nanny.

Grace volunteered to make the picnic, and having sweet-talked Cook she prepared a hamper full of chicken pie, tomato sandwiches made with freshly baked bread, fruit cake, homemade ginger biscuits, sweet juicy green apples and bottles of sparkling pop. Even Nanny was moved to say she'd never seen a picnic like it come up from the kitchens in all her days at Keston. By mid-morning, the party less Dora, who had been given permission to go and visit her sick grandfather, set off for the lake in a state of high excitement.

It was a perfect day, with just enough breeze coming off the water to keep everyone cool. In the fields beyond swallows swooped out of the clear blue sky to pluck insects from the air while not fifty yards away along the bank they saw a grey heron waiting in the reeds, as still as a stone statue. Then, just as Grace was helping Henry and Harriet to launch the smaller of the two rowing boats moored to the jetty, the great bird struck like lightning, shooting its head and half its neck into the placid brown waters of the lake and re-emerging with a shake of its black and white head as the fish it had speared with its yellow beak disappeared down its long curved throat.

'I'm glad I can't catch fish as easily as that,' Henry announced, throwing his discarded shoes into the rowing boat. 'It would be too easy.'

Henry didn't catch anything until just before lunchtime when he landed a small roach which wriggled and flipped in helpless panic while Henry tried unsuccessfully to disentangle the hook. Grace took the fish from him and holding it firmly in her left hand expertly removed the barb in a trice.

'Shall I throw him back, Master Henry?' she enquired. 'Or shall we put him in the keep net until the end of the day?'

'Put him in the net, please,' Henry replied, frowning hard at Grace, who dipped her arm into the cool water of the lake and gently released the fish into the net which hung off the back of the boat.

'I didn't know you could fish, Grace,' Henry said.

'Grace can do everything,' Harriet said, without looking up from her drawing book. 'When she was little, Grace used to fish with her sister.'

'Girls don't fish,' Henry said, still deeply perplexed. 'At least not unless they're like Mama.'

'I fish,' Harriet said.

'Not properly,' Henry replied. 'You couldn't take a hook out like that.'

Grace swished her hands clean in the lake, and then shook the sparkles of water off them away from the boat.

'We used to fish in the same river that runs through the park, Master Henry. Where it flows through the fields at the back of our house. Or rather at the back of where we used to live. An uncle of mine taught me how to tickle trout.'

'Tickle trout?' Henry's frown deepened. 'However can you tickle trout?'

'One day perhaps I can show you,' Grace replied. 'There must be some calm and shallow pools in your stretch of the stream. If you get really good at tickling, you can sometimes catch trout with your bare hands.'

After they'd rowed ashore and had lunch with Nanny who had been dozing under her parasol on the shore, Harriet showed Grace the drawings she had done that morning from the boat, which included an attempt at a heron, a frog which Henry had netted for her, and a clump of magnificent water lilies.

'Those are really very good, Miss Harriet,' Grace told her with perfect truth, because there was no doubt from the sketches that the seven-year-old had real ability. 'I couldn't draw like that at your age.'

'Can you draw now?'

Grace hesitated before answering the question. Since her father had left home, for no reason she had yet understood herself she hadn't once felt any real desire to pick up a paintbrush or a pencil. It was as if her teacher had not only stolen Father, their home, and their happiness from her, she had also stolen her talent. Of course she could still draw, perhaps she could even draw quite well, but first the desire to draw had to arrive, and it just had, if only for a few seconds. But now once more it was gone: like the dragonfly she had been watching earlier the impulse had darted

118

off into the closed part of her mind, behind that door that was now for ever shut marked 'Childhood. Do Not Enter'.

'Yes, I can draw a little,' she found herself saying, but only because she thought she might be able to help Harriet, of whom she was becoming very fond, to develop what could be a considerable talent.

'Draw me something then, please,' Harriet instructed her, carefully turning over to a fresh page in her drawing book. 'Draw me Nanny.'

The old lady made a perfect picture, asleep as she again was under her lemon-yellow frilled parasol, her head nodding on to her chest, her hands folded on her lap. Harriet watched Grace in reverent silence as she drew an exquisite pencil sketch of the scene.

'Wow!'

'Don't say *wow*, Harriet,' Henry sighed. 'It's frightfully childish.'

'I don't care, Henry. Look what Grace has drawn.'

'Hmmm,' Henry said, looking at the sketch. 'Not bad. Not bad at all.'

Henry had decided to polish off the last of the sandwiches, and as he stood over Grace and Harriet who were seated on a rug on the ground, a slice of tomato dropped right on to the middle of the drawing, obliterating Nanny in a spreading sea of pink juice.

'Oh *Henry*!' Harriet cried, jumping to her feet. 'I wanted to keep that!'

Grace had already torn the page out of the book, so that the tomato wouldn't soak through too many pages. Besides, the drawing was quite ruined.

'I'll just have to tell people how good it was,' Harriet grumbled, sitting back down next to Grace.

'It wasn't that good,' Grace demurred, finding herself for some as yet unknown reason surprisingly relieved that the evidence of her talent had been destroyed.

'It was,' Harriet insisted. 'It was perfect.'

The child tried to persuade Grace to draw Nanny again, but instead Grace encouraged the little girl to try drawing the subject herself, promising her that she would help show her how.

For the next hour or so, while Henry fished happily from the edge of the jetty, Grace and Harriet studied the sleeping figure of Nanny while Harriet did her best to produce a good likeness. Grace taught the child how to simplify and as soon as she did, Harriet produced a charming and Grace thought quite precociously talented sketch of the old nurse in her chair.

'That's excellent, Miss Harriet,' Grace told her. 'You see what I mean about concentrating on the outline and not the details. That's the result.'

Without ceremony Harriet duly woke her old nanny to show her what she'd done. As the old lady approved wholeheartedly of her charge's effort, Grace noticed Henry suddenly start to grow restless. She asked him if anything was wrong, but all he told her was he had to speak to Nanny. Pushing his way past Grace and Harriet, he went and whispered for a long time in Nanny's ear, while Grace began to clear up the remains of the picnic.

'Grace?' Nanny Lydiard called as Grace was fastening the hamper back up. 'It seems Master Henry has left his box of floats on top of the nursery chest of drawers.'

'Yes,' Harriet gleefully chimed in. 'And I've left my other box of crayons.'

'Very well,' Grace replied. 'Well, if you both come with me—'

'No,' Henry interrupted. 'No, we want *you* to go and get them. By yourself.'

'Because we can't very well leave Nanny here by herself,' Harriet added with a look at her brother. 'Can we?'

'Of course you can't, children,' Nanny said, settling back in her chair. 'I might run off with a strange man.'

By the time Grace got back from the nursery with the missing items, the small rowing boat was back out in the middle of the lake. Harriet was sitting in the stern, her head down over what Grace imagined must be

120

her ever-present sketchbook on her knee, and Henry was sitting facing the same way, on the second of the three bench seats. While the boat drifted away across the lake towards the weir.

And while on the bank Nanny slept on under her parasol.

There was no one in the boat with the children. Neither did they have any oars. For some reason the oars had been left behind on the bank, right beside the spot where Grace began to undress.

'Henry!' she called. 'Harriet! I'm coming! Wait and don't do anything! I'm coming out to you!'

Grace had her shoes off by now, and her dress and apron.

'Just sit quite still!' Now she was down to just her chemise, her drawers and her stockings, tossing aside her summer petticoat. 'Paddle with your hands! Do you hear me? Paddle with your hands, Henry!'

Either the children were too far from shore to hear Grace's cries, or else Henry was petrified with terror as the boat drifted slowly and inexorably towards the line of foaming water on the top edge of the weir.

Neither of the children could swim.

Grace plunged into the shallows of the lake and started to wade her way through the weed as fast as she could to the clear waters beyond. As soon as she was clear she started swimming, her underclothes clinging to her body, her stockings rolling themselves down as she kicked as hard as she could through the water, shouting all the time to the children to try to paddle the boat away from danger, away from where the lake dropped six feet, first into a foaming header pool, and then cascading into the lower lake.

When Grace was about twenty yards or less from the boat, Harriet suddenly looked round and saw her swimming towards them. Leaning forward she tapped her brother on the shoulder and they both turned back to stare at her. Grace couldn't hear anything they were saying because by now all she could hear was the roaring of the waterfall and her own increasingly hysterical shouts. But she did notice that the children seemed to be curiously unbothered by their circumstances, and when she was only a matter of yards from the boat she could have sworn she saw Henry stifle a grin.

Then at last she had hold of the boat, or at least of the rope at the stern.

'Quickly, children!' she gasped. 'Harriet first! Jump in and hold on to me tight and I can get you to the bank over there!'

Harriet didn't move. She just sat there, frowning at Grace as if Grace were mad.

'*Quickly*, Harriet!'

'Why?' Henry asked. 'Whatever's up, Grace?'

'Can't you see?' Grace cried. 'The boat's heading for the weir!'

'It's all right!' Henry laughed, and leaned past his sister to tug at the rope Grace was holding. 'We're perfectly safe! Look!'

He yanked at the rope, as Grace let go and grabbed the stern of the boat. Grace saw the rope snake upwards, breaking the surface of the water between the boat and the shore.

'We're on a long line! Moored to the jetty!' Henry yelled. 'We often do this with Nanny!'

'You didn't think I'd let them go out on the lake by themselves, did you, Grace?' Nanny Lydiard chided, as a shivering, soaking wet Grace did her best to towel herself dry with her petticoat. 'What kind of a nanny do you take me for? A ninny?'

Henry found this hugely amusing, and started to laugh helplessly and roll around on the picnic rug.

'I thought you might have fallen asleep, Nanny,' Grace explained through chattering teeth. 'And I thought perhaps Master Henry might have gone out in the boat without realizing he'd left the oars behind.'

'As if Henry'd do a silly thing like that,' Nanny sighed. 'Would you, Henry?'

'Of course not, Nanny,' replied Henry, also with a deep sigh. 'As if I'd be so *stupid*.'

'I don't think it was fair,' Harriet said suddenly, her cheeks flushing red.

'Keep quiet, Harriet,' Henry said, sitting up and stopping laughing. 'I'm warning you.'

'I don't mind,' Harriet replied. 'I don't think it was fair so there.'

Grace was too cold and still too shocked to bother about what Harriet considered fair or unfair. Her only concern was to get herself dry and warm.

'Go on, girl,' Nanny suddenly said, as if reading her thoughts. 'Go back to the house and change into some dry clothes before you catch your death of cold. Henry – get up off that rug and give it to Grace to put round herself.'

'What about you, Nanny?' Grace asked as Henry handed her the tartan rug. 'Will you be all right?'

'Will I be all right indeed,' the old lady snorted. 'I can do this job with my eyes shut, Grace. As no doubt you've probably noticed.'

Nanny Lydiard suddenly beamed at Grace, a smile of humour and affection as she took hold of Henry's hand.

'Go on, Grace,' she insisted. 'We can't afford to lose you, can we children? Not now.'

Both the children were sound asleep before Grace was halfway through their story. They were so blissfully tired after their long sunlit day on the lake that their eyes had started to close practically as soon as Grace had started reading to them. They were in Henry's bedroom, and Grace was sitting on the bed beside Henry with Harriet on her knee. The dark-haired handsome boy lay asleep as he always did, flat on his back with both arms stretched out either side of him outside the bedclothes, while Harriet, thumb in mouth and index finger touching the end of her pretty snub nose, lay fast out with her blond head on Grace's shoulder. She never woke for a second as Grace carried her back to her own room and tucked her up in bed.

Not until Grace bent down and, thinking it safe, kissed her.

'Good night, darling,' she whispered.

A little freckled arm still warm from the sun wound itself round Grace's neck.

'Good night, Grace,' the child sighed, before falling back fast asleep.

'Of course I want to retire,' Nanny said. 'What do you think? Wouldn't you? I'm an old woman.'

They were sitting as was now their custom in Nanny Lydiard's sitting room, under the window through which the last rays of the sun were falling, the old lady in her favourite chair, and Grace on the window seat, knees pulled up under her chin as she stared out across the beautiful park.

'Old Lord Lydiard tried once or twice,' Nanny continued after a long but easy silence. 'He used to mutter something about a cottage on the estate. The one down by the mill. But that wasn't for me. I couldn't see out my days turned away in some poky little cottage, watching someone else walk my children out, watching someone else lead my life. Most important, who was that person going to be? Not any of the Boetians they've been sending me up to train. Imagine. All except that poor girl who died. All except poor Meg. The children loved her. The way they're beginning to love you.'

Grace looked round in surprise. She hadn't given a thought to what the children made of her. The fact that she herself had become fond of both of them, surprisingly so in such a short space of time, seemed purely academic. Grace liked children, and she'd always been good with them, so good that Mrs Jenkins had often put her in charge of the younger pupils at school when the occasion arose. But she'd never worried herself as to how the children saw her, either at school or here now at Keston, on the nursery floor. All she had concentrated on was making sure she was doing her new job to the best of her ability, which to Grace did not include setting out to win the children's affections.

'Don't look so startled, girl,' Nanny Lydiard chuckled. 'It'd be a sight worse if they didn't like you, believe you me. Henry has a terrible temper on occasions, and can give you the frost, too. Just like his grandfather. And his father. But it's only shyness. He's a very sweet boy. A very gentle boy. As for Harriet.' The old lady sighed, and closing her eyes made as if to blow her nose in a lace-trimmed handkerchief. 'It's as if an angel dropped down from the clouds.'

The old lady tucked her hankie back up her sleeve, and cleared her throat.

'Time for the other half, Grace,' she said, holding out her glass. 'If you'd be so kind.'

Grace refilled the glass with an inch of brandy and put it back on the table beside Nanny Lydiard.

'They all think I'm an old soak downstairs, you know,' she suddenly said, as Grace was settling herself back on the window seat. 'They think I just sit up here and get squiffy. But I never took a drink in my life, not until I had to. Not until the wretched pain got the better of me.'

'Your hands?'

'My hands. And my neck. And my hips. But then these things are sent to try us, Grace. These things are sent to try us, and as his late lordship used to say, *so, Nanny, is brandy.* He made sure I always had a supply. For when things got a bit too much. There's nothing else that relieves it. Not now.'

'But how have you managed to carry on, Nanny?'

'How have I managed to carry on indeed. Imagine. How could I not carry on, Grace? It was my duty. You don't stop doing your duty because of a few aches and pains. Like Lord Nelson, I too thank God, because I have done my duty.'

They sat in silence then, as the room first turned red-pink in the setting sun, before slowly slipping into darkness. Normally at this point, once she had drunk her first brandy, Nanny Lydiard would fall asleep, and Grace would leave her, returning at bedtime to see whether the old lady had taken herself off or if she needed help. But this evening, although the light was growing ever dimmer, Grace knew Nanny was still awake. But she said nothing, because at times like this silences could be as eloquent as words.

'Don't you want to know about the boat?' the old lady finally asked from the twilight. 'Or the time I came back without the children?'

'Not unless you want to tell me, Nanny,' Grace replied. 'I think I've worked it out.'

'I had to find out about you, Grace. They are my charges after all. I had to be quite certain that you really cared. Besides, it's only common sense. Which you have in abundance. And you care. I could see it all over that pretty face of yours every time you thought something had gone wrong.'

The old lady laughed quietly to herself and then sighed contentedly.

'Good,' she said. 'So that's that then.'

'I'm not quite sure I understand,' Grace ventured. 'Are you saying that my place here in the nursery is secure, Nanny? Is that what you're saying?'

Grace knew the old woman was looking at her, but in the fast fading light she couldn't make out her expression.

'You want to know if your place in the nursery is secure. Yes, Grace dear. Yes, I think we can safely say your place up here is well and truly secure.'

'Thank you, Nanny.'

'I don't think you should be thanking me, Grace. Should be the other way round really. But there you are. And that's that, isn't it. Yes, I think we can safely say your position up here's safe enough.'

There was a long silence, punctuated only by the flight call of a nightjar leaving its hiding place in search of flying insects and the mysterious eerie moan of a distant long-eared owl searching for prey.

'I'm only doing it because it's right,' Nanny murmured

in the dark. 'Not doing it as a favour, you know. I'm only doing it because it's the right thing to do. After all, they are my charges.'

Grace sat quite still until she was certain the old lady was fast asleep, then she let herself quietly out of the darkened room. As she walked through the silent nurseries, she knew she should be happy and proud that she'd won her place on the nursery floor, yet her abiding feeling was one of an almost overwhelming sadness. In her mind's eye all she could see was the lone figure in the chair under the window, an old lonely woman coming to the end of her life, a life which had been solely devoted to the loving care of children who were not her own.

Perhaps she was seeing herself, Grace thought, as she sat at the nursery table in the half-darkness. Perhaps that's why her heart felt so heavy: because if she didn't take care the figure in the half-light could well be her in another sixty years' time, all alone at the end of her life as the light fast faded. *Never mind worrying about where the bloomin' old swallows go in winter*, Cook was fond of saying when things got too much for her. *Never mind the bloomin' old birds. What about us?*

But Grace wasn't like that, she decided, watching the shape of the new moon form through the haze of the warm summer night. She hadn't been born into service. The circumstances of her childhood had been so different from those of the other servant girls at Keston. She simply couldn't see her life – so many of them already could – as going to be spent caring for people who were not her family or devoting herself to children she hadn't birthed. The light that had been first lit by Professor Goodfellow at the art school that morning still burnt bright within her. She couldn't see a tree as someone like Cook might, as being of interest only by virtue of whether or not it was an oak or an ash. To her a tree was, at one and the same time, a host to a thousand different colours, a symbol and a way of being. And yet, if she was honest, already the very idea of moving away from Keston was oddly frightening.

She was so busy daydreaming she had forgotten to return the picnic hamper to the kitchen. Grace remembered it just in time before she went to bed, which was as well since Cook was a stickler for having everything back in its place by the end of the day in case it was needed the following day and wasn't ready for action. Finding where she'd left it in the nursery kitchen, Grace set off downstairs. At least she'd remembered to wash it all up, which was something. All she would have to do once she was in the kitchens would be to unpack it and put the contents away.

She just hoped Mrs Quinn would be asleep, because although initially she had been as good as her word and paid the housekeeper regular teatime visits, as she became more and more involved in the running of the nursery she found conversely she had less and less time to spare, a fact for which she was secretly grateful because for no reason she could quite pin down she still found the poor woman's company oddly uncomfortable.

Since that initial agreement Grace had been careful to try to keep her visits and their cups of special tea together short, and then finally to omit them altogether. Oddly enough the housekeeper had made no comment about Grace's absence, the reason being, as was later disclosed by Dolly, that she was too busy making life hell for the new tweeny, a pretty little flaxen-haired fourteen-year-old sent from Aylesbury Orphanage.

On her way to the kitchens Grace tiptoed her way down the corridor past Mrs Quinn's room in an agony of fear and embarrassment in case she met her and had to explain just why she had left it so long since she had last sat in the parlour and tried to make conversation with her. She felt a great rush of relief when she saw that there was no light shining under the housekeeper's door, but she felt even more relieved once she was past it and securely on her way through the servants' hall and into the kitchens where to her surprise she saw there was a light burning.

Dolly was at the sink, running water into a basin.

'Gawd, you give me a fright,' she said, spinning round

and spilling some of the water. 'Quick – shut that door behind you, quick! I don't want that old bag findin' me 'ere, if you don't mind, Grace.'

'What's the matter?' Grace asked, doing as she was told. 'What's happened?'

'Mrs Quinn's what 'appened, that's what, as usual,' Dolly replied, lifting the basin of warm water out of the sink. 'You bring them linen towels, and that packet of boric, quick, would you?'

'Has Mrs Quinn hurt herself?' Grace enquired as she followed Dolly out into the corridor that led to Grace's old room.

'Would she 'ad,' Dolly retorted. 'An' if she 'ad, catch me runnin' to 'er rescue. It's Sally. The new girl. Mrs Quinn's just given 'er a right larrapin'. Just like she done to everyone when they start 'ere. Edith, poor little Aggie, me. Din't she never 'ave a go at you?'

'No, I can't say that she did.'

'No, well, she wouldn't probably, seein' as she thinks you're gentry. She's an evil old witch, that's what she is,' Dolly declared as they reached the end of the passage. 'Claims she caught Sally nickin' food from the larder. Poor kid wouldn't dare. She's far too scared of bein' sent back to that miserable old orphanage.'

Grace could hear the sound of the girl whimpering before she even opened the door.

'It's orl right, Sal,' Dolly whispered as they went in. 'It's only Dolly.'

Grace lit the candle and held it up so they could see. The girl was crouched on her haunches in one corner of the tiny room, her face awash with tears, her reddened eyes staring dully in front of her.

'It's orl right, girl,' Dolly whispered again as she set the basin down on the small table. 'No one's goin' to 'urt you no more. We just come to see to your back.'

When Sally had removed her blouse and camisole, which she held clutched in one hand to cover her breasts, Grace was revolted to see that the poor girl's back was quite simply a riddle of thin red weals, all of them angry and most of them still bleeding. She couldn't believe her eyes. There must have been at least a dozen cuts.

'I thought a larraping meant a belting,' she said to Dolly, who was carefully washing the welts. 'These look as though they were done with a whip.'

'They was,' Dolly replied. 'The old witch uses a riding cane, would you believe. I think it's somethin' terrible myself.'

'She hasn't the right!' Grace protested.

'What's rights when it comes to servants, I ask you,' Dolly sniffed. 'Needs must, Grace. Down 'ere, right's got bugger orl to do with it.'

'Even so. I'm sure if Lady Lydiard knew of it.'

'Yeah? An' who's goin' to tell 'er, Grace?'

'Nobody has the right to do this to another human being. And particularly not for just taking some food from the larder.'

'I din't take no food from the larder, miss,' the girl whispered. ''Tis more 'n my life's worth. I din't take no food, not even when I was half starved at the orphanage.'

'We'll have to tell Lady Lydiard about this, Dolly,' Grace announced crisply.

'No,' Sally pleaded, 'no please, it'll cost me my position, and then I'll never get another one.'

Her sobs renewed themselves as Grace and Dolly stared at each other for a few seconds.

'All the more reason then why Lady Lydiard should be told, Sally,' Grace finally insisted.

'Like she said, Grace,' Dolly replied for the poor victim as she returned to her ministrations, 'she'll lose her position. Besides, who's goin' to do the tellin'? An' get shown the door, for their pains. Not me, thank you very much.'

'I will,' said Grace.

Edith Crane had arrived unnoticed at the door and was standing with her arms folded, leaning against the lintel as Grace and Dolly went to leave, having made Sally as comfortable as they could lying on her front in her miserable little truckle-bed.

'You really goin' to tell 'er ladyship?' she asked as Grace walked past her.

'Yes, Edith,' Grace replied. 'I am.'

'Us'd all like to see this, us would!' Edith sneered.

Even so, she was still with them as they returned the basin and towels to the kitchen, and then a few steps behind Grace as she hurried quietly past Mrs Quinn's still darkened room towards the pass door and the stairs to the nursery floor.

'Grace,' she called from the twilight, just as Grace was about to go through to the house proper. Grace stopped and turned back. 'You'd better not be going to speak to Lady Lydiard, had you?'

'If I feel as angry in the morning as I do now, Edith,' Grace replied, 'and I find I still have the courage, yes I most certainly am.'

'Yeah,' Edith said, with a sniff and then a long silent look at the floor. 'Well in that case you'd better 'ave this.'

Edith handed Grace a grubby fold of paper which she'd taken from her apron pocket.

'Aggie give it me,' she said. 'The night she 'ung 'erself.'

'I thought Aggie broke her neck falling downstairs?'

'That's as what everyone was meant to think.' Edith looked up, and stared right into Grace's eyes with a look of cold fury. 'I should 'ave said some'at, I know. But I was afraid I'd lose my job, see. Likes of me says some'at about some'at like that, an' it's the work'ouse. So if you're really goin' to see 'er ladyship, you'd best make sure she knows what really goes on.'

Edith was gone back into the shadows before Grace could ask her what she meant. So she put the folded note in her pocket and pushed her way through the green baize door.

She showed the note to Nanny the next morning after breakfast when Dora had taken the children off to wash their teeth and brush their hair. The old woman read the one page of semi-literate scrawl and then put it back down on the table in front of Grace.

'The woman's a monster,' Nanny Lydiard said. 'But then, there you are.'

'There you are?' echoed Grace.

'These things have always gone on, child. Big fleas and little fleas.'

'That doesn't give her the right, surely? To take the law into her own hands and beat anyone she suspects of doing something wrong?'

'Sometimes I have to mete out punishment up here without reference to the children's parents, Grace. We can't all of us be forever running up and down the stairs to ask shall we shan't we, can we can't we, can we?'

'I don't think what happened to Aggie was a matter of punishment, Nanny. I mean, what had she done wrong? This seems much more to have been a case of sheer persecution. And why? That's what I don't understand. What on earth had the poor girl done?'

'It's more a case of what she hadn't done, reading between the lines,' Nanny Lydiard replied, opening up the copy of yesterday's *Times* which had as usual been sent up with breakfast.

'What she hadn't done?' Grace wondered, smoothing the note out on the table in front of her. 'You mean this reference to Mrs Quinn trying to make her do things against her will?'

'She's a most peculiar woman,' was all Nanny would say. 'Most peculiar.'

'*She said if only I would do as I was told,*' Grace read out, '*I should be all right, and she wouldn't beat me no more. But if I don't do as I'm told, she said she'll say I'm nothing but a common thief, and I'll go to gaol for the rest of my days.*'

'The poor girl was obviously frightened out of her wits. By the thought of gaol. And these terrible threats. Little wonder she wanted to end it all.'

'But what were the threats, Nanny? And what exactly would Mrs Quinn want her to do against her will?'

'I told you, child. Mrs Quinn's a very peculiar woman.'

'But peculiar in what way, Nanny?'

132

The old woman put the copy of the newspaper which she was holding up very close to her fast failing eyes down on her knees and removed her spectacles.

'You're as bad as the children,' she sighed. 'Why this, why that. No doubt you heard about the notorious Mr Oscar Wilde?'

'Yes,' Grace replied, wondering what the connection might be. 'Mrs Jenkins, my schoolteacher, she told me about him. That he was a wonderful playwright, and poet. And how he was wronged.'

'Wronged?' Nanny snorted. 'Wronged indeed. Imagine. Well anyway, that's neither here nor there at this moment. Sufficient unto the day, Nanny always says, and that's that. Why I mentioned Mr Wilde. You understand, poor man. But there you are, if you do understand.'

'Yes I do,' Grace replied. 'Mrs Jenkins. Yes, I think I know a little of why he was disgraced and put in gaol.'

'In that case you might know what I mean when I say Mrs Quinn is a peculiar woman. After all she has the married title only by right of her being a housekeeper.'

Grace looked at the old woman sitting opposite her across the nursery table. She felt very much as if she was a child again and wanting to know where Venezuela was, and why God had allowed flies.

'Unfortunately there are people who take satisfaction from hurting people,' Nanny went on, half to herself, giving a small sigh. 'Peculiar satisfaction.'

'In that case,' Grace concluded, folding up Aggie's tragic note, 'I think it's even more important that Lady Lydiard should be told. If that is what Mrs Quinn is, if she's a person who takes peculiar satisfaction in the punishment of others. It's too horrid to think about, even for a second.'

'And you're going to be the one to tell her.' Nanny Lydiard had picked up her copy of the newspaper again and was busy reopening it. 'You don't think perhaps I should.'

'Thank you, Nanny, but no.' Grace stood up and ran her hands down her blue uniform to straighten out any creases. 'No, I think I should, don't you? After all, it's my fight, not yours, and anyway, it wouldn't be fair.'

'You risk everything. You know that, of course.'

Grace nodded. She did know, but about that there really was nothing to be done.

'Why not see Mrs Quinn yourself first?' the old woman advised. 'There's nothing to be lost, and after all, you have no evidence, only the girl's word and this scrawled note. These things can be doubtful, in my experience. Not that I want to deprive you of your chance of martyrdom.'

Grace turned. Old Nanny was right to mock her a little, she was making a martyr of herself, marching off like some sort of latterday Saint Joan. Of course she must confront Mrs Quinn, and at the earliest opportunity.

'It's been so long since I had the pleasure of your company.'

Mrs Quinn leaned forward and handed Grace what the girl knew to be a very expensive piece of fine china, used only by the housekeeper and the butler.

'Nursery life is very different,' Grace told her, smiling, 'very busy, just as busy, but in a very different way. I just never seem to have a minute to myself.'

She laughed although she had said nothing funny, but raising her eyes to Mrs Quinn's she quickly dropped them again, and for no reason found herself blushing at the quite open sadness reflected in the housekeeper's eyes.

'My dear, if you only knew how unhappy your absences have made me,' Mrs Quinn went on, and Grace could feel how intently she was still staring across the table at her. 'Every day, I have wondered what I had done to offend you. You know how much store I set by our friendship, just the thought of it.'

At that Grace was forced to look across at her again.

'Offend me? Good heavens, Mrs Quinn, it's nothing like that, it's just as I say, I've been so occupied. Old Nanny is quite a character, as you know.'

'Old Nanny should be given her wages and told to leave, hanging on like that,' said Mrs Quinn, her voice quickly growing cold. 'She's a silly old woman. A silly, meddling old woman.'

'I'm afraid I can't agree. I find her very wise.'

'She wouldn't appreciate someone like you, my dear, there is nothing in her that could appreciate you.' Mrs Quinn's large roughened hand seemed to come from nowhere and touch Grace's cheek.

Grace didn't know why she found herself getting to her feet so determinedly, or why she quickly backed off down the room towards the door until she had done so, but by the time she reached the door she did. She didn't exactly know why old Nanny had used the word 'peculiar', but it had obviously been advisedly, although what form 'peculiar' took Grace wasn't quite sure, she just knew it wasn't something she wanted to stay and find out.

'Thank you for the tea,' she heard herself saying somewhat incongruously. 'It's been very nice to see you, but I have suddenly remembered. Something I left on the fireguard. Up in the nurseries.'

'But you've hardly been here a minute, child—'

'Nor I have,' Grace agreed, and was gone before Mrs Quinn could say any more.

Shortly before midday, John the footman arrived up on the nursery floor to inform Grace that Lady Lydiard had agreed to see her in the Staircase Hall. A freshly uniformed Grace followed John in silence down the nursery stairs, along the main bedroom corridor where only weeks before she had been forced to hide her face from the late Lord Lydiard, and down the main staircase which led into the hall.

She had only ever seen the hall before as a vast wooden floor to be polished and an enormous fire to be emptied and reset first thing in the gloom of the morning. Coming down the long flight of twenty-four steps below the pillars which ran the length of the double landings and past another pair of pillars which framed the entrance to the hall proper, Grace now saw the hall as it was meant to be seen, a marvellous room at the very centre of the house, rising eighteen or twenty feet to a beautifully carved and ornamented ceiling, below which ran a frieze of panelled paintings of various gods and goddesses. The lower half of each wall was worked in wood panelling, upon which a variety of family portraits hung beneath the dead gazes of a dozen or more stags' heads. There was a huge carved and tassellated stone fireplace, almost the same height as the entrance through which Grace had just come, dominated by the largest of the stags' heads, which over the years had gradually come to rest its nose on the mantel, and either side of which for some reason were arranged two armoured vambraces and gauntlets. There was little furniture besides a low rectangular table which was almost hidden beneath an array of potted plants, a large oak cabinet along one wall, four wooden settles, and two rather worn three-seater six-legged sofas either side of the fireplace.

In front of which stood Lady Lydiard.

She was dressed in her tennis clothes, a hanging white skirt with its hem about two inches off the ground, black boots, a white blouse and matching band, and the very palest of blue ties knotted through a stiff white collar. Taller than Grace, she had softly waving hair the colour of chestnuts swept up from her face into a bun at the back of her head, a skin the colour and texture of eggshell, and the palest green eyes Grace had ever seen. She was perfectly beautiful in every way, from the elegance of her slim and flawlessly proportioned figure to the light in her green eyes and the sweet set of her mouth.

'You must be Grace,' she said in a voice full of good humour. 'Please come in and sit down.'

She indicated one of the old and worn three-seat sofas by her and then dismissed the footman with her thanks and a warm but vague smile.

'I understand that you wish to speak to me,' she said, picking up a half-drunk tumbler of chilled lemonade, the condensation trickling in and out of the pattern of the cut glass. 'Isn't it warm? Really far too warm for tennis, I'm afraid.'

Sipping her drink from the glass in one hand, and gently wiping the pearlescent gleam off her cheeks with a lawn handkerchief held in the other, Lady Lydiard looked at Grace with still smiling eyes before resetting her glass down and going to sit on the sofa opposite.

'Nanny's been keeping me posted as to your progress, Grace,' she continued. 'And well done is all I can say. Well done anybody who can get halfway through one of good old Nanny's obstacle races let alone reach the finishing line. Which from all reports you seem to have done.'

'I really had no idea I was being put to the test, Lady Lydiard,' Grace replied with perfect candour.

'Of course you didn't, Grace!' Lady Lydiard laughed gaily, and opened her eyes wide with the pleasure of her amusement. 'Why of course not! Goodness me, had you known – why Nanny would have spotted you as a fake and a fraud from the moment she'd said play! No, well done, I say. Very well done, Grace. In fact dare I say it absolutely terrific. Nanny Lydiard might be old, but she's lost none of her guile. She's quite an opponent to find oneself facing over the net. She can still put spin on the ball, as no doubt you probably found. Anyway, Grace, the thing is, as Nanny's probably told you – the point being one simply can't go on for ever. None of us can. So there we are. Yes? And I can't tell you how happy I am that it's all been sorted out and with no hard feelings. Don't you agree?'

'Forgive me, Lady Lydiard, but I don't quite follow,' Grace said carefully, completely baffled by the turn the conversation had taken.

'Oh, of course you don't. I'm so sorry. You came to speak to me, and now you want to know what on earth one's talking about because I'm doing all the talking and I can't say I blame you. Would you care for some lemonade? It really is most exceptionally hot,' Lady Lydiard continued at great speed, ringing the bell by the fireplace, 'which is probably why I'm not making much sense. It really is far too hot for tennis. But then of course Lord

Lydiard says the only time I talk sense is in my sleep. Good, here's Harcross.'

In answer to the bell the butler had appeared through a large ornamentally panelled door between the fireplace and the staircase, where he must have been standing ready and waiting.

Grace smiled to herself and thought it was little wonder he was known by all the servants as Harker Harcross, since it was rumoured he was rarely if ever out of earshot, and knew whenever a bell was about to be rung from the conversation he was busy overhearing. Getting up, Lady Lydiard ordered them both some chilled lemonade, and then went out of sight behind Grace's sofa.

Grace was too well mannered to turn and stare, but was momentarily disconcerted by the sound she heard behind her until she realized what it was, moments before Lady Lydiard reappeared bouncing a tennis ball off the highly polished wooden floor with her racquet.

'Is that what those marks were?' The remark was made before Grace had time to consider it.

'What marks do you mean, Grace?'

'I didn't mean to comment on them,' Grace replied. 'It's just that I did often wonder what made the marks on the floor. When I was polishing it.'

Lady Lydiard stopped bouncing her tennis ball and stared at Grace, her pale green eyes opened as wide as they could be.

'Heavens,' she said. 'You don't mean to tell me but how *frightful*. But you didn't do these floors, surely, Grace? I mean that sort of job a girl like you – don't they I mean surely someone else does that sort of thing? Polishing floors and – well. That sort of thing?'

'Not really, Lady Lydiard,' Grace replied. 'Before I was moved up to the nursery, I was a tweeny. I helped with the housework in the morning, Cook at lunchtime, cleaned the kitchens in the afternoon, and then helped Cook again prepare dinner.'

'Yes I do know vaguely what a tweeny does but even so, goodness gracious,' Lady Lydiard said, looking at Grace with complete disbelief. 'I mean good heavens above.'

She then began to bounce her tennis ball up and down once more while she walked around the room.

'Good heavens above,' she repeated. 'Sometimes on occasion, now and then, you know. One has a good think about something or other and when one does, one sometimes gets quite stopped in one's tracks. And I really must stop doing this in here.' She put her tennis racquet and ball on the sofa and sat down beside them. 'It's not the sort of thing one thinks of, day in day out, you see,' she explained after a moment. 'The fact that this sort of thing, the sort of thing one was doing a moment ago, you simply don't think for a moment that it might cause work for someone I mean that is *simply* dreadful. But there you are. It's absolutely typical, isn't it, Grace? When one comes to think about it. There you are. But do tell me, because I simply have to know. How actually did a girl like you ever come to – but then of course that's none of my business, is it? I'm frightfully sorry and it's certainly not something which should concern us here. Besides, I remember now, because Nanny told me the whole story from start to well – you know, and I remember thinking at the time – *how awful*. Good.'

The last remark was prompted by the reappearance of Harcross, who set down a tray of fresh lemonade on a small table by Lady Lydiard. He poured two glasses out slowly and carefully and then, having handed one to Lady Lydiard and one to Grace, he withdrew as silently as he had entered.

'Good,' Lady Lydiard continued, after taking a sip of her drink. 'Anyway. To get back to what we were talking about, Grace. You were saying.' She smiled another vague and enchanting smile while with the middle finger of her right hand she brushed away some stray chestnut hair from her forehead.

Grace, who so far hadn't said one thing she had meant to say since her arrival in the hall, cleared her throat and then fell silent, unable to see where she should begin. It had all seemed so easy in the abstract.

'Yes?' Lady Lydiard said, leaning forward and brushing another stray chestnut hair from her forehead. 'Do go on. Are you not happy here? I do hope not, not after all Nanny's told me. Surely not.'

'It's nothing to do with me, Lady Lydiard,' Grace said, at last finding her tongue. 'Not directly anyway. It's to do with Mrs Quinn.'

'Ah.' Lady Lydiard smiled approvingly. 'Otherwise known as Mrs Marvel. Yes do go on. What wonderful thing – something quite extraordinary, I'm sure. What miracle has she performed now?'

Grace stared at her, finding out not for the first time but certainly for the most telling that things very rarely go according to plan. The very last thing she would have guessed was that the woman who was hated and feared by all the staff should be considered to be something of a miracle worker by her employer.

'I'm afraid you're not going to like this, Lady Lydiard,' Grace said, determined to see it through now if just for the sake of her compatriots below stairs. 'But I think you should read this.'

Lady Lydiard read the note very quickly and straight through without stopping or looking up once. When she finished, she got up without looking at Grace and walked to one of the long windows which overlooked the park where she stood, remorselessly bouncing her tennis ball, but this time from her hand. Then she returned to sit on the sofa, where she read the note again but much more slowly, stopping every now and then to look up and stare at the silent and motionless Grace.

'So. Fine. Yes,' she said, folding the letter in its previous creases and tapping it against her hand. 'This is the word of a servant girl. So. Fine. Yes?'

'That was written by a girl called Aggie, Lady Lydiard,' Grace said. 'A girl you were told met her death by falling downstairs, but who in fact ended her life by hanging herself with her stockings from a beam in her room. Edith Crane, one of the kitchen maids, told me the details first,

140

and then Cook vouchsafed the story, as did all the rest of the junior staff.'

'What about Mrs Quinn?' Lady Lydiard wondered. 'What did she have to say on the matter?'

'I didn't think I, or for that matter anyone, should say anything to Mrs Quinn, Lady Lydiard,' Grace replied, 'until I had spoken to you.'

'In that case I shall summon her up here at once.'

Lady Lydiard reached for the bell and rang it before Grace could say anything.

'Mrs Quinn will deny it, Lady Lydiard,' Grace said.

'Well of course she will, Grace! The whole thing – I mean such a thing, can you imagine? Some of these girls will say anything, you know. Usually to get out of doing something.'

'This particular girl is dead, Lady Lydiard.'

'She fell downstairs, Grace, and broke – good heavens, Mrs Quinn came up here and told me herself! The girl broke her neck. Falling down – I don't know. The stairs somewhere. Mrs Quinn I could hardly get a word out of, she was so upset and I know for a fact she was very fond of the girl because she told me herself. Good heavens I mean heavens. Mrs Quinn stood here with a handkerchief to her – she could hardly get a word out about it she was so upset!'

'Perhaps you should ask Cook, Lady Lydiard,' Grace suggested. 'And Dolly. And Edith. And John, and everyone on the staff.'

'I shall ask – I'll tell you whom I shall ask. I shall ask Harcross,' Lady Lydiard announced as the butler re-entered.

'Last night Mrs Quinn said she caught the new tweeny, a girl called Sally who's just joined the household,' Grace continued, trying her best to remain impervious to Lady Lydiard's astounded look, 'Mrs Quinn said she caught her in one of the larders, stealing some food. No one else saw the girl, who denies taking anything, yet none the less Mrs Quinn beat the girl on her bare back at least a dozen times with a riding crop.'

'Nonsense,' Lady Lydiard said, but quietly and without conviction. 'This has to be a nonsense.'

'Sally's back bears ample evidence that it's the very opposite of a nonsense, Lady Lydiard.'

Looking first at Grace and then at her butler, Lady Lydiard suddenly seized both her knees and started drumming on them quickly and anxiously, while sucking her top lip with her lower one.

'Suppose you're wrong, Grace,' she finally asked. 'What then? I mean you know what then, don't you?'

'I'm not wrong, Lady Lydiard, I assure you,' Grace replied.

'She's absolutely right, milady,' Harcross put in suddenly, to both their surprise. 'She isn't wrong. Something should have been said a long time ago, but alas I fear we were all too intimidated seeing as it's Mrs Quinn's responsibility to run the servants in her care. Seeing as how it is, and old Lord Lydiard didn't like hearing about servants, as you know.'

Lady Lydiard continued to drum on her knees as she listened to the full history of the death of Aggie and of the various punishments meted out by the housekeeper to the young girls in her charge for no other reason, it became increasingly clear, than to satisfy what Nanny had described as her peculiar inclinations, or perhaps, Grace thought wryly, because this was not something she found she could say to Lady Lydiard, because she had been denied some of them.

'It sounds like another world down there,' Lady Lydiard said eventually, and a little unoriginally, since they all knew it was. She continued staring up above her, unable yet to look into the faces of her staff. 'One had simply no idea. What a different world.'

'Might I ask you something, Lady Lydiard?' Grace ventured, while privately wondering if she dare.

'How did she get the doctor – you see I don't understand how she got the doctor to – he signed the death certificate actually it was according to you, Harcross.' Lady Lydiard now looked a little accusingly at her butler. 'According to

142

you, you told me it was accidental. That the doctor, Dr Price, wasn't it? That Dr whoever had signed the certificate as accidental death.'

'Mrs Quinn is most persuasive, milady,' Harcross replied with his usual *gravitas*. 'Particularly when she knows a little something about a somebody.'

Nothing more was said of that particular matter, perhaps because it was unnecessary, or because they all feared to take matters too far too quickly. Cook had already told Grace, when Grace had stolen ten minutes with her midmorning, that Mrs Quinn was extorting money in return for her silence from several members of the staff, up to and including Mr Harcross, whose only real shortcoming was an inability to resist the temptations of his master's wine cellar, temptations which few butlers could resist.

'You wanted to ask me something more, Grace,' Lady Lydiard said, turning her extraordinary gaze on Grace.

'You'll think it impertinent, Lady Lydiard,' Grace replied, suddenly having serious second thoughts.

'After what I've learned this morning, good heavens!' Lady Lydiard cried, putting both hands to the back of her head. 'Good heavens, fire ahead.'

Grace took a deep breath.

'I wanted to know if you've ever been through the pass door.' Harcross frowned at her, as much as to warn her to stop. But Lady Lydiard showed no signs of displeasure. In fact she was looking at Grace with great curiosity. 'I just wondered if you'd ever been downstairs. To the kitchens. And the basements. To where most of the staff live.'

'Yes I've been to the kitchen, of course I've been to the kitchen,' Lady Lydiard replied with a frown. 'Every week to do the menus, and whenever we have a house party planned and at Christmas yes of course I have. You don't think I have?'

'But have you been anywhere else downstairs?' Grace continued. 'Have you seen where we sleep? And where we wash? Have you seen the room poor Aggie had? That I had? Have you seen where Mr Harcross sleeps? Between the boiler room and his pantry, with no window in his room? Have you seen the table in the corridor which John sleeps on in the summer when his room gets too hot and unbearable? Have you seen—'

'Yes, Grace, thank you that's quite enough.' Lady Lydiard put up both hands and then lay back on her sofa.

'Precisely, Merrill,' Harcross agreed. 'I think you've said quite enough.'

'She certainly has, Harcross,' Lady Lydiard agreed, suddenly sitting upright and then springing to her feet. 'Yes much the best thing now is to go and see for oneself.'

The tour was conducted in an almost total silence. Mrs Quinn, all smiles and pleasantries, found herself ordered to her room without explanation, while Grace was instructed to act as her employer's guide. Cook literally threw up her hands in dismay and started to run around her kitchens like a startled goose when Lady Lydiard arrived unannounced, and was only partly mollified when she learned that the object of the surprise visit wasn't to inspect Cook's domain but rather to see first-hand the conditions under which the staff had been expected to live since old Lord Lydiard's time.

Nothing more of any consequence was said as Grace led the way along the labyrinth of murky linoleum-covered corridors, in and out of the warren of windowless bedrooms, through the cheerlessness of the barely furnished servants' hall with its permanent ghostly smell of stale cabbage, the bleak austerity of the sculleries with their huge sinks in which the maids not only washed up endlessly but were also expected to bath, the steam and smell of the laundry room, past the stale-ale-smelling brewhouse and finally out into the courtyard past the unsanitary reek of the dung heap and the row of earth closets.

'Good. Well yes. Fine,' Lady Lydiard said when she and Grace returned through a side door into the hall. 'In what is it? Exoneration, yes, in one's defence all one can say is that if one had started from *scratch*. It's very difficult, Grace, marrying into a family such as this. One marries a

144

house as well, and of course the former Lord Lydiard and his father and so on, particularly Lord Lydiard's father the former Lord Lydiard, he saw places like this quite distinctly. As two separate entities if you see what I mean. Or communities. The family and the servants. And while there's everything to be said because after all just as much as the family require their privacy, so too the servants of course, so while there's a lot to be said for that, it just won't do, I quite agree. Not in this day and age. So I think much the best thing, because it's not the sort of thing that can be done overnight, I'll speak to my husband, who I don't for a minute suppose has been through the baize door I'll bet since he was a boy, when or so I gather he used to spend most of his time in the kitchens. Anyway, jolly good, Grace, and leave this to me.'

Grace thanked Lady Lydiard for her time and made to go, only to be recalled at once.

'Sorry,' Lady Lydiard said, 'but I hadn't quite finished. I mean I haven't said well done, have I? Which was really the whole point of the exercise, wasn't it? But then of course there was all this business.'

Lady Lydiard smiled at Grace and then flopped down on the sofa.

'Phew,' she said. 'It really is going to be another scorcher. I think a swim in the lake's indicated, don't you? We're actually thinking of putting in a swimming pool now. We tried to persuade old Lord Lydiard to build one, but he stoutly maintained that the point of water was for catching fishes. So.'

Another smile was bestowed on Grace, this one even vaguer.

'I really should be getting back to the children, Lady Lydiard,' she volunteered.

'Of course you must,' Lady Lydiard agreed. 'But well done. Really. I'm so glad such a good solution was found, and without whatever. You know. Any sort of recrimination. Because one was beginning to get the heepy-creepies.'

Grace suddenly found herself bursting with laughter

and was unable to control herself. She at once bit her lip and put a hand to her mouth.

'I'm terribly sorry, Lady Lydiard,' she said, 'but I just couldn't help it. You see I honestly don't know what you're talking about.'

Lady Lydiard frowned at Grace as if she was the one double-talking.

'Really?' she asked. 'You mean Nanny didn't *say*?'

'Nanny didn't say anything, Lady Lydiard, except was I sure I didn't want her to speak to you.'

'About?'

'About downstairs. About Mrs Quinn and all the rest of it.'

'She didn't say anything about—' Lady Lydiard frowned even more deeply and poked just a fraction of pink tongue from the corner of her mouth. 'About. She didn't say anything else?' she continued, her beautiful face now puckered in perplexity. 'You mean when you came down here because that was certainly necking it. If you didn't know what had been decided. Good lord, I'll say. Do you mean you really didn't know what's been *decided*?' Lady Lydiard leaned forward, hands once again clasping her knees. 'You funny girl,' she said. 'You do know if – well. If things had been otherwise. Imagine my mother-in-law for instance. If you'd decided to bring this to *her* attention – well, there'd have been no question of it.'

'Of what, Lady Lydiard?'

Still clasping her knees, Lady Lydiard now began to rock backwards and forwards with delighted laughter.

'You'd have been out of a job, Grace!'

'I understood that perfectly well,' Grace replied, unable to see the funny side. 'But I just thought something should be said.'

'Absolutely,' Lady Lydiard agreed. 'And Nanny was absolutely right. What she suggests makes perfect sense. She came down to see me this morning after breakfast and – well. Of course most of what Nanny says makes sense, doesn't it? But then most of what most nannies say makes sense I suppose, which I suppose is why

146

they're nannies. Because they're so sensible. But it's good sense, isn't it? Not common sense that one looks for in one's nanny. And Nanny said you had plenty of that. Plenty of *good* sense. Plus a great deal of pluck – and determination. Which is just the job. So really all in all things could not have worked out for the better. We were really getting to the point when we thought – that's Lord Lydiard and I. Because I mean she was my husband's nanny, and his father's, so you can imagine. My husband just hadn't the heart, you see. Not after all this time just to say well that's it. Thank you very much for all you've done, but I'm afraid that's it. Can you imagine? And then out of the blue the dear old thing volunteers to call it a day, saying she hadn't wanted to before because she was afraid it might upset John, I mean my husband, Lord Lydiard. But now that a solution had been found – and such a *good* one. I mean what better? Just as long of course as you're happy too, Grace. Except that won't do at all, will it? Calling you Grace. No, no – heavens above no from now on, Grace, one is going to have to call you by your proper name.'

From somewhere Lady Lydiard had got hold of another tennis ball and had begun bouncing it quickly and dextrously from one hand to the other without looking, because now she was looking up directly at Grace.

'No from now on, Grace,' she said with a smile of genuine affection, 'everyone's going to have to call you by your proper name. From now on we're all going to have to call you Nanny Lydiard.'

S E V E N

Keston. August 10th, 1911.

Nanny Lydiard had no idea she was being painted. She knew there was a house party because of all the motor-cars which had arrived that lunchtime and were parked in front of the Hall, a dark green 1907 Wolseley, according to Henry who could now identify every vehicle that rumbled and spluttered up the drive, a yellow Sunbeam 12/16, a black Lanchester, a 1907 40/50 Rolls Royce Silver Ghost, a ruby 1906 Vauxhall Touring and the last to arrive, long after the others, a deep red and dashing 1910 25hp Talbot which Henry announced as his favourite, a conclusion with which Grace wholeheartedly concurred, particularly when she caught sight of the driver when he had climbed out and was standing in the drive, looking up at the elevation of the house.

At this point, Grace, Henry, Harriet and Baby John known as 'Boy', who had been born to Serena, Lady Lydiard that March, had been sheltering from the boiling August sun under the shade provided by the huge cedar of Lebanon which dominated the lawns to the west of the house. Harriet as usual had been busy painting, this time a watercolour sketch of Beanie, the brown and white spaniel who lay panting lazily under Boy's pram, while Henry had been idly playing with his diabolo, expertly flicking up the double-coned top from the string stretched between two

148

sticks before recatching it again as it was still spinning.

'I like that motor-car,' Henry had announced, as the latecomer sunk his hands in his pockets and walked a few steps backwards in order to get a better view of the house. 'That's a Talbot. A Clement-Talbot, actually, and it's really very fast.'

'It's not as nice as a horse,' Harriet had concluded, after a brief look up. 'I don't know why you think so much of motor-cars.'

While brother and sister had continued to argue over the respective merits and demerits of motor-cars and horses, Grace had stolen another look at the new arrival from under the brim of her sun hat, a high-crowned straw trimmed with a swathe of white lace frilling. The man was tall and slim, dressed in an unpressed lounge suit made of a lightweight beige material, a white shirt and a large red floppy bow tied very large and loose, and instead of boots a pair of newly fashionable brown shoes above the tops of which could be glimpsed socks which matched his tie. He looked very debonair, Grace had thought, and casual, even more so when he took off his straw boater and revealed a head of thick unkempt brown hair which he attempted to tidy by running a hand back through first one side then the other before replacing his hat. He was as handsome as he was dark, with a pair of straight dark brown eyebrows which seemed lowered in a permanent frown, a wonderful aquiline nose, and a determined mouth which perfectly matched his frown.

'Hello there!' he had suddenly called as he'd turned and noticed the party under the tree, and Grace had looked up, not only because he had called, but because of his American accent. 'I suppose I've missed lunch! But I got ridiculously lost!'

The man had then wandered over to them, sideways like a crab since he was still staring up at the house.

'Seventeenth century, I'd say,' he'd wondered aloud. 'Most probably middle of. And either a Roger Pratt or a Robert Hooke. Whatever, it's quite perfect. One of the

149

best seventeenth-century houses I've seen. Wouldn't you agree, Nanny?'

He had turned to Grace with a frown and for a moment their eyes had met before Grace had dropped hers and returned to her sewing.

'I would find it rather difficult to agree with you, I'm afraid,' she had replied. 'Because I don't know what other seventeenth-century houses you've seen.'

Harriet had got the joke long before the new arrival and burst into a peal of laughter, which had only made the dark-eyed man frown the more. Then he too had suddenly laughed.

'Of course! I see!' He'd turned back to the house and then back to the group, taking his boater off once more to run a hand again through his hair. 'That's a habit of mine I'm afraid, Nanny. Asking the unanswerable. One of the best seventeenth-century houses I've seen don't you agree. Yes, that's pretty typical. And how on earth *would* you know?'

'I haven't seen your motor-car before,' Henry had announced. 'So this must be your first visit here.'

'Almost right, young man,' the visitor had replied. 'My only other visit here was at night. Now then – might I be allowed to see what you're drawing, miss?'

Then he'd gone round behind Harriet and bent down to look over her shoulder. Harriet had paid him no attention except to warn him that he would be late for lunch.

'How do you know they haven't started?' he'd asked her.

'Because someone rings the gong half an hour before it's time to go in,' Harriet had replied. 'Don't they in your house?'

'In my house they ring the gong twenty-seven and a half minutes before it's time to go in,' the man had teased, frowning again as he bent lower to look at Harriet's work. 'And that's very good, young lady. Most excellent. You really have captured the weight of the dog. The substance. That really is quite remarkable for someone your age.'

Harriet had stolen a look at Grace and they'd exchanged

a secret smile. Every time someone saw Harriet's drawing the same remark was passed. The next remark, however, wasn't typical.

'You are working wet-in-wet and dry-brush, I take it?' he asked. 'Because if you are, you want to take a little white gouache here, on a dry brush, may I?'

He had taken a dry brush from Harriet's hand and, dipping it in the white gouache, had started to embellish the watercolour of the dog by painting the coat round the dog's neck with quick, flicking strokes.

'It's called *feathering*, and it's a very useful technique. See?'

Harriet had looked across at Grace again, but Grace had just shaken her head slightly and put a finger to her own lips.

'Thank you,' Harriet said politely. 'And by the way, the gong for lunch went twenty-seven minutes ago.'

Now it was late afternoon, and Grace and her charges had moved camp to the summerhouse at the end of the croquet lawn where Dolly had brought them out a tray of tea, consisting of cucumber sandwiches, scones, thinly sliced lemon cake, and a jug of iced orangeade.

'You're being drawn, Nanny,' Dolly told her, gently rocking Boy's baby carriage now she'd put down the tea tray. ' 'Oo's a pretty boy then, eh?' she cooed, leaning over to take a closer look at the infant.

Grace glanced down to the terrace below them where the house party was also taking tea, but could see no sign of anyone sketching. She knew for whom she was looking, the late arrival, the tall man with the floppy bow tie and head of unruly brown hair, the handsome American.

' 'E's inside,' Dolly said, eyeing Grace. 'The window to the right of the French doors.'

Shielding her eyes from the blazing sun, Grace took another look, and after a moment was able to make out a figure at the open window, seated behind a small easel.

'Here.'

Henry handed Grace a small telescopic spyglass which he opened out for her.

'It's Grandfather's,' Henry explained. 'He kept it here to spy on his guests.'

The American wasn't drawing, he was painting in watercolours. Through the powerful eyeglass Grace could see the small wooden paintbox and the jar of brushes set on the window-sill. She could also see someone else in the room, a woman, who came out of the shadows to stand behind the artist's back for a moment to admire his work. Then she bent slowly forward and whispered something in the man's ear, something which prompted the American to loop one arm round the woman's neck and hold her close to his face so that he could slowly kiss her cheek, while the woman dropped one hand on his shoulder, spreading the fingers out over the top of his chest.

Grace folded the eyeglass back and handed it to Henry.

'Thank you, Henry,' she said, having seen quite enough.

The woman was Henry's mother.

When Grace took the two older children in for their goodnights, the American was sitting playing the piano for several of the house guests who were gathered round him. Grace waited by the fireplace with Henry holding one hand and Harriet the other, having been ushered in by Lady Lydiard who once she had smiled at her children had then pressed a finger to her lips for silence until the American had finished. He was playing a strange and haunting piece which Grace had never heard before, an exquisitely hushed nocturne which seemed to conjure up a dreamlike garden in the moonlight.

The only person in the room who wasn't standing in the group round the grand piano was Lord Lydiard, whose tall, slim figure was draped in a wing-chair the other side of the fireplace. As usual he had taken no notice of Grace and the children when they had come in, and he continued to ignore them, deeply involved in the leather-bound volume he was reading, every so often slowly turning to the next page and carefully smoothing the papers down before continuing to read.

What Grace had at first taken for Lord Lydiard's indifference but now knew to be diffidence no longer troubled her. When they had met face to face in the drawing room on Grace's first day as Nanny, Lord Lydiard had got up and left the room without a word the moment she had entered it. Not unnaturally Grace had assumed him to be the son of his father, as had her friends downstairs who still kept out of his sight at all times despite the fact that no instructions had been issued to that effect. He was very tall and physically imposing like the late Lord Lydiard, but whereas his father had been a heavyweight, the sixth Baron Lydiard was slim and willowy, and in no way conventionally handsome. His chin was good and strong, as was his jaw, but his mouth was feminine, pretty and full-lipped, and his unshaven upper lip long and protrusive, which with his high forehead and large downturned eyes gave him a permanent look of moodish melancholia.

Except when he smiled, which at first acquaintance it seemed he never did. At least that was the impression Grace had formed initially. In fact when she remembered her first year as Nanny, she could only recall seeing her employer smile once. Not that it appeared to bother either of his children, who seemed perfectly at ease in the company of both their parents. Their mother teased and tickled them, laughed with them and played with them, in contrast to their father who never joined in their games but instead listened to what they had to say patiently and seriously, however childlike their conversation might be. Even when they told him of something that had just happened which they considered funny, his response would always be the same. He would listen, nod and tell them that he saw their point and that he quite understood, which only made them laugh the more.

The first time Grace had seen him smile hadn't been with his children, however. It had been one evening when she had been going back upstairs with Henry and Harriet after they had said their goodnights to their father, and they had met Lady Lydiard coming down late, dressed for a party in the newly fashionable Oriental look, wearing a gown of purple and gold, with a pair of 'harem' trousers just visible below the hem of the tight, straight skirt and a plumed headband holding in place her heap of chestnut hair.

'Oh, sweethearts!' she had sighed as they met on the stairs, bending down to kiss her son and daughter. 'I missed our time together. But you know what Mama is like when she's getting ready to go to a party. Like that dreadful white rabbit. Late, late, late – always late! Isn't that right, Nanny? I'm so sorry, really I am, my darlings, and I'll make it all up to you tomorrow, I promise.'

She had kissed them again and then with a smile and a wave to them all, and lifting up her skirts, she rushed down the stairs at a wholly inappropriate speed, taking two at a time, her free hand sliding down the banister until she was at the bottom and face to face with her husband, who had just appeared from the library, fob-watch in hand.

From the look on his face he must have been just about to scold her, but when he saw the wonderful apparition that was his wife, in her purple and gold slave-girl's costume, her fair skin specially darkened, her long slender arms bangled with Persian bracelets, her ears hung with gypsy rings, and her whole being perfumed with musky Eastern essences, his impatience vanished and sinking his hands in his trouser pockets he simply stood back and for the first time in Grace's recollection smiled.

And in the moment that he smiled he was transformed from his usual earnest, introspective and scholarly self into another person, someone Grace had never seen or even glimpsed, a man with laughing eyes and a smiling face so kind and sweet-natured that he could rob any heart. He most certainly had the heart of his wife, who when she saw her husband smiling at her slipped her hand in his and walked away with him as if they were lovers embarking on a courtship.

But now that the man at the piano had finished playing

and everyone around him had burst into applause, Lord Lydiard took no notice, never even raising his eyes. He simply turned over yet another page, smoothed the papers of the book and went on reading.

Someone asked the pianist what it was he'd been playing.

'Ah,' he replied, rising from the piano and running both his hands back through his shock of dark hair. 'Debussy. The man who paints with music.'

'And what was that particular painting called, Brake?' Lady Lydiard asked, giving a name to her guest.

'*Clair de Lune*, Serena,' the man now called Brake replied. 'I'm told he took the title from a poem by Verlaine, which concerns itself with a vision of long dead people returning to dance in the moonlight.'

'It was perfectly lovely actually I thought, Brake,' Lady Lydiard replied. 'And yes – absolutely. It was rather spooky actually. Very.'

'It was far too romantic,' Lord Lydiard said without looking up from his book. 'The playing of Debussy requires a firm touch and a certain coolness in the interpretation. Not such ardent romanticism.'

The pianist smiled, turning his music back to the first page.

'Are you a pianist, Lord Lydiard?' he enquired.

'I play the piano, yes. But I dare say I wouldn't describe myself as a pianist.' Lord Lydiard continued to read while he replied, without looking up once.

'Perhaps you'd like to show me the error of my ways then.'

'Oh, I don't think so.'

A beautiful woman with an oval face and a wonderful mane of brown hair leaned over Lord Lydiard, confiscating his book.

'Go on, John,' she said. 'Don't be bashful.'

'I really don't think so, Marjorie,' her host repeated firmly but with good humour. 'And may I have my book back?'

He held his arm up but instead of returning his book

the woman took his hand and going round to the front of his chair pulled Lord Lydiard to his feet.

'He's a remarkable pianist, Mr Merrowby,' she said. 'You just wait.'

'Do you know the piece, Lord Lydiard?' the American enquired. 'Or are you a good reader? Because I have the music.'

'The music's no good to him,' the beautiful woman laughed. 'John can't read a note.'

'I probably won't be able to play it all the way through,' Lord Lydiard protested as he was led to the grand piano, taking from his short pocket a pair of round spectacles with tinted lenses. 'I've only heard it once.'

'What does he mean?' the American wondered. 'He's only heard it once?'

'Wait and see.' The beautiful woman smiled as she folded the sheet music shut. 'It's John's party trick.'

As Lord Lydiard settled at the keyboard, carefully looping the wired ends of his spectacles behind his ears, Lady Lydiard came over and sat Grace and the children down with her on a long low sofa covered in faded yellow damask from where they had full sight of the keyboard.

'I do so absolutely love this when it happens,' she whispered. 'At least I do when it comes off.'

'I don't see how your father can possibly play a piece like this if he really has only heard it once,' Grace whispered to Harriet and Henry. 'Or is it some sort of a tease?'

'Of course not,' Henry scoffed. 'If Papa really likes something he only ever has to hear it once.'

'It's just the same when he reads something,' Harriet added. 'The first time he reads the story from the book, and the next time he doesn't have to bother.'

'Only if he likes it,' Henry reminded his sister.

'We heard these Debussy pieces, which actually I think or rather I seem to remember are all part of a suite actually,' Lady Lydiard confided to Grace. 'Anyway we heard them – where was it? Yes. In Paris when we were over there last when was it?'

156

'In April,' Harriet said. 'Just after my birthday.'

'You see my husband loves contemporary music, Nanny,' Lady Lydiard continued, paying no attention as Harriet wriggled her way over to sit on her knee. 'We both do. As for the South American tango. It was absolutely sweeping Paris. I can't wait for it to come over here. Anyway to get back to what's he called? Debussy. We went to this recital and at the reception afterwards the soloist told us that the secret of how to play this music is to imagine we weren't living now but in Louis XIV's time which I have to say I found too funny for words because I couldn't see how that can possibly be, can you, Nanny? Because I mean how would they know? You know. What things sounded like in seventeen hundred? Sssshhh. Papa's going to play. So keep your fingers crossed everyone.'

The whole room fell silent as the first notes sounded *pianissimo* from the ebony-black piano. Lord Lydiard sat bolt upright over the keyboard as he played, with his body completely still, his wrists flat rather than arched so that his long fingers were level with the keys, and his head tipped backwards as far as it would go so that his eyes stared fixedly at the ceiling. Seeing that he was in fact looking at nothing, Grace wondered why he had troubled to put on his spectacles.

For a second Grace's eye roamed around the room away from the pianist, and mentally she compared the rich scene around her, the guests in their beautiful clothes made of stuffs of the kind that Father had used to bring back from his travels, the rich decorated oil paintings on the walls, the priceless ornaments and rugs, everything so beautiful and such a contrast to poor Mother and Lottie crouching in their little house only a few miles away. Lottie coming in soaked, as she had when Grace last visited, her nose streaming with cold after cold because she was always trying to eat as little as possible so that she could save for other things. Everything at Keston was rich with age, and everything at home, by contrast, seemed to be only dingy with the same. For a second Grace's heart surged with resentment. It didn't seem fair for so few people to have so much, and for so many to have so little.

But the music was so sublime it soothed away the sudden bitterness she had felt, and almost at once she became intrigued by the difference between the two interpretations she was hearing, even though the composition was totally unknown to her. The first had been, as Lord Lydiard had commented, too romantic and too expressive. Even from her limited knowledge of the piano Grace knew it had been overstated, particularly now as she listened to this the second version, which was almost mathematically detached and deliberately unromantic. As a result the music spoke as the composer surely must have intended it to speak, with a subtle delicacy and a dreamy tenderness, with a special poetry and grace. The room seemed to shimmer with the magic sound, and to be bathed in the paleness of the moon rather than the lessening brightness of the evening summer sun.

There was utter silence when Lord Lydiard finished the nocturne. The audience was enraptured, so much so that no one wished to break the spell by clapping. After a moment Lord Lydiard sighed and carefully unhooked his spectacles from behind his ears.

'The last chord, eight bars from the end,' he said, 'should, I imagine, have been A flat, G flat, C, and just A flat in the left hand.' He demonstrated. 'Simple stuff, but I left out the G.'

'I didn't notice,' Brake protested.

'I did,' Lord Lydiard replied. 'So you win.'

Grace was astonished, as were all those guests who had been unaware of their host's incredible gift. She joined in the applause which had now broken out and watched with wide eyes as her employer resumed his seat and picked up the book of verse he had been reading.

'You can take them to say good night now, Nanny,' Lady Lydiard said, first kissing both her children before allowing them to go.

'Can we say good night to everyone, Mama?' Harriet asked.

158

'Don't be so boring,' Henry groaned. 'You always ask that.'

'You can say good night to whoever you want to,' their mother replied. 'Isn't that right, Nanny? I don't see why not.'

'Good night, Papa,' Harriet said. 'We're going to bed now.'

'I wish I was,' her father replied without looking up from his book, causing Grace to smile.

'Good night, Papa,' Henry said. 'Except if you don't mind me saying—'

'I don't mind you saying,' Lord Lydiard muttered, putting a finger on the page to remind him where he was, and then looking at his children. 'What?'

'You cheated.'

'I didn't. Did I, Henry?'

Lord Lydiard frowned deeply, rubbing the end of his Roman nose so hard he almost flattened it into his top lip.

'You heard that tune more than once, Papa,' Henry informed him. 'Lady Wynant played it last weekend.'

'Well done, Henry.' His father took Henry's hand and shook it very seriously. 'You're right. And you're wrong. Lady Wynant did play it last weekend, but she played it incorrectly. And she didn't play it all the way through. Even so, ask Nanny if you can have a sweet.'

'Can I have a sweet please, Nanny?' Henry asked Grace.

'Can I have one too, please?' said Harriet.

'I don't have any sweets,' Grace told them.

'I only said for them to ask you, Nanny,' Lord Lydiard corrected her. 'I'm the one with the sweets. You're the one with the permission.'

He looked up at her, finger once again marking his place in the book, and opened his mouth as if to speak. Then he stopped and stared at her instead, very hard, almost it seemed to Grace as if he knew her.

'Well?' he finally asked, still looking at her through narrowed eyes although by now he had fished two sweets from his trouser pocket and was holding them out for his children.

'Yes of course, Lord Lydiard,' Grace replied. 'They haven't cleaned their teeth.'

Henry and Harriet took a sweet each and went off to say good night to the guests. Grace was about to follow them when a voice behind her stopped her.

'You are a local girl, Nanny?' Lord Lydiard asked her, no longer looking at her, but back reading his book.

'Yes,' Grace replied. 'I was born and bred in Keston.'

'Your mother must be a very pretty woman.'

'So people say, Lord Lydiard.'

'And your father?'

'My father was good-looking, rather than handsome.'

'A fine distinction, Nanny.'

'Not one of my making, Lord Lydiard. My mother's.'

Lord Lydiard looked up at Grace once more, but this time without expression. Then he returned to his reading.

'Thank you, Nanny,' he said to his book.

Grace waited by the door until Henry and Harriet had shaken each and every guest solemnly by the hand. She caught them just before they started their second round.

'Bed,' she said. 'Monkeys.'

'The man with the monocle,' Henry told her confidentially, 'has a hand like a dead fish.'

'That's nothing. The woman sitting at the piano has a wart on hers,' Harriet said triumphantly.

'Good night everyone!' Henry called from the doorway, before bowing solemnly to the assembled company.

Everyone bowed back except their father, who instead waved a hand as he leaned sideways to take another book from the shelves.

Before she closed the double doors, Grace took a last look into the drawing room. Everyone was busy talking again, or taking drinks from Harcross. All except the American who was sitting beside the woman at the piano. Brake Merrowby was looking across at the door, at Grace, a look of which Grace had been aware as she had begun to usher the children out, a look which had made Grace look back.

A look which, now that she caught his eyes, made Grace blush and quickly pull the doors tight shut, because somehow and for some reason Grace knew what the look was, she had read about it, and seen it expressed in paintings, only now for the first time she had seen the reality.

E I G H T

'Lady Lydiard says it's perfectly all right for me to paint you.'

The artist had found his way up to the nurseries and was standing in the doorway of the playroom, dressed in tennis whites, both hands sunk deep into his trouser pockets. In his mouth he had the stub of a cigar.

'We don't allow smoking in the nursery I'm afraid, Mr Merrowby,' Grace told him as she bustled past with an armful of freshly laundered sheets.

'Excuse me, Nanny,' the artist replied, moving the cigar stub to the other side of his mouth with his tongue and giving an impish grin. 'But it isn't alight.'

'Even so,' Grace replied, 'the aroma. Harriet has a weak chest.'

Dora, who by now followed Grace everywhere like an orphaned sheep, opened the linen cupboard door and took the laundry to put away with her own bundle. Meanwhile Brake Merrowby had wandered over to one of the barred windows where he tossed out the offending cigar butt.

'Bars everywhere,' he said. 'Don't you feel as though you're in prison up here?'

'Quite the contrary,' Grace replied. 'We feel we're very safe.'

'I'd go quite lunatic,' Merrowby mused, still holding

the bars and looking out over the parkland. 'Shut away up in the roof of a house, with no one to talk to.'

'Nonsense, Mr Merrowby,' Grace said crisply. 'There simply aren't enough hours in the day. And as for not having anyone to talk to, really. We never stop, do we, Dora?'

'I don't suppose we do, Nanny,' Dora replied dolefully, before wiping her nose on the crook of a finger.

Brake Merrowby turned and looked at Grace, smiling at her, still holding the bars of the window and leaning his head on them.

'Nonsense, Nanny,' he mocked. 'Sheer stuff and nonsense.'

Grace turned her back on him so he couldn't see her quick blush.

He was absolutely right, of course. There was no one to talk to up here, not for someone as bright as Grace, not once her charges were in the classroom one floor down or tucked up in their beds asleep. And when they weren't, there was a limit to the conversations you could have with children, however intelligent and interesting they might be and as Henry and Harriet certainly were. When the three of them talked it was either question and answer: *Why does such and such a thing happen, Nanny?* Or *What makes such and such a thing do such and such?* Or the conversation was purely instructional, with Grace explaining something to Henry and Harriet, correcting them about certain aspects of their behaviour, or showing them how to do something.

Like all children they were perennially inquisitive and very often their questions got so convoluted and complicated they were almost indecipherable, sessions which Grace enjoyed enormously, but which even so were no satisfactory substitute for proper conversation. The sort of conversation she had used to enjoy so much what now seemed so many years ago, in her former life, when she was 'Miss Grace', not 'Merrill' or 'Nanny'.

Then after Grace had put the children to bed early in the evening, never any later than seven o'clock despite the fact that Henry was now thirteen and Harriet eleven, there were still three hours left of the day before Grace herself retired. Since Boy had been born, she could no longer leave Dora in charge while she paid a visit to her friends below stairs, and although Dolly made an initial effort to come up and have a chat with Grace at some point in the evening, by the time she'd finished her work she was usually so exhausted she often fell asleep on the old nursery sofa, leaving Grace to carry on with her sewing and mending until it was time for Boy's last bottle at ten o'clock.

Most evenings now, however, Grace spent with her workbox, for a large part of a nanny's duties was the making and mending of baby and children's clothes. She took great delight in choosing the materials for Boy's silk suits, and embroidering and smocking them, her tiny stitches requiring every concentration, and her delight in the colours of the silken threads she used replacing any desire she might have once had to paint.

Nowadays therefore it was Grace's lot to sew in every spare moment, while Dora padded round the nursery suite sniffing continuously while she put the final touches to tidying the rooms and preparing them for the next day, before collapsing in a chair to read the latest magazine she'd borrowed from the servants' hall. For the next two hours Grace would sew while Dora read, the silence punctuated only by the nursery maid's incessant sniffing. Conversation between them had long been exhausted, just as Grace had long since abandoned making any further suggestions as to how Dora might cope with her permanently running nose or her complete inability to knit even the simplest garment without dropping stitches and making sudden, large incomprehensible holes in the middle of what Grace could only consider to be a quite ordinary and simple line of knitting.

So the American painter had been right, which was probably why Grace had reacted so prudishly. Shut up in the roof far above the rest of the house with no one to talk to Grace had on more than one occasion thought longingly of a broader horizon.

'To get back to the purpose of my visit, Nanny.'

Brake Merrowby detached himself from the window bars and sat at the nursery table.

'I wish to do a painting of you,' he continued. 'I made some initial sketches the other day, which encouraged me to think there might be a painting here, of you and your youngest charge.'

'Boy.'

'That's the little fellow. Boy. Although he won't be seen. I want to paint you as I saw you on Saturday. With Boy in his baby carriage, and you sitting on the grass beside him reading, or sewing, or whatever it is you do.'

'What I do, Mr Merrowby,' Grace replied, 'is look after Lord and Lady Lydiard's children.'

The artist roared with laughter and leaned back dangerously far in his chair so that he could watch and keep talking to Grace as she circled round him, involved in her morning routine.

'Tell me,' he said, just managing to keep his balance. 'Do all you nannies talk the same? Do they train you to sound alike? To talk to us all, all of us as if we're still children?'

'I suppose the way we talk, if we do indeed talk in any particular way, Mr Merrowby,' Grace countered, 'is for the same reason why you talk as you do. With an accent. It's something that we hear, because it's all around us.'

'I don't think so, Nanny. I think it's something you adopt. I think it's a form of control. Particularly when allied to this use of the first person plural pronoun. We feel perfectly safe up here. We don't allow smoking in the nurseries. It's very daunting. Like dealing with royalty. And I can't believe that a girl like you has always spoken like some imperious monarch.'

By now Grace was the opposite side of the table, facing the artist, and she couldn't help noticing, despite everything she had said, and the way she had worked so hard at distancing herself from him, that he was looking at her again in that same intense and disturbing way, as if he was refusing to go along with the rest of the world and accept her just as 'Nanny Lydiard'. As if he saw that she was a woman.

'Allow me,' Brake said, as Grace managed to drop a jar of pencils.

He reached to help her pick them up and as he did so he quite deliberately, she thought, allowed their hands to touch albeit very briefly.

'It was my fault, I'm sorry,' Grace muttered, wishing she could just stop blushing every time she found him staring at her.

'Don't you know why I want to paint you, Nanny?' Brake Merrowby asked as he rearranged the pencils and crayons in the jar.

'You said you were encouraged by your sketches to think you might be able to make a painting,' Grace replied, turning away and pretending to tidy an already immaculate shelf of books.

'I want to paint you,' the artist replied with exaggerated patience, 'not because you are beautiful, which you are, but because you seem to emanate – no, radiate. Radiate's a much more appropriate word. You radiate warmth and affection. When I saw you, not the first time when I arrived, although that picture itself was charming, no, when I saw you up on the high lawn outside the summer-house, sitting in the half shade with the children beside you, and the unseen baby in his carriage, from where I was, from all that distance away I just got this feeling. There was such composure, such peace. Thank God I got it at the time, in my sketches, I think I got the very essence of the moment, but of course now I must paint it, and capture it fully. And for that I need you.'

Grace dropped a book quite unintentionally, and bent down to pick it up.

'I seem to be all thumbs and no fingers this morning,' she said.

'Lady Lydiard has given her permission.'

Still Grace made no direct reply. In some way, although she was privately excited by the idea, she also felt more than a little irritated by the fact that permission had been sought and granted to use her, as if she was simply a chattel. *Can I borrow your nanny? But of course you can. Just don't borrow her for too long because she does have her duties.* For a moment she considered refusing.

'That's why I came up here, Nanny,' the voice behind her said, in quite a different tone, a tone altogether less assertive and confident. 'It's all very well for Lady Lydiard to say yes, and for me to say I want you to do this. But finally it's up to you. It has to be something you want to do. So that's why I'm here. I'm here to ask you if you'd be so kind as to spare me just a couple of your precious hours today to sit for me. I could do it without you. I could paint from my sketches as I so often do. But in this case I know it would be no good, because I need you. I need your radiance, I need the light that shines from you. I'm not sure I can capture that light, but then that'll be my failing, not yours. Please?'

He was smiling at her when Grace turned, without that hint of mockery she had noticed in his smile before, without even the attractive playfulness to which she had felt herself respond immediately when he walked sideways across the lawn to her when he had arrived, one eye on the house, and then both eyes on her when he saw her. This smile was almost helpless in its honesty, almost hopeless in its sincerity. Grace knew she couldn't refuse him, not because of his candour, but because she knew she couldn't refuse him.

'Would this afternoon be convenient?' she asked. 'About the same time? Around teatime?'

Brake Merrowby rose from his chair, the supplication in his smile now changed to unfeigned gratitude.

'We shall,' he promised, 'be friends for life, Grace.'

He was gone the next morning, without a word. Henry was the first to notice, as he checked the motor-cars

167

from the playroom window after breakfast.

'I think that's rather rotten,' he said in his solemn way. 'Mr Merrowby's gone and he never gave me a drive in his car.'

'How do you know he's gone?' Grace asked, finding herself looking out of the window alongside Henry. 'He might just have gone out for a spin.'

'I saw Harcross and one of the footmen putting his cases in the car when I got up,' Henry said. 'But I thought even so he might be staying for lunch. People usually do.'

There was no way Grace could find out why Brake Merrowby had left so abruptly. All she knew was that his departure could have had nothing to do with her. The two hours she had spent being painted by him the previous afternoon had in the main been silent, with the artist only speaking to her to instruct her as to what she should or shouldn't do. Very occasionally he would ask her a question out of the blue which he immediately forbade Grace to answer lest she broke the pose. The sum of these questions was how come and why a girl such as she had come to be a nursemaid, as the artist had called her job, but since Grace hadn't been allowed to respond to his questioning at the end of the session Brake Merrowby was none the wiser. Certainly no information of a personal nature was exchanged or volunteered, and when the sitting was over, the artist had simply thanked the subject and politely dismissed her without showing her his work.

He had, however, indicated that he would require her for at least one if not two further sittings, and had assured Grace that he would seek the necessary permissions.

Yet now he had left, gone without a word.

More acutely than ever before Grace felt the restrictions imposed upon her by her position. Whereas she could politely enquire of Lady Lydiard if Mr Merrowby had in fact ended his visit, she could not ask the reason why, nor could she ask if he had left any message as to future arrangements regarding the painting. If there was any such information then Grace would have to wait until it was volunteered to her, if in fact it was volunteered at all, since Lady Lydiard might consider it unnecessary to relay such trivia, preferring to keep the matter to herself until Mr Merrowby was next invited, which was precisely the feeling Grace got when the subject was broached.

'Yes, Mr Merrowby was called away, Nanny,' Lady Lydiard had said, but with a laugh. 'Rather suddenly.'

It was the sudden laugh and the impish look in Lady Lydiard's eye as she led Henry off for his tennis lesson that convinced Grace there was more to the artist's sudden disappearance from the house party, and took her down to the servants' hall mid-morning when Harriet was out riding and Boy was being wheeled in the park by Dora.

'Well now 'ere's a sight for sore eyes I must say,' said Cook, who was doing her best to cope with a table full of live blue-black lobsters. 'Just in time to give poor Cook an 'and with this bloomin' lot of nonsense.'

At that moment Dolly hurried in and screamed when she found herself confronted by a couple of lobsters who had fallen off the table and were making their way as fast as they could away from the boiling pots.

'Don't be so daft, girl,' Cook scolded the maid. 'Anyone'd think you'd never seen a bloomin' lobster before. Just grab 'old of 'em and put 'em in the pot before I takes leave of me senses.'

'I don't seem to have chosen the best of times to come and see you,' Grace grinned.

'The best of times, I like that,' Cook grumbled. 'The best of times indeed. What with this 'ouseful of Boetians I haven't sat down for a week.'

Dolly was now trapped in one corner by the two advancing lobsters, which Cook finally grabbed with great difficulty and some pain before consigning them to one of the simmering pots.

'Talking of lobsters,' Cook said, wiping her hands on her apron, 'you look as though you caught the sun, my girl. On that pretty nose of yours.'

'It was while I was sitting for Mr Merrowby's painting,' Grace explained. 'I wasn't allowed to move my head.'

'Oooh that Mr Merrowby.' Cook shook her head wryly and breathed in and out deeply to show her disapproval.

'Has he done something wrong?'

Cook waited till Dolly had gone before she answered Grace's question.

'High old jinks,' she told Grace with relish in a low tone. ' 'Course up there on the third floor I don't suppose you gets to hear much any more about what goes on. But there were some right old high jinks, I can tell you.'

'I know there was a party last night,' Grace said. 'We could even hear the music on the nursery floor.'

'Music?' Cook's eyes nearly popped out of her lobster-red face. 'Cacaphony I calls it.'

'Cacophony.'

'Well. Whatever.' Cook sniffed again, even more disparagingly. It was something at which Cook excelled, passing a comment with a sniff. 'Cacaphony, cacophony, it's off the 'inges. Like somethin' out of the jungle, as you'd expect. Comin' from America. Little wonder they all misbehaves like a barrowload of monkeys.'

'Did Mr Merrowby misbehave?' Grace asked, only to find what she had hoped to be her careful enquiry swiftly greeted with a loud hoot of derision.

'Did Mr Merrowby misbehave?' Cook echoed. 'Mr Merrowby was the leader of the monkeys! He was grinding the organ and dancing to it too!'

It seemed that Mr Merrowby was not only a ring-leader. Mr Brake Merrowby was also rumoured to be Lady Lydiard's latest admirer.

Grace couldn't help herself. She was deeply shocked. Not because Brake Merrowby admired Lady Lydiard, since as Grace well knew from the conversations she had listened to around the table in the servants' hall it would have been more shocking had someone as beautiful as Lady Lydiard not had admirers, and indeed you would fully expect to find a handsome and debonair artist such as Mr Brake Merrowby in their company, and why not? What shocked Grace was the sharp and very immediate

170

pang of jealousy she felt. She had no business with such emotions. None at all.

Pretending she had something in her eye she managed to successfully hide the embarrassment she felt as she found herself blushing at just the mention of his name. It was so silly and schoolgirlish. The colour having eventually subsided she managed to listen to Cook's account of the goings-on with a look of detached interest. At any rate that's what she hoped. As it turned out the detached interest was not to be long held. Small wonder that when Cook had finished Grace found she was left not embarrassed, but deeply shocked.

It seemed the party, with Brake Merrowby and Lord Lydiard taking it in turns to play the piano, had gone on until way past midnight, with those who stayed up late, according to Harcross and John whose task was to keep the guests' thirst quenched, dancing the turkey trot and the bunny hug, of all things, until they practically dropped.

Among those who couldn't stand the pace were Lord Lydiard's brother and sister-in-law, the Honourable Gerald and Cicely Rokeham, who apparently always contrived to get themselves invited to the Keston house parties which they then resolutely refused to enjoy, and of which they were constantly and quite publicly critical.

'Of course I will say they're a couple of stuffed shirts them two,' Cook said, 'but then of course it would have to be them, wouldn't it? That some smarty decided would be the brunt of the joke. And I mean you has to see the funny side I have to say, even though it's somethin' shockin'. But then that's the way they carry on this lot, somethin' shockin', I can tell you. I wouldn't like no child of mine bein' brought up with the likes of these for parents, no thank you kindly. Yours will be no easy task, Nanny, I tell you, no easy task. The haristocracy, as me old mother used to say, is no better than they ought, and a lot less better than they should be, and that's the truth.'

Grace said nothing, preferring not to press Cook for

the full story which somehow she guessed was not going to be either to her liking or her advantage. She'd heard enough stories of what Cook called the *carryings-on-upstairs* to know that whatever had happened the night before was bound to be scandalous at the very least, and from the way the story was shaping the scandal had to involve Mr Merrowby. But Cook was in full flight and not deterred in the slightest by Grace's apparent indifference.

'John saw it all,' she continued. 'Or rather heard the *brouhaha*. Someone rung down for some more champagne, see, and just as John was on his way back downstairs he saw Mr Merrowby coming out of his bedroom and sneaking along the landing in his dressing-gown, but with nothing on his feet, if you please!'

Grace's blood was running colder and colder while her cheeks were once more getting hotter and hotter, but there was nothing she could do now to stop Cook other than get up and walk out, and even then she imagined Cook would follow her, so determined did she seem to be to finish her story.

'So there was John, hiding 'isself behind one of them great big statues they has all along the landing as Mr Merrowby flings open the door of the bedroom next to his where I imagine he imagines lies his lady love. And what do you think happens next? John hears Mr Merrowby laughing and crowing like a regular cock in the yard, before it seems jumping from the door into the middle of the bed. Well, before you could say sixpence the door opens again and back out comes Mr Merrowby and kicked halfway down the corridor by Mr Rokeham! Barely before he's hardly time to get his dressing-gown back on again! Well I asks you, Grace. It's little wonder Mr Rokeham demanded his brother should ask Mr Merrowby to leave first thing this morning.'

'You said it was some sort of joke,' Grace asked rather hopelessly.

'So it was I imagine,' Cook replied. 'The joke being someone switched the name cards on the bedrooms. And put Mr Merrowby next to Mr and Mrs Rokeham. Rather than who he'd been hoping and thinking he was going to be sleeping next to.'

'Yes?' Grace swallowed hard, dreading what was coming. 'And who might that be?'

'Who might that be, you daft girl,' Cook sighed. 'Why Lady Lydiard of course.'

NINE

Grace just wished it didn't hurt so much. There was no reason for it to hurt the way it did. She was nothing of any consequence to Mr Merrowby, nothing more than a model for his painting, she reasoned. When he had talked about her warmth and her radiance he had been talking as a painter, purely and only as such. Not complimenting her as a woman.

She knew that now. And she should have known it then. As a painter herself. People were only part of the panorama of life, their faces and their shapes landscapes of their own to be studied, measured, sketched and then captured in a likeness. In order to be able to paint their subjects, artists had to love them but only in the abstract. Whatever they might say to their sitters, reflecting on their beauty perhaps or their grace, or even their radiance, such remarks had to be purely objective, and prompted by the desire of the artist to see whether he was in fact able to recapture that particular essence of his subject to which he'd been attracted in the first place. Such remarks were not meant as flirtations, otherwise painters would become so infatuated with their sitters that they would be unable ever to put a brush to canvas.

At least that was Grace's considered opinion. She resolutely believed this to be so, and most particularly so in her case, because if she didn't she thought she would not be able to withstand the ache in her heart whenever she thought of Mr Merrowby and how he had looked when he had talked so softly to her about her, when he told her why he knew he had to paint her.

And how he had looked at her when he had promised they would be friends for life.

The very worst aspect was that although Grace knew such a promise would be impossible to keep, and despite the fact that the good sense with which, according to old Nanny, she was so generously imbued told her that the most she could reasonably expect from her relationship with the artist would be a pleasant diversion while she was sitting for him, her heart insisted otherwise. Her head told her Mr Merrowby was a society painter and a man who moved in the best of circles, while she belonged in service and was, as he called her, a nursemaid, employed to look after other people's babies. There was no hope, her head ruled, most particularly and most of all because apparently he was in love with Lady Lydiard. Besides, her head said, she had no right, because she was enthralled, she was servant class. While all the time her heart was saying otherwise. All the time her heart was saying that yes, she had every right, and yes she was enthralled, but in quite the other way. She was enthralled but not enslaved. Grace finally had to admit, after days of self-examination, she was hopelessly enthralled by her mistress's lover.

Brake Merrowby didn't return to Keston for some months. After a week or so, Grace stopped looking out for his smart red motor-car amongst those of the guests, but she never stopped hoping, not even when the Lydiards took off for their yacht in the south of France with a small party of friends. Somehow she knew he'd be back. She knew it not because Lady Lydiard's personal maid Jean had told Grace she had caught sight of the painting in a cupboard Lady Lydiard had left temporarily unlocked in her boudoir when Jean was dressing her one evening, and that the painting was obviously far from finished, nor because

Dora, who loved telling fortunes by cards and tealeaves, kept predicting that Grace would fall in love with and be loved in return by a dark-eyed stranger with the initials BM, but because when she lay in her bed every night before going to sleep something in her heart told her that in spite of everything one day Brake Merrowby would return, and when he did, it would be for her.

'I don't see why,' her sister Lottie said when Grace confided her secret. 'I mean it would be wonderful, of course, but I don't see why. At least why you're so sure.'

'Neither do I,' Grace confessed with what Lottie kept calling her silly smile. 'I just am, that's all.'

'But you're such a practical person, Grace,' Lottie insisted. 'I know how you love to paint, and read poetry, but you never romance about things. At least not like I do.'

'Probably because I've never had good reason to before, Lottie,' Grace replied. 'I've never felt like this about anyone before.'

'You were very sweet on John Batters for a long time.'

'I was only eleven, Lottie. It was hardly the same thing.'

'And you took a terrific shine once to the last parson's son. What was he called? Benedict.'

'Until I sat next to him at the Harvest Supper and heard the noise he made eating.'

Both girls laughed at the memory while Lottie poured them a second cup of tea. Soon they knew they must talk about their mother and their joint future, but for the moment they indulged themselves in reminiscence.

'I wish there was someone I could ask,' Grace said. 'Someone who could tell me what my feelings really are and what they mean.'

'Someone who knows all about love, you mean,' Lottie said, her pretty eyes darkening. 'Someone like Mrs Jenkins.'

While Lottie had never forgiven their teacher for running off with their father and leaving their lives in pieces, Grace had long taken a different view, believing that since they didn't know the reasons behind his flight they had no

176

right to sit in judgement. This had been the only serious
bone of contention between the two sisters, with Lottie,
because she had sworn never to forgive their father, con-
tending that the reason why Grace wished to forgive was
so that nothing might sully the memory and reputation of
their formerly blameless schoolteacher.

'It's fine for you to be so Christian, you can afford to
be,' Lottie always argued. 'You don't have to live here
like a pauper looking after Mother.'

'And you don't have to get up at half past five every
morning and spend the rest of the day on your hands and
knees emptying fireplaces and scrubbing floors,' Grace
had returned. 'It isn't easy for either of us. You never
knew Mrs Quinn.'

'You always say that—'

'Poor woman. Lady Lydiard sent her to their house
in Scotland.'

'Considering what she did that's hardly punishment,'
Lottie snorted lightly.

'No, except it's on a remote island off the west coast.
Somewhere the previous Lord Lydiard bought on a whim.
There's nothing except the house and a fishing boat that
calls once a fortnight, and she's all alone except for an old
caretaker. But with no references and a bad character what
choice had she?'

There was a small silence while Lottie and Grace
considered Mrs Quinn's plight. It was oddly comforting,
and made their own position seem really quite tenable.
Besides which, three and a half years after their father's
fateful disappearance, there was now even a glimmer of
hope regarding their mother's health.

During the long fine summer months she had finally
grown bored with her room and had begun to come downstairs and sit outside in the small but pretty and sunny
little cottage garden. At first she didn't bother dressing
herself, but would sit outside under a sunshade in her
dressing robe over her nightgown. Then as the summer
sun relaxed her, and as the roses bloomed around her,
some sense of her former life must have returned and

she had begun to dress herself, carelessly at first, and then finally with her old fastidiousness, so that now, as her daughters sat inside the cottage talking and taking tea, she sat outside in a pale yellow cotton blouse and skirt the charity had sent and which Lottie had invisibly patched and mended, her hair beautifully done, her Bible open on her lap.

'She still doesn't say very much,' Lottie told Grace. 'And sometimes she looks at me as if she doesn't know me.'

'Like she did with me when I arrived,' Grace replied.

'But then on other days when I have the time to sit and talk to her,' Lottie added, 'she makes perfect sense. We even had a visitor the other day. Miss Tibbs, our piano teacher. She and Mother sat and talked for ages, although after Miss Tibbs was gone and I asked Mother what it was they were talking and laughing about so much, Mother looked blank and said she couldn't remember a thing.'

Although her mother hadn't said a word to her on Grace's arrival, when the time came to say goodbye she took hold of her elder daughter's hand and pressed her to sit beside her for a moment on the garden seat. For a long time she said nothing, but just sat keeping hold of Grace's hand.

'I must go, Mother,' Grace said eventually. 'I have to be back to give the baby his bath.'

'Just remember they aren't your children, Grace,' her mother said, suddenly looking round at her. 'You must have children of your own. Don't make that mistake, I beg of you.'

Then she looked away again, relapsing once more into silence. Grace held her mother's hand for a moment longer, then quietly got up and left.

August passed in a haze of heat. Despite the efforts and skills of the gardeners, the brilliant sunshine blistered the parkland and the drought parched the wonderful flower gardens. There was often thunder in the air as well, threatening storms which never arrived, and irradiating the purply night skies with long silent shimmers of sheet lightning. As the heatwave rolled into September, people's patience grew shorter until tempers frayed and were lost. The kitchens became unbearable, even though the family were away and Cook only had to cater for the staff, small comfort for her since the absence of the Lydiards meant there were only two less mouths to feed out of a total of eighteen. Things got so heated before the weather finally broke that Dora told Grace Dolly had told her that John had overheard Mr Harcross telling Cook that if she didn't stop her scolding he swore he'd lift her up and sit her down on her own stove.

Left behind, the children finally grew bored, bored with the repetition of their days, bored with their games, bored with each other, and finally bored above all by the interminable heat. It was too hot for them to ride except first thing in the morning, but with their parents away the children found it almost impossible to persuade the head groom to get out of his bed and saddle their ponies up before the flies began to swarm and the sun rose too high. The continual bright sun kept the fish at the bottom of the lake, while the trout stream all but dried up completely, leaving Henry no sport at all. Lunchtime picnics were ruined by a plague of wasps and teatime ones by swarms of mosquitoes and midges, until the picnickers gave best and retreated indoors.

Given the run of the house, they soon discovered the coolest place was the hall, which was also admirably suited to the games Grace devised to try to keep her charges amused. It wasn't an easy task since Henry and Harriet were both now too old and sophisticated to play let's pretend games, but still too young to keep themselves amused. So Grace got them playing treasure hunts and organized obstacle races round the hall, but with only two competitors most of Grace's diversions were short-lived. Instead, once it was too hot to play tennis or ride, the three of them would play card games, which mercifully both Henry and Harriet adored. Grace taught them every game she knew, their favourites turning out to be rummy, snap and racing demon, and to make them even more exciting Grace invented her own system of betting, in order not to lead them into bad ways, whereby instead of money the players all bet 'time', the joy and the agony being that winning bets could be claimed whenever the victor wished. Thus just when Harriet was settling down to draw, Henry would claim ten minutes he was owed and make his sister go and tidy his toy cupboard, or Harriet would claim a winning bet by making Henry go and polish her riding boots just as they were undressed and ready for bed, and woe betide Grace if she lost a substantial bet. Her worst loss and the children's greatest *coup* was when Grace had forgotten she owed them a total of twenty minutes, and the children triumphantly claimed them just as Grace was about to go out on her afternoon off, an afternoon of which she spent the first three quarters of an hour changing out of her good clothes and into her old maid's uniform in order to clean and polish her charges' new bicycles.

Perversely enough, the trials and tribulations brought about by losing a substantial 'time bet' never resulted in acrimony between the concerned parties. In fact whenever either Henry or Harriet found themselves caught out, the discovery was only greeted with a groan, and the forfeit was carried out without any further protest, although both the children swore that as a result of Grace's invention they would never be tempted to bet when they grew up.

'At least not like Papa's brother,' Henry informed Grace. 'Uncle Gerald has lost all his money betting on his horses.'

'And Aunt Cicely has never forgiven him,' Harriet added.

In the first week of September the weather broke. A torrent of refreshing rain poured from the skies, starting in the night and continuing for the whole day and most of the next. When the skies cleared, the sun shone again, but it was no longer a summer one but one which carried the first hint of autumn, leaving the sky still clear but a deeper blue, no longer scorching the countryside but drenching it instead in a faint golden haze, with the evening skies brilliantly clear but crisper-aired. Like everyone else, Grace welcomed the change even though it presaged winter, but then September and October had for a long time been her favourite months for their misty blue mornings and their yellowy red evenings. She never felt the melancholy of which so many others began to complain when the leaves turned and began to fall, but then she was still young enough to think ahead to spring, and not dwell morbidly on winter.

Not everyone was happy when September came. Henry suddenly fell silent and sad, and there was nothing Grace could do to cheer him out of his melancholy, although she knew the reason and had been privately dreading it as much as Henry obviously had been. For in only a matter of a week or so, Henry was to leave Keston and begin his first term at Eton. He had told Grace he'd known this since he was a very small boy, when he had been informed by his grandfather that one day like his father and his grandfather himself and like all his forefathers he would go to a place called Eton, which was a school to which all young gentlemen such as he went when it was time. This was a fact, and one which was both so appalling and mercifully so far distant that he had then put it right out of his mind.

Now and then, from what Grace understood and from what she now heard, the odd passing reference had been made to when Henry would start school, and what Henry would do when he went to Eton, but Henry never joined in these conversations, or added to any of the remarks. He remained steadfastly silent on the matter and refused to discuss it or refer to it. Once Grace tried to draw him out on the subject to see how he felt so that she might be able to encourage or enlighten him, but when she asked him what he thought about going away he answered in his oddly mature way that this was not something he ever wished to discuss and he would prefer Nanny never to mention it again. Grace considered this an even more telling reply to her question than a detailed discussion.

She also found a hand-drawn chart on which Henry was marking off his last hours at home. She found it under his pillow one morning when she was putting his nightshirt away, a pillow she also found was wet from what had to be tears. During that day still nothing was said, but in the evening when Grace was doing her last round of the nurseries, she thought she heard the muffled sound of Henry sobbing. At once she knocked on his door and asked him if he was all right and if he wanted anything, and a muffled voice called back that he was fine and that he'd just been blowing his nose. Quarter of an hour later Grace crept back.

'Henry dear,' she said as she let herself into his room and came and sat on his bed. 'Whatever's the matter? Can't you tell me about it?'

There was a long silence while Henry merely stared ahead, obviously so miserable he couldn't speak. Grace longed to pick him up, and hug him, but she knew him too well by now. One step taken towards Henry and he went into retreat. Henry had to be allowed to come to you in his own good time.

It was fortunate that Grace didn't have to wait long, because if she had it would have broken her resolve. Henry suddenly erupted from his bed as if he had touched a live electric wire and threw his arms around Grace's neck with such force that for a moment she could hardly breathe.

'Don't let them!' Henry begged her. 'Please don't let them send me away, Nanny! Please, Nanny, *please*!'

Grace was lost as to what to say and do. She refused to feed him the usual bromides about school, offering him false comfort by telling him he'd enjoy it once he got there, and that although he might not know it now, when he was older he'd appreciate what his parents were doing. She refused to say any of those things, because she didn't believe them. Besides, Grace cared about the truth, and when a child was as deeply unhappy as this she knew that even well intentioned lies were pointless, and that the only comfort that could be given was love.

Instead she gave him a big hug, which normally she

would never do, knowing how reserved he was, and as she held him in her arms she tried to ease the pain out of his body which felt as tight as a drum. And Henry didn't seem to mind at all.

'It's all right, Henry,' she said, 'nothing's going to change. Not here. You have to go away, we know that, but nobody's going to stop loving you just because you're not here. And when you get a bit lonely, what you must do is think of us, and we'll all be thinking of you. As long as we all keep thinking of each other, we'll never break the chain, and it's such a strong chain the one that binds us together invisibly, you and Harriet, and Mama and Papa, and you and me—'

'And Beanie,' Henry reminded her.

'And Beanie,' Grace agreed, smiling, 'that as long as we all are in each other's minds and most of all in each other's hearts, then that chain can never be broken. You just have to reach out in the night and rattle it and it will rattle and shake all the way back here to where we'll all be holding on to it. Out of sight is never out of mind, Henry. Not if people love each other.'

'Harriet doesn't have to go away to school,' Henry said, his tears temporarily stopped.

'Harriet's a girl, Henry,' Grace said. 'Don't ask me why, but girls don't have to go away to school. At least not in families like this.'

'Did you go to school, Nanny?'

'Yes. I went to the school in the village.'

'Why can't I go to the school in the village?'

'I think you know that, Henry.'

'Because Papa's a lord.'

'You wouldn't be very happy at the village school, Henry.'

'Am I going to be happy at Eton, Nanny?'

'I don't know anything about Eton,' Grace replied, tucking the boy back into his bed. 'Except that there'll be other young boys like you there, so you should make friends without too much difficulty. Particularly someone like you who can ride, and fish, and row and shoot so

183

well. You're bound to have a lot in common with the other boys.'

'I wish you could come with me, Nanny,' Henry sighed, as Grace finished tucking him up. 'Then I wouldn't mind at all.'

'I think I'd look a bit silly at Eton, Henry,' Grace smiled, 'following you around like a nursemaid. You'd soon regret having asked me.'

'No I wouldn't,' Henry told her, looking up at Grace with big serious eyes.

But on the fateful day as just the two of them sat together in miserable silence in the back of the Lydiard Rolls-Royce while Parker chauffeured it through High Wycombe and Beaconsfield on the long drive to Windsor, Henry's regret was only too apparent. He sat as far away from Grace as he could, tucked under his travelling rug in the corner of the deep green button-leathered seat, never looking at her once, just staring fixedly out at the passing countryside which from the occasional snuffle and sniff Grace knew he was seeing through a veil of tears.

She had done her best to persuade Henry's parents to travel with him on his first journey to Eton, and on several occasions had been convinced she had won the day, only for one or both of them to slide out of the obligation with yet another new excuse. Unable to ask either Lord or Lady Lydiard directly what their reasons were for not wishing to deliver their son and heir personally to his school, Grace could only guess, and witnessing the misery their continual excuses, last-minute cancellations and ultimate refusal caused, could only conclude that they simply couldn't be bothered.

Seen from Grace's point of view, the Lydiards' lives appeared to be dedicated purely to the pursuit of pleasure, whether the pleasure was to be found as in Lady Lydiard's case in endless house parties, tennis tournaments, horse racing and shooting matches, or in the fine arts as was the case with Lord Lydiard. Nothing else seemed to matter. Certainly they were both kind and apparently affectionate people, and considerate too, when pressed. After Lady Lydiard's now famous progress below stairs a programme of reformation and modernization had been immediately initiated and implemented at Keston, resulting in vastly improved living conditions for each and every member of the staff, so it seemed all the more surprising to Grace that they should consider Henry's departure from the family to be of little enough consequence to merit neither of them accompanying him on what, judging from Henry's expression, must seem to him to be his last journey.

What was even worse in Grace's eyes was their constant prevarication, culminating in their both finally crying off at the eleventh hour. Grace had taken Henry and Harriet down to have lunch with their parents, to find only Lady Lydiard in the dining room, Lord Lydiard apparently having been called away on very urgent business, a reason which surprised Grace, since as far as she knew Lord Lydiard's only business was the running of the estate. Consequently she imagined there really couldn't be anything so urgent that it couldn't be postponed until his son was seen to be safely in school.

'Will he be back in time to come with us this afternoon?' Henry had asked his mother on learning the news.

'Oh I do hope so, my darling boy,' Lady Lydiard had replied, ruffling Henry's carefully brushed hair and sitting him close beside her at the table. 'Otherwise what shall we do?'

'We won't be able to do anything,' Henry said gloomily, smoothing his hair back down. 'But at least you'll be coming, Mama.'

'Absolutely,' his mother had replied, with, Grace noted, a sudden flash of absolute panic in her eyes. 'Let's just keep our fingers crossed, shall we? And all our toes. Harriet darling, do sit up straight like Nanny's taught you.'

'What do you mean, Mama?' Henry had asked, as his sister protested that she was sitting up straight. 'Why should we have to keep our fingers crossed? You *promised*.'

'Of course I did, darling.' Lady Lydiard smiled quickly

and vaguely at her son, and once again leaned over to ruffle his hair.

'So then why should we keep our fingers crossed?' Henry asked, having yet again failed to get out of range. 'Not if you promised.'

'Don't blame me, Henry darling, because it really won't be my fault if I don't make it back in time—'

'Back from where, Mama?'

'Henry darling it's the only day I can see this wretched horse although I made Alice Wynant swear—'

'You're not going to see a *horse* this afternoon, Mama?' Harriet had dropped her knife and fork with a clatter and stared open-mouthed across the table at her mother, who had closed her eyes and sighed as if the whole thing was much too much, before instructing Grace to tell Harriet to remember her manners.

'But you can't, Mama,' Harriet persisted. 'You promised Henry *faithfully*.'

'If by the slightest chance I'm not back and it really isn't my fault, Harriet, it really is absolutely no good looking at me like that – Nanny, I really would rather not have my children staring at me as if I've got two heads or something, thank you.'

Grace had given Harriet the look she had developed to bring the children back in line whenever they went too far, but for once Harriet ignored it and continued to defy her mother by staring at her.

'It's Alice Wynant's fault, for heaven's sake!' Lady Lydiard had protested, her voice rising in panic. 'She promised I could see this wretched animal tomorrow, but now someone else is after it and it has to be today! And the trouble is it's *exactly* what I'm looking for for the new season and Henry?'

But Henry had pushed his chair back and was on his feet, his eyes filled with angry tears.

'You promised, Mama,' he reminded her yet again. 'You crossed your heart!'

'Harriet can go with you!'

'I want you to come.'

'Harriet and Nanny can take you!'

'I don't want to go with either Harriet or Nanny. I want you and Papa.'

Lady Lydiard had thrown her arms open wide either side of her and then slowly and sadly clapped her hands together.

'We will, darling boy, I promise!' she said. 'If we're both back in time and here!'

It was too late. Henry had known it was a lie the way children always do, and as his mother leaned across from her chair to try to embrace him he had turned and run out of the dining room, across the hall and as fast as he could up the stairs.

'How much further, Nanny?'

'I'll ask Parker.'

Grace made no comment on the fact that these were the first words Henry had spoken voluntarily since they had left Keston, but just picked up the speaking tube which interconnected the chauffeur's compartment with the passengers'.

'About quarter of an hour, he thinks,' Grace replied when she had spoken to Parker. 'It's another seven or eight miles.'

'Nanny?'

'Yes, Henry?'

'When we get there, Nanny, I'd rather you didn't come in with me if that's all right.'

'That's perfectly all right, Henry,' Grace replied.

'Parker can carry in my things,' Henry continued, looking back out of the window. 'We can say goodbye in the car.'

Nothing more of consequence was said until Parker drew the car up outside Henry's designated house. The chauffeur waited a discreet moment before he came round to open the boy's door, giving Grace one last chance to make sure Henry was as impeccably turned out at the end of his momentous journey as he had been at the beginning.

'Goodbye, Nanny,' Henry said very formally, as Parker held the door open for his young master. 'I'd better go now.'

The boy made to get out then hesitated when he saw the throng of other boys arriving with or saying goodbye to their parents. After a moment he turned back to Grace, who had been careful and considerate enough to change into her best coat and hat for the occasion, and cleared his throat.

'Perhaps you can come in with me after all,' he said, before sitting back to allow Grace to disembark.

It was obvious which were the new boys. They were all standing holding their mothers' hands as they looked timorously about them at the confident older boys, all casually greeting and joshing their old friends. Everyone was either far too busy or too nervous to pay much attention to anyone else's parents or companions, so after he had taken a good long look at the scene, Henry turned round to Grace and once more slowly cleared his throat.

'Goodbye then,' he said as firmly as he could manage. 'Thank you very much for bringing me.'

Grace could see he was about to hold out his hand which would have quite given the game away, but luckily he hesitated, looking out of the corner of his eye as some of the other new boys paid their farewells. Whether they liked it or not, they were all being kissed fondly goodbye by their mothers.

Henry looked back at Grace, and his eyes widened. But Grace was there before him. Leaning down to him she took both his hands and smiled.

'Goodbye, darling,' she said as loudly as she dared. 'I'll tell Papa and Nanny what a good boy you were.'

She was rewarded with such a brave smile that for a moment Grace was afraid she was the one who would give way.

'Goodbye, Mama,' Henry said back, as brave as a young lion. 'And by the way I forgot to tell you. You look very pretty today.'

He reached up and, putting both arms round Grace's

neck, kissed her sweetly on the cheek. They held on to each other for just a moment, just long enough for Grace to give him one last message.

'Don't forget the magic chain,' she whispered. 'Rattle it whenever you need.'

Then with one more quick kiss he was gone, marching ahead of the laden Parker without ever once looking back.

It was an extraordinary sight, that of Lady Lydiard running out of the great doors and standing where the new housekeeper Mrs Mason was accustomed to stand and greet new arrivals, the moment Parker drove into sight.

'Well?' she demanded, waving interlaced fingers, her face as white as a sheet. 'Well, how did it go, Nanny? You'd better come in. Perhaps you would like some refreshment, because I'm sure you must need it.'

Before Grace could get a word out, Lady Lydiard disappeared into the house ahead of her. As she followed, Grace heard her calling out that Nanny was back and for someone to ring for Harcross, who was in fact hanging back by the door to take Grace's coat.

'You can imagine, Nanny,' he murmured, 'what sort of evening it's been.'

Directed to follow her mistress into the drawing room, Grace went in to find not only Lady Lydiard waiting anxiously, but also a wan Lord Lydiard pacing up and down in front of the fire.

'Well?' he demanded like his wife when he saw Grace. 'Yes, Nanny? Did it all go off all right?'

'No tears?' Lady Lydiard quickly added, nervously plucking at the shoulders of her beautiful maroon evening blouse. 'At least not too many I hope, do please say.'

'Of course there'll have been tears, Serena!' Lord Lydiard sighed, nodding first at Harcross then at the brandy decanter. 'Great heavens, I cried for almost the whole of my first week.'

'Yes, but then you were infernally wet, John,' Lady Lydiard replied. 'Henry's made of sterner stuff. Isn't that right, Nanny?'

189

'There weren't any tears, Lady Lydiard,' Grace replied. 'Not one.'

'The devil there weren't.' Lord Lydiard paused mid-pace to stare first at Grace then back at his wife, then back at Grace, now with a deep frown. 'Not one?'

'Not one, Lord Lydiard,' Grace assured him. 'He was the boy who was bravest of all.'

'Well done, Nanny,' Lord Lydiard said, taking his drink from Harcross. 'Well done.'

'Yes,' Lady Lydiard agreed. 'Well done, Nanny Lydiard.'

'Well done Henry, I think,' Grace said. 'Don't you?'

'Give Nanny a sherry, Harcross,' Lady Lydiard instructed. 'You'd like a sherry, wouldn't you?' she went on quickly without waiting for Grace's reply. 'Only Nanny dearly loved her sherry. And I'll have some more champagne. *What* a day.'

'Not one tear,' Lord Lydiard mused, taking one of his crested slippers off and examining the sole without interest. 'Well I'll be dashed. So you were right, Serena. We could have gone after all.'

'But I thought it wasn't possible,' Grace said after a moment, after looking at both the Lydiards, one of whom was lying back in her armchair with her eyes fast shut, and the other of whom was still staring at the tops of his gold-embroidered evening slipper.

'What did Nanny say, John?' Lady Lydiard asked, without opening her eyes.

'I don't know, Serena,' Lord Lydiard replied, now refitting his shoe. 'Why don't you ask her?'

'If I might ask you something first, Lady Lydiard,' Grace said. 'You said you couldn't take Henry to school because you had to see a horse, wasn't that right? And Lord Lydiard couldn't go because he was called away on urgent business.'

'That what you said, Serena?' Lord Lydiard asked with mild surprise. 'You could have come up with something a bit better than that, surely?'

'So you weren't called away on business, Lord Lydiard?'

'Er – no, Nanny. Not strictly speaking, that is.'

'He was out in the pouring rain with his easel all day. It didn't rain with you, did it? No. It poured here. So dismal. No. And I didn't have to see a horse.' Lady Lydiard opened her eyes now and looked up at Grace. 'Yes I know what you're thinking. You're going to think us perfectly awful and quite right, too.'

Harcross offered Grace her sherry on a silver tray. He had his back to the Lydiards, so as Grace took her drink off the salver the butler breathed in very slowly and deeply while raising both his eyes to the ceiling.

'Thank you, Harcross,' Grace told him, trying to contain her smile.

'Thank *you*, Nanny,' the butler replied.

'I think you'd better tell Nanny or shall I?' Lady Lydiard said somewhat confusingly. 'John?'

'Oh, I think these things are always better coming from a woman, don't you?' Lord Lydiard replied, wandering over to the piano. 'Not one tear,' he repeated, shaking his head. 'I really will be blowed.'

'Sit down, Nanny,' Lady Lydiard instructed, sticking one shoeless foot out to indicate where. 'Sit over there where I can see you although I shall probably see two of you after all this champagne.'

Grace did as she was told and sat down in the armchair opposite.

'Very well,' Lady Lydiard pondered, putting her bare feet up on the chair and pulling her knees up under her chin. 'You know you looked so disapproving all through lunchtime. I mean such disapproval that I nearly explained to you why we couldn't go then except of course I couldn't.'

'Of course you couldn't, Serena,' Lord Lydiard agreed from the piano, where he was now seated, quietly and perfectly playing a Bach fugue which Grace had long ago tried to learn and given up in despair. 'Of course you couldn't.'

'We've been worried about this for months, this day, you know – Henry going to blasted Eton, goodness knows if you'll pardon my language,' Lady Lydiard sighed, resting her pretty chin on her knees. 'But we hadn't a clue, not one, what to do about it, because the poor boy just had to go.'

'Thanks to my father,' Lord Lydiard called over the music.

'That needn't concern you, Nanny,' Lady Lydiard said. 'That's just a family condition sort of thing. It's just that we knew if *we* took him you can imagine. I mean suppose there had been floods of tears—'

'Which perhaps there would have been if you'd taken him,' Grace offered.

'Precisely!' Lady Lydiard snapped her finger and thumb as she spoke. 'Just what I said. Did you hear that, John? I said to my husband, Nanny, absolutely precisely that. Or words to that effect that if *we* took him – did you hear what Nanny said, John?'

'Yes!' Lord Lydiard called back. 'Not a tear, not one! I say that's just very, very brave of Henry!'

'Well you can imagine, can't you, Nanny?' Lady Lydiard asked again for reassurance. 'And if there had been floods of tears well of course there'd have been nothing for it but to bring the darling boy straight home again.'

'Nothing for it at all!' Lord Lydiard called. 'We'd have brought him home at once! Couldn't have stood it for a moment! What a palaver that would have been.'

Grace sipped her sherry and said nothing. She just sat and listened to the beautiful lucid music which was ringing round the room. Moments later when she looked across the fireplace she saw Lady Lydiard fondly smiling at her, her long arms wrapped round the front of her knees, on which she was still resting her chin.

'Well done, Nanny,' she said. 'I really mean it. And thanks.'

'And not one tear,' Lord Lydiard sighed again in the silence that followed the end of the fugue. 'What about that, everyone? What about that?'

In response to a nod Harcross replenished everyone's drink and then retired, leaving the three of them, master, mistress and nanny, all reflecting on the events of the day in the warm glow of the fire and lamplight. After a long silence, Lord Lydiard began to play again, a Chopin nocturne which had always been way beyond Grace's capabilities. After he had finished the piece, and seeing Lady Lydiard had fallen fast asleep in her chair, still in the same position with her knees up under her chin and her arms wrapped around them, Grace got up very quietly and made to go.

As she passed by, she saw Lord Lydiard was sitting quite still at the piano, staring ahead of him. Grace stopped and wished him good night, but he didn't appear to hear her. Lord Lydiard just remained staring into space, while the tears rolled down both of his cheeks.

Almost a year has passed. Nineteen eleven becomes nineteen twelve, with every day carefully recorded in the journal Grace has kept since the time she was put in charge of the nursery floor. At first she keeps account in a series of plain school exercise books Miss Chambers sells her (profitably) at a penny a time until as her gift at Christmas, 1911, Harriet gives Grace a half-bound pocketbook with alternately lined and blank pages. Harriet is the only one who knows that Grace has a talent, but with that strange instinct for extreme sensitivity that children have which appears to become instantly blunted when they reach adolescence, she never refers to it, seeming to know without being told that it is something which Grace had rather she did not mention. Instead she applies herself to the development of her own.

Her mother is charmed by her daughter's efforts, but not unduly impressed, being more concerned with Harriet's equestrian and general sporting skills.

'To be perfectly honest,' Lady Lydiard tells Grace, 'I really don't mind at all, really. It's perfectly all right to be artistic, to have – you know – to have a gift, and know about old things, architecture, and the past and everything. Painting and playing the piano, it's absolutely fine, one hundred per cent so. Just so long as one moderates it with some hunting and fishing. One can't have absolutely no sport at all, and spend all one's time indoors. Heavens no.'

Lord Lydiard on the other hand is of quite the opposite complexion, and follows Harriet's artistic progress with an intense interest. Forever and delightedly described by his wife as 'quite hopelessly artistic', and a man whose favourite pastime is doing petit-point, Lord Lydiard is a more than fair artist himself, and consequently takes great pride in the fact that his pretty and personable daughter is proving herself to be exceptionally gifted.

'Harriet tells me you're her inspiration, Nanny,' Lord Lydiard says to Grace one evening, when just the three of them are alone in the library. 'I know it's difficult to keep a balance, but this is the side of Harriet I'd like to see develop. Much rather this by far than getting a big backside through too much riding. Or losing those pretty looks in a hunting accident.'

Now in her turn this gentle encouragement opens up something in Grace. With that and Harriet's thoughtful gift of the prettily bound book she is suddenly encouraged to start to sharpen her pencils once again, not with any other purpose though than passing the time pleasantly.

So during the long winter afternoons upstairs or outside in early summer evenings, when Henry is away at school (and hating it by all accounts) and Boy is sleeping out or being walked by Dora, the two of them (Grace and Harriet) spend long and happy hours drawing and painting and writing. At first Harriet simply and diligently copies drawings Grace has done for her, but within six months she has begun attempting her own subjects, at first a little warily and still looking constantly to Grace for help and advice, but then, thanks to Grace's sympathetic tutelage, she grows steadily in ability, so much so that now by their second summer together Harriet is working independently.

While she works, Grace sits and writes in her journal, filling the lined pages with detailed descriptions of her life at Keston, and the blank pages with little pencil sketches of the inhabitants of the Great House and its visitors, but most of all with loving studies of her charges, of Henry, Harriet, and Boy, and their ever attendant dogs Beanie and Chipper, an eternally cheerful and apparently tireless stray mongrel Henry found wandering half starved around the park in the spring of that year.

There it all is, the story so far, carefully, lovingly, but accurately recorded in Grace's journal. Little account is given of life outside the estate gates, however, even though the times were becoming ever more troubled, as if whenever the waves on the beaches around their island grew louder they played and sang a little louder not to hear them.

Of course Grace reads the newspapers. Of course she knows there is a war in Europe, and a real danger of its spreading, and that there's even talk of a German invasion. She also knows that there is both social and industrial unrest in the country, with bitter and often violent confrontations breaking out between the bosses and their workers, culminating in lockouts and strikes. The long insufferably hot summer of 1911 seemingly brought matters to a boil, so much so that by 1912 the dockers, miners, and transport workers have all downed tools in protest. Anarchy seems to be rife, or at least the very real fear of it. Two foreigners rob a bank clerk in Tottenham, hijack a tram at gunpoint and shoot a policeman and a boy, wounding fourteen innocent people before they themselves are killed, while in a house in the east end of London three alien criminals are besieged by seven hundred and fifty policemen and a detachment of the Scots Guards armed with a machine gun under the supervision of the new Home Secretary, Winston S. Churchill, a response which is later found to be out of all proportion to the danger, but in keeping with the current state of public near-hysteria.

Grace records none of this, and to read her journals you would think that life within the estate walls at Keston continued unaltered and unaffected by the fight for women's suffrage, the ongoing constitutional and Irish problems, and the increasing industrial unrest.

Nothing of course is further from the truth, because both the Lydiards and their small army of servants are fully aware of the prevailing situation, with many long and heated debates being held both upstairs and downstairs on all the main issues of the day. Grace is fascinated by these discussions whenever she's privy to them, because contrary to expectations all the proposed changes and reforms are generally supported by the upstairs factions and opposed by the downstairs ones. Lord Lydiard in particular is known to be genuinely sympathetic to the workers' current demands for reform, having graduated from a flirtation with Fabianism, and then Guild Socialism (to the private horror of his wife), before finally falling under the thoughtful influence of Hilaire Belloc and his belief in the Distributive State, while Cook, whose work is probably the hardest and most unremitting of all those downstairs, is outraged by the very idea of women's suffrage and subscribes to the notorious Lady Bathurst's published opinion that convicted suffragettes should first be well and truly birched and have their heads shaved, before being deported to the Antipodes.

But while Grace remains perpetually intrigued by the arguments and discussions which seem to rage whenever two or more people are gathered somewhere in the Great House, she is determined to make the record she is keeping of her life a purely personal one.

She knows well enough that the social and political history of the country will be better chronicled elsewhere, while the life she is leading, the life she has been forced into by circumstances beginning with her father's adultery and flight, will go completely unnoticed and unremarked unless she records it herself. Not that she is unhappy with her lot, or considers her life to be extraordinary, far from it. Rather she is intrigued with the position in which she has found herself, and fascinated by the growing sense of involvement she is experiencing with a family to which she bears no familial relationship. So since fate has denied her the right to record her journey through life in a series of paintings, she has decided instead quite simply to paint a picture of her life in words.

References to outside events are therefore only made when they have a direct connection with herself, her family or Keston. H. G. Wells and Hilaire Belloc get mentioned not because they are frequent visitors to the house, which indeed they are, but because Wells refuses to play croquet unless he's partnered by Henry, and Hilaire Belloc always makes the nursery floor his first port of call in the mornings when staying.

Scott's expedition to the South Pole is recorded because he stayed at Keston, briefly, before setting sail for the Antarctic in the Terra Nova, a signed photograph of which he brought with him for Henry. The sinking of the Titanic is written up because Lord Lydiard's aunt only escaped the tragedy by leaving the ship at Cherbourg after the liner suffered a near collision leaving Southampton harbour, an event that the grand old lady considered sufficiently ominous to prompt her fortuitous disembarkation; and the suffragette movement is referred to only because of Cook's aversion to it, and because Lord Lydiard is host to Lady Constance Lytton and Mrs Pethick-Lawrence with whose views he is deeply sympathetic. Happily the kitchens are so deeply buried neither lady is party to Cook's vociferous objections to their cause.

Otherwise the journal concerns itself entirely with the lives of Henry, Harriet, and Boy. Grace writes little about herself

197

and her feelings, unless she or they are directly involved with her charges. Until the summer of 1912, it is simply an intelligent, honest and good-humoured account of life in a great house as seen from the nursery floor. There is no mention of anything or anybody not directly connected with the family, the household or the writer of the journal. For instance there is no mention of Brake Merrowby, nor of Grace's feelings for and about him.

Not, that is, until 17 August 1912, Grace's day off, a baking hot day, which she, as she set off on foot down the long drive, was intending to spend visiting her mother and sister, but which turned out altogether differently, from the moment she heard the motor-car behind her slewing to a sudden halt in the gravel.

T E N

The car which had stopped drove past her once Grace
had stepped aside on to the verge, and the driver gave
a token wave of gratitude. Grace recognized both the car
and the driver at once, although it took Brake Merrowby
another fifty yards or so before he pulled up.

'Nanny?'

He had reversed the dark red car and was now peering
at her across the passenger seat.

'You must think me very rude, but I was in kind of
a hurry,' Merrowby said, reaching over and opening the
door. 'May I give you a ride?'

His manner was perfectly polite and his smile was
friendly, but there was a look in his eyes which didn't
match his cordiality, and a certain nervousness under-
lying his apparent affability. Grace got the impression
that he couldn't wait to leave the house and grounds.

'Thank you,' Grace said, without moving to the car,
'but I'm sure I'm not going your way.'

'My way is your way, Nanny,' Brake Merrowby
answered, opening the car door wider. 'I don't have
a notion as to where I'm headed.'

The chance of being driven to her mother's cottage
instead of walking in such heat was almost impossible
to resist, yet Grace found herself demurring. At first she

had no idea why she should be refusing the offer of a lift, which she did for a second time before beginning to walk off again down the drive. It wasn't until Brake Merrowby called to her and she heard him running after her to catch her up that she realized what her reason was for refusing. She was angry.

As she kept walking, knowing that within seconds he would catch up with her, Grace knew she had no real reason to be angry and yet she found herself seething with inexplicable indignation, and wondering to her great surprise *how he dared*. How he dared quite what she wasn't yet sure, but that was what the voice in her head was saying. How *dare* he?

'Nanny!'

He had overtaken her and was facing her, walking backwards down the drive in front of her. She noticed that he was perspiring, and that his hair was dishevelled and his shirt and necktie were askew, with the tie pulled down from the collar.

'Nanny – please!' he was entreating her. 'I'd be really grateful for the company. I mean it. I'll take you wherever it is you're going.'

Grace stopped and turned to him, without knowing what to say. She knew what it was now, what it was he dared. How dare he just suddenly show up after a whole year without a word and simply stop and offer her a lift as if it was one day later and not three hundred and sixty-odd. As if nothing had happened. She was speechless, finding it incredible that he should behave in such a way, and yet as she stood staring blankly at him she knew at the same time that her feelings were totally irrational and that his behaviour was perfectly natural. So she simply stood her ground, hoping that he would say something, and that her complexion wasn't as red as his, although under the brim of her straw hat she could feel her brow dampening, and under her chemise her skin beading in the heat.

'It really is far too hot to walk anywhere,' Brake Merrowby said, reaching for his handkerchief and mopping his gleaming red face. 'Or maybe you don't remember me?'

He suddenly looked at her, under the handkerchief now held to his brow, and Grace realized that he had mistaken her blank look for one of non-recognition.

'I'm so sorry,' he said. 'Of course you probably haven't the faintest idea who I am. It must be nearly a year. We met last summer. I was painting a portrait of you. Brake Merrowby?' He repocketed his handkerchief and offered her his hand.

'Of course,' Grace replied, smiling over-politely. 'Forgive me for not recognizing you at once, Mr Merrowby. But then so many people visit us here at Keston.'

Grace was happy with the misunderstanding. It saved her from having to explain the reason for her apparent indifference which she felt she would not have been able to do without disclosing some part of her feelings. A pretence of having forgotten who he was seemed much better, and served perfectly well as a valid excuse for her unwillingness to accept a lift.

She was also pleased when she saw the effect it had on the artist. She imagined he must have expected to have been recognized, and then when he wasn't, and when the mention of his name merely identified him as one of the many visitors to Keston, she could see he was quite visibly disappointed. She could see it in his eyes; you did not have to be a painter to see the change in them.

'Perhaps now that you've placed me,' he said with evident control, 'you will accept my offer of a lift.'

'Thank you, Mr Merrowby,' Grace replied, 'it certainly would be a relief in this heat.'

She smiled and turned to walk back to the car which stood in the drive with its engine still running and both doors open, as if abandoned. Merrowby followed and stood by Grace's side as she settled herself on to the dark red leather seat.

'Good,' he said as he got in his own side and selected first gear. 'The last thing we want is anyone dying of sunstroke.'

'Is that why you stopped?' Grace asked. 'Because you were worried about my health?'

'No,' Brake Merrowby answered, turning out of the main gates. 'That wasn't why I stopped.'

He didn't ask her which way he should head nor did it occur to Grace to think to tell him, not until they had passed the crossroads half a mile from the end of the estate.

'You should have turned left there,' Grace said, looking back over her shoulder. 'I'm sorry.'

'No matter,' Brake Merrowby replied, accelerating away rather than making any attempt to stop and turn. 'We've got some time. So why don't we go for a spin?'

'I'd rather you drove me to my mother's, if you didn't mind, that is.'

'How long a walk to your mother's? From the house?'

'It's over two miles. It usually takes me about half an hour.'

'In that case we have time!' Brake Merrowby accelerated even harder, and changed up another gear, raising his voice against the noise of the engine and the rushing of the wind. 'Your mother won't be expecting you yet! And if we stay in the neighbourhood I can drop you there any time you say!'

Grace knew the vicinity well, particularly the areas around the village and the now well trodden paths from Keston Hall to her mother's rented cottage. But in a speeding car she was soon out of her territory and completely disorientated. Brake Merrowby was driving with such determination, however, that Grace assumed he knew exactly where he was going, even though she had only given him the very vaguest of indications as to her original destination. What was more worrying was the speed at which her companion was driving. Grace had never been in a motor-car anywhere near as fast as this.

'Is it quite safe to go this quickly?' she shouted over the noise, leaning forward and holding on to the edge of the dash. 'What speed are we doing anyway?'

'Oh, we can go a lot faster than this!' Brake Merrowby

shouted back. 'Some guy's got plans to do one hundred miles an hour in one of these motors at your Brooklands track! We're not even doing forty yet!'

The road ahead straightened out from a long right-hand bend into an unbroken line that seemed to climb gently and finally disappear into the bottom of the sky. There was nothing but farmland on either side and no other motor-cars or vehicles of any description.

'Sit back!' Merrowby yelled. 'Just sit right back in your seat! And hold on!'

As Merrowby engaged another gear and accelerated hard, Grace was thrown back in her seat by the velocity and all but lost her hat, which she then clasped with one hand on top of it while holding on to the bottom edge of her seat with the other. Neither did she have any option but to sit back, such was the force of the car's momentum. The fastest she had been before had been in a Humber belonging to a big customer of Father's on a trip to Oxford just before Father ran off, when he had terrified the life out of her parents by driving at twenty miles an hour. Yet now here she was being rushed through the countryside at twice that speed.

'Forty!' Merrowby shouted as the motor-car careered along the arrow-straight ribbon of road. 'Forty-two! Forty-four! Forty-five! Forty-eight! *Fifty!*'

Certain that they were both going to die, Grace closed her eyes as tightly as she could and lowered herself down in her seat until her head was below the bottom of the windscreen. She had tried her very best to brave it out, staring fixedly at the road ahead, until unable any longer to accept the rate at which the road was disappearing under the long bonnet of the car she had tried looking at the countryside passing by at the side of her. But that had proved to be even more upsetting, with what had been only moments ago recognizable trees and hedges now just a passing emerald haze. The sky above them streaked by in a rush of azure while the sun seemed to dance in the air, its brilliance flaring in dazzling glints off the paint and chromework and splitting into bright little splinters of iridescent light as it bounced off the polished glass of the windscreen. There was no escape from this roaring rush through space, no respite from the tearing, heart-stopping speed, no lull from the screaming noise and bone-shaking buffeting, so Grace just closed her eyes as tightly as she could and prayed to God to forgive her for her many trespasses so that in a moment when she died as she most surely would she would go straight to heaven.

By the time Merrowby breasted the hill and began to brake Grace was practically to the floor of the car. She eased herself up as she felt the car slowing until she was back in her seat as Merrowby turned the car on to some common land and pulled it up on the brow of a rise which overlooked the countryside beyond.

'That's better,' he said, pulling on the handbrake and turning off the ignition. 'That's just what I needed.'

He seemed to be unaware of the effect of the drive on Grace as he opened his door and giving another long sigh got out.

'And boy,' he added, 'have we chosen some place to stop.'

Grace straightened her hat and sat up to take advantage of the view.

'Do you know where we are, Mr Merrowby?' she called, rearranging her long cream skirt and looking for her other lace glove.

'I don't have the slightest idea!' he called back. 'Does it matter? Look at this view!'

'I have to be at my mother's,' Grace reminded him as she walked across to where he stood with his back to her, his hands sunk deep in his pockets. 'Do you have any idea where we are?'

'Nope. So what time exactly do you have to be with your mother?'

Grace hesitated. Her mother wasn't expecting her to call, but that was not something to which she would admit.

'I really should be there before lunch,' she replied.

'Then we've plenty of time,' Brake Merrowby told her, having consulted his watch. 'Good heavens, it's only a quarter after eleven. Tell you what – let's climb to that hill over there!'

He pointed to a small hill on the other side of the valley and then jumped off the mound on which he'd been standing and started to make his way down the slope away from the parked car.

'But you don't even know where we are!' Grace called as she followed after him.

'It doesn't matter where we are!' Merrowby called back. 'It's only taken us twenty minutes to get here, and your mother is only two miles from Keston! So it can only take us half an hour to get you back there at most!'

Then he was gone, jumping and running down the steep slope until he must have put a hundred yards between him and Grace. Grace picked her way carefully after him, gathering her skirts up with one hand and steadying herself with the other as she made her way carefully down the grassy slope. By the time she had reached the river Merrowby had crossed it. He didn't stop, he just continued his ascent, stopping only to take off his jacket and sling it round one shoulder.

When she reached the river Grace found it was much wider and deeper than it had looked from afar, and there seemed to be not one but several places where it was possible to cross. She looked up the hill beyond, hoping her companion might still be in sight so that she could call to him to find out which route he had chosen, but there was no sign of him. Then she noticed a row of much flatter stepping stones further downstream, and making her way to them she saw they seemed to present much the safest route, because even though they formed the edge of a good four-foot drop into a large and deep-looking pool below, they were flat and closely spaced. Gathering her skirts up above her ankles, Grace started to make her way carefully across the stream, until two stones from the farther bank she slipped on some lichen, lost her balance and promptly fell in.

It happened in a second, the slip on the stone, the helpless tumble sideways, the hopeless grab at the overhanging branch and then the plunge into the water coursing between the stones and over the edge down into the pool below, which was a great deal deeper than it looked so that Grace first had to tread water to stay afloat and then swim in order to reach the bank, where she hauled herself out of the water with the help of a large tree root.

The next thing she knew Merrowby was by her side.

'Are you all right?' he asked.

'No, I'm rather wet, actually,' Grace replied. 'As you can probably gather. Water and I seem to be magnets to each other!'

'Oh,' Merrowby sighed, 'I suppose I must say that was my fault for rushing ahead in that way?'

'I suppose you must,' Grace agreed. 'And it would have been nice to have been shown the way across.'

Brake Merrowby suddenly started to laugh, and then just as suddenly stopped, perhaps prompted by Grace's icy stare.

'I'm sorry,' he said. 'It's just people falling in water. It's always got to me. It's so hopelessly undignified.'

He began to laugh again, but this time more helplessly, so helplessly in fact that he had to sit on the grass to recover himself.

'Oh gosh I'm so sorry!' he howled, rolling on to his side and closing his eyes. 'I guess they should alter that old saying to – in the midst of life we are in comedy! I mean it's just too much to bear!'

Grace felt like kicking him. There he was rolling around on the grass at her feet, helpless with laughter while she stood bedraggled, muddy and dripping with water, her good clothes ruined and her hair in tangles.

'I saw the whole thing!' Merrowby confessed, sitting up and wiping the tears of laughter from his eyes. 'I'd just come back up the hill to see where you'd got to, and there you were! Teetering on the edge and then *splash!*'

'I could have drowned,' Grace said. 'Supposing I'd hit

my head on a stone when I fell. And you hadn't come back up the hill?'

'You know, I never thought of that.' The notion seemed to sober the painter up instantly, and he clambered to his feet at once. 'Forgive me,' he said. 'My behaviour was inexcusable. In my defence I have to say I did run back here as fast as I could, when I saw you fall. But when I saw you were perfectly all right—'

'You couldn't help laughing.'

'No.'

They looked at each other, eye to eye, until Merrowby could stand it no more and began to laugh all over again, mouth tightly closed and with a deep frown as if he wasn't, or certainly as if he was trying his very best not to, until the tears began to run down his face.

'God I'm so *sorry*!' he said, but still laughing. 'You must think me a perfect wretch!'

And then he laughed some more, still with his mouth shut and his eyes half closed, until his whole body shook.

'It's your face!' he whispered helplessly. 'You look as though you're going to stand me in the corner!'

With that he slowly doubled over and wheezing with laughter began to bray like a donkey. It was too much for Grace who unable to hold out any longer started to laugh herself quite helplessly, which made Brake Merrowby bray and wheeze even more, which in turn made Grace almost hysterical, until they both sunk to the ground, Grace ending up on her hands and knees and Merrowby finishing flat on his back with both his arms stuck straight up in the air.

When they could laugh no more, they lay collapsed in silence, both now on their backs.

'I'm so glad you didn't drown,' Merrowby said after a considerable silence.

'So am I,' Grace agreed.

'It would have been quite awful if you'd drowned.'

'It's too nice a day to drown,' Grace said.

'Much too nice,' Merrowby agreed. 'Although it didn't start out that way.'

'Yes it did,' Grace insisted. 'It was beautiful from the word go.'

'For you maybe,' Merrowby replied. 'But not for me. Things were so bad I was seriously thinking of ending it all.'

Grace turned her head and looked at her companion and found him staring back at her with a brooding look in his dark brown eyes. She turned away, and looked once again up at the sky, deciding it wiser to ignore the last remark.

'Do you think if I just lie here I'll get dry?' she asked.

'Good gracious no!' Merrowby was on his feet at once. 'What can I have been thinking? You'll get your death of cold!'

'There's nothing else I can do,' Grace said calmly, trying to find a cloud in the sky. 'It's a very hot day, so I'm sure I won't come to any harm.'

'On the contrary,' Merrowby disagreed. 'The last thing you should do is let clothes dry on you. You of all people should know that, Nanny. Stay there, I have some dry things in the car.'

He was gone before Grace could stop him, jumping sure-footedly across the stream and running all the way up the hill back to the car. Less than five minutes later he was back with an armful of clothes which he placed by Grace.

'There,' he said. 'You can go and change in those bushes. I also brought the car rug. You can use it to dry yourself off.'

Naturally all the clothes were men's: a blue shirt without a collar, a pair of plus-fours with braces, a check waistcoat, a pair of red socks, and a set of long-sleeved and long-legged cotton underwear.

'Très chic,' her companion remarked when Grace re-emerged from the bushes. 'You could well start a fashion.'

'I look like Harry Tate,' Grace said. 'All I need are a moustache and a flat cap. So what do we do now?'

'You want me to drive you to your mother's like that?'

'I don't think so, Mr Merrowby.'

'Very well then, Nanny. So what would you recommend?'

'For a start that you stop calling me Nanny. I'm not
your nanny, and I do have a name of my own.'

'Of course you do. Might I enquire what it is?'

'Grace Merrill.'

'Very well, Miss Merrill. So what do you recommend
we do?'

'I've hung my clothes out on the bushes. They shouldn't
take that long to dry.'

'And in the meantime? What about your mother?'

'My mother isn't expecting me, Mr Merrowby. I was
just going to call on her.'

'So you don't have to go and see her?'

'No. Not necessarily.'

'In that case why don't I take you out to lunch
somewhere?'

Grace laughed, to hide the sudden surge of excitement
she felt.

'Like this?' she asked, indicating her costume.

'If you agree to let me take you to lunch,' Merrowby
said carefully, 'I may take you shopping first.'

'What for?'

'A new dress, a new hat. Even if we wait for your
clothes to dry out they'll be hopelessly creased. Someone
as pretty as you does not deserve to be taken out in a set
of creased clothes.'

'I couldn't possibly let you buy me a dress,' Grace said,
averting her eyes from his penetrating look. 'It wouldn't
be proper.'

'Why not?' Merrowby laughed. 'What's so shocking
about a gentleman wanting to buy a lady a dress?'

'What I meant was that it wouldn't be proper for you
to spend your money on me,' Grace replied. 'We hardly
know each other, and anyway—'

'Yes?' Merrowby prompted as Grace fell to silence.

'Thank you,' Grace said after a moment. 'It was a
very kind offer, but I think we had better wait for the
clothes I have to dry.'

'Oh, what nonsense!' Merrowby was on his feet and pulling Grace to hers. 'I know what you're thinking, and it's a nonsense. We're two people, and that's what matters. That's all that matters. And if I want to take you to lunch and buy you a new dress, then I shall and blow the proprieties! Anyway.' He paused once he'd got Grace to her feet, changing from mock bellicose to a startling intensity, as he kept hold of her hands and looked her straight in the eye. 'Anyway,' he added, 'I think I have every right since if it wasn't for you I might very well be floating dead on the top of that pool.'

'Oh, fiddlesticks,' Grace told him.

He drove them into Aylesbury, although at a much more sedate speed, where he charmed the first well dressed woman he saw into telling him where the best dress shop was to be found.

'I can't possibly go in there looking like this!' Grace protested as the car drew up outside a bow-windowed salon in the High Street.

'Of course you can!' Merrowby replied. 'The whole point of dress shops is for people who don't have anything to wear to be able to go to them and buy something.'

To Grace's further mortification Brake Merrowby threw open the door of the shop and announced to no one in particular that he was sending in someone who had just been involved in a bathing accident and needed outfitting from head to foot.

'Pay no attention to the cost!' he announced. 'For I have the money!'

Half an hour later Grace emerged from the fitting room in quite the most delightful outfit she had to admit to ever wearing, a day dress made of a creamy yellow silk decorated with tiny dark blue flowers with the newly fashionable narrow skirt. Over the dress was a short sleeve silk jacket in dark blue with a thin matching cream stripe, cut to the waist in the front and a rounded tail behind, and on her feet she wore the very latest in footwear, a pair of shoes with two-inch heels held in place by a single leather strap across the top of each foot. From the ends of the short sleeves of the jacket the slightly longer sleeves of the dress were allowed to show, and for a hat they had chosen Grace a velvet turban trimmed with one large upright feather in the front.

'Charming,' Brake Merrowby said the moment he saw her. 'Quite charming. All it needs now is the parasol to match – *et voilà*.'

He took the parasol which was being offered to him by one of the assistants and handed it to Grace, before sitting back for a final appraisal.

'Absolutely perfect,' he declared. 'Sweet elegance personified.'

Grace had never worn such fine clothes. When she and Lottie were growing up the most they could look forward to was one of Mother's outmoded gowns cut down. As for the past two and a half years, they had been spent in uniform, beginning with the rough and demeaning garb of a kitchen maid and then the less shaming but still cheap and unattractive habit of the nursery maid before graduating to the starchy strictness of her nanny's attire. Little wonder she felt so different. Gone were the cheap underpinnings, and in their place she wore pale pink underlinen of *ninon de soie*, smooth against her skin, except where her new lace-trimmed *cache-corset* held her figure in place and in an altogether softer shape. Also gone because of the new narrow skirt line were the heavy petticoats, in fact gone altogether was the need or indeed the room for a petticoat at all with her new dress of expensive silk which brushed the silk of her stockings with every small step she took. For the first time in her life Grace suddenly felt as if she was no longer a girl, but a young woman, and to judge from the looks she was receiving not only from Brake Merrowby but from all the gentlemen passersby as she and her escort strolled to the White Hart hotel for luncheon an attractive woman at that.

'You know I shall have to take all this off before I return to Keston,' Grace told Brake as they approached the hotel. 'I couldn't possibly arrive back at the house looking like this.'

'Why ever not?' Brake stood aside to allow Grace to enter first through the large half-glassed and brass-railed door which was being held open for them by a liveried doorman. 'You have a life of your own. You have the right to do what you please and wear what you like when you're not working.'

'Even so,' Grace said, once again mindful of the stares she was getting from most of the gentlemen in the hotel foyer, 'I think it would take a little bit too much explaining. So if you don't mind—'

'As a matter of fact I mind very much,' Brake replied, his attitude suddenly changing as he tossed his boater to a bell-boy. 'But even so, I suppose I must accept that Nanny knows best.'

Grace felt it diplomatic to let the matter rest until they had found a table. There was suddenly such a wide gulf between herself and Brake. He so obviously knew nothing about being in service, or about the politics of the nursery floor versus the servants' hall, or the attitudes of employers to their staff. Why should he? Unlike her he was a free spirit.

'It wasn't my intention to hurt your feelings. Forgive me if I have,' she said quietly once they were seated. 'I'm more than grateful to you for this beautiful dress and hat.'

'I don't want your gratitude. Believe me, seeing you as you are is quite enough,' Brake told her brusquely.

He ordered champagne and then sat back, looking not at Grace but past her out of the window.

'Something has upset you, Mr Merrowby,' Grace persisted.

'Brake,' her companion reminded her. 'I'm an American. We don't need to be married for fifty years to first-name each other.'

Grace sighed inwardly, but couldn't help persisting, 'Something has upset you.'

'Nothing has upset me, as you put it,' he replied, still

looking past her. 'At least nothing that need worry that very pretty head of yours.'

He said little over lunch. Neither did he eat much. Instead he drank a great deal of champagne while at first Grace tried to make conversation, and having failed to do so ate her way through the lunch which was carefully placed before her. Grace couldn't help feeling disconcerted by her escort's sudden change of mood, but none the less was determined that the sudden darkening of his spirits shouldn't spoil her enjoyment of the excellent fillets of sole and the roast Aylesbury ducklings she had chosen from the menu. Besides the unbecoming monotony of having to wear a uniform on the nursery floor Grace had also to endure the very plainest of fare.

'Aren't you going to eat anything at all?' she finally asked as a freshly made cherry tart sat untouched in front of him.

'No,' Brake replied, 'and nothing you can say will make me, Nanny. All I really want is a cigarette. So if you'll excuse me.'

Calling the waiter over and giving him far too much money to settle the bill, Brake rose to his feet and weaved a slightly unsteady way out. After a moment, and trying to cover the embarrassment she felt at his rather obviously unsteady gait, Grace pushed her chair back before the waiter could help her, and followed her escort out.

She caught up with him just as he was ordering a brandy.

'What exactly do you think you're doing, Mr Merrowby?' she demanded.

'Having a cigarette,' he replied, taking a case from his pocket, 'and having a brandy.'

'You seem to have lost what manners you might have had,' Grace told him, trying to control her anger, 'leaving me alone like that in the dining room. I could just about put up with your silence over lunch, but getting up and leaving me at the table—'

'Sorry, Nanny.' Brake glanced at her as he lit his cigarette, then threw away the match before it was properly out. Grace stood on it before it burnt a hole in the carpet.

'What on earth's the matter with you anyway?' she asked. 'You were as happy as a sandboy before lunch.'

'Nothing's the matter with me. Nanny.'

Grace looked at him helplessly.

'Couldn't you please stop calling me Nanny,' she asked him sotto voce.

'If you will please stop treating me like a child.' Brake shrugged foolishly and drunkenly.

'I'll stop treating you like a child when you stop behaving like one.' Grace took him by one elbow and led him to a quiet corner of the hotel lounge, away from the stares of the residents and other guests. 'Are you drunk?' she asked him.

'Basically,' Brake replied after giving the matter due consideration, 'I would say the answer to that is yes.'

'You should have had some lunch,' Grace scolded him quietly, sitting him down and then seating herself in a chair opposite. 'You should have eaten something, instead of drinking on an empty stomach.'

'Yes. Nanny. Miss Merrill.'

He looked at her without humour, and Grace exactly matched his look.

'If you're drunk, then how am I supposed to get home?' she asked.

'How do you imagine?' he asked. 'I shall drive you.'

'No,' Grace said with sudden firmness, intercepting the waiter who was about to set down the brandy Brake had ordered. 'Mr Merrowby will not be requiring that now.'

'For God's sake—'

'You'd be better advised to drink some strong black coffee,' Grace said. 'I'll order you some.'

But before she could instruct the waiter, Brake was up and gone, crashing his way through the lounge and out of the front door, knocking an elderly gentleman back down into the armchair from which he'd started to raise himself and sending a pageboy laden with luggage flying across the hall. Grace hurried after him, but since her new tight skirt would only allow her to take paces of no more than four or five inches, by the time she was outside the hotel Brake had altogether disappeared from view.

ELEVEN

It was now well past three o'clock, but the heat of the day had barely abated. Grace had no money, so without a lift from her escort she was stranded. With a sigh, and wondering what on earth else this strange day could possibly bring her, she made her way back to where Brake had parked his motor-car in the hope that once he got to it he might at least remember his responsibilities and wait for her. But when she reached the dress shop where the Talbot was parked, there was the car but no sign of its driver.

All she could do was wait, and hope that by the time Brake returned he would have sobered up enough to drive them both. She climbed into the car and sat on the bakingly hot leather seat, raising her new parasol to protect herself from the heat.

By half past four there was still no sign of the errant Merrowby and the back of Grace's new dress was soaked with her perspiration. So were the backs of her silk-clad legs and her hair underneath her beautiful turban. Exhausted by the heat and the tedium she thought she was not unlike a beautiful plant which had been allowed to dehydrate in the hothouse. But there was nothing she could do except wait, so she eased her sticky self further in her seat, pulled the parasol down over her head and closed her eyes.

A few minutes later a French voice woke her from her doze.

'M'moiselle?' it asked. 'Please, why do you not come and sit in the cool of my shop?'

The woman who had fitted her out so beautifully with her new outfit opened the car door and helped the now bedraggled and wilted Grace on to the pavement.

'You cannot sit no longer in that dreadful sunshine,' the woman clucked. 'And oh *mon dieu*! Your beautiful dress!'

Remembering her original clothes were somewhere in the car, Grace told the proprietor, who offered to get one of her girls to iron the blouse and skirt so that Grace could wear them instead of her now saturated dress. They found them in the boot of the car, carefully laid out on top of a painted canvas which was half covered by a sheet. Grace saw the hood of Boy's baby carriage and knew at once what the picture was. It was the unfinished painting for which she had sat.

While the proprietor of the dress shop hurried inside with Grace's old blouse and skirt, Grace turned the sheet back so that she could look at the whole canvas. She had had no sight of the painting while Brake Merrowby was working on it, so she had no idea at all of the composition. All she had known was that it was to be a painting of her sitting on the grass in front of Boy's perambulator.

As it turned out it was rather more than that, as Grace realized as soon as the painting was revealed. Even though it was nowhere near finished it was obvious that Brake had captured the moment exactly. Grace could just feel herself sitting in the shade of the tree on the lawn. She could feel the lazy hum of the baking hot day, and Beanie's head asleep on her knee, she could hear the drone of the bees, the distant clack of the lawnmowers and the voices drifting up from the terrace below where she had been sitting. As for herself she was still only a sketch, her face a splash of pink, her upswept hair a band of black below the upturned back brim of her favourite straw hat, her uniform with its crisp white collar and cuffs half finished in pale blue, with seams and gashes of ultramarine for the folds and creases, while the undetailed hands which were carefully mending a baby garment were very much her hands, just as the figure in the shadow of the large dark blue perambulator was unquestionably herself. The painting was already a small masterpiece. Even in its raw state it was what every painting should be. It was an extension in the art of seeing.

But what astounded Grace more than the brilliance of the composition was the emotion behind it. It was apparent even though the canvas was only half completed, and what surprised her even more was that it wasn't at all how she had imagined the artist would paint. From what she knew of him Brake Merrowby was capricious, unpredictable and temperamental, yet his style of painting was in direct contradiction to his personality. The colours were soft, the line was delicate and the overall tone gentle and loving and sympathetic. It was at such variance with the personality of the man who had practically driven her off the face of the earth that morning, laughed helplessly at her tumble, and totally ignored her while drinking himself all but insensible over lunch that Grace could make no sense of it at all.

'It's not what you see,' a voice suddenly said behind her, 'but how you see it.'

When she wheeled round at first all Grace could see was a wall of flowers. After a moment the flowers were lowered slightly to reveal Brake.

'These are for you,' he said before Grace had time to speak, and handed her the massive bunch of freshly cut summer blooms, smiling shyly. 'With my apologies,' he added. 'You must think me a perfect rogue.'

'I did and I still do,' Grace replied, trying her best not to look at the beautiful bouquet but instead to fix the artist with her best cross look. 'You try sitting in this heat in a motor-car waiting for someone you're not at all sure is going to reappear.'

'What I'd really like is some tea,' Brake replied, ignoring the reproof and looking around him. 'I have a simply dreadful thirst.'

'Please yourself,' Grace told him. 'I have to go and change out of this dress. Which is quite ruined.'

Taking a gamble that Brake wouldn't disappear and leave her once more stranded, Grace went inside the dress shop. After a moment she heard the bell on the door ring behind her as Brake followed her in. Having glanced in a mirror to make sure it was him, Grace then ignored him totally, looking round the shop at the dresses and hats on display while waiting for the proprietor to appear with her newly ironed garments. For his part Brake just sat on a chair by the counter watching Grace. He said nothing as he saw her emerging from the fitting room in her old clothes, and the newly purchased outfit being handed to her in a box. It was almost as if he expected as much. For her part Grace merely carried on as if it was really quite normal being bought one set of clothes, changing into them, and then changing back into something else, and all in the space of a few hours.

'I would still very much like some tea,' he announced about half an hour after leaving Aylesbury. 'I still have this dreadful thirst. From drinking all that champagne, I guess.'

'No one asked you to drink it all,' Grace replied.

'No,' Brake agreed. 'You're right, no one did. Sorry, Nanny.'

'Couldn't you please stop calling me that?'

'I can't help it. You keep talking to me as if I'm *so* high.' Brake took his left hand off the wheel to gesture, without bothering to look at her. 'As if I'm one of your kids.'

'You just passed some tea rooms on your right,' Grace told him. 'If you really are that thirsty.'

They sat outside in a very pretty rose garden bounded by a hedge of box. It was late afternoon, and a slight breeze had got up to ease the heat. This time Grace made no attempt at conversation, but just sat eating her fresh strawberry tart and sipping her tea.

'I imagine you're waiting for me to explain,' Brake said finally, licking the tip of one of his square-ended index fingers to pick the very last crumbs up off his plate.

Grace itched to tap his hand in disapproval, but she restrained herself.

'What do you imagine I'm waiting for you to explain?' she asked instead.

'My perfectly dreadful behaviour.'

Brake tipped his boater to the back of his head and stared at Grace, his eyes half closed, waiting for confirmation. Unwilling to be drawn, Grace carefully finished her cup of tea and smiled back at him as insincerely as she could.

'You don't want to hear why I've been behaving so badly?' he asked her, opening his eyes wider now, and unable to keep the light of astonishment out of them.

'From what I understand,' Grace replied, 'you're not exactly a stranger to bad behaviour.'

The light of astonishment grew brighter.

'I would certainly be interested to hear what you know about me,' he said evenly, never taking his eyes off Grace for a moment.

Grace poured herself a second cup of tea and looked back at him.

'Servants talk,' she said. 'You must know that.'

'And what do they say? About me?'

'I can't remember precisely. As I said to you before, so many people come to stay at Keston.'

'I imagine it was about me and Lady Lydiard.'

This time Grace's urge was to correct his grammar, but she resisted it and simply repeated her polite smile.

'I imagine it could have been.'

'Well that's all past history now,' Brake said, raising his voice slightly. 'So you'll all have to find someone else to gossip about, won't you?'

Grace felt herself colouring at being numbered as one of the servants, but kept her temper in check, picking up her fresh cup of tea and sipping it slowly, careful to avoid catching her companion's eye in case he saw the anger in hers. Even so, she still saw Brake close his eyes as he sighed and leaned back in his chair.

'Lord. I'm sorry. I really am not normally this darned rude, I promise you. I guess it's just because—' After a moment he opened his eyes and looked at her. 'May I tell you about it?' he asked.

'If you think it would help.'

She had meant to say *no. No I don't want to hear about it. Particularly if what you're going to tell me is what I think.* Instead of which she found herself all too politely agreeing, unable to escape her role as confidante and confessor, or perhaps, she thought wryly, too fearful to do so.

Once Brake began to talk it must always be hard to stop him. Certainly his eloquence on the subject of how he had fallen in love with Lady Lydiard was most affecting. He described how they had met at a party in London, and how she had dazzled him with her beauty and her athletic grace, and how he had sat enthralled at Wimbledon the year before when she had contested the ladies' singles title only to lose narrowly in the semi-final, and how he had been invited to stay that fateful weekend at Keston, before joining the Lydiards in France, first to see Lady Lydiard play in the championships at St Cloud, and then to stay on their yacht while they sailed the north Mediterranean, swimming in crystal clear seas and dancing in clubs and cafés along the newly fashionable French riviera.

'So there you have it.'

Brake paused at last, and Grace both wished that he hadn't, and was glad that he had.

'That only takes us to last summer,' Grace said, eventually, as Brake swung on his chair and gazed past and through her, experiencing once more, she imagined, all the emotions that he had described so effectively. 'There has to be more. Particularly since earlier you kept making references to the events of today. And how bad you felt.'

'Let me pay for the tea,' Brake said, getting up suddenly. 'I'll tell you the rest in the car.'

He drove back towards Keston slowly, keeping silence for the first five or ten minutes, gazing ahead at the road, still, it seemed to her, enthralled by the emotions he had described. Grace too found nothing to say, but contented herself with looking out to one side of her at the beautiful Buckinghamshire countryside flowing gently by.

'The problem was,' Brake began again eventually, before correcting himself. 'The *ridiculous* thing and the cause of all the trouble – as it always is – was that I fell in love. Why do I have to fall in love?'

'Perhaps because you're incurably romantic.'

'Well, yes, perhaps, but even so, why? Can you tell me? No one else does, darn it. They all have what they call flirtations, or intrigues or liaisons, and then they all walk away from them unscathed! Can you believe it? Because I can't. But that's what they tell me. That's what Serena – that's what Lady Lydiard told me. I pressed my suit too hard, apparently. I was a little too ardent. I became *a little too serious*. Very un-English. But then I'm an American. I'm not a cool-as-a-what are they called? A cool-as-a-cucumber Englishman. I'm an American, I'm a painter, and I'm a hothead. And I fall in love. And I fell in love with your Lady Lydiard hook, line and sinker. I even asked her to leave her husband and marry me, for heaven's sake—'

'When was this?' Grace interrupted, trying to keep her voice as dispassionate as possible.

'In the south of France last year,' Brake replied. 'I went a little crazy, I suppose. But dammit, love makes you crazy, doesn't it!'

'I don't know.'

'I'm sorry. You must think my language terrible.'

'It is certainly no worse than your manners.'

'There you go again! Is it little wonder that I keep calling you Nanny? I can't help being what I am!'

'And neither can I,' Grace replied. 'I'm sorry if you find me authoritarian.'

'You looked so beautiful in that dress.'

'What's that supposed to mean?'

'You didn't look authoritarian then.'

Brake turned his head to her but he didn't smile.

'Where was I?' he asked.

'You were going a little crazy in the south of France,' Grace replied.

'I shouldn't be telling you this.' Brake slowed down to turn a sharp corner by a signpost for Keston. 'I can't help wondering why I'm telling someone like you all this?'

'Because you want to, I suppose,' Grace replied, ignoring his allusion to her lowly status, and suddenly, and to her astonishment, finding her heart growing heavy at the thought that their day together might be drawing to an end.

'Of course I want to,' Brake agreed. 'For some strange reason I want to tell you everything. Why is that?'

'I don't know. Maybe I remind you of your nursemaid,' Grace teased him.

Brake laughed as he accelerated down the long steep road which led to Keston village.

'Do you know what I mean by *the wrong side of the tracks*? Do you have that saying in England?' he asked, and when Grace told him that they didn't but that she understood what it meant, Brake told her of his poor upbringing in Newark, Ohio, and how he ran away from home when he was fourteen and ended up learning to paint signs in Pittsburg.

'He was a wonderful person, the man I worked for, and I was a terrible painter. At least I was a terrible sign painter, because I always wanted to do it my way. To add things, make the signs more interesting. Anyway, old Will Mencken, the guy I worked for, he thought I had what he called a peculiar ability with paint. So he kept me on provided I promised to study with a friend of his, a woman who really could paint. She did all the covers for the *Post*, which was the town's weekly magazine, and she did them anonymously because she was the daughter of a famous Pittsburg family and it wouldn't have done for it to be known that she was *an artist*.'

Brake said it to make it sound as if she was unclean, and Grace laughed, not because she thought it funny but because she understood perfectly.

'She got me doing covers finally,' Brake continued, 'and then I got some commissions for some portraits, and a benefactor took me to New York, where I did some more portraits and got to study with Ed Dickinson – you know Ed Dickinson? Well of course you wouldn't, but he is a very important painter back home. And one heck of a teacher. I mean the man is a genius.'

'So what happened then?' Grace asked. 'How did you get to England?'

Brake smiled.

'Another benefactor,' he replied. 'She – well. She brought me over and effected some introductions, and I guess they like what I do here. End of story.'

'It was as easy as that,' Grace said.

'Sure it was,' Brake agreed, looking round at her again, but this time cautiously.

'I see.'

'What do you see?' Brake was still looking at her, even though the car was gathering speed downhill.

'Don't you think you should watch the road?' Grace asked.

In reply, Brake pulled the car up to a halt.

'What do you see?' he demanded again. 'Because it wasn't like that, if that's what you're thinking. Sure, I had lady benefactors, a whole handful of them. But I didn't have to – I didn't have to sing for my supper, if that's what you're thinking, Nanny dear.'

'Stop calling me Nanny!' Grace suddenly turned on him, her voice raised, her hands clenched into fists in her lap. 'You're just doing it to provoke me!'

'I can't help it!' Brake protested back. 'You just have this way! This way of implying criticism with your voice! And your – your eyes! You make me feel like a naughty little boy. With your *I sees*, and your scolds. I can't help it! I keep feeling I'm being bad!'

He began to laugh again, just as he had when he'd stood looking at her that morning in her soaking wet clothes, with his lips tightly closed and laughing down his nose. Grace tried to stay angry, but when he laughed

224

like that he looked so appealing she found it impossible.

'Perhaps you'd better just drive me home,' she said without much conviction. 'We seem to be doing nothing but arguing.'

'Poppycock!' Brake laughed out loud, swinging round in his seat to face her. 'And besides, even if we are,' he added, 'I'd far rather argue than be bored. Now. Do you have to be back at any particular time?'

Once she confessed that she didn't, Brake insisted on taking Grace to dinner, to make up for what he called a pretty up and down sort of a day. On her recommendation they dined at the old coaching inn on the Oxford road six miles north of Keston, where although the fare was much plainer than at lunchtime it was a far more enjoyable meal, due entirely to Brake's complete change of mood. He was the absolute opposite of how he had been at midday, talkative, good-humoured, inquisitive, and attentive, instead of silent, drunk and inconsiderate. Even so, Grace kept up her guard, uncertain yet as to how far she could trust a man as impulsive and unpredictable as the handsome dark-eyed artist sitting opposite her, particularly when it came to answering the questions which she knew must finally come, about how and why she had become what she had, where and when she had.

She kept the story simple, because she didn't wish to solicit sympathy. Even in her short spell in service below stairs Grace had soon learned that the personal histories most of her fellow servants had to tell were far worse than her own. At least she had once known the comforts of a proper home and the security of family life, however precarious that security had finally turned out to be. Her initial miseries at Keston were nothing compared to the bewildering exile of the orphanage, or the squalor and distress of the workhouse. Most of all she was still alive and able to enjoy her life, unlike poor Aggie who had been so terrorized she had chosen to end her short and wretched existence hanged by her stockings from a beam in her cell-like bedroom.

All she told Brake was that her family had fallen

on difficult times, which had been aggravated by her mother's consequent illness and meant that Grace had to find employment locally as soon as she had left school. She made no mention of her father's indiscretions nor of her painting and the offer of a scholarship to the London Academy of Art. Brake listened to her account in silence, never taking his eyes off her face, which caused Grace to drop her own more than once.

'There's more to it than that,' he said in conclusion. 'I don't believe that's all.'

'Why not?'

'You've left out something. The something that makes sense of you. Of the person you are,' Brake replied, still watching her carefully. 'I just get the feeling there was something else, something that you'd like to have done, would still like to do. I don't know what. Go into vaudeville, perhaps?'

'It's called variety over here,' Grace corrected him, in an attempt to steer him away from this line of country. 'Either variety or the halls.'

'You just strike me as having a certain determination hidden away in there,' Brake continued, ignoring her amendment. 'And it has nothing whatsoever to do with looking after other people's babies.'

'I love my work,' Grace protested. 'I don't see it as looking after other people's babies. I see it as being part of a family.'

'That's really not my point.' Brake sighed, and leaned his chair back dangerously far.

'You just be careful that chair doesn't tip over with you,' Grace warned him.

For once Brake resisted making his usual retort, but the smile in his eyes still said it. *Yes, Nanny.* Grace saw it but this time she also saw the funny side, and smiled.

'My point, Grace,' Brake continued, 'is that you're *different*. I knew that the moment I saw you, and I guess that was why I wanted to paint you. I don't know what it is. But it's there. Yes, sure, you're very lovely. You have beauty, quite beautiful looks, but then if you don't mind

226

me saying, I see an awful lot of beautiful women, and I've seen an awful lot who were an awful lot more beautiful even than you. So you can say it's not my first visit to the circus if you like. What you have isn't just your beauty. I keep getting this feeling – it's as if you're really someone else, not "Grace Merrill, Nanny" but someone else altogether, but you don't want it to be seen. That's why you climbed out of those clothes I bought you so quickly: too much of that other person was showing.'

He had put both his long square-fingered hands on the table and was rocking himself backwards and forwards on the back legs of his chair while he watched her and waited. Grace carefully finished the last of her fruit salad and wiped the edges of her mouth with her table napkin.

'That was very good,' she said, putting her napkin down on the table. 'Didn't you think so?'

'Very well,' Brake said. 'If you don't want to tell me.'

He left another silence, which Grace refused to fill.

'Maybe one day,' he said, his fingers now slowly drumming on the tablecloth, his chair tipped back as far as it would safely go.

'Maybe,' Grace replied.

'Ah!' He was forward now, and leaning across the table to her. 'So there is something!'

Grace was trapped by his eyes, by the almost wild light in them. She wanted so much to tell him the truth, so that they could talk about painting and share their feelings, to show him some of her work so that he could criticize it, and perhaps help her, teach her some of the lessons she should have had at the Academy. They had this in common, they both painted, they stood on the same ground although at different levels perhaps. But she didn't tell him because she couldn't, because she was afraid. She was afraid that rather than being delighted he would be furious, which she thought was much the most likely prospect if today had been a typical day in the life of Brake Merrowby, furious with her for wasting the opportunity the scholarship had held out to her, and for meekly complying with her family's wishes. And yet, because she was honest, she knew it was not just his sarcasm that she feared, it was her own embarrassment. To look into those fierce eyes of his and have to admit that she had turned away from adventure and challenge – she would not just feel embarrassment, she would feel shame.

Brake wouldn't even try to understand how real her dilemma had been, and there was little reason why he should. When circumstances had prevailed against him, Brake Merrowby had run away from home and at a much earlier age. She could hear him saying it to her – *sure, sure I was a boy and not a girl but so what? There's no real difference between us, not if we both say we're artists!* And she knew it just wasn't true, that there was all the difference in the world between being the youngest boy of a large and poor itinerant family on whom nothing depended, and being the elder girl of a small and auspiciously respectable middle-class one on whom their very survival rested. Worse, she also knew Brake Merrowby would pour nothing but his scorn on her for using her gender as an excuse for her faintheartedness. Even before they had talked so extensively over dinner it had been more than obvious how much Brake cared for his art, and she knew that even if he professed to understand her reasoning, he would still finally have nothing but contempt for someone who had sacrificed her art to look after, as he put it, other people's babies.

So she admitted to nothing. Even though Grace was incapable of telling a bare-faced lie, she was perfectly capable of deferring the truth which she did by remaining silent.

Brake remained silent too, but only for a while, only while he kept looking at her with a smile on his face, while he once more rocked backwards and forwards on his chair.

'Someone as beautiful as you are,' he said, breaking the sentence up into two. 'Shouldn't be a nursemaid.'

'I don't see myself as beautiful,' Grace replied. 'But I can see myself as a nanny.'

'But you are beautiful. I've already told you that.'

'Yes you have. And thank you.'

'That's perfectly all right.'

'What you haven't told me, or rather finished telling me, is about you and Lady Lydiard.'

It was Grace's turn to do the looking, which she did, holding his eyes with hers, until Brake slowly rocked himself to a stop.

'You're right,' he said, banging the table lightly once with both hands. 'You know, I haven't. Where had I got to?'

'I think you'd just proposed to her in the south of France?' Grace offered. 'Then there was something about doing away with yourself.'

'Are you making fun of me, Grace?'

'No more than you have been making fun of me.'

Brake eyed her and then grinned broadly.

'Suddenly it all seems faintly ridiculous,' he confessed. 'Particularly after today.'

'I like the way you say *particularly*,' Grace said, straight-faced. '*Partickerly*.'

'Not quite,' Brake replied. 'But not bad. Not bad.'

'So what was so *partickeler* about today?' she enquired. 'You got any theories?'

'Not *partickerly*.'

'Fine. Then I'll tell you mine,' he replied. 'What was so *particular*—' (he pursed his mouth on the word and over-pronounced it in an absurd English accent. Happily Grace managed not to laugh. So he tried again) 'What was so *particular* about today is sitting right opposite me. If I hadn't met you this morning, Grace, I really don't know what I would have done,' he said, dropping his voice suddenly and seriously, 'or where I would be right now.'

There was such passion in his voice, and he was looking at her with such a sudden fierce intensity that had seemed to come from nowhere, Grace felt oddly breathless. She tried to swallow, but her mouth and throat were too dry, so she reached for her glass of water as slowly as she could and took a long, careful sip.

'First,' she said as soon as she was able, although she had to clear her throat after the first word. 'First you must finish telling me about you and Lady Lydiard.'

'And second?'

Grace just wished he would stop looking at her so fervently, before wondering why such a look was not making her laugh, which it normally would have done.

'Secondly,' she said, swallowing again, 'we may then talk about other things.'

'Done!' Brake banged the table with his fist, startling not only Grace but all their fellow diners. 'I made a total ass of myself with Serena. I didn't know the rules, you see, as I think I might have mentioned before?'

'What rules?' Grace asked back.

'The Rules of the Game,' Brake said, getting up and moving his chair round so that he sat beside Grace, facing out on to a rose garden which was just beginning to disappear into the twilight of a summer's night. 'I didn't know I wasn't meant to *fall in love*. Not that I really fell in love. I was really just infatuated. Intoxicated. Captivated. Bewitched. Knocked off my feet.' He stared out into the darkening garden and then began to smile. 'I'd lost control of my senses. And while I was out of control I asked Serena to leave her husband and marry me. I wasn't serious. At least I don't think I was serious. But I think Serena thought I was. John most certainly did and ordered me off the yacht. In fact he said as long as I was in love with his wife I wasn't to see her or visit either of them. He did it very sweetly. As charmingly and thoughtfully as John does everything, but he meant it just the same. Just the same as if he'd had a gun in his hand. Serena agreed with him, too. She put one of those long arms through his – we were all up on deck at the time – she draped her arm through John's and with that really fetching frown of hers she said that really she thought this was *much the best thing too, don't you?* So at that I jumped overboard, and swam ashore.'

'In all your clothes?'

'Just like Byron when he swam the Grand Canal in

Venice. Except I didn't have a torch in my left hand to give me light, as he did. Oh, I wish I had! I wish I'd grabbed a candle off the table! That really would have been the final touch!'

Still he gazed out in front of him, his smile turning to a slight frown now as he relived the memory.

'So obviously,' Grace said after a moment, 'with you being back here today, at Keston, then I take it you thought you were no longer – that you could come and visit Lord and Lady Lydiard again?'

'Why don't you come out with it, Grace?' Brake laughed, turning back to her, his face very close to hers. 'It's not a dirty word, you know. Love. What you mean is my being here means I'm no longer in love with Serena? No of course I'm not. Or rather I wasn't until I saw her again. Come on.' He got up and held the back of Grace's chair. 'Come on, let's go and stroll in the garden, and smell all those wonderful roses.'

He offered Grace his arm, and she took it, lightly, her hand resting in the crook of his elbow. The night was warm and soft, and the air was musky, sweet with the perfumed tincture of the roses.

'So when you saw her again,' Grace began, feeling her heart sinking as she spoke, dreading his reply. 'When you saw her again—'

'I saw her. And thought – I thought I'm still in love with this woman.'

'Even though you were really just infatuated,' Grace said out of the ensuing silence. 'Intoxicated. Captivated. Bewitched. And knocked off your feet.'

'Quite right, Grace.' Brake turned to her and put his hand over hers, over the one she had resting in the crook of his arm, making Grace catch her breath. 'You're quite right to make fun because I was being totally absurd. Serena thought so too, because she laughed as well. She had a really good laugh and told me not to be so absurd. Not to be such a *puppy*. To run along, and to do some growing up. Then John came in and when he saw me he groaned. He *groaned*, as if the *puppy* had done something

231

it shouldn't have done, which of course it had, and then he told me that my behaviour really *wasn't on*. I just loved that. *Not on.* So once I'd been roundly scolded and put back firmly in my place, we all had a drink, Serena gave me back my painting, which is what I'd come for originally, they both saw me to my motor, Serena kissed me goodbye, chastely, on the cheek, and they both stood on the steps waving to me until I was out of sight, as my grandparents used to do when my dad drove the buggy off after a visit. Is it any wonder I felt suicidal? Wouldn't anyone have done?'

'You weren't really suicidal,' Grace said. 'You were just feeling sorry for yourself.'

'There you go again!' Brake detached himself from her and walked away, hands now sunk in his trouser pockets.

'Yes, there I go again,' Grace said, following him but making no attempt to take his arm again. 'And what you don't like about it is I'm right. If I sound as if I'm scolding you like a child it's simply because you're behaving like one. No. Worse than that. You're behaving like a spoilt child.'

'Spoilt?' Brake looked at her, astounded. 'Me? *Spoilt?*'

'Yes, spoilt. I don't really know how you were expecting to be treated. You run after someone else's wife and ask her to marry you, you misbehave and get asked to leave their house, you get thrown off their yacht, and then as bold as brass you turn up a year later and start all over again! And then claim to be suicidal when both Lord and Lady Lydiard, not just Lord Lydiard but Lady Lydiard as well, when they both ask you to go in the nicest *possible* manner! When what should have happened and would have happened with anyone else, with people less kind and charitable than the Lydiards, is you should have been punched on the nose! Or at the very least chased away with a horsewhip! No wonder you felt suicidal indeed. Quite honestly, I've never heard of such spoilt behaviour.'

'Haven't you, Nanny?'

'No, Mr Merrowby, quite frankly I haven't.'

They were standing facing each other now, Brake Merrowby standing over Grace, Grace standing up to him. She had a look of fierce defiance, he wore one not of irritation or dismay but of patent astonishment.

The evening was turning slowly to night, a half blue half-light with the crescent of a new moon just becoming visible.

Yet it seemed the stars were already out and that they were shining in the soft dark embroidered cloths of his eyes.

Then it was night, and dark, dark blue with stars that danced behind her closed eyelids as Brake gathered Grace up into his arms and kissed her.

Much, much later Grace was to recall this moment in her journal. There was no note of it at the time, in fact there was (initially) only the most cursory reference to the return of Brake Merrowby into her life. That particularly fateful day merited a very brief entry which recorded only the fact that Brake Merrowby (B) had stopped and offered her a lift, and that they had in fact ended up spending the day together. It makes no mention of the incident at the river, the purchase of the new dress, the disastrous luncheon, their reconciliation and least of all the dramatic conclusion to the day.

Surprising really, since it was, after all, Grace's first kiss. And while today few people remember with great distinction their very first kiss, because it is usually followed very closely by even more kisses, and very often by something else, something more physical, in those days kisses and particularly first kisses were so special they were constantly celebrated.

Between lovers there is nothing so intimate as a kiss. Certainly there is nothing so incredibly innermost as a very first kiss, Robert Browning's Moth's Kiss, the kiss taken almost uncertainly —

> *As if you made believe*
> *You were not sure, this eve,*
> *How my face, your flower, had pursed*
> *Its petals up . . .*

and certainly few kisses were ever so innermost, nor so uncertain, as when Brake Merrowby first kissed Grace.

You are surprised to learn this perhaps, because this was Edwardian England, a time and a place where morals purportedly had relaxed so much since the end of Victoria's reign that married women were rumoured to wear specially designed tea gowns (with no underclothes) which permitted their lovers easy and immediate access without the bore (and the possibly disastrous repercussions) of undressing, husbands followed the example of their monarch and openly took mistresses, while at weekend house parties famous society Lotharios took unresisted advantage of unaccompanied wives with the connivance of their complaisant hostesses. So why should a young woman of twenty-two (an age when most eligible young women would be married) be so traumatized by a kiss that she quite literally almost fell into a dead faint? The likely reason is that while in the upper echelons there was most certainly a much greater degree of sexual escamotage, society as a whole remained very moral. Divorce was generally quite out of the question, virginity was an attribute to be admired and not derided (or pitied), and public displays of affection, apart from linking arms, were for the poor, the illiterate and the ignorant. So little wonder then perhaps that Grace was so completely overwhelmed by her first kiss. The greater wonder is that she was able to resist the temptation to make a record of her reaction.

Other, that is, than a beautiful and delicate half-page watercolour of a rose garden at summer's twilight, under which in her lovely sloping copperplate is written not the second verse (which is the verse you would expect) but the first verse of Shelley's Love's Philosophy.

> The fountains mingle with the river,
> And the rivers with the ocean;
> The winds of heaven mix for ever
> With a sweet emotion;
> Nothing in the world is single;
> And things, by a law divine,
> In one another's being mingle.
> Why not I with thine?

Perhaps Grace was afraid lest someone found and read her journal and blew the whistle on her. After all staff were not permitted to marry. At least if they did, they were then expected to cease being staff. Most certainly nannies were not meant to marry, least of all good nannies, and Nanny Lydiard (aka Grace Merrill) had turned out to be the very best of nannies, in fact in a very short space of time she had become totally irreplaceable, so much so that the very best of friendships between Serena Lydiard and Lelia, Countess of Clwydd, had come to an abrupt end because rumour had it that Lelia Clwydd was determined to poach Nanny Lydiard.

Maybe it was Harriet whom Grace feared, even though she trusted the child. She most possibly thought, not from vanity but from common sense, that were Harriet to read that Grace had been kissed and had fallen in love, she would run and tell her mother not from spite but from fear of losing not only her nanny but her beloved art teacher. Who knows? Certainly Grace was discreet and rightly so. Yes, she kept a journal which is in some ways asking for trouble, but she never wrote in it anything of a personal nature (which is probably why it makes such touching reading after all these years. The impression you get from reading it is of a totally selfless and giving person, which would not have been the case had every entry been taken up with her own problems and emotions) so that even if it had been discovered while she was at Keston, the only guilty secret it would have revealed was that she was a remarkably gifted artist.

So we have to wait until Grace was an old woman to learn what she felt that day, and even then the reference only comes from being prompted. Grace was never one to volunteer anything about her life and self.

She was 76 years of age when a young man with long hair and sideburns, dressed in a large-collared yellow ochre satin shirt, a purple jacket and light blue trousers (which were so wide at the bottoms they reminded Grace of Oxford Bags), arrived to interview her for the BBC. He was directing one of a series of programmes called The Way I See It, *which as he explained were first-person films in which an outside contributor was invited to choose a theme and make a film on it. His contributor's chosen subject was* Nannies? Or Nuns?

He had invited his contributor/writer along as well, who arrived after half an hour wearing a cheesecloth shirt, faded blue jeans, sandals and a small bell around his neck. (Both the director and the contributor were later drawn by Grace from memory and preserved for posterity on the page opposite that day's entry in her journal.) He spoke in the same style as his director, their dialogue peppered with plenty of yeahs, OKs, *and* right-ons, *although it was immediately obvious to Grace that he came from a totally different background, a fact she would have known just by looking at him and observing his*

236

behaviour, without ever needing to know his well born name, viz. Nick Melford.

The Melfords had been frequent visitors at Keston, although they were never counted among the family's closest friends, and Nicolas (as Grace insisted on calling him once he had insisted that she first-name him) was Sir Anthony Melford's grandson. His special subject was things upper class, and he announced his intention to write a book about it in the very near future, the projected television film being obviously to test the water. The director and he stayed most of the day, exhausting Grace in the process, although she never once complained, nor wilted for a moment. Even more remarkably, once they had gone she still found the energy to record the events of the day in her journal at once, while the memory was still fresh.

They were for the most part (she wrote) only really interested in what nowadays is referred to as 'sex' but which we liked to think of as love, or at its worst – passion. I couldn't really understand what the one called Ben was trying to say (I never really caught his second name), or what he was trying to ascertain, since he talked very fast and used a great deal of slang, whereas the Melford grandson was as transparent as cellophane. He had quite obviously suffered at the hands of his nanny (I quite clearly remember Nanny Melford in my day being a particularly stern creature) and was determined to revenge himself by ridiculing nannies as a race of people. Hence the derisory subtitle as to whether we were nannies or nuns.

What he most wanted to know from me, and I must therefore suppose from every other nanny to whom he was going to talk, was why I chose to look after other people's children rather than have any of my own, in other words why I had not married. Why I was a nun. Was I frightened of 'sex'? Did I know about it? (as if we all lived on Mars). What did I tell the children when they asked about it, about 'sex'? He was quite obsessive about it, as so many people are nowadays, as if they're the very first generation to know about it. Everything seems to be entirely based on and explained away by 'sex', so much so that all proportion has *been lost in the process. I've always liked to think and I've always taught my children that the only two things that can move mountains are faith and love. Not 'sex'. 'Sex' seems to be so out of context with the truth.*

Finally, of course, this is what he wanted to know. This is what he wanted to ask me but couldn't quite dare. Whether or not I had ever had 'sex', as they say. He was about to put it that way to me I feel sure, from the way the conversation was going (and if anyone knows how a conversation is going to go it's a nanny, believe me), so I just looked at him, as much as to say just you dare, just as I used to do when any of the children took it into their heads to have a go at going too far, and I was delighted to see that young Melford turned very red. Had I ever been in love? he asked instead, thinking I would find it less impertinent.

I was still affronted of course, and I only hope I didn't show it. I would have appeared quite hopelessly old-fashioned, which of course I am. But I just cannot get used to how personal everyone is nowadays. Everyone asks the most particular things now in the newspapers and on the television, and no one seems to mind. But I'm afraid I minded this particular question, and wondered not only what gave them the right to ask it but more especially what made them ever imagine for one moment that I should answer it truthfully, if at all.

The other one joined in here (Ben Whatever). When I declined to tell them what they wanted to know, on the grounds that a person's private life is precisely that, he made a long speech about how impossibly feudal a system it had been, and that no one had the right to own another human being and prevent them marrying or having love affairs. I told them I had never known a case of any nanny being prevented from marrying, nor proscribed from having what they called 'love affairs'. The point was plenty of nannies left to get married, and no one (or very few of us) had 'affairs' because it simply wasn't done. There were such things as morals and they were there to be observed. This second point delighted 'Ben' and he said that was just the sort of thing they wanted and that I must repeat exactly that when I was 'on camera'.

They're coming back tomorrow to talk more, but I don't think I shall do the programme. I know what they're up to, although they don't think I do, but even so I'm quite sure that in this instance they will have the last word, and I'm not at all sure (from what I see on the television) that it will be an altogether fair one. But it's been a very interesting encounter, particularly 'sex' v 'love'. I can't for one moment imagine trying to describe to 'Ben' and young Melford, as well as millions of unseen people, my feelings on love, particularly my first love (B). Can I imagine trying to put into words what I felt when he kissed me that evening in the rose garden? Of course not. I've never told anyone, in fact I've hardly even admitted it to myself. How when I felt his arms round me and we kissed I heard in my head the first fluttering of what Longfellow wondrously called love's silken wings. How when I first tasted that strange sweetness of a kiss I felt so delirious I thought we were suddenly standing somewhere high in the sky. I can remember the sound of my gasp, and how the silence seemed to roar in my ears. I can even call up the smell of the roses.

Of course some will say this is an exaggeration. That if first love is such an elusive emotion for poets then who am I to remember it with such precision? They will say that first love has nearly always been superseded by the time we have acquired the skill (if we're poets or writers) to recount it. That our memory of our first love is coloured by our later romantic experiences, and that it is almost impossible to remember it at all accurately, and not to describe it as being more romantic (or indeed more tragic) than it actually was.

I am no exception to this rule, I'm sure. As far as my love for B was concerned, of course in the passage of time some of the corners have been knocked off, the heights have been heightened and the sorrows deepened. But one thing is certain, locked fast in my memory, and that is that when he first kissed me all I could think about was when he would kiss me again.

239

Had I ever been in love. When B and I were together, I thought from then on I would never be out of love. The magic was it would never, ever end, and even though it has ended, it never really has. Even now, yes, after all this time, and after everything that has happened, sometimes I feel a sudden tug on my heart, and my breath catches in my throat, just when I think of him, just when I remember, when I remember how it all was.

TWELVE

'I simply can't believe it!' Brake cried with his usual mix of indignation and amazement. 'Here we are, it's nineteen-thirteen – and you've never seen a moving picture?'

'Not the sort you're talking about!' Grace confessed, shouting over the noise of the engine and the wind. 'Once when we went to the music hall in Oxford, after the last act they showed a bioscope—'

'I'm talking about real films, with a story! Not some flickering sequence of a train coming into a station, or waves crashing on the seashore!' They were driving away from Aylesbury, where they had as usual met, and on towards Oxford. 'Films you would just not believe, Grace! *The Life Drama of Napoleon Bonaparte and Empress Josephine of France*! *The Voyage to the Moon*! *The Great Train Robbery*! I was a kid of fifteen when I first saw *The Great Train Robbery*! I must have seen it six or seven times!'

'My father wouldn't let us!' Grace shouted back. 'Whenever there was a picture show in the village, Lottie and I were forbidden to go! My father and my mother both thought we'd get fleas! They said moving pictures were vulgar! And not suitable entertainment for well brought up girls like us!'

Brake Merrowby roared with laughter and banged the steering wheel with both hands.

'You just wait and see, Grace!' he cried. 'Moving pictures are going to be just about the biggest thing this century! If I wasn't an artist, that's what I'd be doing! I'd be back home making moving pictures! Like D. W. Griffith!'

When they got to Oxford, to his great delight Brake found that a *Theatre-de-Luxe* in the city was showing the latest film from Universal Studios, *Sheridan's Ride*. Over lunch he insisted that he be allowed to take Grace to see it, assuring her tongue-in-cheek that since it was a *Theatre-de-Luxe* and not a common penny nickelodeon there would be no chance of her catching fleas.

Not that Grace would have minded, once they were settled in their seats and the film had begun. Even the early and conventionally theatrical scenes held her spellbound, but when the famous ride began and the screen exploded into action, Grace was so thrilled and astounded she did everything but hide herself under her seat. She was familiar enough with Cook's story of how Mr Harcross had taken her to the music hall before the turn of the century to see Lumière's moving picture of a train arriving at a station, and how Cook had fainted when the train, in reality peacefully steaming to a halt, seemed to hurtle out of the screen, but nothing had prepared her for the excitement and sheer amazement she herself was now experiencing as the camera furiously tracked Sheridan's cavalry and then the screen filled with scenes of the Union army being routed and put to flight by the Confederate onslaughts. By the time the film had been shown, without remembering where or how, Grace found not one but both her hands in Brake's.

They were both silent as they walked down through the city, past honey-stoned colleges with snapdragon on the walls and under silent fingered spires dreaming high above under a summer sky, on down hollowed steps beside a bridge and then along by the cool dark shaded water of the Isis. Grace was silent because she was speechless, still

242

filled with wonder and incredulity, but Brake was silent for another and quite different reason.

They walked for a long time, until they were in a meadow far below a distant college. Brake swung his jacket off the one shoulder on which he had been carrying it and spread it on the riverbank for Grace to sit. He settled beside her, both knees drawn up under his chin, idly backhanding stones picked from beside his feet into the water.

'Grace,' he said as yet another stone flopped into the river, his chin resting on his knees. 'What are we going to do?'

He said it very flatly, without any inflexion, as if he was suddenly without hope, and she knew how he felt, because whenever she herself thought about their predicament, which she did with an ever increasing frequency, the futility of their situation became ever more apparent, so much so that Grace thought now only of the present, and of each moment they were able to share together, rather than wondering what the future might bring.

'Oh for heaven's sake!' Grace mock-groaned, trying to lighten what was obviously about to become a heavy atmosphere, just as she did with the children. 'Not another attack of the mulligrubs, surely! Not on such a lovely day as this?'

'*Mulligrubs?*' For a moment the spark was back in Brake's eye as he turned to her, matching his astonishment to her groan.

'It's what Harriet calls the blue devils,' Grace explained, still hoping she might sidetrack him away from his original question. 'It comes from old Nanny Lydiard. Apparently bad moods or an attack of the dismals were known as the mulligrubs. Or the mubblefubbles.'

'Really?' Brake said, lying back on the grass, arms behind his head and staring up at the sky. 'Well I've got them both, the mulligrubs and the mubblefubbles, and no kidding.'

'You were perfectly all right when we were in the

picture house,' Grace reminded him, knowing as she did it was a mistake as Brake rolled on to one side, propping his handsome head up on one hand to look at her balefully, his small but full-lipped mouth now pursed into a childish pout.

'I was perfectly all right as usual until I held your hand,' he said, after a long silence broken only by the *kittick!* of a scavenging moorhen. 'Why should holding someone's hand be so potent? I could hardly watch the screen. All I could feel was you. There. Right there. You – in my hand.'

'Brake—' She wanted to stop him, or at least deflect him from asking the question to which she knew there was no answer. But he just shook his head at her and continued as if she hadn't spoken.

'So. What are we going to do?'

There was no point in feigning ignorance any more, in asking him *about what?*, in pretending she didn't know what he meant, and then when he started to explain yet again having to find another excuse for putting the matter to one side and making him concentrate purely and simply on the time they had together. Sooner or later Grace knew as well as Brake that some sort of a decision would have to be made. What sort she refused to specify, preferring instead to speculate only as far as that, as far as the point of decision. She was afraid to imagine beyond that point in case the only course open to them was the severance of their relationship.

During the past year she had only once thought of that possibility, and finding the prospect unimaginable she had never again contemplated it. As long as they could see each other there was no need to worry. As long as she could be with Brake at some time, and it didn't matter how much time she had with him, or how long she had to wait between their trysts, just as long as Grace knew she was going to see and be with him then that was all.

But the real reason why Grace never allowed herself to entertain such a notion was that inside, privately, deep down in her heart of hearts she knew the final truth. At some point and for some reason (neither of them properly defined) Brake would move out of her life, and once more Grace would be alone. She knew this would happen, because never once in all the long and deep conversations they'd had about their relationship over the months they had known each other, not once had Brake ever suggested or even hinted at any degree of permanency. He was passionate, and he was serious. After he had kissed her for the first time in that magic, moonlit rose garden, he had told her he loved her. He had whispered it into her hair, his lips softly touching her cheek as he spoke, as he explained how he had fallen in love with her that morning, as he stood high on the hill above the river, as he had watched her picking her way across the water with the sunlight dancing in diamonds at her feet, and how he had known he loved her as she stood soaking wet before him, how even as he had laughed at her all that he'd wanted to do was sweep her up in his arms and make love to her. He had told her then as he kept on telling her now that he had never loved anyone as he loved her. She must believe that, she must listen. She was beautiful, she was wonderful, she was sweet and she was pure, but above and most of all she had a pilgrim soul. And he was the one man who loved her not just for her beauty, and her wonder, for her sweetness and her purity, but for her very special soul.

'So come on – what are we to do?'

They could marry, that's what they could do. He was an artist and so too was she. She could understand him, she would understand him, as she was learning to understand him now, to fathom his moods, to read his despair and celebrate his exhilaration. If ever two people were made for each other, it must surely be the two of them. They loved with a love that was more than a love, and their life blood flowed from the one heart that beat between them. Grace had only to see him for her head to swim, and she knew it was the same for Brake. Whenever they remet, when he walked then ran to her when she got off the train at Aylesbury station, he would take her by the hands, or sometimes by her forearms and he would hold her with such a passion, just hold her hands or her arms, looking at her as if he was possessed by a form of wonderful delirium. Such was his emotion his jaws always seemed to be clenched almost as tight as the hands which held her, his eyes searching hers to make sure she was real, that she was there, while past them and unseen by them people walked by as life went on in a blur, in a ribbon of haze.

Yet never once did he suggest a solution as to what they should do, beyond wondering, as if it was a puzzle to be solved in an examination, or a nursery riddle.

If two people, a man and a woman, fall in love, and one person is the former lover of the other person's employer, and the recipient of many favours in the form of introductions to her society friends and resultant commissions, and that other person is in a job which expressly demands that she neither falls in love with a member of the opposite gender and certainly not leave to marry the same, what are they to do?

'Stop seeing each other, I suppose,' Grace said, staring out across the river. 'That's what we should do really, I suppose.'

'You don't mean that?' Brake replied, getting to his feet and coming round between Grace and her view of the river. 'You can't really mean that?'

'You keep asking me the same question, Brake,' Grace said, 'over and over again. And that's all I can think of by way of a reply. If you think we ought to do something—'

'That's because we can't go on like this, Grace!'

He stared at her for a moment, then strode off away from her along the edge of the riverbank, hands sunk deep in his pockets. With a sigh, Grace got to her feet, picked up his jacket and followed him. Brake was impossible when he became truculent, which he was just about to do as Grace knew only too well, but she had learned by now that the best thing was to ignore the changes of mood and say nothing, at least nothing that would provoke him. So she allowed him to stride on ahead, knowing that he would soon get bored and engage her in conversation once more. Brake Merrowby could never stay silent for long.

In the meantime, while he walked on, kicking the occasional stone into the river, or plucking a long fresh grass to chew, Grace reviewed her situation.

Throughout the winter and the spring it had been difficult to meet. Grace didn't have much time off, and what days she was allowed had to be taken to suit not Grace but Lady Lydiard. Consequently at one point Grace and Brake didn't see each other for over two months. Nor could he write to her very frequently, in case Dora noticed an abundance of letters for Grace written in the same hand and put two and two together, making a tale to tell downstairs which inevitably would find its way upstairs and possibly straight to milady's chamber. Of course any direct visits were right out of the question.

Right from the outset they had known they had to keep their association secret. Besides the fact that Brake had been one of Lady Lydiard's most ardent admirers, so a subsequent romantic relationship with the family nanny would not be taken well, Lady Lydiard had also made it quite plain what her feelings were with regard to her nanny's private life when Grace had won her promotion.

'While of course I fully understand because I wouldn't be human otherwise, Nanny, would I?' she had said to Grace. 'That is to say I wouldn't be human if I didn't realize you might wish to have a life of your own outside of ours, and a – well – that you have an entire life of your own which is entirely nothing at all to do with me. And us. The family. But even so I have to say because it's just one of those things, you see, which is just one of those things, and it's true, isn't it? Wouldn't you agree? That romance as it were, romance and the nursery floor don't really mix. *Tout l'un ou tout l'autre*, as they say in France, one thing or another, Nanny, nothing in between. That is to say, which is only common sense after all, that obviously it's either the children, or it's you. But then I really shouldn't be telling you this, should I? Because if you hadn't realized this, you really wouldn't have become a nanny.'

Although Grace was tempted to tell her employer that she had become a nanny by default rather than through a vocation, and that until the day her father disappeared her ambitions had had nothing to do with looking after other people's children, she had felt so relieved that she no longer had to work in the kitchens, and so proud at her promotion, that she found the temptation very easy to resist.

But just how serious Lady Lydiard was about her not having admirers or beaux Grace never really knew until Cook told her.

'It's an unwritten rule, you mark my words, Grace,' she'd said. 'Same goes for all these big families. It's a bit like being a nun, see? They expects you to give up everything to look after their kids, body *and* soul, my girl, you best believe me. Old Lady Lydiard, she was a right caution. Used to spy on old Nanny, when they was both young, this is. She got to hear from one of the nursery maids that old Nanny 'ad this soldier boy in tow, so one evening she pretends she's going out, and instead 'ides herself in an airing cupboard. Up comes Nanny and her beau up the nursery stairs and out springs old Lady Lydiard! Well you can imagine, can't you? Did them feathers ever fly. And that was an end to Nanny's romancing, I can tell you. So you be careful, Grace. You do any canoodlin', you just make sure it's not where any of this lot 'ere can see.' She'd jabbed a thumb vaguely in the direction of some of the other servants who were having their tea in the hall. 'And if you ever think of gettin' married,' Cook had added, 'just make sure you 'as the ring on your bloomin' finger before you go tellin' anyone about it. They don't like even the thought of their nannies gettin' married.'

But now, one year on from the beginning of their romance, with her employers away on holiday in Ireland, it was much easier for Grace and Brake to meet since the Lydiards had taken both Henry and Harriet away with them, assuring Grace there was no need for her to come since their friends had more than enough staff. So

Grace had been excused, ostensibly because Lady Lydiard insisted that she needed a break from her duties, but in reality, Grace suspected, because Boy was teething again and was being extremely fractious, which was why he had been left behind. None the less, Lady Lydiard generously urged Grace to take as much time off as she could since she would still have Dora to help her. Grace had taken her at her word, as indeed she had every reason to do.

'So? *What are we going to do, Grace?*'

She'd caught up with him now and he had taken her hand and slipped it through his arm in a gesture of such romantic intimacy, such familiarity that as always it made Grace's heart turn over.

'We're going to carry on doing what we've been doing so far,' Grace replied, hugging his arm to her since there was no one else anywhere in sight. 'We're going to carry on seeing each other whenever possible, that's what we're going to do.'

'That is *feeble*,' Brake protested. 'That is feeble, and that is no answer! I am a man, Grace, and I cannot go on like this. That is no answer. At all.'

He had thrown his head back and was looking up at the heavens in despair.

'Of course it's no answer,' Grace retorted, withdrawing her arm. 'And of course you're the man. So you're the one who's meant to have the answers!'

It was Grace's turn to walk on, which she did, hurrying away from him, biting her tongue for being so outspoken. What if he should urge her to tell him precisely what it was she wanted? What should she say then? What could she say?

She could hear him running behind her now, running to catch up the hundred yards or so she was ahead of him. She quickened her step to show that she was in no hurry to be caught, but in a moment he was by her side, taking hold of her arm and swinging her back to face him.

'Very well,' he said quietly, and breathlessly. 'Very well then, I shall tell you what we're going to do. We're going to – we must – run away together. We shall run away to Italy! And live together in Florence, you and I! We shall run away this instant! Tonight! Tomorrow morning! Whenever you say! As soon as you can!'

'But I can't!' Grace said, even though her heart was pounding like a pile-driver. 'How can I run away? I couldn't!'

'Why ever not?' Brake was looking at her as though she were mad. 'What else can we do? Of course we must run away!'

'I can't, Brake! What about Boy? I can't just run off and leave Boy.'

'Why ever not? There's Dora. Why can't she look after him?'

'Dora's a nursery maid, not a nanny.'

'You were only a kitchen maid.'

'It's not the same thing!' Grace argued. 'Dora's not very – well, she's not very bright. Dora would never make a nanny. And besides, Boy is my responsibility.'

'Your *responsibility*?' Brake's look now turned to one of total incredulity.

'Yes!' Grace insisted. 'You don't understand, but if I left, if I just suddenly ran away and something happened to him, I'd never forgive myself!'

Brake took her by both her arms and stared at her hard, as if to try and find the truth in her eyes.

'Right. When they return then,' he said, loosening his grip. 'The family are due back from Ireland at the end of the week and we'll go then. You must say yes, Grace. Please. I want you to come with me to Italy. I want so much for us to run away together.'

Suddenly Grace could feel the wheels beneath her, ready to take her feet from under her, standing where she was on top of a very steep and dangerous hill. She had to hold on, she knew she must hold on and stay where she was, she had to steady herself and stand firm, because she knew if she didn't that the voice in her head was right, that she'd plunge down this slope down into what had to be a deep, dark and bottomless void.

'I couldn't leave my children,' she said in a whisper. 'Not now.'

'They're not *your* children, Grace,' he reminded her.

'It doesn't matter,' she replied. 'I couldn't leave them.'

'Yes you could. They'd forget about you in a week. Sooner. As soon as they got a new nanny. *They're not your children.*'

'So just suppose I did? Supposing I did leave Henry, and Harriet, and Boy, and run away with you, then what? What would happen then?'

'We'd be together, Grace,' Brake said, with an air of faint irritation, as if he was explaining the obvious and she was a small girl. 'You wanted to know what we were going to do—'

'*You* wanted to know what we were going to do,' Grace corrected him.

'Fine!' The note of irritation was rising to one of desperation. 'So I'm telling you, Grace! We're going to go to Italy and live together!'

'In sin.'

'It won't be sin!'

'Well of course it will be sin. That's what it's called when people live together without – outside wedlock. It's called living in sin.'

'Well I like to think of it differently! I like to think of it as – as—'

Grace waited as he stumbled into silence.

'Yes?'

'As living in love!' he cried, his voice a half roar. 'Does it matter? Does it matter what it's called as long as we're together?'

'Yes it does matter,' Grace said. 'I know you don't have much faith, in fact you keep saying you haven't any, although I don't altogether believe that, but you see I do. I was brought up to believe that love out of wedlock is wrong and I still believe it. It may be romantic, running off and living together, and I'm quite sure it's wonderful—'

'It would be with me,' Brake assured her. 'No kidding.'

'I don't doubt you, not for a moment.' Grace smiled

and took one of Brake's hands in both of hers, turning him to start walking back the way they had come. 'But you see when it was all over—'

'When what was all over?' Brake demanded, taking his hand away, and stopping in his tracks.

'When you were bored with me,' Grace replied, walking on with his hand once more in hers. 'Which you would be, you'd grow bored with me. People soon tire of their mistresses if they come by them easily.'

'How the heck do you know?'

'My teacher told me,' Grace replied airily, wondering at the same time if her father had yet grown bored with his mistress. 'And I've read about it. Lots of times.'

'I won't get bored with you.'

'You will, and when you do, what then? What of me? You – you're a successful painter, and a man. You can go on working, and you can find another mistress, and everyone will cry *bravo! What a splendid fellow! He fights, he drinks, he paints and he has a succession of mistresses – bravo!* What a great chap! What a *man!* But what of me? If I do as you're suggesting and run away with you, when the day comes that you stop loving me, where do I go? Not into the arms of the next man, or the one after him, or the one after the one after him. Because that's not the sort of person I am. I'm not a *bohemian*, like you, and I would really and truly believe that what we'd done was wrong, unlike you. But I wouldn't be able to get another nanny's job, at least not one like this. Everyone would know, every would-be employer and every other nanny, because they do. They know everything about everybody, and they'd soon have heard about Nanny Lydiard running off with one of Lady Lydiard's ex-admirers, the society painter. So even if I didn't believe it was wrong, I'd still be a fool to do it, to let my heart rule my head.'

'But I wouldn't grow bored with you!' Brake protested. 'I could never grow bored with you!'

'I won't say of course you would, because I would hope you wouldn't,' Grace replied. 'But you might. Or I might grow bored with you.'

'Never!' Brake assured her. 'You couldn't get bored with me! How could you? I'm far too interesting!'

Even so, some of the heat had already escaped, and the balloon Brake had been flying high above the mountains was now slowly but inexorably coming back down to earth.

'I won't make this offer to you again,' he threatened. 'This is a once in a lifetime chance.'

'Of course it is,' Grace replied, 'because you don't really mean it.'

'Don't I just!'

For a moment Grace thought she might have provoked him too much as he stood glowering at her before turning on his heel and once more walking off ahead of her. But by now she could tell from his back whether or not he was serious, and the back going away in front of her was not Brake's serious, dark-minded round-shouldered back. He was walking too straight, too upright and with quite a spring in his step, as if he was relieved, just as Henry walked when he'd got away with something.

Grace made no effort to catch him. She just let him walk on ahead of her, and when he began to slow down in the obvious hope that she would catch him up, she too slowed down so she remained exactly the same distance behind him.

Before they reached the bridge, Brake stopped altogether, with a visible and audible sigh. Grace stopped as well, busying herself by adding to the long daisy chain she was making.

'Very well.' He had been forced to walk back to her and now stood in front of her, one hand on his hip, the other holding the jacket slung over his shoulder.

'Now what?' Grace asked, looking up. 'Very well now what?'

'Very well then, we'll have to get married,' he replied.

'Why?' Grace asked as calmly as she could.

'Because if you won't run away with me, then that's what we'll have to do,' Brake replied. 'Get married.'

'No we won't,' Grace told him. 'Not if we have to. I would hate you to marry me because you felt you had

253

to. People should only get married if they want to.'

Brake eyed her, without moving, without changing his pose. Then he swung his jacket on to his other shoulder and changed hands.

'Very well then,' he announced. 'We won't get married.'

'Very well then,' Grace agreed. 'We won't.'

'Good,' Brake said, throwing his jacket round both his shoulders and running a hand through his dark unruly hair. 'At least we agree about something.'

Then he ran up the stone steps beside the bridge leaving Grace, not for the first time, to find her own way back to the railway station.

He found her compartment just as the guard, flag in hand and whistle in his mouth, was making sure all the carriage doors were shut.

'You're wrong!' he shouted through the open window which he had grabbed with both hands as the train started to move, much to the astonishment of the other passengers in the Ladies Only compartment. 'We do have to get married! Because if we don't – I shall kill myself!'

The train was slowly beginning to pick up speed, but Brake had a fast hold on the top of the window and was breaking into a run alongside the carriage.

'Let go, Brake,' she urged, leaning forward from her seat. 'Let go before you hurt yourself.'

'No!' he shouted back at her. 'I shall hold on until you say yes!'

'Don't be ridiculous,' Grace said as quietly as she was able, with a glance at her fellow passengers who were all staring at her with amazement. 'Let go at once.'

'No!'

Brake was having to run faster now as the train accelerated. But still he had hold of the carriage window. A glance to her right told Grace he was just about to run out of platform.

'Let go!' she pleaded with him, trying desperately to unhook his fingers from the window with hers. 'You're going to kill yourself!'

'So say yes before I do!' he yelled back above the increasing noise from the steam engine and rattle of the carriages. 'Because I'm not going to let go!'

The train had reached the part of the platform now where it sloped steeply off to the track, but instead of letting go, Brake jumped on to the carriage step and, tightening his hold on the window, pressed himself as hard as he could against the door.

'Now will you say yes!' he yelled.

'This is blackmail!' Grace found herself shouting, standing up now and leaning her face as close as she could get to him. 'And I'm going to pull the emergency cord!'

'You do that,' Brake shouted back, 'and I'll jump in front of this oncoming train!'

Neither locomotive was going very fast as they passed each other, but their combined speed would have been more than enough to kill Brake outright. As the incoming train rumbled its way past Grace grabbed Brake round his shoulders and head to try to stop him falling or being sucked under its carriages.

'You're mad!' she yelled. 'Quite, quite insane!'

'Of course I am!' he yelled back. 'Mad about you! Mad enough to die for you! Now say yes because I won't be able to hold on much longer!'

Grace hesitated, her arms now holding his forearms, while the train really began to pick up speed and the increasing wind blew Brake's hair into his eyes and ballooned inside his jacket, making it ever harder for him to keep his hold.

'Pull the cord, someone!' a voice said behind Grace. 'Will someone pull the emergency cord!'

'If anyone pulls the cord,' Brake howled, 'I jump! Now for pity's sake, Grace, will you please say yes!'

Still Grace hesitated. For a second, or two seconds maybe, that was all, but long enough for it all to flash by her, the children, Henry, Harriet and Boy, her safe life at Keston, the Lydiards, the family, her part in it, her part of it, the children, Henry, Harriet and Boy in

255

time with the train wheels, Harriet telling her secretly that when Henry grew up he was going to marry Grace and have lots of children, Henry, Harriet and Boy, Harriet's wonderful drawings, Harriet's hand in hers, Boy asleep on her lap while Harriet draws them, Henry kissing her at Eton, Boy's little pink hand grabbing hold of her cheek and him smiling at her, the children, her life, and Brake, hanging on quite literally for his life, hanging on a second away from death because he loved her, he wasn't fooling, the train was going too fast, the train was going Harriet, Henry and Boy, the-children-and-Brake the-children-and-Brake the-children-and-Brake—

'For God's sake, Grace!' the voice was shouting, breaking the hypnosis. 'Grace you must say yes!'

'Yes!' She heard herself, her voice calling back, she heard her voice agreeing. 'Yes, Brake! All right – yes!'

Someone was by her side, another man, someone in a uniform, and Brake was being hauled in through the window by a large ticket collector, a big strong fellow with a countryman's face. There were voices, too, voices which were telling the guard the story all at once, but all Grace could see was Brake, smiling at her like a boy, like Henry when he was rescued from the oak tree, smiling at her from the floor of the carriage where he sat propped up now against the door, his clothes awry, his thick hair tangled, his handsome face smudged black with soot.

'You said yes, Grace,' she heard him saying through it all, the noise of the voices, the rattle of the carriages, the clatter of the wheels on the rails. 'You said yes,' he said. 'And remember, I have witnesses.'

But as she sat down, as he smiled up at her and then got up and sat beside her, as the man who loved her took her hand and she took his, Grace had the feeling that this was all a looming, a trick of the light.

The two things could well have been coincidental, but that is something of which no one will ever be sure. Not that it is of any importance as far as the story goes, in so far as one event did not cause the other to happen, or vice versa, although one of the incidents had a profound effect on the other. What is curious, or possibly remarkable, was that these two quite separate occurrences happened on the same day, and there is a possibility that they might even have happened around the same time of day, although there is little reason to suppose (as Grace did, and continued to do for the rest of her life) that they did so simultaneously. Even if that was the case, only the superstitious or those obsessed with the phenomenal could possibly believe that Grace by finally agreeing to marry Brake Merrowby could in any way have been responsible for an accident that happened two hundred and fifty miles away in Ireland.

THIRTEEN

Mr Harcross summoned her as soon as she was back from the station. No sooner had she reached the top of the nursery stairs than Dora had redirected her back down again.

'I don't know what's 'appened, Nanny,' Dora said, for once forgetting to sniff. 'But somethin' has 'cos you've never seen such faces. Mr 'Arcross he even come up 'ere 'isself.'

The butler was in his pantry, sitting in an old armchair by the window, smoking a cigarette which he held halfway down between his first two fingers, the tips of which touched the end of his nose. He stood up when Grace came in but said nothing until he had taken one last draw from his cigarette, exhaling the long blue plume of smoke with a deep sigh.

'You're to go to Ireland at once, Nanny,' he said, stubbing his cigarette out in the saucer of his teacup and picking up a timetable. 'Since you're home in time—'

'What's happened, Mr Harcross?' Grace interrupted. 'Has there been an accident? And why must I go?'

'One thing at a time, please, Nanny,' the butler replied, never taking his eyes from the page he was now studying. 'First we have to see which boat we can get you on. I've marked the times down.'

'Please, Mr Harcross,' Grace beseeched him, automatically unpinning her hat and taking it off. 'Please, I must know what this is about.'

'There has been an accident, Nanny, you are quite right,' Harcross told her, looking up and consulting the clock on his mantelpiece. 'There has been a serious accident, and his lordship telephoned late this afternoon to inform me and to request that I despatch you to Ireland with the greatest possible speed.'

'Then it must be one of the children.' Grace sat down suddenly as her legs gave way. 'Which one is it, Mr Harcross? Is it Master Henry or Miss Harriet?'

'It is neither of the children, Nanny.' Harcross glanced at Grace over his spectacles before returning to his time-table. 'Now if we can get you to Swindon—'

'Mr Harcross, you have to tell me what's happened,' Grace insisted. 'Please.'

The butler carefully removed his spectacles and tapped them on the railway timetable.

'It's her ladyship, Nanny,' he said, with a shake of his head. 'I regret to inform you she has suffered a fall.'

How and from what Harcross couldn't tell Grace. All he knew was what he had been told by Lord Lydiard on the telephone, namely that Lady Lydiard was injured and in hospital. The reason why Grace was to be sent over post-haste was because the Lydiards had moved on to stay with other friends who were childless and so had no one to look after Henry and Harriet while their mother was in hospital. Grace, however, as the train sped through the late summer night suspected that this was not all. If Lord Lydiard was simply worried about the children's welfare she felt sure he could have hired some help locally. Henry and Harriet were now of an age when they barely needed supervising, so there had to be something else, and the only thing Grace could imagine was that the accident must have been much more serious than as reported to Harcross.

Lord Lydiard met Grace off the boat himself. He was alone and driving his host's Rolls-Royce. As soon as she saw him Grace knew that she had been right and that Lady Lydiard was grievously injured.

'She's fractured her skull, Nanny,' Lord Lydiard said in answer to Grace's enquiry, while they sat on the quay in the stationary car. 'Of all the things. She's fractured that lovely head of hers.'

He had a hold of the steering wheel as if he was driving the Rolls, but as yet had made no move to start the motor preparatory to driving off.

'How did it happen, Lord Lydiard?' Grace asked, looking ahead of her, afraid to look at him and instead fixedly watching the gulls swooping down to feed off what the ship's kitchen crew were throwing out on to the harbour waters.

'Catching Harriet's pony.' Lord Lydiard seemed now also to be watching the gulls, although Grace knew that like hers his thoughts were somewhere else. 'You see they'd been racing each other on the sands, my wife, Henry and Harriet, on horseback. And Harriet was riding this rather nice little Arab. Which duly won. But it had taken hold, d'you see? Harriet couldn't pull it up and it took off with her, along the beach. Which one would think was safe enough. Gracious me, they'd been galloping up and down it all afternoon to beat the band. Anyway. Serena. My wife galloped off after Harriet, her horse must have put its foot in a hole or something, and down it went. And there were some boulders, not many, a sort of outcrop. She cracked her head on one. Then the wretched animal kicked her as it got up, because she's got internal injuries as well. Of all the things.'

Once more the gulls swooped and shrilled as they fought for food while the occupants of the car watched them without seeing. After a moment, a long moment while Grace searched for the right question, for the right thing to say, Lord Lydiard started the car and drove them away from the sea.

'What do the doctors say?' she asked as calmly as she could, the hands in her lap clenched so tight it felt as if her nails were puncturing her skin.

'What do the doctors say?' Lord Lydiard wondered wearily, pushing a long sweep of hair away out of his eyes with one gloved hand. 'Not much, Nanny. There's not a lot anyone can say. They don't think she'll live, do you see.'

Grace said nothing. She knew there was nothing to say. Lord Lydiard wasn't someone to be comforted by hollow reassurances, so she sat without speaking while he drove in silence through the city to the hospital. The tragic news had cut Grace off from the real world, and as the huge silver car made its way along the cobbled streets what passed by her eyes might have been scenes from one of Brake's beloved moving pictures: lines of strong-limbed horses pulling everything from carts to trams, barefoot urchins with candlestick noses begging from passersby, black-shawled women with large empty baskets crooked on their arms moving slowly along the pavements or gathering like so many blackbirds waiting to cross the road near street corners where men smoking homemade pipes stood propping up the buildings taking notice of nothing except their own importance. Grace saw it all, she saw all the pictures that went to make up Cork, but she heard none of the noise of the city, none of the shawlies' cries, none of the pleas of the urchins nor the constant clatter of the horses' hooves, because all she could hear were the sweet small voices that had cried out to her the previous afternoon.

Lord Lydiard asked Grace to come into the hospital and see his wife, but Grace declined, thinking he was only offering the invitation out of politeness and that he would far rather spend the time at his disposal alone with his mortally stricken wife. But he insisted, kindly but firmly, until Grace was persuaded.

'She would want to see you, Nanny,' he assured Grace as they walked down the wax-polished corridors. 'She's very fond of you, and would give one a dreadful drubbing were she to discover – you know.' He walked on in silence for a moment, his feet echoing on the wooden floors. 'Were she to discover,' he continued after briefly clearing his throat, 'that you were here and hadn't come to see her. Besides.'

He fell to silence again, but this time it seemed deliberate because he stopped and turned to Grace, who in turn stopped and waited to hear what he had to say.

'You probably know all this anyway,' he said, 'being a nanny. Old Nanny Lydiard was a great believer in this sort of thing, do you see. Children giving old or ill people energy. People one loves and who love one do the same sort of thing. But then you probably know all this anyway. Point is, it's really why I want you to visit her. In case your presence might make a difference. Don't you think? One really never knows.'

'I don't understand,' Grace said. 'At least I do, I understand what you're saying. But – but is that why you sent for me? I thought it was the children.'

The two small voices calling from far off. Just as I said yes.

'Absolutely, Nanny. I can't give them what they need. Not the way you can.'

He had started walking down the corridor again, without meeting her eyes once. He didn't even look at her as he opened the door they had come to, holding it for Grace to go in first in front of him, but gazing past her, back down the corridor as if there was someone else behind them.

The room had only the one white-painted iron bed in it, beside the head of which sat a nurse. There was a black blind at the window, but it wasn't pulled so the almost bare room was flooded with sunlight, giving it a dreamlike quality, particularly to Grace who was exhausted after her long and mostly sleepless journey.

'Would you mind if we had the blind down?' Grace asked. 'It is very bright in here.'

'There's no point, miss,' the heavily uniformed nurse told her, briefly looking up from the book she was reading. 'The patient's unconscious.'

'I think that's the right idea, Nanny,' Lord Lydiard said, walking over to the window and pulling down the blind. 'It wouldn't do to wake up and have the sun in your eyes.'

The nurse looked at him briefly, as if to say there was very little hope of that happening, before reluctantly closing her book.

Having shut out most of the sunshine, Lord Lydiard walked to the end of the bed and once again cleared his throat.

'Nanny's here, Serena,' he announced.

Then without another word he left the room.

There was another chair against the wall behind where the door had opened. Grace fetched it and sat down at the side of the bed opposite the nurse. Lady Lydiard lay between them, her long slender arms outside the bedclothes, her skin white and translucent, her fingernails seemingly bloodless, her beautiful mouth slightly open, her lips dry and puckered. Around her head was a swathe of thick bandage which ran across the top, round the temples and down under her chin. To look at her she seemed not to be breathing, so shallow was her respiration, but when Grace listened hard, in the silence of the darkened room she could just hear the faint *huh* of expiration.

'There's really no hope,' the nurse said suddenly in her normal voice. 'She's a depressed fracture and a subdural haemorrhage.'

'What does that mean?' Grace asked.

'It means there's really no hope.' The nurse eyed her, and then consulted the watch pinned to the front of her uniform. 'Good,' she said, rising. 'That's the end of my shift.'

She walked to the door, with her book clasped to her flat chest.

'Aren't you meant to wait for your relief?' Grace asked.

'On the contrary, Nanny,' the nurse replied, building a small sneer into Grace's title, 'my relief is meant to be here on time.'

Once she was alone, Grace took Lady Lydiard's hand in hers and gently squeezed it. There was no response, and the hand felt dry and barely warm. Carefully replacing the hand back on the blanket with the tips of two fingers

Grace searched for the pulse at the base of Lady Lydiard's thumb, and could only just find it. It was very faint and ominously slow.

The door opened quietly behind her and another nurse appeared, a young girl with pink cheeks and green eyes.

'Hello,' she said softly. 'I'm Kathleen. You must be Nanny. Deirdre's skipped off again, has she?'

'If you're referring to the last nurse,' Grace whispered back, 'she said you were late.'

'That'll be the day.' The young nurse grinned and settled herself down to start her watch. 'Deirdre's forever cutting corners and then blaming everyone else. Search me why she ever became a nurse. Now then, you poor darling.' She turned her attention to her patient, beginning by doing what Grace had just finished doing.

'She seems very weak,' Grace ventured, once the nurse had taken Lady Lydiard's pulse.

'While there's life, Nanny,' the nurse replied. 'Miracles can happen.'

No miracle happened while Grace was there. By the time Lord Lydiard returned to take Grace away there had been no sign of life from the patient other than the faint and regular *huh* of her expiration.

'Goodbye,' Lord Lydiard wished his unconscious wife from the end of her bed. 'We'll be in again at the same time tomorrow.'

At first when they saw each other, none of them knew what to say, or what to do. They were standing waiting at the top of the steps of the house, with a small slender blonde woman who had her arms round each of their shoulders, and when their father drew the borrowed Rolls up they freed themselves to run down and greet their father first, and then their nanny.

'Hello,' Henry said after an unconscionable pause. 'Awfully good of you to come over.'

Harriet said nothing. She just suddenly ran to Grace and threw her arms around her, burying her head in the softness of Grace's stomach.

'It's all right, darling,' Grace said, stroking her hair, 'everything's going to be all right.'

But she knew from Harriet's hug that Harriet knew it wasn't really.

'Come on, Nanny,' Henry said, using the fact that he was leading her up the steps as an excuse to take her hand. 'Let me introduce you to Lady Hillier. Lady Hillier, this is our nanny Grace.'

Lady Hillier was a china figure of a person, delicate, small, perfect, and perfectly beautiful. She extended a hand.

'Hello, Nanny,' she said in a voice as deep as a man's. 'I'm so sorry to welcome you here in such sad circumstances. Come in and have a drink because you must be quite exhausted.'

With Henry still holding her hand, and Harriet still clasped to her waist, Grace followed her hostess into the large rambling house.

'How's Mama?' Henry asked Grace as they walked into the drawing room.

'She's no better, Henry,' Grace said, 'but then I understand she isn't any worse either.'

'We're saying prayers all the time,' Henry told her. 'And Lady Hillier who's a Roman Catholic is very kindly having a mass said every day in the village church.'

A butler in an old white coat and sandals asked Grace what she would like to drink after she had been offered a chair by the open French windows. She asked for a lemonade, at which Lady Hillier immediately insisted that she at least had some gin in it otherwise there was simply no point. Harriet climbed first on to the arm of Grace's chair and then during the conversation gradually slid herself over until she was sitting on Grace's knee, with her head resting on Grace's right shoulder. Grace, her drink held up in her right hand, her other arm round Harriet, with Henry sitting at her feet stroking the grey grizzled head of an old and sleepy lurcher, told them all about her long journey while from another room somewhere came the sound of Lord Lydiard playing some Liszt on an old piano.

Later they all dined together in a room whose walls were decorated only with fishing trophies, glass cabinets full of long dead trout and salmon caught by Lady Hillier's husband, Sir Anthony, a man with a face like an eagle, as tall as his wife was small. The conversation was studiously idle, concerned only with gossip and salmon flies, tennis and the foxtrot, while outside the walls of their holiday house the world was growing more dangerous by the minute. Yet no mention was made of the Balkans or the worsening of relations between France and Germany, and above all none at all of the matter which concerned them all most, of the life that hung on a thread, the life of one they all loved most dreadfully.

At one point during a brief lull in the conversation the telephone rang in the hall. No one moved, neither was any reference made to it. Instead Lady Hillier enquired of the children whether or not they'd had enough summer pudding, while her husband began a discussion with Lord Lydiard about the prehistoric remains of a human skull with an ape-like lower jaw which had been found the previous year at Piltdown in Sussex. Meanwhile Grace saw the butler answering the telephone and taking a message, which he delivered to Lord Lydiard only once they had all left the dining room.

Grace overheard it.

'No change, your lordship,' the butler said quietly. 'Her ladyship still sleeps.'

There was no change the next day either, nor the one after that.

'It was my fault, Nanny,' Harriet suddenly confessed that third night when Grace was tucking her up in her bed. She had barely spoken a word more than a yes or no since Grace's arrival, preferring instead either to sit by herself reading in the garden, or to go on long walks with Grace and Henry around the lake during which she would hardly speak. Grace never pressed her to say anything, nor did she try to engage her in idle conversation. She could imagine well enough what the child was going through, and understanding Harriet as

266

she did, she knew that when she needed to talk she would.

'I don't see how it can have been your fault,' Grace said, smoothing the creases out of the crisp linen sheet before sitting on the edge of the bed.

'Harriet thinks it's her fault for suggesting we should race,' Henry said from the window seat where he was sitting in his dressing-gown reading *The Innocence of Father Brown*.

'It was my fault, Henry,' Harriet replied, very quietly, slipping herself down between the sheets. 'If I hadn't suggested the race—'

'If *if* and *ands*,' Grace said, plumping up the child's pillows. 'There's always an *if* or an *and* to everything.'

'If I hadn't suggested the race,' Harriet said from under her covers, 'my horse wouldn't have bolted, so it was my fault.'

'From what I know of horses, which isn't a lot,' Grace said, 'if a horse bolts that surely isn't your fault?'

'It is if you were showing off.'

Harriet's dark round eyes looked up at Grace over the sheet, full of limpid tears.

'You were racing each other,' Grace said, finding one small hand under the bedclothes and taking it in hers. 'Racing isn't showing off.'

'Of course it isn't,' Henry agreed, carefully turning over a fresh page.

'It is if you were showing off how much you could win by,' Harriet said. 'I was on easily the fastest horse, but I had to try and win by miles. Instead of just winning.'

'That's understandable, Harriet. In the heat of the moment.'

'That's what I said,' Henry agreed again. 'Absolutely.'

'That's not the point.' Harriet took her hand away, and turned on her side, away from Grace. Grace stroked the waves of her soft blonde hair and then bent down to kiss it. It smelt of the warm sun and the sea.

'The point is,' Harriet said, turning her head back to

Grace, 'he wouldn't have bolted if I hadn't kept jabbing his mouth.'

'Nonsense,' Henry said without looking up.

'I rode him all wrong, Nanny,' Harriet persisted. 'One minute I was kicking him on and throwing the reins at his head, and the next minute I was hauling him back, like a dead fish as Henry calls it. No wonder he bolted.'

'People who admit things are never the guilty ones,' Grace said. 'You're only feeling guilty because you're afraid. Don't be. Don't feel guilty, and don't be afraid.'

Harriet now turned her whole body round and lay on her back, facing Grace.

'Supposing Mama dies?'

'We must pray that she doesn't, darling.'

'But suppose that she does?'

'It won't be your fault. It won't be anybody's fault.'

'Is she going to die, Nanny?'

'I don't know, sweetheart. Only God knows that.'

Grace stroked Harriet's cheek. As she did, Henry came and sat on the other side of the bed.

'I can still hear her laughing, Nanny,' Harriet whispered. 'Behind me. She was laughing as she was trying to catch me up. Laughing so that I wouldn't be afraid, and calling to me to hang on. That was the last thing I heard, Nanny. Mama laughing. You know that laugh of hers. It always makes me laugh.'

'Me too,' said Henry.

'I'd just hate never to hear her laughing again, Nanny.'

Grace got up twice in the night when she heard someone crying. The first time it sounded like Harriet but when she hurried barefooted into the bedroom she found it was Henry who was sitting up starey-eyed in bed. She changed his soaking wet pyjama jacket for a dry one, and hugged him to her until he told her that he was all right and settled back down in bed. The second time it was Harriet, whom Grace found huddled and sobbing under her bedclothes.

Grace took them both back with her and tucked them up in her large double bed. Then she turned up the lamp, pulled up a chair and read to them until they fell back to sleep. There was a chill to the night air now, so Grace wrapped herself up in a rug over her dressing-gown and curled her legs up under her in the chair, and then when she found sleep wouldn't come, reached for her journal which was beside her bed, and finished the entry for the day which she had started when she'd first retired.

I told Harriet not to feel guilty which she mustn't, and yet here am I suffering from pangs of guilt myself. I knew what the conditions were when I accepted the post of nanny, she made it clear, yet at the first opportunity I disregarded what I'd been told and fell in love. Not only that, I had to go and fall for B, and by doing so I feel I have betrayed her in some way.

It's half past three in the morning in a strange house in a strange country. The children have at last fallen asleep in my bed while I sit wrapped up in a chair wondering what is going on in their young heads. They haven't said anything really, apart from H's confession of guilt, but from their embraces and their looks I can more than guess at their thoughts. What will they do if they lose their mother? What will happen to them? She really is a mother to them. Lady L adores all three of her 'smalls' (as she calls them) and they love her back. Lucky them. Lady L is the most wonderful woman I've ever met. What it must be like to have a mother like her.

So now I must pray, as everyone else who loves her is praying. I must pray God that she survives this terrible accident, although from what I heard the doctors say it seems that there is very little chance. But I shall still pray. I really don't know 'whether or not more things are wrought by prayer than this world dreams of', but tonight more than ever I must try to believe it.

'The children want to see their mother,' Grace told Lord Lydiard the next morning after breakfast. 'They asked me when I was getting them up, and I said I would ask you.'

Lord Lydiard said nothing for a while. He just chewed the corner of his bottom lip as he stared out of the window and then found something in his jacket pocket which he examined thoroughly without, Grace suspected, an idea of what it was.

'Well,' he said, replacing the unregistered object back in his pocket, 'what do you think, Nanny?'

'I think it would be a good thing all round, Lord Lydiard,' Grace replied, having thought it all through long before she had come downstairs. 'Particularly in the light of what you said to me when I first arrived.'

'Very well,' Lord Lydiard agreed, still staring out into the garden. 'Whatever you say, Nanny.'

Kathleen, the pretty young nurse, was on duty when they all arrived. She got up at once and walked quietly to the door.

'I'm sure you'd rather be left alone,' she said. 'I'll be just outside the door.'

There were flowers in the room now, flowers the children had carefully collected from Lady Hillier's garden and given to their father to bring in and more flowers they had picked today, tall daisies, phlox and the last of the pinks, hollyhocks, briar roses, a profusion of asters and racemes of wild honeysuckle gathered from the hedges, all in vases and jars which Henry and Harriet carefully placed on the table either side of their unconscious mother's head, as if the vigour of the still fresh flowers would act as a life-giving transfusion.

Then they all sat around the bed, Henry next to his father, and Harriet by Grace, her hand in hers.

No one spoke, they just sat and waited. At the beginning there was a square of latticed sunlight on the cover of the bed, which by the time Grace glanced at her watch had moved off the bed and become a rectangle on the polished floor halfway to the window. They had been sitting there for over an hour.

Lord Lydiard cleared his throat, very quietly and slowly, and stretched both arms straight out in front of him.

'I think the best thing, don't you?' he said in a hushed but conversational tone, 'is for us all to have a chat with her. I'm not sure it's going to do all that good us just sitting here, everyone. She may be in a coma, but that's not to say she can't hear us. Henry?'

'Yes, Papa?' Henry had hold of one of his mother's hands, Harriet the other, and their eyes never strayed from her face.

'Why don't you tell her about that fish you caught with Sir Anthony?' his father said. 'You know what a mad keen fisherman your mother is.'

'Very well, Papa.' Henry composed himself much the way he did in the nursery when he had decided to recite something (usually Kipling). 'Sir Anthony took me to a stretch of the Lee we'd never fished before, because Mr Mac the gillie said there were some good salmon there. It was quite sunny, not too bright, you see. That hazy sort of sun you always say is much better for fishing, particularly river fishing, and there was a nice breeze too, which kept the water ruffled. Mr Mac told me to tie on a Jock Scott with a blue hackle, because I'd been fishing with a butcher, and as soon as I changed flies I rose a salmon three times.'

Henry stopped suddenly and then looked at his father, rolling his tongue over his teeth behind his bottom lip.

'Go on,' Lord Lydiard said. 'Everyone's listening.'

'Well.' Henry began again with a deep frown. 'The weather changed then, you see, Mama.'

He stopped again, but this time looked at Grace. Grace smiled at him, opening her eyes wider and nodding for him to continue.

'The weather changed, Mama,' Henry said, gradually recovering his confidence. 'We had some showers, the wind changed direction, and they stopped rising, or were rising short. Then the wind changed again and the rain stopped, but there was plenty of cloud still, which Mr Mac said was perfect, and pointed out where he said a big fish was rising, under the far bank. I hit the rise with my first cast and struck him at once, except there was such a pull I thought I must have snagged a log or something.' All the fear in Henry's eyes was gone now, and they were shining with the memory. 'But it wasn't a log, it was a fish and a big one, too, he was so big I couldn't hold him so Mr Mac and Sir Anthony told me to let him run, which I did. They wouldn't help me, Mama, they both said I had to land him myself, and I fought him for an hour. He was such a brave fish and he fought so *brilliantly*, I really didn't want to land him, Mama. But Mr Mac said we had to see what size he was at least, so I netted him, and he was absolutely huge. Mr Mac weighed him on his pocket scales, and he was eighteen pounds.'

'They didn't kill him, Mama,' Harriet said. 'Henry put him back.'

'Just like you, Serena,' Lord Lydiard sighed, rubbing his knees with both hands. 'It could have been you.'

'He was so brave, Mama,' Henry said. 'And so beautiful. I couldn't bear the thought of him being eaten.'

'Just like you,' their father sighed again.

'Lady Hillier's cook was furious.' Harriet grinned, pushing a lock of blond hair from her eyes with her free hand.

'I don't think she was really,' Lord Lydiard said. 'They caught half a dozen other decent fish. Anyway. Wasn't that something?'

Lord Lydiard looked at his wife who lay as still as a statue, and smiled.

'Good,' he said. 'Well done, Henry. You told that very well. Your turn, Harriet.'

'What shall I tell her, Papa?'

'Any ideas, Nanny?'

Grace bent over to Harriet and whispered something to her. Harriet frowned and looked back at Grace.

'I don't see what there is to tell, Nanny,' she said. 'At least I don't know how to describe it.'

After another whispered conference, Harriet pulled a *well-if-you-say-so* face and took a deep breath.

'I did this painting,' she began. 'It's only a landscape. It's the trees and bushes at the bottom of Lady Hillier's garden, but I don't know. Nanny seems to think it's rather good.'

Harriet shrugged and looked at Grace, as if wondering what else there was to say.

'Tell your mother how you did it,' Grace advised. 'Remember how you described what you were trying to do to Lady Hillier?'

'I was trying to make it sort of fuzzy,' Harriet told her unconscious mother. 'Rather than real. To give a sort of impression, the way I *felt* it looked. Rather than exactly *how* it looked. So I drew it out in pencil first, awfully lightly of course, then I worked over the shapes with light washes and let all the colours run together, you see. To make a sort of soft, out of focus thing. Then I built it up with more layers, and painted the shadows in with these great broad streaks of blue and green, and strengthened all the dark bits in the background with blue and black. And finished it off by washing the grass all over with yellow, which sort of lifts it. The grass, that is. It's turned out quite well really, I suppose.'

'It's wonderful,' Grace said. 'It's turned out more than well.'

'The best thing is for your mother to see it,' Lord Lydiard said to his daughter, before turning to address his wife. 'We'll bring it in for you to see tomorrow.'

'What are you going to talk to her about, Papa?' Henry asked.

'I don't know actually,' his father replied. 'Perhaps she'd like to hear this thing I've just written.'

Lord Lydiard got up and walked over to the window, raising the blind and looking out across the hospital grounds.

'I wrote it last night, Serena,' he said, a minute or so later. 'It's a nocturne.'

Once again he cleared his throat slowly, stroking back his hair with both his hands, which is how he stood while softly he whistled his air, both hands on the top of his head, fingers lightly clasped at the back, eyes firmly fixed on some far distant point. It was a slow and pretty tune, sweet as birdsong in a morning garden, but he faltered before the end, and finished it instead with his voice, singing it to its conclusion in a soft, clear tenor.

No one spoke when he'd finished. No one moved. Finally Lord Lydiard broke the spell himself, coming to the end of the bed and consulting his fob-watch.

'I think we should go now, everyone,' he said, 'in case we tire the patient.'

Grace took the children to the door ahead of their father who lingered a moment longer by the bed.

'Goodbye, Serena,' he said. 'We'll come in again and see you tomorrow.'

They were by the door and about to leave when they heard it, as faint as a sigh on the wind.

'*John?*'

All of them looked back, Grace holding Harriet's hand, Henry by his father's side. They looked back at the bed where Lady Lydiard was lying quite still, just as she had been, her eyes closed and her arms straight by her sides. Lord Lydiard took one step nearer the bed then stopped, frowning deeply and putting a hand to his brow, as if to try to smooth out his confusion.

'I thought I heard—' he said, before falling to silence. 'I could have sworn I did.'

'I thought I heard it too, Papa,' Henry said, moving back to his father's side.

'Me too,' whispered Harriet. 'Didn't you, Nanny?'

'I can't be sure,' Grace replied, knowing now she couldn't have imagined it, not if they all thought they had heard it.

Then Harriet's hand tightened on Grace's as quite suddenly, just like a butterfly opening its wings, Lady Lydiard opened her eyes.

'Serena?' Lord Lydiard moved to the foot of the bed where he leaned on the footrail, holding it with white-knuckled hands. 'Serena?'

But although Lady Lydiard had opened her eyes, they were unfocused and staring out as if at nothing. But then her lips parted slightly, pale dry lips which she

274

then slowly moistened with the tip of her tongue before her eyes dropped closed once more.

'Mama?' Harriet was by her mother's side now, her hand free from Grace's. 'Mama?' she whispered, bending over the bed. 'Mama, can you hear me? It's Harriet.'

'And Henry,' her son said, joining his sister. 'And Papa. Are you awake, Mama?'

'Perhaps I should fetch the nurse,' Grace suggested quietly.

'*Who is that?*'

The voice was so weak that the four of them instinctively all leaned closer, watching and listening breathlessly.

'Mama?' Harriet was closest to her, sitting by the bedside, her mother's hand now in hers. 'Mama, it's us,' she whispered. 'Harriet, and Henry, and Papa.'

'*I can't see.*' Her voice was less than a whisper, the words softer than the faintest breath. '*I can't see anyone.*'

'If you stand up,' Grace told Harriet. 'I think it's perhaps because your mother can't look round. Go and stand at the end of the bed with your father. Henry, you too.'

The three of them stood together at the foot of the bed, while Grace remained where she was. Lady Lydiard, propped half upright on a pile of pillows, narrowed her eyes slightly as she tried to focus on what was in front of her.

'You're in hospital, Serena,' her husband said after a moment. 'You had a fall.'

'You didn't, Mama,' Harriet corrected her father. 'The horse you were on fell. You didn't fall.'

Lady Lydiard's eyes didn't move. They seemed to stay fixed in front of her while once again she slowly moistened her lips.

'Would you like a drink of water, Lady Lydiard?' Grace moved closer to the bed so that Lady Lydiard might possibly see her.

'*Yes,*' Lady Lydiard whispered. '*Please.*'

Carefully Grace held the water glass to Lady Lydiard's mouth, tipping a sip of water up, and then brushing the drops away with the ends of her fingers. As she did so

Grace had an image of a beautiful woman in her tennis clothes, standing bouncing a ball on the polished floor with one hand, and sipping lemonade out of a frosted glass held in the other.

'*Who is that?*'

'It's me, Lady Lydiard,' Grace replied. 'It's Nanny. Grace.'

As Grace took away the glass and put it down beside the bed, Lady Lydiard turned her head slightly to her.

'*Nanny,*' she whispered, and a smile came to her eyes. '*Dear Nanny.*'

Grace sat down in the chair beside the bed and then took the white and slender hand that was being offered to her.

'Mama—' Harriet began.

'Sssshhhh.' Her father gently cautioned her, putting his arm round her shoulders. 'One person at a time.'

'*Nanny?*' Grace had to lean in as far as she could to hear. '*It's so dark, Nanny,*' Lady Lydiard whispered. '*Could I have my light on?*'

The hand in Grace's was so cold, cold as the hand of someone who has been swimming in a deep lake, cold and for such a slender hand so very heavy.

'Of course,' Grace said, not moving, just holding the hand in both of hers.

'*Just until I go to sleep,*' Lady Lydiard whispered. '*That's all.*'

'Of course,' Grace said again.

Lady Lydiard looked and slowly found Grace's eyes, and as she did the clouds rolled away from the sun and for a brief moment the light shone brightly again in her own, in those wonderful pale green eyes. Then a darker cloud blew up, from a great bank of black cloud, and began inexorably to blot out the sun.

'Would you like someone to read to you?' Grace whispered, as she saw it wasn't a cloud but a shadow, a Shadow cloaked from head to foot. Lady Lydiard, her head still turned towards Grace, the smile still just alight round the edge of her eyes, nodded slowly, the once.

Grace stood up and went quietly to the end of the bed.

'Lady Lydiard wants you to read to her for a while, Lord Lydiard,' she said. 'And while you do, the children and I will wait outside.'

Henry and Harriet both looked from Grace to their father but before they could say anything their father intervened.

'It's all right,' he told them. 'Just do as Nanny says.'

'Your mother's very tired,' Grace whispered as she led them both back round the bed. 'So just say goodbye both of you, very quietly now, and then slip outside with me.'

She stood back while Henry and Harriet approached the bed where their mother lay, still with her head turned as it had been, a little to her right.

'Goodbye, Mama,' Henry said, before bending over carefully to kiss his mother's alabaster cheek. 'We'll come in again tomorrow.'

'Goodbye, Mama,' Harriet whispered as she too kissed her mother. 'I'm so very glad you woke up.'

For the last time in her life, their mother looked at them and smiled at them both.

'*That's better*,' she whispered. '*Oh, yes, it's so much lighter now.*'

Before the light went out for ever, before their mother slipped off into the dark and breathless void that was waiting at the Shadow's feet, Grace turned Henry and Harriet away and took them to the door. By now Lord Lydiard had taken his place beside the bed, with the one book that was there already in his hand.

As she held open the door, Grace heard him begin to read in a quiet but steady voice.

'*If I take the wings of the morning and remain in the uttermost parts of the sea; Even there also shall thy hand lead me: and thy right hand shall hold me. If I say, Peradventure the darkness shall cover me: then shall my night be turned to day.*'

Gently she ushered the children out ahead of her, holding the door open a moment longer.

'Yea, the darkness is no darkness with thee, but the night is as clear as the day: the darkness and light to thee are both alike.'

Then she closed the door.

'I'm so glad Mama woke up,' Harriet said, taking Grace's hand. 'I think it was the flowers that did it.'

'Yes.' Henry nodded very seriously as they walked off away down the corridor. 'I agree.'

FOURTEEN

There were flowers by the score when they buried Serena,
Lady Lydiard at Keston. The fourteenth-century village
church was full of autumn flowers, vivid blooms of purple,
and carmine asters, clear pink and orange-bronze chry-
santhemums, apricot and clear yellow dahlias, banks of
double white gypsophilas and the last roses of the summer
now gone, the family's choice of flower which were piled
high on the casket, a bank of pale pink and mauve, faded
salmon, soft lemon and creamy golden buff.

And just one single blood red rose, not on the casket
but dropped into the grave when the mourners had gone
by a man with a wild mane of hair and dark flashing eyes,
a tall man with the collar of his long black coat turned up
and pulled high against his unshaven cheeks.

Grace had sensed his arrival, glancing behind her as
the service began and seeing him slipping into the back of
the church where he disappeared beyond the font, tucked
into the shadows by the door. She couldn't see his face
clearly, she could hardly even make out his outline, but
she knew it was Brake.

She couldn't see him in the graveyard either yet she
knew he was there as well, hidden most likely behind
the huge yew tree or one of the other tombs. Then as
the carriages drew away from the churchyard, through a

279

fine veil of early September rain she saw him come out of the porch and walk to the grave where the gravediggers were getting ready to cover the coffin. She watched as he opened his coat and for a moment she thought he had been shot, so vivid was the circle of red against the white of his shirt. Then she saw what it was, she saw it was a rose, a rose which he put to his lips before holding it out before him and letting it drop into the grave.

Someone else had seen him, too, because the carriage in front of theirs stopped, the first in the line, stopping all the others behind it, while Lord Lydiard alighted and walked back into the churchyard. The horses drawing Grace and the children's carriage stamped impatiently and shook themselves, rattling their highly polished harness, their black plumes nodding in the breeze while George the coachman hissed through his teeth at them to be quiet and while Grace watched Lord Lydiard approaching his wife's grave and her former lover.

The two men stood for a minute or so in conversation. At one point Brake made to move away in an opposite direction from the line of carriages, but Lord Lydiard took hold of his arm and stopped him. Then after another brief exchange of words, they walked side by side back to the cortège and together got into the leading vehicle.

On their return to the Hall Henry insisted on attending the reception to give his father moral support. Grace asked Harriet if she wanted to accompany her brother, knowing full well what the answer would be, and sure enough Harriet shook her head and stood staring at the ground.

'Harriet,' Henry said, with that note of exasperation which seemed now to be ever present in his voice when he was dealing with his sister. 'You really are going to have to do better than this.'

Harriet didn't even look up. She just stood with her head bowed, and her hands behind her back.

'Nanny—' Henry turned to Grace for help.

'No, that's quite enough, Henry,' Grace said, cutting him off before he could continue. 'If Harriet would rather

280

do something else, you know what your father said. Everyone must be allowed to try to cope with what's happened in their own way.'

'Papa will need us all there,' Henry insisted.

'No, Henry.' Grace was quite firm, as firm as Lord Lydiard had been when the matter had first been raised on the journey back from Ireland, when it had become obvious that Harriet's way of dealing with the loss of her mother was by retreating into near total silence.

'For goodness sake!' Henry said with barely contained fury before walking off. 'Don't you understand, Harriet? *It wasn't your fault!*'

Harriet walked off in the other direction.

'Harriet?' Grace said as she caught her up. 'Harriet darling, where are you going?'

The child didn't answer. She just turned to stare at Grace before disappearing into the library.

Grace knew the best thing was to leave her alone, but she was so worried by the change in Harriet that she kept fussing the child, which only made her worse. If Grace tried to talk to her, Harriet walked away. She wouldn't eat, she didn't sleep, and if Grace tried to comfort her, Harriet shook her off as if she was a bothersome pest. Worst of all was what had happened to Harriet and Henry's relationship. Before their mother had died, Grace had never heard them quarrel, at least never seriously. They sometimes disagreed, and whenever they did they argued good-naturedly. Henry was very much the protective elder brother, and Harriet the adoring and admiring younger sister. Now however not even her brother could comfort her in her sorrow, and because he felt helpless Henry had become angry, angry with his sister because she blamed herself for the death of their mother, angry with Grace because she couldn't make Harriet see sense, and angry most of all with a world that had taken his beloved mother from him.

Fortunately he clung on to his father, and even more fortunately his father embraced him. Grace had feared that the loss of his wife might make Lord Lydiard even more introspective and reserved, but Henry's passionate attachment to him and his fierce dependence on him meant that Lord Lydiard had little time for introversion. Since the loss of a wife and a mother, Lord Lydiard and Henry had ceased being father and child and had become father and son.

As for Grace, rather than being uncertain of her future as might have been expected, instead she found that she was surprisingly confident. Knowing that all sorts and sizes of problems lay ahead and having only the vaguest inkling of what they might be and how she might cope with them didn't deter her in the least because she knew she now had a purpose, which was to look after her charges and prepare them for their maturity. While Lady Lydiard was alive Grace could have been replaced at any time and for any reason, on a whim or quite purposefully. It might not have been very likely but it was still perfectly possible. Anything could have happened. Grace herself might have grown dissatisfied and left to take up another post; her mother's condition might have worsened, forcing Grace to sacrifice her position in order to return home to nurse her; the children might have grown tired of her and demanded a new nanny, again unlikely but again still possible.

Or she could have left as she had been just about to in order to marry Brake Merrowby.

He was standing there, right by the drawing room doorway, glass of whisky in one hand and a cigar in the other, as Grace made her way back from the library. He had his shoulders up against the architrave, pensively smoking and watching the blue smoke as it curled up above him. Grace turned, back the way she had come, hoping that he hadn't seen her because she knew this wasn't the time or place for them to talk, for their first exchange of words since she had left for Ireland, gone the same night that Brake had threatened to throw himself off the train if Grace didn't agree to marry him.

But he had seen her, because Grace heard her name being called out after her.

'Grace!'

She didn't turn, just kept heading down the long corridor.

'Nanny!'

It was louder now, almost a command. Grace stopped and turned back and saw Brake in the doorway, steadying himself with one hand against the frame. Now he was fully in the light Grace could see he looked dreadful. He was unshaven, his hair was dirty and unbrushed, his clothes appeared to have been slept in and even from where she stood Grace could see how red his eyes were. He was also even more obviously drunk.

'Please,' he said slowly. 'I have to talk to you.'

A woman appeared at his side, a tall woman dressed in black as all the women were, a woman who should have been beautiful had her eyes not been too small and her mouth too thin-lipped. By now Grace knew her of old, since she was one of the most regular guests at Keston and still one of the most disapproving. Brake knew her as well, although he was paying her no attention, because the woman now taking his arm was Cicely Rokeham, Lord Lydiard's sister-in-law, the woman into whose bedroom Brake had burst that infamous night.

All seemed now forgiven as she turned the artist back towards her with a smile.

'I simply cannot imagine what you of all people would need to talk to Nanny about, Brake,' she said. 'Now come back in here because there's someone you must meet.'

'Let go of me, will you?' Brake sighed. 'I have to talk to Nanny here.' He shook himself free, but at once Cicely Rokeham caught hold of him again.

'You must come and meet the Earl of Hungerford,' she instructed him. 'He wants a portrait done of his wife who's extravagantly pretty and frightfully stupid, and he'll pay you very handsomely. So do come along.'

Brake stood his ground, staring drunkenly at Grace. Cicely Rokeham now stared at Grace as well, but in a totally different way.

'And you, Nanny, you may go,' she said icily, before

turning Brake away from Grace and leading him back into the drawing room.

Henry handed her the note at teatime.

'Mr Merrowby said could I give you this,' he told Grace, holding out a folded white envelope. 'You know, the painter. The man who owns the Talbot.'

Grace calmly thanked Henry, slipping the note into the pocket of her uniform before sitting down with Harriet and Dora at the table.

'Mr Merrowby got very drunk at the reception,' Henry announced, carefully cutting open his scone. 'Papa finally locked him in his study, and he went to sleep.'

'I don't think that's any of our business, Henry, do you?' Grace said. 'And don't take *all* the strawberries out of the jam.'

'Why has he written you a note?' Henry asked. 'Why didn't he just tell me what he wanted to say?'

'And that's none of *your* business, Henry,' Grace replied, rescuing the jam and passing it to Harriet. 'It's probably to do with the painting. He still hasn't finished the painting he was doing of your baby brother.'

'And you,' Harriet said without looking up.

'That's right, Harriet,' Grace agreed. 'And me. And Beanie.'

'The one Mama wanted him to do.'

Grace looked quickly at Harriet, who was sitting with her hands in her lap, staring down at the table beyond her plate.

'I didn't know that,' Grace confessed. 'That your mother wanted the painting done.'

'Well she did,' Harriet replied, still not looking up.

'If you don't want your scone, Miss Harriet,' Dora began.

Harriet pushed her plate sideways to Dora who took the uneaten bun.

'I don't want any tea, thank you,' Harriet said. 'May I get down, please?'

'No you may not,' Grace said. 'If you don't want

284

to eat you must wait until those who do have finished.'

'Not today, surely?' Harriet now looked at Grace, her eyes ringed with darkness. 'I don't know how any of you can eat today.'

She was down from the table and out of the room before Grace could stop her.

'Harriet?' Henry called after her. 'Harriet – you heard what Nanny said!'

In reply, Harriet slammed shut her bedroom door on them all.

'Leave her alone, Henry,' Grace said. 'Remember what your father said.'

Now it was Henry's turn to push his plate aside.

'Actually I don't think I feel like any tea either, thank you, Nanny. May I get down?'

'Yes,' Grace agreed reluctantly. 'Very well, Henry.'

Henry got up and went and sat on the old sofa, picking a book up on his way, leaving Grace to feed Boy fingers of bread and egg, and Dora to feed her face with the pile of unwanted scones.

Meanwhile the note was burning a hole in Grace's pocket.

Meet me in the summerhouse at midnight. B.

It was just one line, scrawled hastily in an artist's soft-leaded pencil, a note which Grace finally got to read once everyone was bathed, changed and put to bed. By then it was only just after eight o'clock, but even so after such a long and harrowing day Grace herself would have been more than happy to have gone to bed with her book and a glass of warm milk and honey.

Instead she sat up with her book and a pot of strong tea, and waited for midnight, knowing she must keep the rendezvous but curious as to how she was meant to have responded if she had found the time and the place unsuitable. Knowing Brake she'd have to have sent a message back down with Henry, Grace thought as she opened her well thumbed copy of *The Pickwick Papers* at a beautiful hand-painted bookmark which Harriet had made her, and she sighed. She sighed at Brake's whimsicality, but she sighed even more as she wondered how exactly she was going to tell him.

The rain had stopped and there was now a bright moon in a sky full of scudding clouds. As she approached the summerhouse Grace could smell cigar smoke on the night air so she knew he was there.

He was sitting on a deck chair in the corner, among the bric-à-brac, the croquet hoops and mallets, rolls of spare netting, cricket stumps and bats, and the heap of visitors' tennis racquets.

'You got my note then?' he asked, getting up.

'I would hardly be here if I hadn't,' Grace replied.

'That was a rhetorical question,' he said irritably as he got up. 'Asked for effect. Not to elicit information.'

Grace was relieved when he suggested that since it was a fine night they should walk, because she had sensed his mood even before he spoke, and was afraid she might not be able to deal very well with him were they to remain in the dark confines of the summerhouse. Instead they walked away from the Hall, out of its long shadow cast by the shifting moonlight, up the steep top lawn down which Henry and Harriet loved to tumble, down the other side and then along the tree-lined path that ran along the edge of the lake. Night birds called out across the dark waters, and as they passed a large laurel bush some unseen creature slipped from under its branches down the bank and away into the depths.

They said nothing to each other until they reached the Chinese bridge at the top end of the lake. Brake stopped halfway across it, drew on his cigar for the last time and then dropped it into the still waters below.

'You realize things have changed, Grace, don't you?' he asked, putting his hands on the rails and staring at the night.

'Is that another rhetorical question, Brake?' she asked. 'For effect and not for information?'

'I don't think you understand, Grace,' Brake replied darkly, leaning further forward and looking directly down into the water. 'I don't think you understand at all.'

'What I understand is that a circumstance such as this—' Grace began.

'A circumstance?' Brake stood up and wheeled round, grabbing Grace by the arms. 'A power passes from the earth and you call it *a circumstance*? Is that what you call death in the nursery, Nanny? *A circumstance*? As if it was some sort of formality?'

He walked away from her, his feet clattering on the planks before he jumped off the end of the bridge and began to head off down the far side of the lake. Grace hesitated, unsure of whether or not there was any point in following Brake when he was in one of his despairs, but then when she remembered how when he was at his most belligerent Brake was generally at his most vulnerable she knew she could not leave him.

He was lying out at full stretch on his back when she reached him, a huge dark cross on the night blue of the grass.

'You'll get your death of cold if you don't get up,' she said. 'That grass is soaking wet.'

'Yes, Nanny,' he sighed, first covering his face with both hands and then getting to his feet. 'You must forgive me, Grace,' he said, taking her hand. 'I'm very drunk.'

'There's nothing to forgive,' she replied. 'I only wish I could get drunk.'

'That's better!' He turned to her as they began to walk. 'Sometimes when you're so – so *restrained*, sometimes you don't seem to be human.'

'And sometimes when you're so boorish you're not very human either,' she replied.

'*Touché*,' he said. He stopped and turned to her, taking hold of both her hands. 'Grace, you do know because of what's happened, you do know that I can't marry you.'

'That's not even a question, Brake,' she said quietly, after only the barest intake of breath. 'That's a statement of fact, isn't it?'

She had felt alone before, but never as she did now.

'I can't, Grace.' He was looking her in the eyes,

287

intensely, gripping her hands as hard as he was staring at her. 'You have to understand—'

'Do I?' she asked. 'I have to understand?'

'Yes, Grace! If you love me!' He was almost shouting now, loud enough for his voice to echo across the lake, loud enough for it to frighten some birds in the reeds who crashed away into the night, their wings first flapping on the water as they fled.

'You're not making any sense,' Grace said quietly, wishing he would ease his grip on her hands. 'Try to explain what you mean.'

'What I mean?' he wondered. 'What I mean. What in hell do any of us *mean*?' He let go of her, and walked ahead again, still talking. 'When I heard the news it was bad enough,' she heard him say as she reluctantly caught up with him, while secretly wishing herself a million miles away. 'When I heard what had happened – when I heard she was dead – I knew then I'd been lying! To myself! To you! I knew it – and then when I saw her in her grave – *oh, God*, I nearly asked them to bury me there with her – to bury me alive by her side – that's all I wanted. I loved her so much!'

She was in his arms now. He had grabbed her to him and he was holding her with both his arms around her while he sobbed, and Grace found she could do nothing. She had never heard a grown man cry before. It was somehow shocking. But even if she had known how to begin to comfort him she couldn't have because she was held fast in his arms, trapped in an embrace that locked her to his shuddering frame. And still she wished herself a million miles away from him. Safe from the tidal force of his emotions, and her own.

She was desperate to try to think of something to say to him, but all she could think of were nursery bromides, meaningless *there-theres* designed to soothe away the pain of small bruises and minor cuts, but not to console the despair of grief or mitigate the agony of loss. It was as she was trying to find some words to say to him that the reality of it all descended on her, as she remembered the mistress of Keston, with her newborn baby in her arms, then holding Boy aloft on his second birthday, turning him round and round and laughing while he gurgled in delight, then Henry and Harriet running across the lawn on either of her hands, while her pile of chestnut hair became unpinned and tumbled down, a great mane of hair which all at once was like a girl's, which all at once made Lady Lydiard look like a girl, kicking her shoes off to run barefoot on the grass, then the games of tennis, the elegance of her game and the sheer ferocity of it, images of her white upper teeth embedded in her lower lip as she backhanded the ball past her opponent, or reached up for a smash, her grace about the court, and her nonchalance as she lay on the grass between games, sucking sugar lumps soaked in brandy, her impetuosity, the rushing stuttering tumble of her speech, her beauty, her eggshell skin, her pale green eyes, her perfect figure, and her laugh, the laugh Harriet had heard behind her, the last laugh she gave, a wonderful infectious sound.

Happily for them both Brake let go of her, and having bathed his face in the lake he turned to her in his usual impetuous way and demanded her company.

'Let's walk some more,' he said, pulling his coat around him and extending a hand to her. 'I haven't finished yet.' He went to take her hand, but Grace evaded such intimacy, preferring instead to slip her hand into his arm, and walk decorously beside him, beginning what she knew would have to be an increasing separation.

'It has to be perfectly possible to love two women,' he said. 'Two women, three women, who knows – ten women perhaps. By this I mean that when I said I loved you, I did, Grace. And I still do. But where I was wrong, where I lied was that I thought I didn't love *her* any more. While all I had done was talk myself out of it, or think that I'd talked myself out of it. It's relatively easy, you know, when you don't see someone. To kid yourself that you really don't love them any more.'

'I know,' Grace said, almost to herself.

'You'd be surprised how easy it is,' Brake continued,

without picking up. 'Then when you see each other, when you do see that other person again—' He fell to silence, walking on and staring at the ground in front of him. 'You know, I never knew pain like this,' he said, very factually. 'Not until today. Not until I stood by her grave.'

'I know,' Grace said. 'I think I understand.'

'That's why I can't marry you, Grace. Not because I still love Serena, or because I don't love you, but because I love you both.'

'I see,' Grace replied. 'It's very much the same as why I can't marry you, Brake.'

'What do you mean?' Brake stopped again, turning to her alarmed and fascinated at one and the same time. 'You can't marry me?'

'I can't,' Grace told him. 'Even if you had still wanted to, even if you had been free to – I couldn't have married you, not because I don't love you, but because I love the children more.'

'That just isn't possible!'

'It's perfectly possible, Brake. Not only that, but they need me more than you need me.'

'Sure! Which is why you love them, Grace. *Because they need you!*'

'No, Brake.' Grace was quite firm. She knew what she felt, why she felt it, and how she had arrived at her decision, and none of Brake's pugnacity could shake her belief. 'I love them more not because they need me, but because I think about them even more than I think of myself, even more than I think of you, or you and me. I couldn't have deserted them even before they lost their mother. But now—' Grace shook her head, almost proud, shoring up her crumbling pride. 'Nothing can take me away from them now, Brake,' she said. 'I'm afraid not even you.'

They walked on further, even longer this time without saying anything.

'Supposing,' Brake said at last. 'Supposing it was possible for us to marry and you still to have charge of the children . . . ?'

'That wouldn't be possible,' Grace said, looking at the moon reflected in the water of the lake. 'If I married you I would want your children. You can't have two families, Brake, it's just not possible.'

They had reached the end of the walk, back at the top of the upper lawns. Below them the Great House slept in its sorrow, while the moon hid its face in the clouds.

'But if it was possible—' Brake asked quietly from behind her.

'But it isn't, Brake,' Grace replied. 'There's no point in saying *if*.'

'Grace – you can't just stop loving someone,' he protested. 'Not just like that. In favour of someone else's children.'

'Not in favour, no,' Grace agreed. 'I can't stop loving you, but I can stop thinking about you.' Grace wanted so much to turn back to him, to look closely on his face once more and watch the expressions in his eyes, but she knew she didn't dare. 'And now that I know we are not to be married, I know I must.'

Brake said after a moment, 'Don't think I shall ever stop loving you, Grace, because I won't. Never. Not for a moment.'

'Oh, I think you will, Brake,' Grace said, keeping her eyes firmly focused on the house below her. 'I hope you will.'

'And you?' he whispered. 'Will you stop loving me?'

'I shall have to, Brake,' she replied. 'I must.'

He put both his hands on her waist. 'If only things had been different,' he sighed, so close to her now.

'But they aren't, Brake, they weren't.' Grace tried to ease herself from his hold, from the way his hands seemed to burn through her clothes.

'We could still be lovers, Grace.'

'No, Brake.'

'Yes, Grace. We should be lovers, just once, you and I.' His mouth was by her ear, in her hair, his breath was on her cheek, and his hands were holding her more tightly by her waist as he began to turn her to him. 'One kiss and then tell me,' he whispered, 'just one and tell me then we weren't born to love each other.'

She broke free just in time and swung away from him, running off into the night without another word, off down the rolling grass bank, on to the flat of the top lawn and on, on down the flight of stone steps which connected the two levels, turning past the stone urns full of trailing flowers at the bottom, across the velvet croquet lawn and finally out under a pergola covered with still fragrant musk roses. Noiseless bats winged past her while somewhere in the distance the night owl whooped as Grace ran on, her skirts held up in front of her, footsure and never once looking back to where she knew he was, high above her, silently silhouetted against the cerulean sky.

She ran into the side door she had left open, and all the way up the service stairs until she reached the passage which connected with the back stairs to the nurseries. She ran up these too, until she was half a dozen from the very top, where at last she stopped to catch her spent breath. The moon was out again, casting its clear cold light through the rose window at the end of the passageway, and as Grace climbed the very last stairs she heard the baby crying.

Such was the tenor of his howls Grace knew he must have been crying for some time as she hurried past the still senseless Dora, whose cormorant snores sounded roundly through her half-open door, and on into Boy's bedroom. The child was standing holding one side of his cot, which from the way he was rattling it he intended to shake to pieces.

'There,' Grace said, hurrying to him at once. 'It's all right, darling, no need to cry now.'

As soon as the child saw her and heard her he stretched his small arms above him to be lifted up.

'There then, sweetheart,' Grace whispered, lifting the hot-cheeked infant into her arms. She cuddled him to her, smelling the warmth, the scent of soaped and powdered baby skin, and as she hugged him he stopped crying, instead feeling the soft face that was now kissing him better with stubs of pink fingers, little hands which squeezed Grace's cheeks and pulled at her lips.

'It's all right, my darling, it's all right.' Grace kissed him some more, gently on his baby cheeks. 'No need for any more tears,' she whispered. 'Not ever ever any more. Nanny's here.'

FIFTEEN

For the next week Grace saw Brake every day. She saw him more regularly than she had seen him over the whole of the past year, yet she didn't speak to him once. She didn't speak to him until the eighth day and then it was only by chance, certainly not design.

Parker was driving Grace back from Eton where she had left Henry to start the Michaelmas term, a routine which had been repeated since the first traumatic but successful expedition exactly one year before. They had just driven through the village of Lower Tatling which lay approximately ten miles to the south-east of Keston when they passed a familiar blood red Talbot sports abandoned on the verge. Two miles further up the road Grace could see a tall dark-coated figure walking dejectedly up a steep hill ahead of them. Before she could unclip the speaking tube to instruct Parker, he had started to slow the Rolls up, having obviously reached the same conclusion as his passenger.

'It's Mr Merrowby, I reckon, Nanny,' he said, sliding the dividing window open behind his head. 'I dare say from the look of things he could do with a lift.'

Brake hesitated for a moment when he saw who was sitting in the back of the Silver Ghost and then climbed in as Grace smiled politely and made room for him.

294

'Of all the good fortune,' Brake said, as he settled in the corner behind the chauffeur.

'Indeed,' Grace replied. 'You were still a long way from home.'

'Would you believe the luck?' Brake asked the question away from Grace, watching the countryside pass by his window. 'I got not one flat tyre, but two.'

'I suppose you were driving too fast as usual,' Grace said, also staring out of her window.

'I really don't know what I was doing,' Brake replied.

'No, I don't suppose you did,' Grace agreed. 'But then that wouldn't be at all unusual.'

'I don't get the innuendo.' Brake was looking at her now, she could feel it, just as she could guess his expression, one of very definite mockery, eyebrows slightly raised and dark eyes widened deliberately for effect.

'Exactly how long do you intend staying on at Keston?' she asked, now turning to him, looking at him as coolly as she could, the very opposite of how she was feeling. 'Word has it you've been asked to stay indefinitely.'

'Word has it?' Brake nodded. 'Is that right?'

'Mr Harcross overheard you and Lord Lydiard arguing.'

'We weren't arguing. I was maybe just a little drunk.'

'You seem to be a little drunk most days, so I hear. And most nights.'

'Tut tut, Nanny,' he said, shaking a finger. 'We mustn't be rude to the guests.'

'Brake,' Grace said in a tone of voice quite different from any Brake had heard her use before, 'I want to know how long you intend staying at Keston—'

'I was going to tell you, Grace,' he said quickly.

'I want to know how long, Brake,' Grace persisted, 'but above all I want to know *why*.'

She had taken the precaution of reclosing the window between Parker's compartment and the back, but something must have got through to the chauffeur because Grace saw him look upwards and half over his shoulder.

'And keep it conversational,' she said, mock-smiling. 'After all, it wouldn't do to have the staff gossiping.'

There was a long silence while Brake went back to staring out of the window.

'Actually I don't think you'd understand,' he said finally.

'Why not?'

'It's an artistic matter. And you're not an artist.'

Grace bit her tongue, and to help contain herself began to rummage in her reticule, searching for nothing in particular.

'If you explain it simply,' she said, between almost clenched teeth, 'I might be able to follow.'

'Perhaps.'

'And if I don't, there's no harm done.'

'Even so.' Brake paused, rubbing his rough chin with the flat of his right hand. 'Artists take a terrible risk talking about art, you know,' he said. 'As soon as you begin trying to explain what your problems are to ordinary people, you can see it in their eyes. They think you should be locked up.'

'This ordinary person will try to be a little more sympathetic,' Grace assured him, doing her level best to keep any sarcasm from her voice. 'I'm listening.'

Brake looked out of his window some more, idly playing with the tasselled strap which hung by his hand. Then he turned to her, settling himself back in his corner, as if he was about to tell her a story.

'I don't want to do any more portraits,' he said. 'It's as simple as that.'

'Then don't,' Grace replied.

'I have no money, Grace. Every penny I earn, I spend. I spend an awful lot I don't earn as well, as maybe you can imagine. So.' Brake sighed. 'If I don't paint portraits, I don't earn my living,' he continued. 'And that's too awful for words, because I like to travel. I like to gamble. I like to eat and drink. And buy beautiful clothes for beautiful women.'

Their eyes met and held. The beautiful outfit he had bought her hung in her wardrobe next to her spare uniforms, unworn since that day.

'There are all sorts of things happening in the world of art, Grace. Things you won't know about, things you wouldn't understand. And I want to be part of it, I want to be involved. Not in the *avant-garde*. I'm no Vorticist, or Futurist or even Cubist – but I'm fascinated by what they call Post-Impressionists. These artists are making statements, about how they feel. Which is what I want to try and do. I want to tap the emotions, Grace, I want to paint from the heart, you see. From my heart. I don't want to spend the rest of my life painting pretty pictures of pretty women to order. I want to break away like the paint-ers are doing in France! I want to stop being judicious, and I want to startle! It's so hard to explain, and I don't expect you to understand. Why should you? It sounds like crazy talk. But if you knew anything about painting. If you did and if you'd been with me last time I was in Paris, and seen what I'd seen. The courage, and the brilliance, the use of colour – they're not *afraid* of colour, you see! The colours leap out at you, as if they'd been freshly invented! Combinations of colours that would make the previous generation of painters blush! Pinks and reds, oranges, turquoise, green! It's as if they're reinventing nature, as if they're physically grappling with their subjects, and as if by doing so they'll get closer to them. That's what I want to try and do, Grace. I want to connect. I want to try and communicate my excitement, the excitement I have with life.'

Grace had felt the wind leaving her sails, felt the blow in the plexus of her soul as soon as he had opened the conversation, as soon as he had told her it was an artistic matter, and so therefore one she wouldn't understand. But she held her tongue and stayed lying low, digging her fingernails deep into the palms of her tightly clenched hands, while she sat and listened to him telling her things he thought she wouldn't understand because he thought she knew nothing about painting, that she was a philistine. If she did know something about painting (and was there regret in his voice as he'd said it?) *if she did and if only she'd been with him when he was in Paris last . . . If only,*

Grace thought, if only then or if only when he was in Paris next, if only if only. If only she had said yes the first time he had asked her to marry him, if only she hadn't been so dogmatic, so self-righteous. *I would hate you to marry me because you felt you had to. People should only get married if they want to.* If she had said yes then which she should have done, because that was what her heart was saying, then everything in the world might have been different. If she had said yes and not no to Brake on the steps of the bridge in Oxford, the rhythm of life might have been universally altered, and a horse on a far distant beach in the south of Ireland might not have stumbled and thrown its rider. Lady Lydiard would still be alive and Grace might now be engaged to be married to the man by her side.

No, Grace thought, shutting herself off from the rest of Brake's passionate declarations, no, it was worse than that, something Grace had known from the day of the accident. What was far, far worse was that she knew she was directly responsible for Lady Lydiard's death. The truth was she had agreed to stay behind in England not because Boy was teething, but because she wanted to be with Brake. Grace had used Boy as an excuse. When Lady Lydiard had expressed some concern over her youngest son's welfare, and wondered aloud whether or not the journey and the holiday might actually be the best thing for a teething toddler, although never for a moment directly suggesting that they should stay behind, Grace had been only too happy to let the idea take root and germinate.

'Yes, what a good idea!' Lady Lydiard had finally enthused, after much arguing with herself. 'By staying behind because of course baby Boy's really too small, don't you think, Nanny? To enjoy a holiday as it were and particularly if his little teeth are hurting him, poor little small. No, I think it's a very good idea, absolutely. For you both to stay put because that way you can have a bit of a holiday too, Nanny dear. Which you certainly won't get if you have to struggle over to Ireland with all of us lot and this fractious little fellow here.'

So Grace had stayed behind, and just as she thought,

and feared, and hoped might happen, Brake had proposed to her, a proposal which Grace had known full well was something she could not accept. Whereas if she'd done as she should and not as she wanted, she would have gone to Ireland with the family, and the whole pattern of events would have been different. Harriet and Henry and their mother might not have gone riding that day at all, or if they still had they would certainly have left the house at a different time because everything would have been different with Grace there, with one more person present, and even if they had raced that day on the sands, the horses would not have run the same route. They would have started out at a different place in the sands, it might even have been a matter of only a foot or so, an inch maybe or two, the precise difference didn't matter. What mattered was that the pattern of the day would not have been the same, it couldn't have been the same, and because of that the horses would have run a different route, Lady Lydiard's horse would have missed the hole, it wouldn't have stumbled, she wouldn't have been thrown, Lady Lydiard would still be alive, and Grace wouldn't be sitting here next to Brake trying to pretend she knew nothing about what he was saying to her, and doing her very best to conceal the fact that the more passionately he talked the more passionately she wanted to take back everything she had said and run off with him that very moment to Paris.

There was a moment, one moment as the car slowed down on the road approaching Keston, as she found Brake staring at her with all his old, familiar and burning intensity that Grace nearly weakened.

But then Brake sighed and looked away out of his window.

'You haven't understood one word I've been saying,' he said. 'You're looking at me as if I'm mad.'

'I'm looking at you—' Grace began and then petered out.

'Yes?'

But the moment had gone.

'You're looking at me as if I'm mad,' Brake repeated.

'I told you. Ordinary people think artists are *loco*.'

'I was looking at you like that,' Grace countered, just managing to contain her anger, 'because I was wondering how you were going to achieve your ambition of experimenting with your style and "communicating your excitement" by remaining here at Keston. After all, what could be more staid and sedate than life in an English country house?'

Brake looked at her without replying for a moment.

'Lord Lydiard is going to be my benefactor,' he announced. 'He's going to pay me a certain amount of money a year so that I can work exactly how I want to work.'

'And in return?'

'Nothing.' Brake shook his head, bemused. 'I keep him company. He needs company right now, and I guess so do I.'

Yes, and what about me? Grace nearly asked as the car turned into the drive, past tall stone pillars topped with carved falcons. *What am I meant to do? Seeing you every day yet not being able to see you. Knowing that you're here but that you're here not for me but for yourself and your patron, a man who wants you there for the same reason, the real reason why you want to be at Keston, to help mourn the loss of his dead wife.*

'There's no problem,' Brake said as the car drew up, somehow pre-guessing Grace's worry. 'I won't get under your feet.'

But it wasn't her feet Grace was concerned about as she sat tired and lonely in her sitting room up under the roof, it was the state of her poor old heart.

SIXTEEN

It was odd, to look out of the window and see him there, his easel set up on the terrace when the weather was still fair, or in the conservatory once autumn began to turn to winter, or to glimpse him the other side of the park when Grace was out walking Boy, his hands sunk deep in the pockets of his great black coat, his collar turned up against the wind, wandering along with his chin on his chest trailing a thin vapour of cigar smoke behind him. He never seemed to see her, at least he never gave any sign of seeing her, never looking in her direction, not even when Beanie would chase a rabbit barking loudly and excitedly, not even once when they passed within feet of each other.

On that occasion Grace guessed he had seen her because by the time their paths crossed Brake had taken a book from his coat and was holding it up to his face, reading it closely as they passed each other by, she pushing Boy in his baby carriage, Brake Merrowby behind his book. Had Harriet been with her it would have been different. Harriet would have approached him and Brake would have had to have noticed and talked to her, and by doing so would have had to talk to Grace. But Harriet never came out on walks any more. Harriet didn't do anything any more. Harriet stayed inside the house, cocooned in silence.

It was in fact Harriet's mutism that helped Grace

through what might otherwise have proved to be an impossible time, that and the disorder which was gradually becoming manifest in Europe. Had all the circumstances been more normal, had Harriet shown signs of recovering from her grief and had the world not seemed to be on the brink of war, then Grace might have had too much time to concentrate on the bizarre circumstances of her own existence. But because Harriet seemed to be slowly withdrawing into silence, while the world outside their windows seemed about to explode into chaos, once Grace had recovered from the initial shock of Brake's being part of the fabric of her daily life without as it were being any real part of it, she gradually became too absorbed in Harriet's problems and too concerned with what might be about to happen in the outside world to indulge herself in her own somewhat less significant unease.

It also helped that no one else really saw things the way Grace did either, no one that is with whom she had any direct and constant contact. Dora was totally uninterested in the state of both Harriet and the world outside. According to Dora Harriet would soon 'snap out of it, 'specially if she knows what's good for 'er', and the same went for Europe.

'My dad don't 'old with foreeners,' she'd say whenever the subject arose at table. 'My dad say we should send the army and navy over there and teach 'em Germans oo's 'oo and what's what, that's what 'e say. Afore it's too late, an' afore they gets any fancy notions.'

There was little more sense made of the state of the world downstairs in the kitchen or the servants' hall, either. Not that any of her former colleagues was prepared to spend much time with Grace any more, even though since Lady Lydiard's death Grace had tried to spend more time with them, because through no fault of their own or Grace's but simply because of the system of which they were all a part, over the past two and a half years Grace had gradually ceased to be one of their number and had become Nanny, and Nanny to them was a member of another and superior household echelon, and therefore not necessarily any longer on their side.

Cook was the least resistant to the changes, and whenever she had the time would find a moment to sit down and have a cup of tea and a gossip with Grace. The trouble was that Cook was more interested in sounding off, as Mr Harcross called it, than in finding a real cure for any ills, so every time Grace brought up the subject of Harriet back would come a set of answers similar to Dora's.

'It's only a phrase, Grace,' Cook had malapropped the last time Grace had broached the subject. 'It's only natural the girl's upset, but it's only a phrase. You mark my words, my girl, what's best left is soonest mended. Dogs and children never starve themselves, and the more attention you give them the more trouble they cause.'

Added to that Grace's trouble was that she was too kind, she fussed too much, and that she'd long forgotten the efficacy of a good slap administered at the right time and place. So none the wiser and considerably sadder, Grace had once more climbed the long haul back up to the nursery, to end her day sewing and mending with only the perpetually sniffing Dora for company.

This was the time of day Grace always felt most alone, detached from the activity of the house and with no one to whom she could discuss anything of real interest. Since falling in love with Brake, and since their separation, these evening hours had become even more desolating, particularly since Grace knew he was somewhere in the house, pacing the library or the drawing room and talking about the things which interested not only him but her too, the unending fascination of colour, of trying to reshape nature, of seeing with the heart, while she sat trapped in a room under the roof mending the children's clothes and half-listening yet again to Dora's ill-determined plans to escape somehow from her servitude to find fame in the music halls.

So it was little wonder that Harriet's disorder perversely was the saving of Grace's reason. She had never seen anyone, adult or child, change as much as Harriet did in the three months following the loss of her beloved mother. Harriet had gone from being a happy, carefree, beautiful and nicely plump twelve-year-old to a silent, heartbroken, and already painfully thin little girl who ate and drank hardly anything and who by the end of November had given up any attempts at communication whatsoever. The most Grace could get out of her now was a nod or a shake of the head and then only after repetitive questioning. Harriet no longer painted or drew, and flatly refused to go out of doors. After her lessons with Miss Chambers were over for the day, all she did was sit in the nursery reading or staring for hours out of the window across the rainswept park.

Her governess became as concerned as her nanny. Miss Chambers, who wasn't a resident but came in daily from the village once term had begun, became a frequent visitor to the nursery floor, retiring with Grace into her sitting room after teatime was over to discuss the ever increasing degeneration of Harriet's condition. According to her governess there seemed little point in trying to teach Harriet any longer because all the child did was sit in the classroom in silence, refusing to do both her class and her home work. At first she had still done her written work, albeit minimally, but now she just sat with her exercise books closed, staring at nothing in particular and deaf to all her teacher's remonstrances.

'You'll have to call Dr Granger in again, Nanny,' she advised one cold dark November evening as the two women sat warming themselves by Grace's fire. 'Get him to try her with another tonic. Some iron, or something. The child is just wasting away.'

'I don't think this is something the doctor can cure, Miss Chambers,' Grace replied. 'I think time is going to be the healer here, the worry being how to get her through the next six months, or year, or however long it's going to take.'

'Surely not that long?' Miss Chambers said with dismay. 'She's only a child, Nanny. Children are very resilient.

304

They get over these things very quickly, not like adults. No, no, Nanny, I'm sure that if you call in Dr Granger and if he can just get her eating again, and put her on some iron—'

'I think it's more than just grief, Miss Chambers,' Grace said. 'Harriet's a deeply sensitive child, and for some reason she's decided that she was to blame for her mother's accident. Of course she wasn't, not in any way, but she won't accept that, and consequently she's feeling guilty.'

'Guilty?' Miss Chambers' expression now changed to one of total astonishment, as if Grace had said something vulgar. 'How can a child that age feel guilt, Nanny? This sounds like some of this latest Viennese nonsense.'

'I don't think it's nonsense, Miss Chambers.'

'Children have no idea of guilt, Nanny. They know what is right and what is wrong, and if they have done something of which they should be *ashamed*. But they know nothing of guilt. Guilt is a purely adult emotion.'

'I'm afraid I must disagree with you, Miss Chambers,' Grace replied, leaning forward to heap some more coal on the fire. 'According to a friend of mine' – *Brake on one of their long sunny August walks* – 'who admittedly had just been reading something by some Austrian neurologist—'

'That Sigmund Freud I should imagine,' Miss Chambers interrupted with a disapproving sniff.

Three Treatises on the Theory of Sex. Brake had the book in his pocket, and had taken it out to show it to her, saying that she mustn't be shocked, that this Viennese doctor's theories were going to change the whole nature of our thinking.

'The point is, Miss Chambers,' Grace continued, 'that some people now believe that what we feel and think, and how we behave, that all these things are controlled by unconscious wishes, and conflicts. And that if we don't resolve these conflicts or fulfil these unrealized wishes, that is the cause of our troubles.'

'Dangerous and indecent nonsense,' Miss Chambers said, making ready to leave. 'Mr Freud is a Jew, and Jews have some very peculiar notions.'

'They have some very brilliant ones,' Grace argued. 'I can see lots of good reasons to believe that the suppression of certain memories and the conflict between our conscious and unconscious minds could affect not only our behaviour but our health.'

Miss Chambers sat back in her chair once more, suddenly intrigued and so prepared to listen a little longer.

'Are you saying that Harriet's problems go deeper than just the loss of her mother?' she asked.

'I can't be sure of it,' Grace replied, 'and I probably have no right to suggest it. She was always such a very sweet child, so easy to be with and so willing to please. Yet there was always a sadness somewhere there, somewhere not very far away, as if any moment it might take over this gentle, loving little girl and turn her into a melancholic.'

'As she is now.'

'Just as she is now. I really don't know what, Miss Chambers. It's only a feeling, but it's as if something happened to her somewhere along the line, something or perhaps someone. Perhaps somebody said something to her once which somehow sowed the seeds of a guilt. I really don't know. I'm not nearly clever enough to understand these things.'

'Perhaps your friend can explain it,' Miss Chambers said, with a small tight smile.

'Unfortunately not,' Grace replied, returning the smile. 'It was only a casual association.'

'So you have no further theory as to who this person might be? The person who could have sowed your so-called seeds of guilt?'

'It could have been you,' Grace said evenly, 'or it could have been me.'

'I doubt very much if it could have been me,' Miss Chambers replied, adjusting the bun on the back of her grey hair. 'My job is to teach, not to waste time theorizing.'

'I think it's more likely to have been my predecessor.'

'Old Nanny Lydiard?'

'Yes.' Grace paused and stared into the fire. 'Either

her old nanny,' she said quietly, 'or perhaps her mother.'

On the following Monday during lunch, Harriet, who as usual hadn't touched her food, suddenly got up from the table and rushed from the room. Grace looked at Dora, only to be met with Dora's *don't-ask-me* shrug, and then followed Harriet out of the room to see where she'd gone. She was in the bathroom with the door bolted shut, being violently sick. Grace knocked urgently on the door but Harriet ignored her, refusing to let her in until she had finished vomiting.

'Are you all right, Harriet?' Grace asked as the white-faced child opened the door. 'What on earth can have made you sick?'

In reply Harriet just shrugged and wandered off to her bedroom.

Grace followed and tried to talk to her, but the child just lay face down on her bed and ignored her. Her pulse was perfectly normal, and she showed no signs of running a fever, so Grace pulled Harriet's eiderdown up over her and left her to sleep, coming back every half-hour and then every hour to make sure she was still all right.

On Thursday the same thing happened, except this time at tea. For some reason Grace had begun to suspect that Dora knew more than she was saying, but it was only a suspicion. As far as Dora admitted to knowing, Harriet hadn't eaten or drunk anything at all except the couple of mouthfuls they'd both seen her take at lunchtime. Yet once again Harriet suddenly got up and dashed from the room to be violently and extensively sick in the bathroom.

When Harriet got up from the table at Saturday teatime Grace was ready and got to the bathroom just ahead of Harriet, preventing her from locking herself in.

'If you're going to be sick again, darling,' she said, 'I'll hold your head.'

Harriet stood her ground by the open bathroom door, not moving and not saying anything, her eyes downcast.

'Harriet darling?' Grace tried to take the child's hands,

307

but Harriet quickly withdrew them, putting them behind her back.

'Harriet,' Grace repeated her offer slowly. 'If you're going to be sick, darling, I'll come in and hold your head.'

There was still no response.

'Are you going to be sick, Harriet?'

Harriet shook her head, without looking up.

'So what is it?' Grace asked. 'Why did you rush off from table to the bathroom if you're not going to be sick?'

The answer was a single shrug.

'Did you think you were going to be sick?' A nod. 'But you're not going to be sick now?' A shake of the head. 'Well if you're not going to be sick, darling, why don't you come back to the nursery and sit by the fire?'

Harriet looked at her once from under her blond fringe and then shrugged her acceptance. Grace knew better than to try to take her hand so she waited until Harriet had begun to walk off down the passage ahead of her and then followed. But as Grace opened the door of the nursery Harriet ducked under her arm and ran as fast as she could back to the bathroom, locking herself in with time to spare before Grace was halfway back down the corridor.

Grace pushed on the door with all her strength, trying to force it open, but the bolt, fixed to the door out of the reach of infants but well within the range of a twelve-year-old, was strong and held fast. Reckoning that she knew exactly what Harriet was up to but without yet knowing the reason why, Grace hammered as hard as she could on the door, hoping to frighten the child into opening it, but without success. When she stopped, Grace could hear Harriet retching, so she dropped to her knees, hoping to see the evidence she needed through the keyhole, only to find the opening had been solidly blocked with paper. Even so, from what she could hear Grace knew the child was being far sicker than could be justified by the tiny amounts of food she'd eaten in the past forty-eight or so hours.

'You're not goin' to call the doctor in then, Nanny?' Dora asked after both Boy and Harriet had been put to bed and the two of them were clearing up the nursery.

'No I'm not, Dora,' Grace replied. 'I don't think this is something for a doctor to solve. I think this is a case for detection. And an interesting enough one I'd say for Sherlock Holmes.'

'I don't know what you can mean, Nanny,' Dora said, avoiding Grace's long, cool look across the table they were clearing. 'If som'un's bein' sick, then surely 'tis the doctor you should be callin', not a detective like.'

'I'm not so sure, Dora,' Grace replied, folding the tablecloth and handing it to Dora to put away. 'After all, when it's a case of theft—'

The nursery maid stopped dead in her tracks, her back to Grace.

'Theft, Nanny?' she asked, her voice rising a tone. 'There's nothin' been stolen, 'as there?'

'I'll find that out as soon as I ask Cook,' Grace replied. 'Cook will soon tell me what's gone missing.'

Dora turned round to face Grace, the folded tablecloth still in her arms, her big round eyes slowly filling with tears.

'She made me swear not to say, Nanny,' she moaned. 'She made me promise on my life.'

'How long have you been feeding Miss Harriet, Dora?' Grace asked. 'The truth, mind.'

Dora put the tablecloth down to blow her nose, in a long sad trumpeting sound.

'She only started askin' a couple of weeks or so back,' she said. 'Miss Harriet asked me to bring what I could up from the kitchens like. When you was out walkin' Boy. Then she'd wolf it all down so I knew there was nothing wrong with her, see. I mean sick childrun don't eat like little pigs, do 'ey, Nanny?'

'It depends what they eat, Dora.'

'Miss Harriet'd eat 'alf a chocolate cake sometimes, Nanny. T'other day, Monday, weren't it? When she

309

was that sick? She ate 'alf a chocolate cake, two chicken drumsticks, three or four slices of beef, I don't know 'ow many scones, some sausages and two bowls of fruit salad. Oh yes, and three or four cream horns.'

'No wonder she was sick.'

'She's always sick, Nanny. You din't notice afore 'cos you was usually still out with Boy. Miss Harriet used to make me bring her food up then. But then I nearly got caught, see? So I had to choose my times more careful. When Cook was busy getting 'is lordship's lunch, when 'er back was turned. Which meant Miss Harriet was 'avin' 'er secret feast like just afore you come back, rather than as usual just when you'd gone out. Or while you was busy say givin' Boy 'is bath.'

'It's what I thought,' Grace said, more to herself. 'What I don't understand is why.'

'You won't say nothin', will you, Nanny? I don't want Miss Harriet thinkin' she can't trust me. That I betrayed 'er.'

'No, I won't say a thing, Dora,' Grace promised. 'And neither will you, nor will you bring one more illicit scrap of food up here, not if you know what's good for you. Not unless you've already been offered a part in one of Mr Edwardes' Gaiety shows.'

When Grace knelt to say her prayers that night she prayed for strength, that she might have enough resolve not to weaken and having chosen the toughest path sufficient determination not to waver from it. She knew she had to remain strong and resolute, because she knew it wouldn't be easy and there was a very real chance that the course on which she had determined might well jeopardize all the love, the trust and the friendship she and Harriet had between them.

She also knew it was the only way to stop the child from destroying herself.

The instructions to Cook were simple and clear. Everything that was sent up to the nursery had to be as appetizing as possible, and the tightest security had to be maintained in the kitchens at all times. In between meals the larders must be kept locked, and no food must be left around anywhere it could 'walk'. Grace knew Dora wouldn't dare break the embargo, but she thought that Harriet might, so having let Cook in on the secret, Grace stressed the importance of vigilance. If there was any way Harriet could break the siege, Grace knew the day would be lost and she would never discover the reason for Harriet's subterfuge.

Somehow Grace got through the first day, although how she did she never really knew. As soon as she removed the first plate of untouched crisp and succulent bacon, perfect fried eggs, homemade sausage and fried bread from in front of the silent Harriet and saw the sudden sad look the child gave her, Grace nearly threw the towel in there and then, because all at once she believed that Harriet knew, not what Grace was up to and why, but that things had changed, and because they had then Grace must be betraying her. It was a heart-stopping moment, and although Grace later told herself off for overreacting, and reminded herself that she was acting from the best possible motives, these private admonishments still did little to mitigate her private agony.

It was so cruel, and it was all there in her change of tone.

'If you're not going to eat that, Harriet,' she'd said, 'I'm not having you sitting here staring into space any more. If you don't want to eat, then there's no point in putting good food in front of you. You've got to stop feeling sorry for yourself, and just get on with it like everyone else.'

It was then that Harriet had looked up, her big corn-flower blue eyes searching Grace's dark brown ones, with a look on her thin pale face which was saying *am I hearing right? Are you really the same person?* while Grace ordered Dora to send the uneaten food straight back down to the kitchens, before banishing Harriet from the table to her desk under the window where she was set to read the first chapter of *Nicholas Nickleby* before being sent down for her first lesson of the day with Miss Chambers, and while Grace, Dora and Boy tucked into similarly appetizing breakfasts with undisguised enthusiasm.

This then was the strategy which Grace pursued remorselessly. All Harriet's favourite foods were set in front of her, only to be whisked away the moment Harriet professed indifference. She was given the chance to eat every course, lusciously thick broths, steaming golden-pastried pies, homemade tarts topped with whirls of fresh cream for lunch, freshly baked scones, eclairs, chocolate cake and cream horns for tea, then more steaming broths and stews for supper, but she was never given the time for them to go cold. Cook was appalled and grumbled constantly to Grace when she hurried down to the kitchens to thank Cook especially at the end of each day.

'You should do what old Nanny Lydiard used to do, my girl,' Cook would grouse. 'Make 'em sit there in front of their food until they bloomin' well eats it. And if they still don't eat it, put it back in front of 'em next meal.'

As far as this was concerned Grace was certain she knew better. If it seemed that she was punishing Harriet for not eating, as would appear to be the case if she kept rehashing the food she had left, then that would defeat her purpose because it would give Harriet good reason for not eating. It would also give her cause for complaint, not that Harriet had anyone to whom she could run and tell. Henry was still away at Eton and her father, who since the day of the funeral had been notably absent from the nursery floor, and who in the first few subsequent weeks had barely noticed when Grace brought the children down to wish him good night, was away somewhere now in Switzerland, walking the lower reaches of the Alps Grace heard, still in the deepest mourning, and not due home again until just before Christmas.

So Harriet had no one to run to, and no way of breaking the siege. If her refusal to eat really was a bluff then Grace was prepared to call it. If on the other hand Harriet was seriously intending to starve herself to death then under this new regime it would only be a matter of days before the truth of her intentions was revealed.

'Most like she's aping them suffragette women,' Dora volunteered on the morning of the third day after Harriet, still steadfastly refusing everything that was put in front of her and taking only water for nourishment, had been sent down for her lessons. 'Cook says they 'as to feed 'em in gaol with a funnel and tubes. Is 'at true, Nanny?'

'I'm afraid so, Dora,' Grace replied, 'and like a lot of people, men and women, I think it's a dreadfully wrong thing to do.'

'Yes, but then aren't you doin' the same sort of thing to Miss Harriet, Nanny?' Dora asked sly-eyed. 'Forcin' 'er not to eat, as 'twere?'

'No, Dora, not at all,' Grace replied. 'I'm seeing if what Miss Harriet says she wants to do and what she really does are one and the same thing. The forcible feeding of suffragettes in gaol isn't the same thing at all. That's doing something directly against someone's will. That's interfering with people's freedom.'

'If you say so, Nanny. It just seems that if Miss Harriet don't *want* to eat—'

'We don't make her, Dora. But then we don't think that's the case, do we? Otherwise why would she have asked you to smuggle food to her? Nor do I think she's doing it to gain attention, because that is just not in Miss Harriet's character. I don't know why she's doing it, but I think we stand a very good chance of discovering the reason this way. I think this way we're bound to flush it out.'

By the end of the fourth day of her stratagem, Grace was having the most severe doubts and was on the verge of conceding defeat. To her almost certain knowledge Harriet had eaten nothing at all since just before the last time she had been sick, the evening of the previous Saturday. It was now suppertime the following Wednesday and a hollow-eyed, white-faced, lank-haired Harriet was sitting mutely facing her untouched second course of boiled chicken breast on a bed of creamed potatoes. The tension was now such that even Dora's seemingly insatiable appetite had deserted her and the maid was sitting with her knife and fork upright in either hand, staring slack-jawed at the battle of wills which seemed just about to reach its climax in front of her.

'Are you quite sure you don't want to eat this, Harriet?' Grace asked for a second time, something she hadn't done since the beginning of the campaign. 'Cook made it specially for you.'

Harriet stared steadfastly back at Grace and shook her head. She remained looking at Grace as Dora removed the full plate to the dresser and while Grace began to try to eat her own helping. Watched steadfastly by a pair of blue eyes which seemed to be fast losing their brightness, Grace found the food sticking in her throat and after taking a couple of barely digested mouthfuls, she put her own knife and fork down and motioned for Dora to clear. None of them ate their helping of steamed pudding either. By the time they had said their grace and got up from table, it seemed the battle had been lost.

SEVENTEEN

As she did every night, once Harriet was in bed Grace sat and read to her, and as she did every night, Harriet turned her back on Grace and pulled the covers high over her head. Tonight, however, Grace read Harriet's bedtime story automatically, without any thought to the content, unable to get the image of Harriet's thin, haggard face and her deep sunken blue eyes circled in grey out of her mind. All at once she felt so foolish and so heartless, foolish because she had misread Harriet's strength of character so badly, so much so that she'd believed the child would give up within a day, and heartless because she herself had refused to admit defeat and as a consequence had caused the grieving child to suffer even more and needlessly. She wondered how she could ever have been thoughtless and arrogant enough to believe her ill-thought strategy would ever work, and as she did, she finally wondered by what right and by what conceit someone as inadequate as she had ever accepted so blithely the responsibility of bringing up someone else's children.

Just at that moment, just when Grace was about to put down her book and begin trying to explain to the child she had begun to think of as her own what she had been doing and why, Harriet began crying, huge and racking sobs half muffled beneath the blankets, big enough to shake the heavy bed, heartrending enough to bring Grace to her feet and the tears to her own eyes.

'Harriet?' she said, reaching out to the shape in the bed, putting her hands on the child's arched back, able to feel her emaciation even through all the blankets. 'Harriet darling, please talk to me, Harriet. Please say something.'

Suddenly the child's face was in front of hers, deformed with fury and anguish.

'Go away!' she screamed, grabbing and clawing at Grace's arms, spitting at her, seething with rage. 'Go away from me! I hate you! I hate you, do you hear! I hate you I hate you I hate you so *go away*!'

Grace was astounded, taken aback by the ferocity of the attack and by the sheer force of the child's anger. For a moment she simply didn't know what to do, whether to try to comfort the still sobbing child, or to sit back down and wait for the worst of the storm to blow over. The moment she decided on the first option she knew she was wrong as Harriet, summoning up the last of her strength, hurled herself out from under the bedclothes at Grace like a dervish, catching her hair and screaming hatred at her, tearing at her face with her fingernails and punching Grace's chest with tightly clenched fists.

Then as suddenly as the attack had started it was over, and Harriet fell back on to her bed exhausted, her eyes now red and rolling upwards under eyelids swollen by tears, her mouth half open, her skinny little body heaving for breath, her once beautiful blond hair a mat of lank tangled strands.

'Harriet?' Grace said carefully, afraid for a moment the child might have had a fit. 'Harriet darling? Are you all right?'

'Of course I'm all right,' Harriet replied thickly, numbly, her eyes fixed on the ceiling. 'Now please go away.'

Grace was still awake well after one o'clock even though Harriet had fallen into a deep fast sleep shortly after nine, a rest from which she hadn't awoken once according to the regular checks Grace carried out every quarter of an hour. The child's screams had brought Dora running to the bedroom, and it was Dora not Grace whom Harriet allowed to settle her down. Realizing the mistake she had made the first time, Grace retreated and left Dora to make sure Harriet fell asleep, waiting in the shadows of the corridor in case another crisis should arise, but after just over half an hour Dora re-emerged and told Grace Harriet had finally fallen asleep and had been that way for ten minutes.

At first Grace had wondered whether or not to call the doctor, but seeing the child still sound asleep after an hour, she thought there was little point until the morning, when she knew she would have to call him in to find out what to do about Harriet's continued hunger strike. Instead she decided that she and Dora should keep watch over Harriet until the night was through, and if during that time there was any cause for alarm then they would wake Parker and get him to drive Grace and Harriet to Dr Granger.

Grace was on watch from one o'clock until three, although the actual sharing of the vigil was purely academic since Grace knew she wouldn't be able to sleep for one moment until it was light once more. Even so, she must have dozed off for a minute or two because she heard or saw nothing until she was suddenly aware of a small figure standing by her bedside.

'I'm sorry to wake you, Nanny,' Harriet said. 'But I wondered if it would be possible to have something to eat?'

Not even Cook minded being woken at the unearthly hour of ten to two once she realized the patient was actually asking for food. When Grace first shook the overworked woman out of her well earned sleep, she expected to be roundly scolded and at the very least to receive one of Cook's renowned *didn't-I-tell-you-so?* diatribes. Instead once Grace had explained the situation Cook hurried out of her bed, ordering Grace to go and wait in the kitchen and while she was waiting to put on the kettle.

Dora and she had brought Harriet down to the kitchen with them, wrapped in several warm blankets. The kitchens were always the warmest place in the house, and if the child was going to eat it was only common sense to make sure she did so in the most comfortable surroundings. While Grace had been rousing Cook, Dora had rekindled the fire and sat Harriet by it in Cook's large wooden armchair.

Harriet said nothing, but at least she now smiled when any of them looked at her and talked to her. That was more than sufficient for Grace, who considered the only reason the child was now silent was because she was exhausted both physically and emotionally. Fortunately neither Cook nor Dora was the sort to press Harriet for explanations, perfectly content instead simply to fuss around her and spoil the little white-faced scarecrow huddled up in her swaddling of thick white woollen blankets. Cook had warmed up some clear chicken soup which Harriet sipped slowly from a toby mug, after which Grace instructed Dora to feed her the next course of coddled egg and fingers of soft buttered bread.

Harriet refused these with a slow shake of her head as Dora pulled her chair up alongside hers.

'No,' she said and Grace's heart sank. 'If you don't mind, Dora, I'd like Nanny to feed me.'

Dora didn't mind one bit, and Grace's heart stopped sinking and once more soared.

'What did I tell you, Nanny?' Cook whispered after she had served Harriet a slice of her favourite hot jam roll. 'I told you it was only a phrase.'

Dora carried the half-asleep child all the way back upstairs without one murmur of complaint, while Grace followed carrying a jug of hot milk chocolate. When they reached the nursery floor Harriet whispered to Dora to stop because she wanted to ask Grace something.

'What is it, darling?' Grace asked. 'Do you want me to read to you till you go to sleep, is that it?'

'No.' Harriet looked shyly at her over Dora's shoulder.

'I wondered if it would be all right if I could sleep in your bed tonight?'

She slept in Grace's arms all night long and into the morning without changing her position once, her cheek on Grace's breast, her left arm looped around her waist. Grace fought sleep for as long as she could, in case once she was asleep she moved or turned over and woke the child up. Finally she drifted off into a deep sleep, only to find when Dora woke her with her early morning cup of tea both she and Harriet were still in the selfsame positions, Grace on her back propped up by her pillows, with Harriet fast asleep across her.

'You stay right where you are, Nanny,' Dora whispered as she set down the tea. 'I'll get Boy up and give 'im 'is breakfast. We don't want nothin' upsettin' nor disturbin' Miss Harriet.'

'Thank you, Dora,' Grace whispered back. 'I think in the circumstances—'

She glanced down as Dora was doing at the child fast asleep in her arms, and she smiled, just as Dora was doing.

'Funny, in't it, Nanny?' Dora whispered, with a *sotto* sniff. 'Till somethin' like this 'appens, well. Takes somethin' like this to 'appen for a person to know 'ow they feels.'

'I know, Dora,' Grace agreed. 'I know exactly what you mean.'

'That's it. So blow the music halls,' Dora said before she went. 'There's more to life 'n just fame and fortune.'

Grace and Harriet slept until midday, when Harriet awoke complaining, very happily, that she was hungry. Grace suggested a nice hot bath while lunch was being prepared as well as offering to wash Harriet's hair, an offer which Harriet accepted on condition it was after she had bathed. Grace readily agreed, not giving a second thought to Harriet's proviso, remembering only too well her own shyness at that age when she had suddenly and to Lottie inexplicably started to refuse to get undressed let alone bath in front of her younger sister. So she did as Harriet wished, helping Dora to set the lunch table before going to the bathroom where Harriet was waiting for her, her thin frame discreetly wrapped in a thick bath towel.

Grace had enjoined Dora not to pass any comment on the return of Harriet's appetite, because she somehow felt while they might well be on their way out of the woods, they were still a long way from home, and any undue remark, even if intended as praise or encouragement, might easily lead to a setback since although her distress had obviously been triggered by the loss of her mother, Grace felt that was not the only reason for Harriet's behaviour. She still clung to the belief that there was a deeper-lying cause, something subconscious perhaps, some latent fear which had only now been brought to the surface by the trauma following Lady Lydiard's death.

In the exceptional circumstances, Miss Chambers had naturally excused Harriet from attending lessons until Grace was confident she was fully recovered.

'I think we should agree on sufficiently recovered,' Grace had argued. 'From what I've seen and from what Harriet's been through, at which I can only begin to guess, I don't really think Harriet will be fully recovered for quite some time yet.'

Miss Chambers was happy to accept the qualification, just as she was perfectly happy to excuse Harriet from class. With only a week of the school term left to run, the teacher was more than content to pass the last few days of the Christmas term quietly reading by herself in the schoolroom while one floor above her pupil set about her recovery.

'Could we go for a walk this afternoon, Nanny?' Harriet asked when she had finished every scrap of her lunch. 'It's rather a nice day, and I really would like to go out.'

'It will have to be only a short walk,' Grace warned her, as she wrapped the child up warm. 'We'll just walk round the lake and back.'

It was a clear bright December day, cold but dry with hardly a cloud in the pale blue sky. Dora led the way with Boy in his pram, while Grace and Harriet followed hand in hand slowly and some distance behind. Harriet had little to say so Grace did most of the talking, keeping up a flow of light-hearted chatter, or remarking on what wildlife they could see round the lake, until they reached the Chinese bridge, which Grace could still not cross without her heart's missing a beat. When they were halfway across, Harriet held back, her hand still in Grace's, so that they remained behind on the bridge while Dora wheeled Boy on ahead of them obliviously.

'Is something the matter, darling?' Grace asked. 'Are you tired? Do you want to go home?'

Harriet shook her head and took her hand from Grace's, walking over to the rail where she stood watching a family of moorhens darting across the water, their heads jerking backwards and forwards as they swam looking for food.

'Have you ever seen *Peter Pan*, Nanny,' she asked when Grace moved to her side.

'Yes,' Grace replied. 'My Uncle Edward took my sister Lottie and me to see it the first year it was on. Why?'

'Did you like it?'

'I thought it was wonderful. Much the best thing I had ever seen.'

'How old were you, Nanny?'

'I think I was thirteen,' Grace replied. 'Yes I was.'

'I've seen it five times,' Harr. t said. 'I was four when I first saw it, I think.'

The moorhens had now circled back, heads still jerking as though they were the birds' source of propulsion and not their feet.

'What made you think of Peter Pan?' Grace asked, as the birds turned to swim in line under the bridge.

Harriet bent over and through the planks watched them passing under her feet.

'I don't know really,' she said downwards. 'I just did.'

They walked on then, round the .op end of the lake, where Dora was sitting on a bench rocking Boy's pram and waiting for them. Boy was sitting up in his harness, pointing at some greylag geese whiffling down in a spiral high above him.

'Rook, Nana!' he was saying. 'Rook!'

'Yes, I can see, darling,' Grace said as she and Harriet reached the bench. 'Aren't they lovely? They're geese. Can you say that, darling Boy? Can you say geese?'

'Geez,' Boy burbled happily, grabbing a handful of Grace's cheek as she bent to straighten his little red scarf. 'Geez.'

'Isn't that good?' Grace smiled, kissing his chubby hand. 'Well done, darling. Another new word.'

'Geez, Nana,' Boy repeated. 'Geez.'

The party resumed its gentle stroll around the edges of the lake, Dora humming one of her favourite songs of the moment to the baby in the pram, while Grace and Harriet, hands linked, walked along swinging their joined arms as one.

'What was that bit in *Peter Pan*?' Grace wondered aloud. 'About the very first baby laughing for the very first time?'

'That's how fairies began, Nanny,' Harriet replied solemnly, as if it was something everyone should know. 'When the first baby laughs, the laugh breaks into thousands of pieces which all go skipping around, and each of those pieces turns into a fairy.'

'Of course,' Grace said. 'I remember now.'

'Do you believe in fairies, Nanny?'

'Of course,' Grace said, letting go of Harriet's hand for a moment to clap hers together. 'Dora?' she called. 'Do you believe in fairies, Dora?'

' 'Course I does, Nanny!' Dora called back.

'In that case you must clap your hands!'

Dora let go of the pram for a moment and clapped her gloved hands together, much to the delight of Boy who with a huge grin immediately clapped his.

'Harriet?' Grace turned to the child beside her. 'You haven't clapped yours.'

'That's because I'm not sure,' Harriet replied. 'I'm not sure if I believe in fairies any more.'

'Of course you do,' Grace said mock-crossly. 'And you know what happens every time a child says they don't believe, don't you?'

322

'Yes of course I do, Nanny.'

'Then you better clap your hands, darling, just to be on the safe side.'

Harriet did as she was told, although without much enthusiasm, a worried frown.

'Can I ask you something else, Nanny?' she said.

'Of course you can. You can ask me anything you like, darling.'

Harriet remained silent for a moment, and then stopped, looking up very seriously at Grace.

'Do you think everybody has to grow up, Nanny?' she asked.

There was something in the way the child asked the question, something in the look in her eyes and in the tone of her voice that made Grace take care how she answered what seemed to be just a plain, straightforward question. Not that she knew the answer, on the contrary. All she knew was what she mustn't say. Whatever happened she mustn't say *yes of course they do, darling. Of course everyone has to grow up.* How she knew she hadn't an idea, at least she had but it wasn't an explanation which everyone would find acceptable. A voice warned her, a voice inside her head, but it wasn't her own voice. For some inexplicable reason Grace believed (and did so for ever after although the only reference she ever made to it was the one small entry in her journal) that the warning voice in her head was Lady Lydiard's.

'*If you say yes she'll die,*' the voice said. '*She'll stop eating again but this time for good.*'

The sensation was so disturbing that Grace had to close her eyes and draw a deep breath before she replied.

'Well?' Harriet said. 'Does everyone have to grow up or don't they, Nanny?'

'No, I don't think they do, darling,' Grace replied slowly. 'Not everyone, not altogether I mean.'

'What do you mean?' Harriet asked. 'I don't understand.'

'What I think I mean is that although we all grow, we

323

don't all have to grow up,' Grace said. 'Does that make any sense?'

'So you mean Peter Pan could be real.'

Brake spoke to her then. *Tell her the truth*, he was saying. *Explain that the boy is symbolic. That what he represents is something that most of us wish. Those of us who are in love with innocence want it to last for ever. Tell her that, tell her that's what fantasy means. But don't tell her lies. It's the truth that doesn't hurt. Deception does.*

'So Peter Pan *could* be real, Nanny?'

'Yes, yes of course he could, darling,' Grace replied, truthfully, having just remembered Mrs Jenkins' words. We should live our lives according to our beliefs, she had told Grace in her last school term, not form our beliefs from the way we live. If what you believe you believe to be possible, then your belief is an image of the truth. So yes, if you believe a boy who never grows up to be a possibility, then that is the truth. When Grace had seen the play herself, nearly ten years older than the age Harriet was when she had seen it, she had believed in Peter Pan. So had her Uncle Edward. She could see it in his face, the face of someone who had never grown up. Uncle Edward had clapped his hands for the fairies and shouted with the other children young and old in the audience for Tinkerbell not to die. Everyone she saw around her in the packed auditorium believed absolutely in the story of the boy who never grew up.

'Yes, of course Peter Pan could be real,' she repeated.

'I'm glad you think so,' Harriet replied quietly, slipping her hand back into Grace's. 'Mama thought so, too. Mama was quite certain.'

That was all that day. Grace knew she was almost there, she could sense it. Harriet was about to tell her why, and most probably was about to do so quite inadvertently, but Grace must hold back. If she pressed Harriet, Harriet would know, just the way Harriet had sensed the shift in mood the moment Grace took away that first plate of food, before Grace had even addressed a word to her. So all in good time, in the child's time. Harriet would arrive at the truth herself, if she hadn't already done so, and Grace would learn what it was at the appointed time and not a moment before.

The child slept in Grace's bed that night, and the following night as well. Nothing more was said. There were no more allusions, no more questions. In fact as Grace lay awake on the third night that Harriet shared her bed, while the child lay fast asleep once more in her arms, Grace was afraid that although she appeared to have won the battle, her victory might be essentially a Pyrrhic one, for that very evening when Grace was reading to her and just before she fell asleep Harriet had seemed surprisingly at peace, as if she had at last found the real key to her troubles and come to terms with them. Grace could sense her sudden serenity and instead of making her feel happy it made her feel excluded, because it seemed that the child no longer needed her, and if that was the case, then Grace might never learn the reasons for her charge's aberrant behaviour, a state of ignorance which would prevent the two of them from re-establishing their former harmony.

Round about midnight Grace finally fell asleep into a night troubled by vivid and disturbing dreams. Some time and somewhere she was a child again without any clothes, trying to hide her nakedness in a huge house that was full of people. The house wasn't one she knew, it wasn't Keston and yet both Lord and Lady Lydiard were there and so was Harriet who had grown up. Then some time somewhere still in this unknown house Harriet found Grace and when she saw her in her nakedness, a state Grace was suddenly and unaccountably unable to conceal any longer, she began to scream and scream, which was when Grace woke up and found Harriet sitting up in bed beside her screaming.

'No!' the child was shouting. 'No, Nanny – please help, Nanny, help! Please it's happening again please help me, please!'

In the first light of dawn Grace could see Harriet sitting bolt upright in the bed, her blond hair falling

325

either side of her head as she sat bent forward, pushing handfuls of the sheet up between her legs. Even in the half-light Grace knew at once what the dark stains were.

'It's all right, darling,' she whispered, slipping out of bed. 'Just stay where you are, there's nothing to worry about.'

'Yes there is!' Harriet cried. 'I'm bleeding, Nanny! I'm bleeding from inside me! And it won't stop!'

'It's *all right*, darling,' Grace assured her. 'There really is nothing to worry about, I promise you.'

'It hurts me, Nanny,' Harriet whimpered. 'It hurts most dreadfully.'

Why didn't I think? Grace chided herself as she hurried to her chest of drawers to fetch the child a towel. *I can't have been thinking. Before she went on holiday, before she went to Ireland I thought she was beginning to develop, and then when she wouldn't let me bath her—*

'Please, Nanny,' the child was moaning behind her. 'Please do something quickly, Nanny! I don't want to die.'

'You won't, darling,' Grace told her as she opened the bottom drawer of the chest. 'Just wait one minute until I've found what I'm looking for.'

I suppose I assumed her mother would tell her, Grace thought, hurrying back to the bed. *I suppose I thought when they were on holiday, and because Harriet was so obviously developing – and then when her mother died, it must have just gone from my head. Or maybe I just presumed she knew.*

'Why me, Nanny?' Harriet was sobbing now, still frozen in the same position, head forward, bedsheet packed tight up under her nightdress. 'Why should it have to be me, Nanny?'

'What do you mean, darling?' Grace sat on the bed by Harriet's feet. 'What do you mean by it having to be you?'

'Why does it have to be me!' she sobbed almost in a scream. 'What have I done? I haven't done anything, Nanny! So why did God have to pick on me!'

'God didn't pick on you, darling,' Grace gently re-assured her. 'What's happening to you happens to every young woman.'

'No it doesn't! Roberta told me! She told me that it's a curse! That it only happens to girls who are cursed!'

'Who's Roberta, Harriet? Who'd tell you such a wicked thing?'

'Roberta's my cousin,' Harriet told her, starting to rock slowly backwards and forwards in the bed. 'Where we stayed first in Ireland. It has to be true, she knows it's true because her best friend is at a convent and she was told by a nun! So it has to be true, it has to be.'

The rocking went on, backwards and forwards, backwards and forwards, the sobs now a series of plaintive moans. Grace put a hand out to comfort the child, but as soon as she felt Grace touch her Harriet recoiled as if stung.

'Listen to me, darling,' Grace said quietly, making no further attempt at contact. 'What your cousin told you is wrong.'

'It isn't,' Harriet moaned. 'It isn't. Roberta never tells lies. Roberta's the nicest girl I know.'

'Of course she is,' Grace replied. 'I'm sure she is. And I'm sure she told you what she thought was the truth.'

'It is the truth, Nanny. I'm cursed. I know it. Otherwise—'

Grace waited, not saying a thing, feeling that this must be it, this had to be the moment of truth.

'Otherwise—' Harriet started again, not rocking any more, sitting quite motionless, her head still bowed.

'Yes?'

Grace held her breath. It was so quiet, so still, that from far away below the sound of someone shooting a door bolt carried up through the window, followed by the sound of a horse snorting and the clop of hooves on the cobbles.

'Otherwise,' Harriet said in a whisper, 'Mama wouldn't have died.'

Even now Harriet didn't look up. Grace wanted to hold her, to take her in her arms and cuddle the child to her, to hug away the pain, to kiss away her tears. But she stayed strong, and even though what Harriet had just said had made the breath stop in her throat, she waited a moment until she was calm again before speaking.

'Why do you think that, darling?' she asked. 'You know what happened, sweetheart. That it was an accident. So what makes you think that?'

'Because it happened that night,' Harriet whispered back. 'The night Mama – Mama passed away, it happened. Just like it's happening now. And because of what Roberta had told me I thought – I thought—'

Harriet began crying again, silently this time, mute tears that shook her body and seemed about to choke her.

'Don't,' Grace hushed her. 'Sssshhhh. You don't have to think that, sweetheart, because it isn't true. What's happening to you is perfectly natural. Of course it's frightening, particularly if no one's ever told you what to expect—'

'Roberta told me,' Harriet interrupted. 'She said that if you're cursed and it happens to you, you can bleed to death.'

'It's not true, Harriet, believe me.' Grace took hold of one of Harriet's hands, and this time the child gave it to her, a small warm hand that was soaked with tears. 'When you start to grow up—'

'But that's it, Nanny!' Harriet was looking up at her now, her blue eyes wide open and filled with fear. 'That's why I don't *want* to grow up! Not ever ever *ever*! And that's why Mama didn't want me to grow up! That's why she said so! Because she knew what could happen to you when you're a little girl! She knew you could be cursed!'

'Did your mother ever say anything to you about such things, Harriet?' Grace pushed some soaking wet strands of blond hair out of Harriet's wild eyes and stroked her cheek. 'I don't think your mother could ever have put any

328

such idea into your head. Your mama was far too kind and far too wise for any such nonsense.'

'No she didn't,' Harriet agreed, some of the fear going from her eyes. 'But she did say—'

'Yes?' This time Grace felt she could prompt the child out of her silence, because she knew now that Harriet wanted to tell her, and that she was going to tell her.

'It was after we'd been to see *Peter Pan* again,' Harriet said eventually, her hand grasping Grace's the tighter. 'I think it was the third time. And when we got home to our house in London, I said that I didn't ever want to grow up. Like Peter Pan. And Mama took me on her knee. I remember it so well, Nanny. I can remember Mama's green velvet dress, and she had a sort of feathered cap, and I can remember her scent as well, and her beautiful brooch she had on. I said I didn't ever want to grow up, and she kissed me and said I didn't have to. Then she kissed me again and hugged me and said that she didn't want me to grow up either, not ever. Because she loved me just as I was and would always love me like that, so I wasn't ever to grow up. She made us both wish it, you see, Nanny. We closed our eyes and she said I wish I wish that Harriet will never ever grow up and I did too.'

'So when you were aware you were changing, darling, that you were growing up—'

It was later now, an hour after breakfast. They were on their favourite walk, just the two of them, Grace and Harriet walking round the lake, a cold morning with the frost still in the ground and a sheet of thin ice lying over the water, both of them scarved and muffled against the cold, Harriet close by Grace's side.

Grace knew what had happened, why Harriet had begun to starve herself, but she wanted Harriet to know why, she wanted the child to see for herself.

'You know what happened, Nanny.'

'No I don't, darling. If I did, I wouldn't be asking.'

'I thought if I stopped eating—'

'Yes?' Grace had to bite her tongue to stop herself pre-empting Harriet, who shrugged.

'I thought I'd stop getting fat,' she said.

'You thought that's what it was, Harriet? That you were just getting fat?'

'Well I was, Nanny,' Harriet retorted. 'I was getting fat all over. Everywhere.'

They walked on in silence, past unseen frogs resting in the mud of the lake, past butterflies hibernating in the cracks of trees, bees hidden in their nests, dens of entwined adders dormant in the grasses, past siskins and marsh tits concealed in bushes, over toads sitting the winter out in holes in the ground, their footsteps crossing tracks in the frost made by the feet of scavenging badgers and rabbits, hedgehogs and voles, their breath hanging on the freezing air, a silent air broken only by a robin's sad little winter soliloquy.

'So then when you got hungry,' Grace said as once again they walked across the Chinese bridge.

'I know,' Harriet chimed in. 'I got Dora to bring me up food which I know was wrong, but I was so hungry.'

'So I gather.' Grace smiled to herself, recalling the slabs of cake, the slices of pie, the plates of cream cakes. 'Then you were sick.'

'Then I made myself be sick,' Harriet corrected her, cautiously as if afraid of being reprimanded for the revelation. But Grace had long known what Harriet had been doing. She just hadn't known why.

'And since the night your mama passed away—'

It was Grace's turn for prudence. Even though she had finally convinced Harriet by the time the sun had risen that what was happening to her was a fact of every young woman's life, she knew she still had to be circumspect, because not only did Harriet have to adjust to the changes which were happening to her body, much more important she had to accept the inescapable truth that she had already started growing up.

'Since the night Mama passed away, it never happened

again,' Harriet said. 'Not until last night.'

'That can only have been because your body wasn't getting the nourishment it needed,' Grace replied. 'You see once you start, darling – and you've missed two, nearly three months.'

'So if I'd kept on not eating—'

Grace saw the last look of hope in Harriet's eyes and wished she didn't have to put it out, but there was no point in prevarication, not once they had come this far together.

'If you'd kept on not eating, or eating and then making yourself sick, all you would have done is make yourself chronically very ill, sweetheart,' Grace assured her. 'We can't expect to do things like that to our bodies and for all to be well. Or in your case, to stop something normal from happening, something which is perfectly normal.'

'I see.'

Harriet walked a little away from her, to the bank of the frozen lake, kicking flakes of frost off the grass as she went.

'It's all right, sweetheart,' Grace said. 'You don't have to grow up.'

'You just said I did.'

'Your body has to, but what I mean is you don't,' Grace explained. 'Being an adult, a grown-up, it's just what people call an attitude. An attitude of mind. Some people are born old. I'm sure you must know some children your own age or even younger perhaps who seem as if they were born grown up.'

Harriet thought for a while before agreeing.

'Yes, well, yes I suppose I do, actually.'

'So what about some grown-up people who seem not to grow up at all?'

'Mama wasn't really grown up,' Harriet said, which was exactly the answer Grace had wanted to hear. 'She wasn't really a grown-up at all. And Papa's not always that grown up either.'

'So you know what I mean then.'

'You're not very grown up either, Nanny. In fact I

331

don't think of you as a grown-up at all,' Harriet said shyly. 'I think of you as my best friend.'

'Do you know something, Harriet?' Grace said as they stood looking out across the lake. 'I think that's the nicest thing anyone has ever said to me.'

They stood for a while longer, before turning to walk back towards the house, and when they did the woods they passed by were not just full of somnolent birds and insects and reptiles and animals. In them Grace liked to think she could hear the rustle of gossamer wings and the laughter of a boy who would never grow up.

E I G H T E E N

One week short of the sixth anniversary of his defection, George Merrill dropped dead in the streets of Rome from a coronary thrombosis. He and his mistress had been walking back from dinner when he had fallen without warning as if shot, dead it was surmised before the surprised look on his face hit the rain-sodden pavement.

Grace learned the news the day after the tragedy happened. Summoned into the library by Mr Harcross she found Lottie waiting for her, all dressed and veiled in black. At first she thought it must be their mother, since to Grace her family now consisted only of her and her younger sister, since she never thought of their father at all, but Lottie soon corrected her misapprehension.

'I didn't telephone,' Lottie explained after Mr Harcross had gone and she had given Grace the news, 'because I thought I ought to come and see you.'

'How do you feel, Lottie?' Grace asked her sister, staring at the telegram Mrs Jenkins had sent from Italy. *Regret your father passed away suddenly last night. Letter following.* What, Grace wondered as she read the message over and over again, were her teacher's regrets about Grace and Lottie's family passing away, if any? What were her regrets for the murder of their security, for the near ruination of their young lives? Was there a letter following that would cover that as well?

'It's dreadful to say, Grace,' Lottie replied, 'but after the initial shock I find I hardly care at all. Oh, I'm sure God will punish me for it, for thinking as I do, but to me Father died the day he walked out on us all.'

'I feel exactly the same, Lottie,' Grace said, taking her sister's hand. 'And I don't think we'll be punished for it one bit. Haven't we been punished already? And after all, we weren't the ones who did the wrong. Now tell me, how has Mother taken it?'

Lottie looked at her, and bit her lip.

'You have to remember Mother has been ill for a very long time,' she said with undue caution.

'Yes I know,' Grace agreed, 'but she has made considerable improvement over the last year or so.'

'Of course she has, Grace,' Lottie replied. 'It's just as long as you remember that she has *been* ill.'

'So?'

Grace took her sister's other hand and looked into her eyes, eyes which were immediately averted.

'So?' Grace repeated.

Lottie breathed in deeply and dimpled her pretty chin before replying.

'After she had read the telegram,' Lottie said, now frowning and screwing up her face as if she was about to get into trouble for saying it, 'she took me in her arms and kissed me, and then went upstairs to her room.'

'Yes?' Grace waited patiently, knowing there was more to come.

'I thought she wanted to be alone,' Lottie continued, sinking on to the brown velvet cushions of the old leather sofa while Grace sat down beside her. 'I thought she was probably overcome with grief, quite obviously. But not a bit, Grace. Not half an hour later she comes back down wearing her best red silk evening dress, you know the one. The one she had made just before Father bolted and never wore. She came back down with her hair all piled high, and in her jewellery, a necklace and bracelet and brooch she'd managed to hide away from the creditors, looking as if she was going to a society ball. Of course I thought – I thought she was ill, and she must have guessed what I was thinking because she said, "It's all right, Lottie, I'm not mad. I know exactly what I'm doing," and poured us both a large glass of Madeira. Then she looked at herself for a long time in the mirror above the fireplace, smiled at me in the glass, twirled herself slowly round and said with a deep sigh, "We must thank God, Lottie. For God has granted me a second chance." '

Grace stared at Lottie and Lottie stared back at her for what seemed an age without speaking.

'I think she's right, Lottie,' Grace concluded. 'Yes, absolutely. I think she's absolutely right.'

'That's what I thought as well, Grace,' Lottie replied. 'And not only that, but we both have a second chance now as well. I'm afraid once she had explained her feelings, I started making plans for myself as well.'

'But I don't understand, Lottie. Even so, this doesn't change things, surely? Mother will still need looking after. She can hardly live by herself.'

'That's all you know, Grace. Mother,' Lottie told her with glee, 'has been receiving a gentleman caller, so how about that.'

'What?' Grace made no pretence at containing her astonishment. 'What do you mean, Lottie? Mother's hardly been in a fit state to entertain.'

'It's all right,' Lottie assured her. 'There's nothing in the slightest bit indecorous about it. It's brought about such a change in her. She no longer sits about like a witch predicting dire things, she's just so, well, perky really. There's no other word for it. Dr Granger told me that in Italy they say an unloved woman is like a dead branch, no life to her, even her hair dies. Apparently there's even something in the Bible about it, Dr Granger says.'

'I don't see why Dr Granger should know so much about it, considering he's a widower,' said Grace tartly.

'Dr Granger knows quite a bit, Grace,' said Lottie,

giggling. 'He should do, considering it's he who has been calling on Mother!'

'Dr Granger?' Grace echoed, still quite unable to grasp the situation.

'It couldn't be better, could it, Grace?' Lottie said. 'Dr Granger being a widower, and because he's been treating Mother he understands her, and is sympathetic to her state. I think it's ever so dear, really I do.'

'But don't you see, Lottie? The fact that he's Mother's doctor, and that until yesterday, or the day before or whenever it was, Mother was still married. Doctors have to be very careful, Lottie, as far as relationships with their patients go.'

'It's all right, Nanny.' Lottie patted her sister's hand and smiled. 'I told you, there's nothing indecorous. I'm always there whenever he calls.'

'Well. Thank heavens for that, Lottie Merrill.'

'Until Mother finds me something to do in the kitchen, or an errand to run,' Lottie added mischievously. 'Just think, Grace. I mean I know this isn't really the time or the place, but just imagine if Mother continued to make such a good recovery, and if she and Dr Granger *did* marry, just think, Grace! We'd be free! We would! We'd be *free!*'

Grace got up and walked over to the fire, to try to buy a little time in which to sort out her feelings. Only minutes ago she had been reading a telegram which told her of her father's death, and now she was learning of her mother's outlandish reaction to the news and the fact that while she was still a married woman she was to all intents and purposes being wooed by Keston's general practitioner.

'That's not all either, Grace, is it?' Lottie said from the sofa. 'They'll obviously have to give you some time off from your duties, which means we can spend Christmas together. Just like old times.'

'Yes of course,' Grace agreed. 'Yes, I suppose it does.'

Grace kept her back to Lottie, her hands on the mantel, as she stared down into the fire.

'Is something the matter, Grace?' Lottie asked, getting up and coming to her sister's side. 'Is it Father?'

'No.' Grace shook her head. 'Perhaps I'll feel differently later, although I doubt it. I know he was our father, but because of what happened, his death might just as well have been that of a total stranger.'

'So what is it, Grace? I hope I haven't been too presumptuous, have I?'

'No, Lottie, of course you haven't.' Grace took her sister's hands before kissing her fondly on the cheek. 'I understand exactly how you're feeling, and you mustn't for a moment think I haven't considered everything that you're considering now.'

'So what is it, Grace?' Lottie asked again, with a helpless shrug.

'It's too late, Lottie,' Grace replied. 'That's what it is. It's just too late.'

'Why? How can it be? I don't understand what you mean.'

'It's not too late for you, Lottie. You're – what are you? You're only just seventeen, and if Mother should marry, you can do what you want to do. It's not too late for you.'

Lottie kept hold of Grace's hands, holding them more tightly and frowning deeply as she began to make sense of what her sister was saying.

'You're wrong, Grace,' she said. 'It's not too late for you either. This is just a job.'

'You know better than that, Lottie.' Grace smiled and squeezed Lottie's hands in return. 'This stopped being a job the day Lady Lydiard died.'

'That's not fair, Grace. That just isn't fair.'

'It's perfectly fair, Lottie. I could have said no.'

'You couldn't. You had to support Mother and me.'

'I could have said no and stayed below stairs, Lottie, in the kitchens. I could have stayed as a kitchen maid and that way if circumstances changed I could have left at any time. But I didn't, and the reason I didn't must have been because I didn't want to. It's as simple as that.'

'You make it sound as if it's a vocation,' a mystified Lottie said.

'When you think about it, Lottie,' Grace replied, 'I suppose it is. And if it is, then I'm lucky to have found it.'

'What about your painting, Grace? What about your real talent?'

'I don't know,' Grace replied simply. 'When I see someone like Brake Merrowby painting I think the world would not be much the poorer if I never drew. Perhaps there are too many painters already, and I would be just another, whereas through children something else will go on, something much more valuable.'

Grace tried to deflect the conversation away from herself and on to her sister, but Lottie was not to be so easily deterred.

'I don't think there are too many painters in the world, Grace,' she said, looking steadfastly into Grace's eyes. 'I think you're just trapped by your own goodness.'

'Nonsense.' Grace laughed. 'Nonsense,' she repeated briskly. 'Now I want to hear about you.'

'What about me?'

'You said something about plans,' Grace reminded her. 'If it's true that you have been given a second chance, what do you think you might do with it?'

Lottie suddenly looked astounded, as if the reality of what she'd been contemplating had only just dawned on her, a look of astonishment which widened her eyes and slowly changed into a childish smile.

'Well?' Grace prompted, noting the smile had now become a puzzled frown.

'You're not to laugh,' Lottie said, now perfectly serious. 'But I was thinking of becoming a nurse.'

Grace didn't laugh, but she did smile, and doing so she took her sister's hands once more in hers.

'But how dear,' she murmured.

She didn't hear the door open behind her, she only knew from the look in Lottie's eyes that someone had come in. When she turned she saw it was a young man she

338

hardly recognized, so much had he grown in so few weeks, a young man now of nearly sixteen years, a handsome young man instead of a sweet young boy, dark-haired, steady-eyed, athletically built, and already fast growing out of his tail-coated Eton suit.

'Henry!' Grace exclaimed. 'I thought you weren't due home until tomorrow.'

'There's some sort of bug, Nanny,' Henry said in a newly broken voice. 'So they let us home a day early.'

He was staring past Grace now, over her shoulder to where Lottie was standing and doing her best, Grace saw when she looked round, not to stare back at him. Lottie had forgotten she had raised her black veil to talk to Grace, so her pretty, wide-eyed and open face was fully there for Henry to see, beneath her hat and upturned veil, and framed by her lightly curling blond hair.

'Henry,' Grace said, noting the pinkening of the young man's cheeks, 'allow me to introduce my sister Miss Lottie Merrill. Lottie, this is Lord Lydiard's elder son, the Honourable Henry Rokeham.'

It was only after they had been introduced and had shaken hands that Lottie suddenly remembered her veil, a little too late for Grace who had already also noted the pinkening of her younger sister's cheeks as well.

'I'm most awfully sorry,' Henry said, looking suitably abashed. 'Has there been a bereavement?'

'It's all right, Henry dear,' Grace replied. 'I'll explain to you later. Now did you want something in particular?'

'Yes I did, Nanny,' Henry said, unable to stop himself eyeing the now veiled figure beside Grace. 'Which was why I intruded, sorry. You're wanted up in the nursery apparently. Apparently Boy's got something wrong, or something.'

Grace made to go at once, and then stopped, remembering Lottie.

'It's all right, Nanny,' Henry said. 'I can show your sister out.'

It wasn't anything serious, but Dora had been well trained

by Grace into responding to the slightest alarm so that as she put it there wouldn't be any cause for any regrets later. Boy's temperature was nearly 100°F and he showed all the signs of running yet another cold, with flushed pink cheeks and a constantly running nose.

'I've never known a child who had so many colds,' Grace said, blowing and wiping Boy's nose for him. 'Not that I've known that many children,' she added. 'It's just that Boy seems to have more than his fair share of the snuffles.'

'It's just that he seemed to be 'oldin' his ear, Nanny,' Dora explained as she remade Boy's bed. 'When 'e woke up from 'is rest, 'e was cryin' and 'oldin' 'is little ear, and that's why I called you up.'

'He did that last time,' Grace remembered. 'When he had that bad cold in August. What we thought was a teething cold.'

Grace stared anxiously at Boy. He had a dreadful tendency to colds and earache. How many times she wished that she could turn to old Nanny Lydiard, or Lady Lydiard, and ask them if Henry or Harriet had suffered from the same. But old Nanny had followed shortly after her mistress, slipping off peacefully in her sleep. Gone to look after her ladyship, George the coachman had said, and his eyes had filled with tears as he gave Grace the news.

'I think he's all right, Dora, I don't think he has a fever, at least not a very high one. We'll keep him in today even so.'

'Very well, Nanny.'

Dora smiled.

'It's best we do that,' Grace intoned, and she turned away trying to think only of Boy and what was best and not of Father lying dead in some Rome cemetery, and Mrs Jenkins writing to her.

The letter lay on the table where Dora had placed it for some few hours. Grace ignored it and busied herself around the nursery in her usual way, tidying and arranging, making everything look pretty and fresh.

'When you've finished with the envelope, might I have the stamp?' Dora wanted to know. She looked across wonderingly at Grace. A letter from abroad and she hadn't even opened it, Grace could see her thinking.

'I – yes, of course, you can have the stamp.'

Grace walked to the table. What could the letter contain? Thank you for lending me your father? Thank you for letting me ruin your chances of becoming an artist, however inferior? Thank you for letting me be happy at the cost of others? She picked up a knitting needle and inserting it into the envelope split it open, and holding the letter, with care, as if she thought it might explode in her hand, she handed the envelope to Dora.

'Thank you very much, Nanny!'

Grace left the letter on the table, and turned away. Just the sight of that woman's writing on an envelope made her stomach turn over. To think how hard she had tried to please her, all that time she was growing up she only wanted to please her, not her mother, but Mrs Jenkins. And now Father was dead, she obviously felt it was all right to write to her and perhaps try to make amends. Salve her conscience.

Dora hurried away, and Grace returned to the table, and picked up the letter. If she read it and it was nice and said something that might give her feelings of compassion for Father and Mrs Jenkins, it would make things impossible. If she read it and hated her the more for reading it, it would make things even worse. She picked it up, and determinedly walked to the nursery fire, and pulling the guard away threw it on to the hot coals. As she did so something fell out from the leaves of the thin foreign writing paper, a large Italian bank note. Money. She had sent her money! Grace replaced the guard, and carefully watched both the money and the letter blacken and finally disappear. Now she was even more glad she had done as she had done. What sort of woman would send a man's daughters money to make up for nearly destroying their lives? Grace turned away from the fire. At least Dora had got her stamp, that at least was something.

With the newly returned Lord Lydiard still in mourning, there was no house party that year. In fact there were no guests at all, other than Lord Lydiard's brother and sister-in-law and of course Brake Merrowby, who had been away somewhere (Paris, Grace thought, the once she had given the matter any consideration) and had now also returned to Keston in time for Christmas.

On the evening of his return home, Lord Lydiard summoned Grace down from the nursery to the drawing room where she found him sitting at the grand piano wearing an odd knitted cap on his head and a loose embroidered oriental robe over his suit. He glanced up but only for the briefest of moments as Harcross ushered Grace into the room, and then continued to play a very intricate and modern-sounding waltz which Grace couldn't identify.

Over his playing he expressed his condolences for Grace's loss, briefly but sympathetically, and agreed without being asked that she must take off whatever time she needed, telling her that she must suit herself because personally he hadn't much of an idea of how these things were organized. Grace thanked him, and said she would only take off the days which were absolutely necessary which she assumed wouldn't be much more than the Christmas holiday since her father had already been buried abroad. She had to shout most of this information over the music which Lord Lydiard was now playing *fortissimo*, in his usual style with his head thrown back and his bespectacled eyes staring straight up at the ceiling. Lord Lydiard was forced to shout back his responses as well, calling to her again that she must please herself and then once more and apparently finally how very sorry he was.

Grace remained where she was, however, not taking her cue to leave. She was still standing exactly where she had been when Lord Lydiard finished playing, having repeated the long and difficult piece *in toto*, right from bar one.

He looked amazed when he rose from the piano and

saw her, since he had obviously assumed she had left when they had finished shouting at each other, and wouldn't have noticed that she hadn't because all the time he had been staring fixedly at the ceiling.

'Yes?' he enquired, taking his spectacles off and gazing at her in total bewilderment. 'What's going on? I thought you'd had your say, Nanny.'

'I thought you might like to see your children, Lord Lydiard,' Grace replied.

'Yes?'

Grace could see the light of panic brought into Lord Lydiard's eyes by the suggestion.

'I've only just got back, Nanny,' he said helplessly, suddenly stretching his arms out wide. 'Good heavens above.'

'That's why I thought you might like to see them, Lord Lydiard,' Grace persisted. 'You haven't really seen them or spoken to them since September.'

'Yes I'm sure,' Lord Lydiard said shortly, going and ringing the bell by the fireplace. 'Now look here, Nanny.'

'Yes, Lord Lydiard?' Grace was determined to stand her ground. Saying good night to his children was not the only matter about which she wanted to speak to her employer.

'I've been away, Nanny,' Lord Lydiard sighed, sitting by the fire and staring at his feet. 'I happen to have been away.'

'Of course you have, Lord Lydiard,' Grace agreed. 'But you're back now, it's Christmas, and your children would like to see you.'

'I saw Henry when he was getting out of the car,' Lord Lydiard muttered. 'Waved to him, and he waved back. And I saw Harriet when she was out with you. From here.'

He pointed to one of the huge windows which over-looked the winter parkland.

'They know I'm here,' he said. 'Same way as I know that they are.'

'That's not quite the same thing, if I may say so, Lord Lydiard,' Grace replied. 'Besides, Henry and Harriet are both of an age now when they should be taking a fuller part in the family's life.'

'Is that so?' Lord Lydiard said, without a trace of interest. 'Really?'

'Henry's been sleeping downstairs ever since he started at Eton, but Harriet's still on the nursery floor.'

'I didn't leave the nursery floor till I was fifteen, Nanny. Fact of the matter was I didn't want to. I was much happier upstairs with all the other young.'

'I don't think it's good for Harriet to be shut away with just Boy, Dora and me,' Grace persisted. 'I think she should sleep downstairs now as well.'

'What on earth's happened to Harcross?' Lord Lydiard stretched out to ring the bell again.

'Is there something I can do for you, Lord Lydiard?' Grace asked.

Lord Lydiard looked at her round the wing of his chair, as if at someone who was stalking him.

'Hmmm,' he said, sitting back. 'I doubt it. Doubt it very much.'

'Do you want a drink? Is that it?'

Again he looked at her round the wing of the chair, stroking either side of his chin with the crook of his index finger and the inside of his thumb, before disappearing from view again, saying nothing.

'If you only want a drink,' Grace continued, 'it seems a little silly to make Mr Harcross come all the way up to pour it for you. When I could do it just as well. You drink gin at this time of day, don't you?'

'Yes. Usually.'

'Gin and water I seem to remember.'

'With a little pink.'

Grace was by the drinks table now, looking at the decanters.

'Pink?' she said. 'A little pink what exactly?'

'For goodness sake, Nanny,' Lord Lydiard sighed. 'Pink.'

He got up, came to her side and held up a small bottle of angostura bitters.

'Pink,' he said, and put the bottle back down again, before retaking his seat.

'You'll forgive me for wondering, Lord Lydiard,' Grace said, 'but surely if you can get up and walk over here to show me which the pink is, isn't it also possible for you to pour your own drink?'

There was such a long silence Grace thought she must have gone too far. She hadn't made the suggestion out of pique, nor from any revolutionary motives, but simply from a sense of what was practical. Unless he was waiting outside in the corridor it took Harcross the best part of five minutes to climb up from his pantry to the ground floor and walk the length of the house to the drawing room and another five minutes to retrace his steps just to pour his employer a drink. To Grace that seemed like a bad arrangement all round.

Still Lord Lydiard said nothing, so Grace decided on silence as well, standing by the drinks table and looking at Lord Lydiard rather the way she stood by the nursery table waiting for everyone to be seated. Finally Lord Lydiard, who was not looking at Grace but most resolutely at his feet, suddenly got to his feet, hurried over to the table and poured himself a large pink gin.

'Was there anything else, Nanny?' he asked on the way back to his chair.

'Yes there was, Lord Lydiard,' Grace replied. 'If Harriet's to move downstairs, which she obviously must do straight away, then I think that we all should. Boy, Dora, and I.'

Grace had given it a lot of thought. Even when fully occupied the nursery floor was a white elephant. It was impractical for all purposes, too far from the kitchens and all the household amenities, as well as being exceedingly dangerous, unquestionably the most dangerous part of the house excepting the roof, to which inquisitive and adventurous children could obtain access from certain parts of the nurseries. Fire, however, was the greatest risk, and this was the argument which won Grace's day. There had been a fierce fire that year in a large house on the borders of Buckinghamshire and Oxfordshire, and ever since she had learned of it, and the tragic consequences (two children perished in the conflagration, as well as four members of the staff) Grace had realized the folly of housing anyone let alone children high up and out of reach under the roof. So when she made this her main reason for wanting them all to move down a floor, Lord Lydiard immediately conceded the point and instructed Grace to make the appropriate arrangements.

There were other reasons why Grace thought the move necessary, but these she kept to herself. Quite independently she had come to the conclusion that while there was nothing intrinsically wrong with the nanny principle, there was a great deal lacking in a system which enforced an almost total separation of children from their parents, particularly for the sons of such families, who were not only brought up at home on a separate floor and within a separate regime from their parents, but spent the rest of their young days away at boarding schools. Grace considered this could only be storing up trouble for the future, and was determined within her domain to effect as many salutary changes as she could.

Everyone on the nursery floor was delighted with the changes, particularly Harriet who suddenly realized that there might be benefits in growing up if it meant being neighbours with her brother, with whom she was once again in total harmony, and taking an active part in the family's life. For Grace and Boy, however, the best was yet to come.

On the day before Christmas Eve, when Grace was in the middle of helping to organize Harriet's move downstairs, Harcross called to her from the hall as she and Dora were hauling a mattress along the first floor corridor that Lord Lydiard wished to see her in the library.

When she opened the door Grace was delighted to see Lord Lydiard pouring himself a drink from the sideboard.

'Good,' he said as she closed the door and came in.

'Nanny. Right. Well now you've got me trained, perhaps I can pour you something. Sherry?'

Grace accepted the offer and sat down by the fire as Lord Lydiard indicated she should with a vague and backward flap of his hand.

'I've been thinking since we talked,' he said, 'about moving everyone about. About moving the smalls.'

He knew at once he shouldn't have said it and he wondered why he had. Grace could see by the look on his face. It was as if he'd been hit without expectation, right out of the blue. Two words did it, just two little words, seven letters of the alphabet which assembled in their particular order had taken the shape of a bullet and shot straight to his heart.

'Yes?' Grace prompted him, keeping her voice as calm as she could. 'What about moving the smalls?'

She said it to show him that the word was in her lexicon as well, that it didn't just belong to the woman who had gone, that she'd left it for them all to use, so that by using it they would be reminded of her which meant in turn that she would never be forgotten.

Lord Lydiard was staring at her numbly, stupefied, as if in a trance.

'You were saying something about moving the smalls, Lord Lydiard,' Grace reminded him again.

'Yes, yes of course.' Lord Lydiard suddenly snapped out of his stupor and sat back in his chair, looking up at the ceiling. 'I think you should have for the nursery, that is, since there's only you and Boy, otherwise I don't know what we're going to do with it. It'll turn into some sort of memorial, which wouldn't do at all. Not one bit. No, I think much the best thing is for you and Boy to have it as your nursery.'

'What exactly?' Grace asked out of the ensuing silence.

'Didn't I say?' Lord Lydiard looked down from the ceiling straight at Grace, his pale grey eyes meeting hers. 'Her *boudoir*. My wife's *boudoir*.'

It was a room of infinite charm, redolent of the warm

and vibrant woman who had sat at its white wood writing desk scribbling hasty notes and menus, making endless telephone calls to fix up house parties and tennis matches, every available space cluttered with photographs of family and friends, of dogs and horses, of her children through their various ages and of her husband since the time they had first met. It was a room full of light, a feeling heightened by the amount of white-painted furniture Lady Lydiard had used, wooden chairs, tables and screens, some of them colourfully decorated to relieve the large expanses of blond, others hung with pieces of ribbons, or hats, or masks, and carpeted by a huge faded blue Persian rug. In one corner was a large leather wing-chair, to which Lady Lydiard had given a tented effect by draping and knotting a big tartan rug over the top, and on a heavy oak chest along the wall behind the tented chair was her collection of sporting trophies, not arranged but in a heap, some standing, some on their sides and some in a state of disrepair, trophies for tennis, for golf, for shooting, for riding point to point. There were tennis racquets propped up in one corner along with hickory-shafted golf clubs, a pair of shotguns lay in the fireplace, there was even a horse bridle hanging on the corner of the fireplace bound with a purple ribbon to which was strung a faded card which read *RIP darling Fred*.

Yet for all the sporting memorabilia, the boxes of shotgun cartridges and the tins of salmon flies, it was a woman's room, not just because there were beautiful and expensive dresses draped over the white screens and on the backs of chairs, as well as hand-sewn underwear dropped on cushions or half hanging from dresser drawers, but because of the very atmosphere, the fragrance of the person gone, French scents and English silks, powder and the faint sensual tang of hair. Grace could see her at her white desk, her chair only half turned to it, in her stiff collared blouse, semi-undone black tie and ankle length white tennis skirt, her long legs stretched out in front of her while she leant sideways to write a note for Cook, her pile of gorgeous chestnut hair beginning to come undone after her tennis match and fall in long coils at the back of her slender neck, while she talked to Grace, always talking, quickly and in short bursts like the machine gun fire about to come, wild snatches of conversation always and forever punctuated by that laugh, a laugh like bubbles, a laugh which never failed to infect the listener, a girlish gurgling peal which laughed any sense of misery away.

But even the first-time visitor to her *boudoir* would know its former occupant at once, because she was immortalized in a portrait which hung fixed to the wall above the fireplace in a decorated white oval frame, a perfect and brilliant painting of her sitting casually on a chair turned back to front, her slender hands folded on the top of the chair back, her long slim arms disappearing into folds of white silk which again disappeared into the half sleeves of her claret dress, her beautiful long face half serious and half good-humoured but turned slightly away to look at something to the left of the onlooker, some most special memory to judge from the look of faint dreaminess in her lovely eyes, with her famous chestnut hair not quite hidden under a big-brimmed carmine-coloured hat, whose matching veil she had pulled back and allowed to fall in perfect folds behind her head.

Grace had seen the portrait before, but never this close. Somehow whenever she had been in the room she had always stood the other side of the white desk so that the painting was only visible to her at an angle, the fireplace being almost in line with where she usually was. So she had no real idea of the beauty of the work, of the way the artist had captured his sitter's character so absolutely, but she had guessed since who the artist might be, and now that she was standing looking at the portrait full square and head-on she had absolutely no doubt, long, long before she ever saw the signature scrawled in the bottom right-hand corner. *Merrowby. 1912.*

For a while as she stood looking at the painting, Grace wondered whether Brake had loved Lady Lydiard more for painting it, or whether the brilliance of the painting was because he loved her so utterly. The portrait spoke of little else except the artist's passion. Of course its audience would be aware of the technique inasmuch as the painting was flawless. But that wasn't the first impression. The painting's perfection became apparent afterwards, after the audience had sufficiently recovered from the assault on its emotions. Love, the painting said, love, and beauty, intimacy (that most thrilling of words), shared secrets, quiet after passion, but most of all, love. It was as if the brush was a caress, each sweep of colour a stroke on the skin, a sable *buss*, a camel-haired kiss. For once this portrait was no portrait of the artist, in fact it wasn't a portrait at all. It was a painting, and it was exactly the sort of painting Brake had expressed such a desperate and heartfelt desire to do the day he shared the car back to Keston with Grace, when he had professed his need to paint from the heart.

And Grace was jealous.

Until that moment, Grace had been on the verge of turning down Lord Lydiard's offer of the room as her new nursery. Standing in it, seeing and feeling what Lady Lydiard had left behind, she had felt it would be a sacrilege to disturb the smallest thing let alone to turn out the entire room, but now, overcome by a dreadful feeling of blind resentment against both the woman in the portrait and the man who had painted it, Grace couldn't wait to start clearing the place out.

She turned to go, intending to summon Dora to help her and George to fetch up some boxes, and as she did so, someone appeared in the doorway.

'Forgive me.' It was Brake, Grace saw even before he spoke. 'I'm sorry,' he said. 'I didn't realize—'

He left the sentence unfinished, making to leave, his back turned to her already.

'I'm just going,' Grace said, 'if you want something from here. Or have you just come up to admire your work?'

She was by him now, standing her side of the doorway, waiting for him to clear the way.

'You must have seen it before,' he said, looking over

350

to the painting, guessing at once the way lovers do what the other is thinking, what the other one has found. 'It's been hanging there over a year.'

'When did you do it?' Grace wondered, making sure she sounded matter-of-fact. 'It must have been that year. During the time – it must have been the same year.'

'It was a commission,' Brake replied, employing the same tone as Grace. 'I can't exactly remember when Lydiard first asked me to execute the commission – but anyway.'

He kept staring at the painting, any excuse Grace felt rather than look at her. He stood still blocking the doorway, stroking his stubbled chin with the palm of one hand.

'Needs must,' he added. 'I've never been one to live by bread alone.'

'Why don't you tell the truth?' Grace asked, knocking the wind from his very full sails.

Now he turned to her, and there was a dangerous light in his dark eyes.

'Why don't you leave well alone?' he asked back. 'You were the one who said no, if you remember.'

'That's not true.' Grace was angry rather than upset, furious with Brake once more for the way he so conveniently distorted the truth. 'It was you who said no first.'

'I was drunk.'

'You're always drunk! At least you're always giving that as your excuse! Now if you'll kindly get out of my way, I have work to do.'

Grace made to walk past him, but Brake didn't move.

'I *was* drunk that night, Grace,' he said, dropping his voice. 'I was drunk, and I was hysterical, and if you'd only fought—'

'Yes?'

'If you hadn't just given in the way you did—' Brake gave a deep sigh. 'I could have been persuaded. If not then—'

'Ha!' Grace laughed out loud, surprising him but

351

surprising herself even more. He stopped talking and looked at her in astonishment.

'Please.' Grace made another attempt to get past him. 'I have a great deal to do.'

'You never tried to talk me round, Grace.' Brake frowned, his hand now on her arm. 'You never once made it seem that it mattered.'

Grace carefully removed his hand.

'How dare you?' she hissed. 'How *dare* you? Try to remember, *Mr Merrowby*, just try to remember the reasons I gave for why I said no. It wasn't a case of me talking you round. It was a case of quite the very opposite. Now please move out of my way.'

This time he took Grace by both her arms and held her fast.

'Don't you find this very difficult?' he said. 'Aren't you finding this intolerable? Living on top of each other like this?'

'It wasn't my idea,' Grace replied, struggling to get free, hoping that no one would come round the corner in the corridor and see them. 'Besides, I have no choice. I happen to work here. But you – you did have a choice. You could have gone anywhere you wanted, because you're a free agent. You can set up your easel wherever.'

'Not without money,' Brake interrupted.

'I disagree,' Grace said. 'You could have enjoyed Lord Lydiard's patronage without having to live here. But you chose otherwise, in the full knowledge that you and I would be living under the same roof. So please don't ask me whether or not I find such an arrangement intolerable, because the question is purely academic.'

Again Grace struggled to be free, but Brake refused yet to let her go.

'I had no idea, Grace,' he said. 'It's one of my many faults, as I'm sure you know. The inability to think ahead. I imagined that in a house this size, and with your work – and mine—' He stopped and shrugged hopelessly, his dark eyes meeting hers, his look suddenly so forlorn and miserable that if Grace hadn't known him better she might have weakened and listened not to her head but to the heart she could now feel pounding in her chest.

'I really must get on,' she said, pulling her arms away from his hold. 'If you'll excuse me, I do have work to do.'

'Certainly,' Brake agreed, letting go of her all at once with an over-flamboyant gesture intended to mock. 'I am sorry to have taken up so much of your valuable time.'

He continued his mockery by dismissing her with a formal half bow, before turning his back and wandering into the *boudoir*. Grace hesitated for no reason other than she felt he had won, that he had been in control of the situation from the word go, whereas she had let too much emotion show. He had played her the way Henry played the trout he caught so expertly, he had made her rise to his bait, he had hooked her, he had let her run with the line as if she were free, and then he had snapped the line taut and the hook had held. *Look*, his dark eyes had said as he had fallen silent. *See? You're still mine.*

Stifling an almost irresistible urge to run into the room after him and pummel his back with her clenched fists while calling him every imaginable name, Grace took a deep breath and closed the door behind her, resolving from now on to adopt a totally disinterested attitude if and whenever their paths should again cross. None the less as she walked away down the corridor she was unable to stem her curiosity. What exactly was the reason for Brake's visit to Lady Lydiard's *boudoir*? she wondered. He had offered no reason nor made an excuse, even though she had asked him. *Do you want something from here?* she'd said. *Or have you just come up to admire your work?* But he had remained silent on both counts. *You must have seen it before*, he'd replied. *It's been hanging there for over a year.* That was the extent of his reply. No reason, no excuse, no embarrassment. She might just as well have been one of the servants.

What was she talking about? She was one of the servants, at least she certainly was to Brake with his *Yes-Nannys* and his *No-Nannys* and the way he always included her in his generalizations about life beyond the green baize door. Grace stopped at the end of the corridor, at the point where it joined the main landing, and looked back, fighting a losing battle with the sea of resentment that was welling up inside her. *Very well*, she determined, looking round and making sure there were no other members of the staff about, *very well, Mr Merrowby. If you like to think of me as a servant, then I shall behave like one and find out why you are up here shut away in a room where you have no right to be.*

Retracing her steps on tiptoe, she waited outside the *boudoir* door, flat against the wall, a position she knew was perfectly ridiculous since if Brake came out he couldn't fail to see her at once. Yet for some reason she continued with the childish pantomime, feeling as infantile as the position she had adopted, until for some quite illogical reason she decided it was safe to spy and bent down to look through the keyhole.

At once she regretted her curiosity, just as she had always warned the children they would if they looked at something which had been deliberately kept from them. *If you look*, she'd warned Henry and Harriet, *then you must be prepared to find*, and now here she was looking and here she was finding.

Brake was sitting at the white-painted desk in front of a scattered pile of opened envelopes. She could see him perfectly clearly, framed by the keyhole as appropriately as his painting of Lady Lydiard was framed by the ornamental oval. He had one elbow, the far one, on the desk and his face was resting in the cup of his hand almost at right-angles, while in his left hand, his left arm at full stretch, he held the pages of a letter which he was reading while unabashed tears ran down his face.

Grace didn't move. There seemed to be little point now the damage had been done and she'd found that for which she'd had no right to look. She had no idea how long she stayed there on her knees at the keyhole, it might have been seconds or it might have been half an hour. Time no longer mattered. All that mattered was that

Brake was reading the letters he had written to the woman he had loved, watched by the woman who had loved him, and who had just found out to her horror when he had looked at her with that long dark look not that she had loved him but that she still did.

Extracted from Grace Merrill's journal.

6 August 1914

No one seemed to be expecting it, no one in the whole world, although with hindsight I realize someone must have been, the politicians, the generals, they all must have known it was inevitable. But we didn't. No one in our world which was of course our whole world because we never really ventured very far afield, not those of us in service, none of us expected it in the slightest, all except Cook of course, who has been imagining a German invasion for as long as I have been here at Keston. The very first time I joined the table in the servants' hall I remember Cook warning everyone that there were spies in the streets. But war, never. And a European war? Never ever.

It has been an odd year, however. Looking back on how we all were from January to now, to August as I write, it's as if somehow we did know, because otherwise how else to describe (as B called it one evening over sherry) our headless-chicken behaviour? A quite horrible metaphor certainly, but a ruefully accurate one since everyone seems to have spent the last few months running around and around in circles doing absolutely nothing, as if propelled by some form of compulsion. At least that again was B's conclusion. He's been to London and Paris since the Season began, and he told Lord L (and myself indirectly who was there on account of John and Harriet) that the Fancy Dress Balls were even wilder and more foolish than those of last year. It was like a swan song to the old world, he said, a world which he likened to Pompeii before Vesuvius erupted, our volcano (according to B) being the quite unbreachable gap between the rich and the poor.

Shame to say I am hardly aware of this now, being part as it were of the fabric. If I go anywhere it is always with the family, chauffeured in ever larger motor-cars to visit or stay in other grand houses owned by other rich people, where I meet their nannies, who are invariably greater snobs than their employers, but seldom their staff who are where I once was, far away and out of sight below stairs. Yet wherever I have been this year I have never once heard talk of war. Even as late as June when I took Harriet to Henley to see Henry row for Eton (and win) the families talked only small talk, of dances and parties, of princesses riding through Roman ballrooms escorted by leopards and lions, of a thousand guests at the British Embassy Ball, of tableaux vivants and the latest dance craze, fashion and Russian émigrés. But nothing about war. At least not 'above stairs'.

The only real mention I have heard has been in the servants' hall, but the war concerned was not the one which has now broken out all over Europe but the civil war which Mr Harcross was convinced would follow the proposed granting of Home Rule to Ireland 'as surely as night follows day'. Germany was mentioned only by Cook, and only up until March this year when after a particularly violent altercation between herself and Mr Harcross (which ended in Cook throwing her largest saucepan at him) Cook was banned from bringing the subject up again in company.

Yet somehow I have the feeling we all knew, and that this was the reason it was never seriously discussed. Somehow we all knew there was going to be a war which was why we all pretended to look the other way, as if by diverting our gaze it would pass us by. But it hasn't. By 11 p.m. on 4 August we were at war with Germany.

History will relate why. None of us here pretends to know the answer or understands the reason. Cook is delighted to be proved right, naturally, and George and Peter and the other young male members of the staff say they can't wait to pick up a rifle and show Fritz (as George has christened our enemy) the way back home. Myself, I simply can neither grasp it nor understand it, influenced perhaps by the conversations to which I have been a (silent) witness of late between B and Lord Lydiard at 'goodnight' time. (Here I must confess that I quite deliberately time the moment I bring John down to say goodnight to his father to coincide with the moment B downs his brushes to have

357

his first drink of the evening with Lord L, in order to catch up on events outside, if nothing else.) B says that it is a senseless conflict, and that the reason we are at war is because we were prepared for it. He also maintains that alliances pull their members into war regardless of the members' own feelings. None the less he declares his desire to fight, even though this isn't his country. He wants to fight, he says, because it feels as if it is.

Lord L says little on the subject. It seems to induce one of his major melancholias. While B talks and argues, he plays the piano, staring all the time at the ceiling, and then asks B which composers does B think he's been playing, and of course they are all and always German. This usually leads to an argument about patriotism, during which Lord L stubbornly maintains that patriotism only flourishes in a nation torn by strife, and that without patriotism there wouldn't be any wars. The other evening B maintained the war was by popular demand because of the way the cheering crowds had gathered outside Buckingham Palace, forcing His Majesty and the queen to come out on to the balcony, but Lord L dismissed this as 'poppycock', saying the reason the crowds had formed and the cheering had started was not because they wanted war but because the thought of a foreign and common enemy united everyone. Moments of supreme danger such as this, he said, give the people a sense of fellowship, of being part of a whole, a feeling which is particularly welcome at times of strife such as now. The people don't want war, he said. What they want is unity. Which is what they must have sensed in the Mall, with the king on the balcony of the palace and everyone around united in their cheers. All at once, Lord Lydiard said, all at once a country which had been on the verge of civil war miraculously was a family again.

20 August 1914

I don't want them to fight. I don't want any of them to fight, because when they do, when they fight they will be

358

*killed, and when they fall each one who falls is a mother's
son. B is right – it is senseless. All war must finally be so.
They make a desert, Lord L said the other night, and they
call it peace. Henry was given 'A Shropshire Lad' by his
father to read out loud.*

> Into my heart an air that kills
> From yon far country blows.
> What are those blue remembered hills,
> What spires, what farms are those?

*B left the room and Lord Lydiard wept openly when
Henry read:*

> They carry back bright to the coiner
> The mintage of man.

*The only ray of hope is the experts tell us the war will
be over before Christmas.*

N I N E T E E N

'Kitchener said three years at the very least,' Lord Lydiard announced. 'Told them at the first cabinet meeting he attended. You do know they've appointed him Secretary of State for War, Brake, do you?'

Brake was standing by the fire, facing it, hands on the mantel, head down. Grace was sitting at the piano with John on her knee, playing a simple tune which the child was doing his best to follow without success.

'Do we have to have the background music?' Brake asked the fire. 'For want of a better word?'

'Child has to express himself, of course we do,' Lord Lydiard replied. 'Anyway, that's good. From you, I mean. A proponent of Free Expression. You fire ahead, Nanny. Anyway. As I was saying. I got it all first-hand from William. My cousin. Who's in the cabinet. Made them all sit up apparently. Three years at the very least.'

Brake straightened up and turned round.

'Give John to me, Nanny,' he said, reaching out. 'I'll keep him quiet with some tricks.'

Grace handed John over to Brake without meeting the eyes she knew were trying to catch hers, if only to reprimand her, and Brake sat on the sofa with the child on his knee.

'It's caught everyone on the hop,' Lord Lydiard continued, sorting through some music on the top of the piano. 'Got a card from my brother in Switzerland a few weeks ago saying the war scare was a lot of nonsense. Still stuck in Switzerland. Can't get out. Can you read, Nanny?'

Lord Lydiard was holding out a sheet of music to Grace who was still sitting on the piano stool.

'Yes, I can read,' Grace replied. 'Why – what is it?'

'Something I want to learn. Fauré. A barcarolle.'

'It looks quite difficult.'

'Does it? Oh. Well. Do the best you can.'

Grace sat and studied it while the two men continued talking, Brake entertaining a delighted John with a trick with a penny which he was making disappear into the child's ear and reappear out of his own, while Lord Lydiard sampled a selection of wines Harcross had been instructed to bring up from the cellar.

'Yes,' Lord Lydiard said, returning to his theme. 'No one really seems to have given the war much serious thought. We're severely undermanned. Not that it's my subject, but I had all this from my cousin. Apparently we can only muster five maybe six divisions to send over to France, so Kitchener's plan, it seems, is to build a volunteer army. Haven't fought on the continent since Waterloo, know that, Brake? That's practically a hundred years ago. We won't have a clue. How are you doing there, Nanny?'

'If you don't mind a few mistakes,' Grace replied, taking the music from her knee and setting it up on the stand.

'Imagine they'll think it's going to be fought with cavalry,' Lord Lydiard mused, sampling another wine. 'Like the Crimea. Like Waterloo. Gracious heavens.'

'That directed at the wine, John? Or the notion of cavalry warfare?' Brake asked.

'Latter,' Lord Lydiard replied. 'Wine's right on the mark. Fire ahead, Nanny.'

Grace played the barcarolle through with only one

mistake. When she finished, she looked up to find Lord Lydiard staring at her from the end of the keyboard, his mouth pushed forward into a pout, his brow deeply furrowed.

'Hmmm,' he said, sitting beside her. 'That, wasn't it? That what you played? Instead of this.'

His left hand reached across her, across her starched apron, stretching for a chord which he sounded, the arch of his wrist against her breast.

'That's it,' he said, now easing himself on to the stool and Grace off it. 'Good. Well done. You can read as well as that, there's quite a lot we can learn.'

Putting his glasses on, Lord Lydiard then stared up at the ceiling and played through the piece himself. Whereas Grace had only made one mistake, he made several, but whereas Grace had played the piece precisely, Lord Lydiard played it perfectly, at once capturing the French composer's elusiveness and expressing the poetry without a trace of sentimentality.

'One of the Romans said and I can't remember which one,' he said in the silence which followed his rendition. 'One of them always said don't ask what your country can do for you but what you can do for your country. But you know, I'm not so sure. I'm really not so sure.'

They all sat in silence for a while, a quiet observed even by the child who was half falling asleep on Brake's lap. Grace reached out for him and took him gently from Brake who held one of the boy's hands to his lips to kiss.

'Good night, young man,' he whispered.

Grace carried the child to his father, but Lord Lydiard saw neither of them. He was staring up at the ceiling, at a war which was to come as he began to play the barcarolle again, this time faultlessly as well as perfectly.

From then on it seemed there was no talk of anything but war, and the more everyone talked the less confident they became, all except Cook who still firmly subscribed to the belief that 'one good push would do it'.

'You mark my words,' she would stoutly maintain in

the face of her fellow servants' scorn. 'Soon as they send the cavalry in it'll all be over. There's no cavalry in the world like the British cavalry. Look what they did to the Boers.'

Everyone in the servants' hall begged to differ, led by Mr Harcross who argued that the wide open spaces of the *veld* were a very different proposition from the populous countryside of the Franco-Belgian borderland. Besides, as everyone knew, he further contended, any war fought now would be a war of the guns. The cavalry was dead. Not according to Cook, whose own father had been killed at Balaclava in the charge of the Light Brigade. *All that was needed was one good push.*

'I'm glad you're so young,' Grace would sigh as she hugged baby John to her before putting him down for the night. 'Thank God you're too young to fight. And thank God you're a girl, Harriet,' she added one evening when Harriet came in to say good night to her brother.

'What about Henry?' Harriet asked as she sat dandling John on her knee. 'He's not too young.'

'What are you talking about?' Grace looked back sharply from the chest of drawers where she was busy putting the child's clothes away. 'Henry's far too young. He's still only sixteen, Harriet.'

'Henry doesn't think that's too young, Nanny,' Harriet replied, getting up as John made his own way upside down into his bed. 'He and Papa were talking the other night at dinner about whether or not they would or should fight, and Henry said if the war wasn't over quickly then he'd join up as soon as he could.'

Grace was speechless. As she turned John back the right way round in his bed she found she didn't know what to say. It had never entered her mind that Henry might volunteer because to her Henry was still the boy on the lawn watching for motor-cars, the boy fishing from the bank of the lake, the boy in her arms as she kissed him goodbye at school. Sixteen years old was no age to fight. It was far too young, she had assured herself the only time she'd allowed herself properly to contemplate the implications of a war as far as her charges were concerned, and by the time Henry might be old enough to fight the battle would have long ceased to rage. Even if the war wasn't over by the end of the year and Cook was wrong, as seemed most certainly to be the case, then surely with the combined might of France, Russia and Great Britain ranked against them the Germans couldn't possibly hold out for longer than another six months? Just as everyone was saying?

'You know what Papa said right from the beginning,' Harriet continued, as if reading Grace's thoughts. 'What Lord Kitchener said.'

'Yes,' Grace said curtly, not wishing to be reminded of the fact. 'But that's at its worst. He's a soldier, not a prophet, and he's only trying to warn people just in case.'

'In case of what, Nanny? In case the war does go on and on?'

'In case of complacency, darling. In case we underestimate the task ahead.'

Grace collected a book from the shelves for John's bedtime story.

'I'll read to him, Nanny,' Harriet volunteered. 'I enjoy reading. And John's so sweet.' She took the book from Grace and sat on the edge of her brother's bed. 'Not Peter Rabbit *again?*' she asked with a smile as she pushed a loop of blond hair back over her ear.

'I like Peter Rabbit best,' John said, snuggling down under his bedclothes. 'I know it by heart.'

While Harriet read the Beatrix Potter tale, only stopping on demand when John insisted on seeing the pictures, Grace tidied up the child's clothes and fussed around the room over nothing. Although they now had less space than previously in the nurseries, Grace far preferred the new arrangement. John slept and played in the same room now, the room which had been his late mother's *boudoir*, while Grace slept in the bedroom off it. They had their own small bathroom, beyond which Dora

slept in a room which had formerly stored junk. Next to
Dora was Harriet's room, then Henry's, and finally at
the very end of the corridor was Lord Lydiard's suite of
rooms. Everyone was very happy where they now were,
because as Harriet said at last they felt like a proper
family, albeit a family with only one parent.

'Actually that's not strictly true,' Harriet had said
one afternoon when she and Grace were both painting.
'Strictly speaking we might only really have a father, but
that's not how it feels.'

There were guests that Christmas: Lord and Lady Ducarn
who had originally both been friends of Lady Lydiard
but who had since become devoted to Lord Lydiard; John
Chaburn, a writer of adventure stories and his beautiful
and elegant wife Marie; the diminutive and charming
Irish portrait painter William Child and his wife Mercy;
Lord Lydiard's brother and sister-in-law Gerald and
Cicely Rokeham; his mother-in-law Diana, Lady Hythe;
and last but by no means least Brake Merrowby, close to
whom Grace found herself sitting at lunch on Christmas
Day.

Brake was drunk, but for a change neither dramatically
nor miserably. There had been a drinks party after matins
and before lunch at which according to Henry the male
guests had all consumed the best part of a bottle of champagne each, so by the time everyone was seated around the
beautifully laid table none of the men and not all of the
women were entirely sober and everyone was certainly in
festive spirit, a condition in which they remained thanks
to the continuing and seemingly endless supply of wine.

'Oh come on, Nanny!' Brake cried when Grace refused
his offer of champagne. 'This is Christmas and you're *not*
on duty. Isn't that right, young John?'

The wide-open eyes of the child sitting between Grace
and Brake reflected not just the dancing lights of the candles but the whole wonder of the moment as he smiled and
held a cut glass up to the handsome man beside him.

'I'll have some, please,' he said.

'Sure you will,' Brake agreed, pouring out enough to fill a soup spoon. 'And so will Nanny. The best of life is but intoxication.'

Grace's glass was refilled and Brake turned away to offer the wine to Cicely Rokeham who was seated to his left. There were no servants present. Grace knew Lord Lydiard had granted leave to anyone who wanted to spend the rest of the day with their own families, particularly the younger male members of the staff, and she knew why.

'Just in case,' Harriet had surmised to Grace before lunch when she had noticed the absence of Harcross and the two footmen.

'Exactly, darling,' Grace had agreed. 'Just in case.'

There was no further reference to the war throughout the entire meal. It was as if there had been a tacit agreement between all the guests and the members of the family not to mention the subject. The only time the war had been alluded to was on the walk back from church, when behind her and the children Grace had heard Brake sounding off to Lord Lydiard.

'That's what gets me about the church, John!' he had protested. 'It's so damn' infallible! There you have some guy, some ordinary guy and in this case an extremely ordinary guy – getting up to preach at us and telling us God is on our side! How *does* he know? Did he have a vision? Did God appear to him and tell him so? Did He say I want you to put it around that I'm with you guys? And not the Boche? Because Fritz prays too, you know. And not to a different God.'

'Well you know what they say, Brake, don't you?' Lord Lydiard had replied. 'The French, that is. The nearer you get to a church, the further you get from God.'

'They never said a righter thing, John!'

'No, I don't think they did, Brake. Well perhaps they did, in fact they said lots of things, very germane things, but that happens to suit the moment.'

'What do you think, Nanny?' Harriet had asked, her arm looped through Grace's. 'Mama used to say she preferred going to church in her mind.'

'I wonder what God would build churches of?' Henry had mused, every day it seemed a little bit taller, every day that bit more handsome. 'I'd say if God were left to build his own churches, he wouldn't use stone.'

'What do you think he'd use instead, Henry?' Grace had asked, intrigued.

'I don't know, Nan,' he'd answered, using his new abbreviation for her. 'I'm not sure. Light probably. Lots and lots of light.'

Henry was next to Grace at lunch, talking to Lady Ducarn who was on his right about his still unabated passion for motor-cars, and from the enraptured look on the beautiful American woman's face Grace thought he could be talking about the works of Michelangelo.

'I see young Henry's in love,' Brake said with a grin, putting an arm on the back of young John's chair. 'But then who isn't?'

Grace stole a glance to her right and then looked back at Brake.

'You mean Lady Ducarn?' she asked.

'If you want charm made manifest,' Brake replied, 'if you want to see woman as a thoroughbred, if you want sunshine in your garden, electricity in your air, a room full of unpremeditated music, if you want *evanescence*—' Brake held out a hand to indicate the slender brunette still engrossed with Henry.

'Obviously Henry's not the only one who's smitten,' Grace smiled.

'Everyone loves Ruby Ducarn,' Brake sighed, tousling John's hair. 'Everyone except the self-important. Who after five minutes in her company suddenly find they are wearing no clothes.'

Grace found herself drawn once again to look at the exquisite and languorous beauty who was now laughing with unconcealed delight at something Henry had told her, one hand resting lightly on the young man's arm. When she stopped laughing she caught Grace's look and smiled, not a polite smile, but a dazzling wreath of sheer and sweet enchantment.

'Henry is a gem, Nanny,' she announced. 'Congratulations.'

Grace blushed and smiled back, straight into the eyes of the woman who was finally going to deprive her of Brake for ever.

After the distribution of presents and while the younger members of the family examined or played with their gifts, the war was mentioned again for the first time since church. The subject was mobilization.

'Something will have to be done,' Lord Ducarn was saying when Grace came back into the room. The men were grouped by the fireplace drinking port and brandy while at a table in the window the women had begun a card game. 'This concentration on the navy will be our undoing if we're not careful. This war is not going to be won by naval power, mark my words.'

'We don't have enough trained soldiers,' Gerald Rokeham said. 'The Germans had five million they could call on. Five million.'

'The French had nearly as many,' Lord Ducarn added. 'They had over four million. And what did we have?'

'Less than two hundred thousand,' Gerald Rokeham said gloomily.

'One hundred and sixty thousand to be precise,' said Lord Ducarn. 'Over fifty thousand of whom were killed or wounded at Ypres.'

'The Children's Massacre,' Lord Lydiard declared, to the surprise of his companions and Grace, who was nearby tidying up the discarded wrapping papers. 'Didn't you know?' Lord Lydiard then asked. 'I thought you must know. William told me. My cousin. That's what the Germans called Ypres. There were so many young men killed, you see. From the volunteer regiments which were used in their frontal attacks. Absolutely dreadful.'

Grace saw where he was looking. He was looking at Henry who was sitting on the floor with his brother, playing with the brightly coloured wooden train Grace had given John.

'It's a war, John,' Lord Ducarn said. 'These things happen in wars.'

'You don't send boys into the front line, Herbert,' Lord Lydiard replied. 'Not boys.'

'If there's no one else to send,' Lord Ducarn persisted. 'If you volunteer to be a soldier, you must expect to be shot at.'

'They're not trained,' Lord Lydiard argued. 'They're just cannon fodder. They're under-equipped, many of our volunteers don't even have uniforms yet—'

'There were over three quarters of a million volunteers by October, you know,' Lord Ducarn interrupted. 'The most tremendous response.'

'And they're being drilled with wooden rifles,' Lord Lydiard replied. 'Which really won't stand them in very good stead, will it? When they get to France.'

'That would be funny,' Brake said from deep in his armchair, 'were it not so goddamn tragic.'

'And what says the New World in the matter?' William Child chimed in. 'Or are you going to sit this one out?'

'We have troubles of our own in Mexico,' Brake replied. 'They had to send the fleet to Tampico, or didn't you read? President Wilson ordered the marines in to Vera Cruz.'

'All because Huerta wouldn't salute the Stars and Stripes,' William Child laughed. 'Dearie me.'

'You think the European war is any less senseless, Bill?' Brake asked. 'Are you willing to put your life on the line because some half-crazy Hapsburg got himself assassinated in Bosnia?'

'I think I suppose I am, yes,' Lord Lydiard said out of the silence that followed the laughter. 'Although my decision has nothing to do with the Hapsburgs. Or Austria.'

Everyone was looking at their host, their relative, their parent and their employer now. Gravity had suddenly overtaken festivity.

'You're too old to fight,' Lord Lydiard's brother announced, as if to close the debate. 'Unless of course you're talking hypothetically.'

'No,' Lord Lydiard replied carefully. 'No no, I'm not supposing, Gerald. No ifs or buts. And one can always lie about one's age. Which I gather some fellows are. Lot of people are actually, so I gather. The point is Belgium, you see. I don't think anybody at least not if they're in their right mind, I don't think you can just sit by and twiddle your thumbs after what they did to Belgium. Do you?'

There was another silence, during which William Child took a cigarette and lit it, striking the match down the side of the stone fireplace.

'I still say you're too old,' Gerald Rokeham insisted. 'You're what – forty-two. You don't shoot. You've bad eyesight—'

'There's nothing really wrong with my eyes,' Lord Lydiard interrupted. 'I sometimes wear glasses for reading, that's all. Nor is there any point in trying to make me change my mind, Gerald, because it's something you should consider as well. You're three years younger than I am, and you can shoot. I think you ought to at least think about it. Now then. I think some sort of entertainment is called for. Henry? Henry, we should organize a game or something. What do you think? Harriet?'

Lord Lydiard gathered his two eldest children to him and began to confer with them as to what they might play. The group around the fireplace slowly dispersed, Lord Ducarn and Gerald Rokeham helping themselves to more port, while Brake fell into conversation with his fellow artist William Child. Grace cleared the floor of all John's toys in preparation for the games which were to follow, and after she had put them away on top of a window seat, Lord Lydiard's mother-in-law Lady Hythe summoned her over to where she was sitting alone to one side of the Christmas tree.

'We've never really spoken, Nanny, have we?' she asked as Grace took her place beside her. 'Not at any great length anyway.'

The older woman, who was almost as tall and still as slim as her dead daughter, talked without looking at Grace, her face concealed as always behind a dark veil.

Rumour had it variously, most people subscribing to the supposition that she had been badly burned as a child when trapped by a fire on the nursery floor, and certainly Lady Hythe was never seen without either a veil or gloves. That was all Grace knew, because that was all she had ever heard propounded in the servants' hall, and because Lady Lydiard had never once talked about her mother or the mystery surrounding her in Grace's presence.

In fact Lady Hythe was a very infrequent visitor to Keston. Even when her daughter had been alive she rarely called and certainly to the best of Grace's knowledge she had never once stayed as a house guest during the seven years Grace had been there. Her appearances had in the main been limited to birthdays and Christmas, during which sojourns as she had correctly indicated she had hardly exchanged more than a greeting with Grace.

'Your charges do you proud, Nanny,' she said. 'Children nowadays by and large are so ill-mannered and determined only on getting their own way.'

'I think children have always been like that, Lady Hythe,' Grace replied. 'When you're small you're quite ruthless when it comes to satisfying your needs. You have to be, don't you think? Because you depend for everything on other people, and if you can't make your voice heard life soon becomes impossible.'

'Not when it comes to manners, Nanny,' Lady Hythe said. 'Perhaps we are indeed monsters when we're children, but not when it comes to manners. You must surely agree that as far as good manners go, today's child leaves a lot to be desired.'

'I was reading some G. K. Chesterton recently,' Grace said, 'and he inclined me towards his way of thinking. As far as manners go. That morals are more important because they belong to all mankind, whereas good manners always mean our own manners. And that we only enforce them as a convenience.'

Lady Hythe turned and looked at Grace directly for the first time. Even though she couldn't see them, Grace could sense the eyes behind the look, large dark eyes which seemed to burrow into her very being.

'Do you always beg to differ, Nanny?' she enquired, still holding the look.

'Yes, I'm afraid so, Lady Hythe,' Grace replied with a sigh. 'It's a habit I seem to have had since I was a child.'

'Well, there's no need to despair, I assure you,' Lady Hythe said, turning away. 'I have exactly the same habit myself.'

Grace laughed, and brushed some imaginary crumbs from her skirt.

'None the less,' Lady Hythe continued, accepting the offer of a cup of tea from Cicely Rokeham, 'your charges do you proud. In spite of your perversity, or who knows? Perhaps even because of it. Henry and Harriet are delightful company, and they both adore you. I cannot bear to imagine what might have happened had they not had you to look after them.'

'They've done for me twice as much as I've done for them,' Grace replied with complete honesty.

'Then perhaps it's true, Nanny,' Lady Hythe said. 'That as far as children go a model is better than a critic. All Harriet wants for herself, so she tells me, is to be as fair and as good a person as you.'

Grace said nothing, looking instead to where Harriet was standing with her father and brother busy choosing teams for the game about to be played, no longer a child but a growing young woman, blonde, bright-eyed and beautiful.

'What would you want for her, Nanny?' Lady Hythe enquired, her gaze also on Harriet.

'Oh, I think the right or just the chance, Lady Hythe, to express herself,' Grace replied without hesitation. 'Harriet is very gifted. I would want her to have the chance to enjoy her gift.'

For a while they sat in silence, Lady Hythe sipping her tea, and Grace watching as the two teams were formed by the two captains, Henry and Harriet. Harriet's first choice was Grace.

'It's terrible to have regrets, isn't it, Nanny?' Lady

Hythe asked, as they watched Henry asking Lady Ducarn if she would be on his team. 'That's what you're talking about, I take it? Not having the chance to take your chance. Or simply missing out on something. I missed out on my daughter, you see. We were never very close, at least not since her childhood. But now that she's gone—' The older woman paused while Harriet chose Brake. 'It was so very kind of John to ask me here,' she continued. 'I would find it difficult to explain how much it means.'

Both teams had been selected now, Lady Hythe having been chosen by Henry. Grace straightened her skirt and went to get up, putting both her hands on the arms of her chair.

'No,' Lady Hythe said suddenly, stopping her before she could rise. 'Show me your hands.'

A little puzzled, Grace first looked down at her hands on the arm of the chair and then back at Lady Hythe, who was now holding out her own. Grace held her hands out, and Lady Hythe took them, holding them lightly, both palms down against her black gloves.

'You have the hands of an artist,' she said after a long, steady examination. 'Do you play the piano?'

'Yes I do as a matter of fact,' Grace replied.

'Do you paint?'

The older woman raised her head, and once again Grace felt a look she couldn't see.

'Yes,' Grace said. 'Or rather more correctly I used to paint. Once.'

Lady Hythe put her right hand on top of Grace's left one and held it there.

'Yes,' she said, 'and so did I. Strange, don't you think? That it seems to be the lot of so many women to bury what they really are. You must come and visit me, Nanny,' she added, 'with the children.'

Then they both rose and went to play their game of charades.

On the morning of 25 May the following spring, the day after the second Battle of Ypres had finished being fought at a colossal cost in human lives and for no real gain or loss in territory, Lord Lydiard called Grace into his study and asked her to dye his hair.

At first Grace thought she had misheard her employer, then when he repeated his request that he was teasing her.

'Why should you want to dye your hair, Lord Lydiard?' she asked him.

'Because most of it's grey, Nanny,' Lord Lydiard replied. 'Why else do you think?'

'If I may say so, Lord Lydiard,' Grace ventured, 'it's been grey for quite some time now.'

'Which is precisely the reason I wish to dye it, Nanny,' Lord Lydiard replied, with more than a little irritation. 'Now either you can or you can't.'

'I suppose I can,' Grace replied. 'Not that I've ever dyed anyone's hair before, but my mother dyes hers. I could ask her for the recipe.'

'This isn't a laughing matter, Nanny,' Lord Lydiard said, seeing Grace's Cheshire cat grin. 'And I don't want you broadcasting the information, so do you have to ask anyone? Surely you can just go into the chemist's, can't you? Can't you just go into Herbert's and ask for whatever it is you have to ask for and there's an end to it?'

'I could,' Grace agreed. 'You could.'

'I'll be blowed, Nanny.' Lord Lydiard was now becoming distinctly edgy, not so much fiddling with the loose coins in his trouser pockets as crashing them. 'Not the sort of thing at all. Catch me. No no, either you go into Herbert's and get the blessed concoction or we forget all about it.'

'What colour were you thinking of going?'

'What colour, Nanny? What *colour*? I don't want to go a colour for goodness sake, woman! I just want my wretched hair dyed! The colour it was! Sort of black! Sort of dark brown! Colour indeed.'

Long before she applied the brown tinge to Lord Lydiard's thick greying hair as he knelt over his handbasin with a towel around his shoulders Grace knew why he was doing it. *One can always lie about one's age*. And the lie would be a far more plausible one if there were no grey hairs showing.

'This can have the opposite effect, you know,' Grace told him before she applied the dye. 'It can sometimes make people look older.'

'Just carry on, will you?' Lord Lydiard ordered. 'And let me do the worrying.'

He had a beautifully shaped head, just like Henry's, a slender neck and small perfectly shaped and set ears. He was also much stronger across his shoulders and back than Grace had imagined. Because of the way he moved he always gave the impression of being very much a lightweight, but his physique, although only visible at the back and where he had rolled up the arms of his undershirt, was that of a much stronger man.

Carefully Grace rubbed the pigment into his hair, her hands protected by the thick pair of household rubber gloves Mr Herbert had directed her to use. Lord Lydiard knelt perfectly still, one hand holding a dry flannel tightly over his eyes and the other hand keeping the towel in place.

'It's like being a boy again,' he said suddenly. 'This is how old Nanny Lydiard used to wash my hair. Exactly like you're doing. I heard from her sister the other day, you know. She wrote to me to tell me her grandson fell at Ypres. During the first battle. He was nineteen. The woman's only grandchild.'

Grace applied some more dye, cupping her gloved hand at the front of Lord Lydiard's head so that none should spill over.

'*The mintage of man*,' Lord Lydiard said from behind his towel.

'I'm sorry?' Grace said, not having heard.

' "A Shropshire Lad", remember? You remember Henry reading it to us. *They carry back bright to the coiner the mintage of man*.'

'I remember it very well.'

'Wrote it in eighteen ninety-six,' Lord Lydiard said.

'Little ahead of its time, way things are going.'

She combed his dark wet hair out carefully, while he held the white towel to his face. He smelt faintly of shaving soap and stephanotis. And all at once Grace wondered whether he would have asked her to dye his hair for him had she not been his children's nanny.

'Right,' she said. 'We have to leave it now for an hour, and then wash it again before we dry it.'

'An hour?' Lord Lydiard's eyes looked at her over the top of his fleecy towel. 'What am I going to do for an hour, Nanny? Just sit here?'

'You can read.'

'Or you could read to me.'

They were still in the bathroom. Grace held open the door and smiled politely.

'I'll be back to wash it out in exactly an hour,' she said. 'I have to give John his lunch.'

Because his face was still so youthful, Lord Lydiard looked younger not older. In fact the dye had taken so well that only the closest inspection revealed any telltale grey hairs. The operation had been so successful Grace assured her employer that he could pass for ten years younger than his real age.

'Why should I want to do that, Nanny?' he said. 'I didn't say I wanted people to think I was younger.'

'You have thought about your children, haven't you?' Grace asked as she began tidying the bathroom while Lord Lydiard stood in front of the mirror retying his necktie. 'I'm allowed to ask that because your children are my concern.'

'You sound very strict, Nanny,' Lord Lydiard said, chin raised as he flicked his tie through. 'I'm not sure I want to see that side of you.'

'You're sure this isn't a quixotic gesture?' Grace asked, ignoring the sidetrack.

'Gracious.' Lord Lydiard eyed her in the mirror and Grace caught the look. 'Old Nanny Lydiard would never have read Cervantes.'

'I'm only thinking of your children,' Grace insisted, hoping she sounded more convincing to Lord Lydiard than she did to herself. 'They've already lost one parent.'

From the stunned look on his face Grace guessed this was the first time such a thought had occurred to Lord Lydiard. With his tie still not tied he sank slowly down into the white wicker chair behind him and stared into space, while Grace pretended not to notice, folding towels and washing out the handbasin.

'I don't think perhaps that was very fair, Nanny,' Lord Lydiard said finally.

'It wasn't intended to be,' Grace replied, putting a dye-stained towel in the linen basket. 'It wouldn't be very fair on Henry and Harriet and John to be left with no one at all.'

'Henry and Harriet would manage. Henry's nearly seventeen, Harriet's practically a young woman, and John has you.'

'I was older than Harriet when my father left,' Grace said. 'He wasn't killed in a war. He just left my mother, and even though we still had a mother, my sister and I have never really recovered.'

Lord Lydiard looked up at Grace and frowned. Grace thought he must be seeing a lot of things for the first time that afternoon.

'You probably think like a lot of people that nannies grow on trees,' she continued, the wind now well and truly in her sails. 'That we don't have homes or parents, and consequently that we don't have feelings. Or rather not the same sort of feelings that other people have. Well, whoever we nannies are, and wherever we come from, and speaking for myself, as a somebody, as a person who has become a nanny, and not *vice versa*, I know what it's like when you lose a parent. I know what can happen, what the effect can be. The consequences. I also know what your children went through when they lost their mother, better than you do, Lord Lydiard. Better than anyone, and if they lost you, I don't think it would be *fair*. I don't think they could survive another such mortal blow, and still remain themselves.'

'Of course they would,' Lord Lydiard muttered. 'Non-sense. This is complete nonsense.'

'They couldn't.'

'You can't hold this sort of gun, you just can't.' Lord Lydiard looked at the floor. 'You simply cannot hold this sort of gun to one's head.'

'I'm not holding the gun,' Grace said. 'It's not my finger on the trigger.'

'They probably won't send me anywhere near the front line.'

'In that case, what's the point?'

'What's the *point*?' Now he looked up at her, as if she was mad.

'What is the point in volunteering if you can't fight?' Grace asked. 'That's what it was all about at Christmas after all. To avenge Belgium. To beat the aggressor, as far as I could gather. But if they won't allow you to do your bit, to fight like a man could and should, and you get killed sitting in a tent writing a supply sheet, what's the point? Someone like you, with your intelligence and wit, there must be other ways, better ways that you can serve your country and help defeat the enemy.'

Lord Lydiard sat stroking his chin thoughtfully with the tips of his fingers for a long time before replying.

'Hmmm,' he said once, before relapsing again into silence. Grace meanwhile wiped the brass taps clean with a dry face flannel.

'Hmmm,' Lord Lydiard said again. 'Lady Ducarn said more or less precisely the same thing to me at Christmas. The only difference between her and you – well, there's a lot of difference really. She's a very intelligent woman, but nowhere near as intelligent as you. Not in the same way. But she did have a suggestion. I mean, her argu-ment was nothing to do with Henry. And Harriet and John, she wasn't at all concerned with the smalls. I still think of them like that, don't you? Suppose we always will really. Anyway she was saying, Lady Ducarn, more or less what you've been saying. That there's more than one way to skin the famous cat etcetera. And of course there is, you're both absolutely right, there's absolutely no question about it. Not only that, Gerald's right. I'm an absolutely useless shot, I can't see a thing without my glasses, and they'd probably put me in charge of peeling potatoes.'

He smiled at Grace, just as Henry would smile, suddenly, the way the sun appears from behind the clouds on a showery day in April. Grace smiled back and sat down on the edge of the roll-topped bath.

'Only thing is,' he said after a moment while he looked Grace in the eyes, 'if that's the case, we needn't have bothered about the hair.'

TWENTY

By June, all the young and able-bodied men at Keston had left to join up. *There's Room For You!* the posters had announced, picturing troops leaning out of a packed railway compartment smiling and waving their hats and beckoning to the unseen conscripts. *Join Up Today!* But the men would have gone without Kitchener's saturation campaign. The reality of the war had dawned on them before Christmas, and by the New Year Lord Lydiard had already lost both his footmen, six foot one George and six foot two Tom, to the Guards, and Arthur his valet to the Royal Artillery.

Throughout that spring the rest of the fighting men had taken the shilling, the under-gardeners, the grooms, Parker the chauffeur, Toddy the handyman though he was well into his thirties, the stablelads and even Tim the pot boy who was hardly sixteen. They were all gone to fight for King and Country and before the last had signed up the first lay dead in the mud.

George fell first, George known as James upstairs because he was the first footman, George known as James fell at Ypres, not during one of the set battles, but the victim of a sniper's bullet. George who was loved by everyone for his good humour and his unending patience died from a cowardly shot, a bullet in the back of his head which killed him outright as he was hauling the wounded body of a comrade back to the trenches. George loved by Clara the maid, pretty dark-eyed Clara who was to be married to George just as soon as they had saved enough between them to run the small public house of their dreams. Little Clara barely five feet tall who sat and cried her heart out for a week when they broke the news, news that made Cook privately declare to Grace that she doubted then if any of them, if any of her brave lads from Keston would ever come back.

Not only the Great House was deserted. By midsummer the village of Keston itself had given up most of its youth. One day in March there had been a rally, with a band and flags, and a well known music hall artiste speaking from the back of a hay wagon and leading the villagers in patriotic songs, a well oiled demonstration which enkindled the hearts of the audience, so much so that when the singer in her scarlet and gold dress and her vividly made up face threw out her arms and implored the young men to come to her, to come up to the wagon and join the great fight, there was practically a stampede as young men barely out of boyhood leapt on to the hay cart to be rewarded with a kiss and an embrace, some of them pushed up there by their mothers, their sisters and even their wives, there to be kissed by a woman in scarlet and gold, the last embrace most of them would feel before the grave.

Grace was there. She saw it all. With Lottie they stood and watched as boys who had pulled their hair at school only later to fight each other in the playground for the right to walk them home jostled and elbowed their way through the throng on their way to extinction. Not that everyone saw it that way. Most people were cheering, as if the place the boys were going was a holiday resort rather than a battlefield. Only the older ones held back, those with clear memories of South Africa and even the Crimea, those who had seen the wounded returning, and those who had waited in vain. There were few cheers from them for the youth that was to pour its red sweet wine away, that was to vanish, *rose-crowned into the darkness.*

'I shall have to go,' Lottie said as she and Grace walked away up the high street after the rally was over. 'You do know that, don't you?'

'Yes,' Grace said, slipping her arm through her sister's. 'I keep feeling I should go as well.'

'You can't, Grace,' Lottie said. 'What about the children?'

'They're not my children,' Grace said. 'And this is a war.'

'They might as well be your children, Grace,' Lottie replied. 'And anyway, you're not a nurse like me. You're only a child's nurse.'

'It wouldn't take long to pick up what I need to know,' Grace said, waving back at some of their old classmates who were running on past them up the hill, waving their Union Jacks. 'They're going to need an awful lot of nurses over there.'

'You told Lord Lydiard he shouldn't fight because of the children,' Lottie argued. 'Neither should you nurse, for the selfsame reason. Harriet and Henry might be old enough to survive without you, but who would bring up John?'

'Another nanny,' Grace replied half-heartedly. 'I'm not indispensable.'

'I'm afraid you are,' her sister replied. 'And you know it.'

'Yes, I suppose I do,' Grace confessed. 'Which is what makes it even more impossible.'

'Why?' Lottie stopped and turned Grace to her. 'You can't be mother to us all, Grace. There's a limit to what one person can do. You've found your role in life, something to which you're ideally suited, perfectly so. Something which you do wonderfully, which enhances the lives of those in your charge. It doesn't matter that they're not your children. Because they're not, they probably love you all the more, more than children of your own would ever love you. You're lucky, Grace, you should count your blessings. Because you've found your purpose in life. You don't have to be anything or anybody else.

Remember what Mrs Jenkins used to say? Blessed is the person who has found his work, and let him ask for no other blessedness. Anyway, you only envy me—'

'Who said anything about envy?' Grace retorted. 'I don't envy you.'

'Yes of course you do.' Lottie smiled. 'You envy me because what I do is the same as you. People only ever envy likes.'

'Do you know something, Lottie?' Grace asked as they resumed their walk. 'I think you're absolutely right.'

The next day Lord Lydiard returned from London where he had been for a week. Grace was sitting out on the terrace having tea with Harriet, while Dora and John played catch with a ball on the lawn.

'I'll call Clara to get you some fresh tea,' Grace said as Lord Lydiard sat down with them. 'This will be cold.'

'We're going to have to close up Keston,' Lord Lydiard said later, after he had shared a plate of fresh cucumber sandwiches with Harriet and Grace. 'Because we're going to have to live in London.'

'I shall like that,' Harriet said. 'Perhaps I can go to art school.'

'Perhaps you can,' her father agreed. 'The point is they've found me something to do.' He looked at Grace and smiled his sudden quick shy smile. 'Not peeling potatoes, something fairly interesting really. It came via my cousin, via William, you know, the one in the cabinet. He knows this fellow Head, you see, and he's put him in charge of what you'd have to describe as – well – a propaganda department, pure and simple, do you see. It's all a bit haphazard, as well as early days. But the point is something needs to be done if we're not to have a repetition of what happened in the Boer war. You won't be aware of this, but during that particular conflict we were very unpopular right across the globe, and no one wrote anything or said anything to persuade people otherwise. It's not really propaganda as such – more the what do you call it? The dissemination of the truth. At least that's what cousin William calls it.'

'What will you have to do, Papa?' Harriet asked. 'Will you have to write things?'

'They've got some bods already, H,' Lord Lydiard replied. 'Writing bods that is. That chum of mine who was here for Christmas funnily enough. John Chaburn. He's been roped in. Arthur Lees-Boyle. Some historian chap with a Russian-sounding name, and some museum men. And a couple of artists which reminds me. Is Brake about, H? You seen him today?' Lord Lydiard looked about him. 'Because of course he'll have to be informed,' he added.

'Why?' Harriet enquired. 'Will Mr Merrowby be coming to London too, Papa?'

'That depends,' her father replied. 'Unless he prefers to stay here.'

In the event Brake came with them. Keston was left in the charge of Fred Pilgrim, the only remaining groom, Herbert Carroll, the head gardener, and Mr and Mrs Campion who lived in the gate lodge and acted as caretakers when the need arose. The horses and ponies were turned away, the contents of the house were put under dust-sheets, the windows were shuttered, and the female staff who weren't accompanying them to London were sent home to their families until further notice, still however on their full wage.

To the house in Cadogan Square they took Mr Harcross, Mrs Mason the housekeeper, two parlour maids, Clara and Rebecca, Edith from the kitchens, Dora to help Grace, and of course Cook, plus the two dogs, Beanie and Henry's mongrel Chipper. The servants were sent ahead to open up the house while the family, Brake and Grace stayed at the Savoy. They were now into July and a week after they had moved into Cadogan Square the summer term was over and Henry joined them.

It was a very serious Henry who moved in, an even more serious-minded Henry than ever. Much as he was obviously pleased to see his father, sister and brother, and warmly though he greeted Grace, Grace could sense his distraction the moment he stepped over the threshold.

'Everything all right?' she asked, putting her head round his bedroom door after he'd gone to bed that night. 'Did you have a good term?'

'It was fine,' Henry said, looking up from his book. 'Nothing remarkable.'

'Thanks for all your letters.'

Henry looked up again and pulled a face.

'I'm sorry, Nan,' he said. 'We had exams. And what with one thing and another. And I had a lot on my mind.'

'I'd say you still had,' Grace said. 'What is it? Have you fallen in love?'

'Don't be a tease,' Henry said. 'But if you're that interested, no I haven't.'

'Good,' Grace said, coming in and pretending to tidy his perfectly tidy room. 'There's still hope for me then.'

For once Henry ignored the provocation. Normally when Grace needled him about girls, and remarked that there was still hope for her, Henry would invariably respond, usually by throwing a pillow at Grace, but this time there was no return. Instead he just rolled on his side with his book and chose to ignore the bait.

'What are you reading?' Grace asked.

'Nothing,' Henry answered. 'Just a book.'

'Excuse me for asking,' Grace said. 'Will that be all, sir?'

'It's a book of poems,' Henry said carefully, still not looking round. 'By someone called Rupert Brooke.'

'Yes,' said Grace. *'Fish say, they have their stream and pond, But is there anything beyond?'* That's Rupert Brooke, isn't it? And *And I shall find some girl perhaps, and a better one than you, with eyes as wise, but kindlier, and lips as soft, but true.'*

'And I dare say she will do.' Henry finished off the quotation, and turned round to look up at Grace. 'What *don't* you know?' he asked.

'I don't know what's on your mind,' Grace replied.

'Shut the door then,' Henry said after a moment, sitting up in his bed while Grace did as requested and closed the door.

'You hardly said a word over dinner,' Grace said, sitting on the end of his bed. 'Normally when you come home for the holidays no one can get a word in edgeways for days.'

'You should read these poems, Nan,' Henry said, handing her the book. 'I'll lend them to you when I've finished.'

Grace turned the volume over to look at the spine. *1914 and Other Poems*, the title read. *By Rupert Brooke.*

'He quite expected to die for England, you know,' Henry said. 'From the moment he went to war. He never had a moment's doubt about this country's cause, and yet, so Mr Steane my English master at school said, his heart was devoid of hate. The poet-soldier.'

'Poetry can be very persuasive, you know, Henry,' Grace said, slowly turning the pages of the book. 'It can make things that are not seem as though they are.'

'What I feel hasn't been affected by what I've been reading, Nan,' Henry said, turning on to his back to stare at the ceiling. 'Rupert Brooke's poems are just a reflection. An expression of what most of us feel.'

'Most of who?'

'Us. People my age. My friends. It's not to do with things that are not. Really, it isn't, I promise. It's very much to do with things that are.'

Henry smiled at Grace and took the book back from her, obviously sensing her growing concern.

'One of my friends at school,' he said, 'who's also called Rupert, funnily enough. He was head of our house.'

'Was? You mean he left this term, did he?'

'Yes.' Henry's eyes swivelled round and caught Grace's. He looked at her for a moment before continuing. 'Well, no. He left at the half actually. To enlist.'

'If he was head of your house he must be older than you, obviously,' Grace said, as factually as she could.

Henry shrugged. 'Not much. A year. He's eighteen.'

'I think perhaps we should talk about this in the morning, Henry.' Grace got up, and shook out her skirts, anxious to curtail the conversation now she knew what was on Henry's mind, now he had confirmed that it was precisely what she had suspected. 'I'm not saying what you're thinking isn't very brave and noble, because it is. But you're just seventeen, Henry. You're still only a boy.'

Grace tucked Henry's sheet in and straightened his counterpane, remaining as resolutely literal as she could, which was the very opposite to what she was feeling.

'Sleep on it,' she said. 'When you've had a good night's sleep, and now that you're home with your family, things will look very different in the morning.'

Henry clasped his hands behind his head and shook it.

'They won't, Nan,' he said. 'But thanks anyway.'

Grace took a book off his shelf and opened it.

'Here,' she said, walking back to the bed and handing it to him. 'If you're not sleepy yet, read some Sherlock Holmes. You know how much you love Sherlock Holmes.'

Henry suddenly smiled up at her.

'Yes of course I do,' he said. 'I really like Sherlock Holmes, but reading him never made me want to be a detective. It really isn't anything I've read, Nan.'

Grace just held the book out to him, unable to say anything. Henry took it from her, and put it beside him on the bed.

'I have to fight,' he said. 'Same as every young man does. Because I'm me doesn't make me any different.'

'We'll talk about it in the morning,' Grace said, turning away quickly so he might not see her eyes. 'Or rather you can talk about it with your father. Good night, Henry. God bless you, and keep you safe from harm.'

'Good night, Nan,' Henry said as she closed the door. 'God bless you as well.'

Grace held out until she got to her room, even though by the time she was climbing the stairs she could barely see them. When she opened her door she didn't even bother with putting on the light and getting undressed. She just went straight to her bed and lay down, clasping a pillow tightly to her face, which was precisely how she stayed until she finally cried herself to sleep.

She woke later when Brake came in and went up to his room which was unusual for her. She had got so used to him walking the floor above her bed that it no longer disturbed her. Besides, Grace slept very deeply, although conversely a child had only to cry out once for her to be wide awake.

But there were two things unusual about Brake's behaviour that night. First, he made far more noise than usual when he came in, running up the stairs with no consideration for anyone who might be sleeping on the floor below his studio, and second, once he had closeted himself away up on the third floor he remained there for the rest of the night, intermittently walking the floor again with no thought for the person sleeping below him. Lord Lydiard had suggested that Brake might have most of the third floor of the house for himself, so that he could paint and sleep whenever he wished, undisturbed by the normal routines of the rest of the family, and Brake had settled in there at once, unwittingly choosing the room immediately above Grace for his studio. Grace never mentioned this fact to him because after the initial aggravation of having someone walking above her head at all and any hours had worn off, she began to enjoy his invisible presence as he walked and worked above her.

Sometimes he would be up there for hours after Grace had retired to bed, not finishing his work until two or three in the morning by which time Grace had long gone to sleep, her head full of her imaginings as to what and how he was painting. She knew when his work was going well by the long silences, and when it wasn't by the rhythmic and ritualistic pacing of the floor. Sometimes she could even smell the paint, the mix of turpentine and linseed oil which made her head swim as she relived the excitement of mixing the bright globs of paint on her own palette and stroking the colours on with a flat-bristled brush. She would ache with curiosity as to what Brake was painting, yet she never enquired, not even when they passed each other on the stairs or in the corridors, as Brake was on his way up or down to his studio and Grace was going about her duties.

They would stop and talk, always. Oddly enough since they had all moved to the infinitely smaller house in London, Brake and she now got along, if not better (since they had always *got along*), then much more easily. Once their new life had taken shape they had found a kind of easy intimacy, the sort of affection it is sometimes possible to build on the remains of a once passionate association. Not that Grace's passion had completely abated, as Brake's appeared to have done. Every time she saw him her heart still seemed to miss, and whenever he fixed her with one of his dark brown-eyed looks, beneath the orthodoxy and formality of her immaculate uniform, under her many layers of clothes, beneath her warm skin and inside her very self Grace melted.

For his part Brake treated Grace like a sister, like a best friend. They knew each other well, they understood each other, and he could talk to her frankly and she could answer him honestly. In some ways, because their relationship was no longer pressurized by love, it had become more easy-going and more easy to enjoy.

No doubt due to this shift of emphasis, Grace also found it easier to deal with Brake's sudden outbursts or abrupt descents into melancholia or inebriation. When the *Lusitania* was torpedoed by a German U-boat off the Irish coast in May and twelve hundred people including over a hundred and twenty Americans had been drowned or killed, Brake had been beside himself with rage for over a week at the callous massacre of innocent civilians.

'This has to bring America into the war!' he kept declaring. 'Atrocities such as this have boundless repercussions! The Germans are changing the whole nature of warfare! With their poison gases, their torpedoes and their bombing of innocent civilians! These people have become brutes, believe me! Left to their own devices there's absolutely no saying what a nation like that is capable of! A nation like that is capable of genocide!'

He became even more agitated in July when a bomb

389

planted by a German instructor at Cornell exploded in the buildings of the US Senate and the selfsame terrorist consequently shot and killed an American dignitary.

'It's as if they want to goad us into the war,' he declared. 'Though God alone knows why. Because if Uncle Sam gets rolling they'll disappear off the map.'

This was the mood which still prevailed on the second day of Henry's summer holiday. Things were looking ever more grim. The Allies' plan to outflank the Central Powers by forcing the Dardanelles strait and occupying the Sea of Marmora had gone disastrously wrong, the German U-boats had begun enforcing a blockade of Britain at sea, and their airships had instilled a new sense of panic into the population when they dropped their first bombs on Tyneside and London.

'What hope, John?' Brake said at breakfast, putting down *The Times*. 'Mr Churchill's plan to end the war by snipping off Fritz's tail seems to have backfired somewhat.'

'I don't think Churchill was altogether to blame,' Lord Lydiard replied, helping himself to some kedgeree. 'In fact as a matter of fact I don't think he was to blame at all, and history will probably prove me right. Or rather prove him right rather.'

'The ships were too old, John!' Brake protested. 'What was the thinking behind it? You know what they've been saying. A civilian plan, foisted by a political amateur on reluctant officers and experts.'

'I don't think that's necessarily so,' Lord Lydiard replied, sitting back down at the table next to where Grace was seated by John. 'I don't think that's so at all. For a start the navy couldn't split itself in two, and the wretched man was first of all told there were no troops available and then they sent troops out but in woefully inadequate numbers and according to cousin William appallingly staffed. Churchill couldn't work miracles.'

'The wretched man would appear to have no feelings,' Brake said, buttering his toast. 'What about the famous or rather infamous *stakes we can afford to lose*? Is that how he qualifies human life? Stakes to be gambled with?'

'I think as a matter of fact he wasn't referring to troops, in fact I'm quite sure he wasn't,' Lord Lydiard said.

'No he wasn't,' Grace agreed, remembering what she'd read in the newspaper. 'He says he was referring to the old battleships that were sent to the Dardanelles.'

'Is there *anything* you don't know about, Nanny?' Brake asked her, with deliberate over-emphasis.

'Exactly what I asked her last night, Mr Merrowby,' Henry said.

'I think it has to do with the company I keep,' Grace replied. 'The conversations to which I'm party nowadays are so erudite.'

She smiled back at him before turning her attention to John who seemed intent to wipe his jam-laden knife on the tablecloth.

'Even so,' Brake said, sitting back in his chair, still with his eyes on Grace. 'Even so, these are bad times. The worst times I can remember. Suppose we – you – suppose you lose this war?'

'I don't think we will,' Lord Lydiard said. 'Wars aren't decided any longer by what you might call episodic victories. You know what I mean, I'm sure: like Philippi, Waterloo, Naseby. We could well win the war without winning any sensational victories. The Germans are too far over their borders. They're way out of their ground. So if we do beat them which I really think we might you see, they'll suffer a much more crushing defeat than if the Allies had gone into Berlin in 1914 as some would have had it. Don't you think?'

'No I don't,' said Brake. 'I think we've – I think you've had it.'

'No we haven't,' Lord Lydiard argued, holding up one finger as his son tried to speak. 'In a minute, Henry. I just want to put America here to rights. I don't think we've had it because I don't think we're fooled like some of those other small countries. As far as Germany goes, I mean. What was it Mr Churchill said? *They see the glitter, they see the episode*. Germany's like a snake-charmer to them, they're simply hypnotized by German might. Whereas the British who've understood these things for centuries, being an island race, the British know how to endure misfortune, how to cope with bad government of which we've most certainly had our fill, and how to come back fighting, how to fight on, how to renew our strength, which is precisely why we won't be defeated. Because even though we shall probably have to withstand appalling losses and untold suffering, I think we shall probably triumph because we are fighting for the greatest cause for which men fight.'

He had the eyes and the attention of everyone round the table, even though while he talked Lord Lydiard had rarely looked up, preferring instead to attend to the matter of cutting his buttered toast into very small squares.

'Bravo, Papa.' It was Harriet who broke the silence. 'Bravo,' she repeated. 'You should stand for parliament.'

'Yes, well spoken, Papa,' Henry agreed, looking his father in the eye. 'So you will quite understand when I tell you that I want to enlist.'

'I don't think this is quite the time or place, Henry,' Grace said quietly, when she saw the look of blank astonishment on Lord Lydiard's face.

'It's perfectly all right, Nanny, thank you,' Lord Lydiard said. 'I don't think either time or place ever mitigated this sort of thing.'

Lord Lydiard was looking fixedly at his son, without expression, as fixedly as Henry was regarding him.

'Perhaps I should take John upstairs,' Grace volunteered, trying to keep any panic out of her voice. 'If you want to talk. Harriet can help me. Harriet darling?'

Grace went to move, but Lord Lydiard stopped her.

'No, I think you should stay, Nanny,' he said, 'I think this is something that affects you as much as anyone.'

'If I don't enlist now, Papa, if you think I'm still too young,' Henry said as Grace sat slowly back down, 'then I shall enlist next birthday, when I'm eighteen. It's only a matter of time.'

'The war might be over by then,' Harriet said.

'Exactly,' said Henry.

'I didn't mean that!' Harriet was on her feet now, leaning across the table. 'What I meant was if you just wait until you're eighteen then the war might be finished!'

'It might be,' Henry replied. 'In fact if we don't all join up now, those of us who can I mean, then I think Mr Merrowby's right. The war could be over because we could have lost it.'

'You don't think your father's right?' Grace asked. 'That we'll win this war come what may because of the sort of people we are?'

'Only if we the people fight it, Nan,' Henry said. 'You can't fight and win a war without soldiers.'

'Papa?' Harriet turned pleadingly to her father. 'Papa, he can't enlist, not if you forbid it.'

'Oh, I don't think it's the sort of thing really that you can really forbid, H,' Lord Lydiard replied with a frown. 'It's not as if Henry wants to do something wrong, something of which we and he would all be ashamed. Is it? No, I don't think so. This is the sort of thing you have to make your own mind up about. One's life is – well. What you do with your life you have to decide yourself.'

'But Henry's only seventeen, Papa!' Harriet said. 'He hasn't even finished at school yet!'

'Wars don't take account of school terms, Harry,' Henry said. 'Hundreds of people my age are joining up and anyway I'll be eighteen in October.'

'OK, that's enough,' Brake announced, suddenly getting to his feet. 'I'm out. If you all want to go and get yourselves killed, you do just that. You just carry on. I'll leave you to it.'

'Wait a moment. A minute ago you were rattling your sabre, Brake,' Lord Lydiard said, cutting a small square of toast into an even smaller one. 'Sometimes I really don't – I can't actually follow your reasoning.'

'Henry's a kid, John, for God's sake!' Brake came back to the table and leaned on it with knuckled fists. 'Have we all gone crazy? That we have to have our kids fight our wars?'

'That's always been the way, Brake,' Lord Lydiard replied, still not looking up. 'Old men make wars, and young men fight them. If I stop Henry, or try to stop him, then I must try to stop every young man. Henry's not being conscripted, do you see. Henry is making a choice, and if my children don't have a choice, then I shouldn't have had children. You know as well as I do that any regrets we have are for things we chose not to do, not for the things we chose to do. Which is why this is Henry's decision. That's what conviction is.'

Lord Lydiard still didn't look up. Instead he began to feed the minute portions of carefully dissected toast to Beanie who was lying at his feet. Brake stared across the table at the top of Lord Lydiard's head, then with one bang on the table with one clenched fist, a blow which sent cups and plates spinning, he turned and stormed out of the room.

'Pay absolutely no attention,' Lord Lydiard said to Beanie, although intending his words for his family. 'He's like this because he's going through exactly the same thing himself. And he's not even English.'

So it was that Henry enlisted. That very morning he took himself off and joined the same regiment as his friend Rupert, the 13th London Regiment, otherwise known as the Kensingtons, not knowing that only two days earlier his friend Rupert had been killed in a dawn raid at Laventie.

Six weeks later along with the other recruits he was ordered to join the rest of the regiment in France. Before he left he was granted a day's embarkation leave.

'I have to say you look very handsome,' Grace told him when she saw him in his uniform, although all she could really see was a boy on the lawn of Keston with his dog. 'I don't know why but it makes you look even taller.'

I don't know why you have to do this, was what she wanted to say. *It simply isn't fair. It seems so pointless, it's such a terrible waste.*

Instead she picked a piece of lint off the lapel of his jacket and smiled up at him.

'How was the training?' she asked.

'All right,' Henry smiled. 'Cakewalk after Eton. Some of the others found it a bit tough, but then as our squaddie said, we're not off on a something picnic.'

'Do you know where you're going?' Grace asked. 'Or aren't you allowed to say?'

'Name, rank and number only, Nan,' Henry said, flopping down in a chair and lighting a cigarette. 'France, somewhere. Not Turkey, I'm glad to say. Not much fun out east, I understand.'

'When did you start smoking?' Grace enquired, wondering how much fun it was in Flanders. 'It's so strange to see you with a cigarette.'

'Everyone smokes in the army, Nanny,' Henry replied. 'If you don't, they think you're a *mauve*. Except that's not what they call it.'

'What?' Grace sighed and sat down opposite him. 'That's not what they call what?'

'Never mind. Nothing that need concern you, Nan.' Henry stretched out a long arm and taped the ash of his cigarette into the fire.

'I must be getting old,' Grace said. 'All this slang. Squaddies, cakewalks, what was it? Mauves. And now you smoking.'

And off to war. The boy with his dog on the lawn.

'What time is your train?' she asked out of a silence. 'And who's going to see you off?'

'I hoped you'd all come,' Henry said. 'Train leaves about six.'

'From Charing Cross?'

'Victoria. I have to report back to the barracks by four.'

'Harriet wants to come,' Grace told him.

'Oh—' Henry laughed. 'I thought she was still not speaking to me.'

'As if Harriet wouldn't speak to you, Henry,' Grace said. 'It's just – well.'

There were the two of them now, playing wheelbarrows on the top lawn, then rolling slowly all the way down the slope with Beanie joyously barking at them, running round them in

*circles. Grace scolded them when they came and collapsed on
the tartan rug she had spread out under the chestnut tree, where
Boy was taking one of his first, slow, careful crawls. 'Look
at those grass stains,' she'd sighed. 'I've told you both before
about sliding down that slope.' What was it? Five years ago?
Brake was saying the fields of Flanders were now just a sea
of mud.*

'Harriet's talking of becoming a nurse,' Grace said.

'Harriet's not old enough,' Henry replied.

'And of course you are.' Grace couldn't stop herself.
Everything was too close to the surface.

'Yes of course I am, Nan,' Henry said. 'Most of the
recruits were about my age. Some were younger. There
were some boys from the east end who said they were
sixteen but I'll swear they weren't. One of them hadn't
even started to shave.'

Grace got up, checking her watch.

'I'd better go and see Cook,' she said. 'I'm not sure
she knows how many there are for dinner.'

'Will Papa come?' Henry asked her before she reached
the door. 'I mean to the station. Is he going to be here
tomorrow? Or does he have to go to Wellington House?'

'He has to go in every day, Henry,' Grace replied.
'But I'm sure in this instance – have you not spoken to
him?'

'I've only seen him briefly,' Henry said. 'As I arrived
he was dashing out with Mr Merrowby. They had some
of Mr Merrowby's paintings and he said they were off to
see Lady Ducarn.'

'You can ask him at dinner,' Grace said. 'Now I'd
better go and see Cook.'

'You can come to the station, Beanie,' he said to
the dog on his knee. 'As long as you don't bark.'

As she closed the door over, Grace saw the boy on
the lawn throw his finished cigarette in the fire and light
another. '*Look, Nanny!*' he was saying. '*A Riley Speed!
It's really fast and it's got twin cylinders in a V!*'

'What's Cook making?' the soldier boy asked just before
Grace closed the door. 'Hope it's one of my favourites.'

Over one of Cook's delicious chicken and mushroom pies they talked of everything and anything, anything but the war, Lord Lydiard, Henry, Harriet, Brake and Grace, who had been included in every family meal since the move downstairs from the nursery floor at Keston. Brake wanted to know how and why they could put a woman in gaol for writing a book on birth control, and whereas Grace wasn't at all sure this was a subject which should be discussed in front of Harriet, Lord Lydiard thought otherwise although all Harriet wanted to talk about was the Charlie Chaplin film she'd been to see with a friend the day before. Henry told everyone that after the war his ambition was to break the automobile speed record which had just been set at over one hundred and two miles an hour in New Zealand by someone called Gil Anderson driving a Stutz. A friend of his from Eton was apparently a brilliant mechanic and another one an inspired designer, and together all three of them planned to make a team and a car to capture the blue riband. Lord Lydiard made everyone guess how many runs had been scored and how many wickets had been taken by the recently deceased W. G. Grace during his eighteen-year career and Grace came closest with an out of the hat guess of fifty thousand runs and three thousand wickets, while all Brake wanted to discuss was how anyone could put a woman in gaol for writing a book on birth control.

After dinner Henry said he wanted to do something mad, which Lord Lydiard said he thought was a sensible idea, so he and Henry then disappeared to return with half a dozen masks which the Lydiards apparently used to wear at dinner whenever they found their guests particularly boring. Everyone, including Grace, was ordered to put one on, while Harcross was instructed to summon one of the new motorized cabs which took them all to the Ritz where they sat and drank champagne without one adverse comment being made. Then to make Henry's evening, on their way out of the bar his father, still in his mask, was recognized by a rather elderly countess who engaged him in a long and tedious discourse about the merits and demerits of Somerset Maugham's latest novel, *Of Human Bondage*.

After that, with aching sides they all returned to Cadogan Square, where they played 'Murder' all around the house until long after midnight. In the last game Grace was murdered in the kitchen, where she was found by a horrified Cook who had come to make herself a late night beverage, and was on her way to call the police when Grace 'woke up' and explained. Cook thought it was such a lark that she insisted on being murdered as well, much to everyone else's surprise when they discovered the bodies.

'A wonderful evening,' Henry told Grace on his way to bed. 'I'm dead from laughing.'

'Did you sort out with your father about the train?' Grace asked. 'I mean who's coming to see you off?'

'Yes of course, Nan,' Henry replied. 'I told him before dinner. In the library.'

'And?' Grace asked.

'He said fine,' Henry said. 'Fine. Absolutely.'

'Meaning?'

'Meaning fine.' Henry shrugged, a little hopelessly. 'Meaning fine. Absolutely.'

It was too late to talk to Lord Lydiard now because he had already gone to bed, so Grace decided she would catch him in the morning at breakfast, before anyone else was up, and find out then whether or not he was intending to come to the station. Now she just took one of Henry's hands and wished him good night.

'Good night, Nanny,' Henry said, bending down slightly to kiss Grace's cheek. 'And thanks.'

Grace was up earlier than usual to make sure of catching Lord Lydiard, only to learn from Harcross that he had already left.

'But it's only half past seven,' Grace said. 'He never leaves for Wellington House until nine o'clock at the earliest.'

'He said he had to call on someone first, Nanny,' Mr

Harcross replied. 'But that he should be home as usual for lunch.'

They waited lunch until half past one, when they could wait no longer. There were just the four of them, Henry, Harriet, John and Grace, and only one of them ate anything, the one who was still too young to know anything of what was going on, young John who cleared everything Grace put before him while keeping up a constant barrage of questions to his brother, wanting to know all about his uniform, what sort of gun he had, and whether or not it had a *baynet*.

Henry answered every question patiently and with good humour while not touching his food. Harriet said and ate nothing. By three o'clock when there was still no sign of Lord Lydiard, Henry threw his last cigarette into the drawing room fire and began to get ready to leave.

Harriet went to get her coat and Grace rose to follow her, only to be called back by Henry.

'Look,' he said. 'You're coming, aren't you?'

'Would you like me to?' Grace asked, removing the invisible piece of lint from his lapel again. 'I'm sure your father will be back in a minute.'

'No you're not,' Henry said, without trace of a smile. 'You know as well as I do, Nan, he's not going to show.'

'On past form I'd have to agree,' Grace said. 'But I don't know. I'm not sure. They keep him very busy at Wellington House.'

'I telephoned his office after lunch,' Henry said. 'His secretary said he hadn't been in today.'

'Perhaps he had business elsewhere,' Grace said. 'It's all terribly hush-hush, you know. What he does.'

A taxi drew up, drawing Henry at once to the window.

'It's Mr Merrowby,' he said. 'He appears to be drunk.'

They both listened as one of the maids opened the front door and let in Brake, who went straight upstairs, running up them from the sound of it, and missing the occasional step. Harcross came in and told Henry the cab was here and waiting with his bags already packed on board, handing Henry his cap.

'Beanie's getting fat,' Henry told Harriet as he bent down to pat his dogs goodbye. 'Tell Cook to stop feeding him so many scraps, and perhaps if you could give him a bit more exercise.'

'It's not Cook who feeds him scraps,' Harriet said. 'It's Papa.'

'He comes out every day with me, Henry,' Grace said. 'When I take John to the park. But he's getting on, you know. He can't run quite like he used to.'

Beanie knew he was being talked about and with a good three inches of pink tongue flopping out of his mouth looked happily backwards and forwards from Grace to Henry and Harriet.

Henry then stroked the top of the mongrel's wiry head, who was trying to push Beanie out of contention.

'Life would be a lot easier,' he said as he straightened up, 'if we didn't have dogs. See you at quarter to four. Platform two.'

When the time came for them to leave, Grace went upstairs and put on her best coat and hat, taking off her apron and cuffs and powdering her cheeks with the face powder Henry had given her for Christmas. On her way downstairs she collected Harriet who Grace could see had been crying.

'It's all right, Nanny,' Harriet said to her as she shut her bedroom door. 'I got it out of the way here so as I won't let him down on the station.'

Victoria was a mass of people, the majority of whom were in uniform. On the adjacent platform to the one where Grace and Harriet waited, Scottish soldiers in tam o'shanters, their packs and helmets strapped to their backs, were disembarking from a train, on leave back from the front. People were handing them hot mugs of tea from trolleys nearby, nurses and volunteer workers who went about what had now become a ritual with maximum efficiency and minimum fuss. The wounded were being helped and carried away, some walking with crutches, some blindfolded with bandages, others supine and motionless on stretchers, their amputated limbs out of sight beneath rough blankets. Grace turned Harriet away from the scene, but she kept looking back, staring at the groups of comrades in arms who were drinking their tea and smoking their cigarettes before leaving their friends to hurry off to their homes. Train doors banged resoundingly and steam hissed from the engines, fogging the air and smarting the eyes, while porters and private soldiers hurried to load up the next train to leave for the battlefront.

Then the men of Henry's regiment arrived fully armed and equipped, newly recruited and as keen as mustard, the studs of their spit and polished boots pinging the platform, belt brasses gleaming, Lee Enfields slung on their shoulders, enamel drinking mugs clanking against the helmets slung on their packs. *Goodbye Dolly I must leave you!* some were singing, while from another platform came the poignant full-throated sound of others singing *Tipperary*. Not the men back from Flanders, however. They just stood and listened, some with a sad smile on their weary faces, others too battle-weary and numb to respond. Grace couldn't help noticing how different their expressions were from the Kensington recruits, who were about to take up their first posting at the front. The men in Henry's regiment looked almost delirious with excitement, their eyes bright and shining as they joked amongst each other while they began to climb aboard the train. *They look as if they're the ones coming home*, Grace thought, *while the ones who have come home look haunted and full of fear*.

'How was it, Jock?' a young soldier called out to one of the Balmorals, as he swung open his carriage door.

'I canna wait to return!' the Balmoral shouted back across the platform. 'Make sure they keep it warm!'

'Henry said he'd meet us by the Officers Only coach,' Grace said, taking Harriet's arm and leading her up the platform. 'That must be it up there.'

Ahead of them was quite a different scene from the mêlée round the third class carriages. At the top of the platform alongside coaches reserved for officers of various ranks and seniority there was almost a cocktail party atmosphere, as groups of officers in their breeches, their Sam Browne belts, their red-ribboned caps and their burnished brown boots stood idly chatting to each other or those who had come to see them off. Most of them were smoking cigarettes which when not in their mouths were held in their gloved hands behind their backs, while others stood surveying the embarkation of their various troops idly tapping their boots with their swagger sticks. Here and there the predominantly khaki colour was relieved by the navy blue and white of a nurse's cape and uniform, or a splash of red or yellow from the hats of the officers' wives. All the older officers had thick moustaches which gave them an air of grave responsibility while the junior officers were clean shaven and fresh-faced.

Among their number Harriet spotted Henry.

'There!' she said to Grace, pointing. 'Come on!'

Grace had both the dogs who as soon as they saw their young master began to bark excitedly and tug at their leads, almost pulling Grace off her feet. Henry was standing looking very much at ease with some fellow lieutenants, none of whom appeared yet to Grace to have reached his majority. He spotted them, and detaching himself from his group, strolled towards them as if it was the Fourth of June and they were about to picnic on the playing fields of Eton.

'Any sign of Papa?' he asked casually, taking his cap off and smoothing back his hair. 'Did he come home?'

'We sent Mr Merrowby round to his club,' Harriet said. 'Nanny found out that's where he's been.'

'We haven't long,' Henry said. 'Train pulls out in a couple of minutes or so.'

As if to underline the fact there was a sudden loud and prolonged *siss* from the huge dark green engine as it built up a head of steam. Beyond their group a guard consulted his watch and shouted the last call to entrain. With his call reality suddenly seemed to strike home as boys in their first uniforms realized the time had actually come to go. All along the platform men and women embraced, some in the arms of their young wives, some with their fiancées, some with their mothers and sisters while older men stood by with their hats in their hands, looking hopelessly and helplessly on. As the latest mintage bade their last farewells, the returning troops all seemed to pause in their hurry to get home to watch and wait while the boys clambered on board the crowded train to slam the doors shut and jam the open windows with their bodies and heads and arms, all to get a last sight of their loved ones.

Somewhere in the mass of soldiers and their loves a brass band played Ivor Novello's latest song and voices rose above the din and the commotion. *'We'll keep the home fires burning!'* they sang. *'Until the boys come home!'*

'Papa!' Henry suddenly exclaimed, more in surprise than anything else. He pointed down the platform where all three of them could now see him, being hurried through the throng by the wildly dishevelled figure of Brake Merrowby. Lord Lydiard himself was as immaculate as ever, although when he drew near Grace could see the state he was in from his red-rimmed eyes and his bloodless cheeks.

Beside them the guard unfurled his flag and prepared to blow his whistle. As if on cue there was a last frenzied bout of farewells while another guard began a long walk along the train to make sure all the doors were shut.

'Goodbye, Henry!' Brake shouted from ten yards away, tactfully keeping himself apart from the family. 'God speed!'

Henry smiled and saluted him.

'Cheerio, Mr Merrowby!' he called. 'Goodbye, sir!'

Harriet threw her arms round her brother's neck and kissed him fiercely.

'You're to write as soon as you can,' she said. 'I shall write to you every day.'

As Henry released his sister from his arms, Grace waited while he cuffed his dogs round their ears and patted their rumps while doors slammed up and down the train.

'You'd better hurry,' she said. 'The guard has his flag up.'

Henry took both her hands and kissed her on the cheek.

'Goodbye, Nan,' he said. 'Take care of them all, won't you?'

'Well of course I will,' Grace said as crossly as she could, straightening her perfectly straight hat and tugging at her coat. 'And you take care of yourself.'

All his fellow officers were on board now, all except one who was in a fast embrace with a beautiful young girl whose hat had tipped backwards off her head. Harriet turned away, and took the dogs from Grace, brushing the end of her pretty nose with the back of her wrist.

'Henry,' Lord Lydiard said, frowning hard and extending his hand. 'Better say goodbye then.'

'Goodbye, Papa.'

The two stood facing each other, man and boy, father and son, a duo being duplicated up and down the platform, a parting paralleled on stations all around the world as men sent their offspring off to fight and kill the progeny of other men.

The guard blew his whistle and the train hissed and rattled and suddenly jerked to life with one massive clank. Henry unclasped his hand from his father's, adjusted his cap, smiled shyly and turned to go.

'Henry?' his father said. Henry stopped and turned back to him.

'Yes, Father?' he asked.

'Your mother would have been very proud,' Lord Lydiard said, and then turning quickly walked away.

The train was moving now, and for a moment Henry hesitated, before turning and running towards a door being held open for him by his colleagues. He hopped into the carriage and swung the door shut in one easy move. 'Goodbye everyone!' he shouted, his head reappearing at the window. 'I'll see you all very soon!'

The train began to gather speed and Grace and Harriet walked alongside it until they were outpaced. They stopped by the last empty baggage truck, by a boy selling magazines from a tray, and stood as everyone behind them was standing, silently watching the train clatter and steam out of the station while the band played on and someone somewhere called for three cheers.

They stood there still until the departing train was a dark square in the twilight, and then it had gone, vanished from sight, taking with it their sons and their lovers, their husbands and their charges. Slowly the crowd disbanded and melted into the dusk, mourners it seemed without a funeral, with grief already heavy in their hearts.

Thirty-six hours later Second Lieutenant the Honourable Henry Rokeham of the 13th London Regiment was on his way with the flower of England to the battlefront at Loos.

TWENTY-ONE

Occasionally there would be people to dinner, not often as most of Lord Lydiard's time was taken up with his work at Wellington House, but perhaps once a week, certainly no more. At these small unostentatious gatherings there was one regular guest, Lady Ducarn, who would arrive long before the others and shut herself in the library with Lord Lydiard and Brake, and who would stay long after everyone else had left, sometimes talking until long after midnight with her host and his friend. On these occasions Grace would eat in the kitchen where she would be brought up to date with news of *our boys*, as Cook called the former staff from Keston who were out at the front. By the end of 1915 besides George known as James three more of their number lay dead, Harry Theobald one of the gardeners, Jack Welton one of the grooms, and young Tim the pot boy, the first two killed on the Ypres salient and young Tim falling at the desperate battle fought at Loos that September, a battle which was Henry's first engagement and from which although thrown straight into action he miraculously escaped unscathed.

'Poor Mr Parker weren't so lucky,' Cook had told Grace the night they sat discussing the outcome of the first battle fought by Kitchener's new army. 'Stepped on a mine, I gather, and lost a leg. They're bringin' him home for Christmas.'

In one year Cook had aged dreadfully. Grace thought it must be because she looked on all the young staff as her children because that was the way she had always treated them, clucking round them and scolding them like a mother hen, and yet always finding time to talk to any who were unhappy or worried or homesick. She always had something to hand for such occasions, a slice of pie or a chicken leg, a cut of homemade cake or a portion of plum tart, which she would produce from one of her many hiding places and place before a sobbing scullery maid or a black-eyed pot boy. *There*, she'd say. *Just you get that inside you and you'll be ready for anything.*

But now she was a shadow of herself, grey in the face and drained of energy. Gone was the talk of *one good push* doing it, and even longer gone her belief in the cavalry. The truth had dawned on her exactly what sort of war it was and it seemed she could hardly bear the reality. Over the last six months of the year she lost a considerable amount of weight and began regularly to complain of pains in her chest. Time and time again Grace would come down to the kitchen to find her sitting at the large scrubbed table staring into space, a cup of tea gone cold in front of her with the latest letter from one of her *boys* clenched in one fist. As the scale of the carnage sank home she became more and more stunned, and after Henry enlisted she began to drink heavily, although in typical Cook style she didn't open the bottle until her day's work was done, when she would set out a glass and a bottle of gin beside her place at the fire and slowly drink herself into stupefaction.

Grace neither condemned nor upbraided her because she understood. A part of her wanted to be where Cook was by ten o'clock each night, all but out to a world where people's sons and lovers were being blown to pieces at a rate of six thousand a day. Every night she found it harder to sleep, afraid that as soon as she closed her eyes she would once again dream of Henry, or as she often did of a thousand

Henrys, all lying dead in the Flanders mud, their faces and limbs blown away, stubs that were once men, young men who had walked the hillsides and swum in the rivers of England and who had kissed their girls and run free but who now to preserve their liberty were being asked to face the bullet and the bayonet. *And the guns*, she had heard Lord Lydiard saying. *They say the noise of the guns is so terrible it is driving men mad.*

So when Cook drank Grace drank with her in spirit, occupying herself with anything and everything which would tire her out and make her drop into sleep before she had any time to think, working herself endlessly during the day and reading rapaciously at night. Harriet and she had an unspoken agreement between them not to mention either Henry or the war. After his train had drawn out of the station and disappeared down the track until it was a speck and then finally no more they had all travelled back in silence to the house where over a half-eaten supper Lord Lydiard had finally spoken and suggested a *modus vivandi* for them all.

'Look,' he had said, his food untouched before him. 'These are difficult times for everyone, for us all and everyone else. No, they're not difficult, they are well nigh impossible times, but nothing is going to be altered by our despair. It isn't that I believe or rather subscribe to the *what-will-be-will-be* school of thought because I certainly don't and I doubt very much if anybody round this table does either. I don't think things are going to happen regardless of what we do or don't do, all that predestination nonsense, I've never gone along with that for one moment. But I do believe that things will or may happen to us if we don't act, in other words Fate as such can be circumvented if you will, if you see what I mean. What I'm trying to say is that what happens or doesn't happen while being something we can't prevent from happening, or not happening, what I mean is as human beings our greatest advantage is that our destiny is not fixed. Just because I run across the road doesn't mean I'm going to be run down. There are no definites in this life, except that we die, and even that is an indefinite, a matter perhaps of terminology rather than a spiritual state. Life's a series of indefinites, otherwise there'd be no point in running races. We know the moving finger writes fine, yes of course we do, but we don't know what it writes so therefore any apprehensions we may have or a sense of despair say, these things aren't any use to us. The way to survive and to cope is I really do believe to take each moment as it comes. Let me see if I can remember it. Yes. *Grief has limits, whereas apprehension has none. For we grieve only for what we know has happened, but we fear all that possibly may happen.*'

With that he set his plate down on the floor for the dogs to enjoy and then got up and walked from the room.

After that the subject was never raised between any of them. The family went about its business not with an air of resignation but with a sense of perspective. At least as far as Grace was concerned they did as long as there was something to do, which was why she made sure both Harriet and she were constantly occupied. She had managed to talk Harriet out of her determination to become a nurse not by arguing that she was too young, which Grace indeed considered she was, but by convincing her that she could play just as important a part by using her talents as an artist.

'You can bring the sorrow and tragedy of war home to people by painting it, Harriet,' she'd argued. 'You know how much more powerful a painting can be than say a photograph, because it expresses what the painter feels. A photograph only records an image.'

'I agree, Nanny,' Harriet had replied, thinking she was winning the argument. 'But then to be able to do it properly I need to go out there and see for myself.'

'Later perhaps,' Grace had replied. 'In the meantime there's plenty for you to paint here. You could do worse for instance than to start with painting what happens at the railway stations. I could see what an effect those scenes were having on you when we saw Henry off.'

Luckily for Grace her argument coincided exactly with the argument Lord Lydiard was having at Wellington House, where they were already finding that words were not enough. In league with Lady Ducarn, Lord Lydiard was now arguing that they should appoint official war artists to detail and record the most monumental war ever fought, since the few photographs they were getting back were by and large useless and of inferior quality, thanks to a combination of the flat countryside of northern France, the technique of trench warfare, and the hopelessly cumbersome cameras being employed by the photographers. There was nothing particularly new about the concept, Lord Lydiard argued, pointing out that as long ago as the seventeenth century Dutch artists had sailed with and recorded the action of the Royal Navy.

So when Lord Lydiard told them round the dinner table of his attempts to get his scheme floated, Harriet saw the merit in Grace's suggestion and set to her task at once, taking herself off daily to Victoria and Charing Cross stations to try to record the scenes of battle-scarred men returning home for leave and their heartbreakingly poignant departures a few days later.

'While all they want me to do are portraits.'

Brake intercepted Grace one evening as she was on her way up to bed. He was looking even more harassed and unkempt than ever, with his hair unbrushed and matted, his beard half shaven and with big dark circles of fatigue under his eyes.

'Come on,' he said, opening the door to her room. 'I need to talk to you.'

'Perhaps we should go downstairs to the library, or the morning room,' Grace replied. 'Everyone else is in bed.'

'This will do just fine,' Brake said, going in ahead of her and leaving behind him a less than faint aroma of cigar smoke and brandy. He flopped down exhausted in an armchair, closing his eyes and stretching out his long elegant legs.

Grace waited for a moment, then leaving the door

wide open she followed him into the room and sat well away from him, on a hard chair at her desk.

Brake opened one eye, looked at her, at the open door, and then back at her. He grinned.

'It's OK, Nanny,' he said. 'I'm not going to try and have my wicked way with you.'

'Just in case,' Grace replied. 'Where you're concerned there are no certainties.'

Brake grinned at her again, and then flopped his head back against the chair, closing his eyes once more.

'You were saying something about "them" only wanting you to do portraits,' Grace said after a moment. 'I don't understand who "they" are. Unless you're referring to Lord Lydiard's enterprise at Wellington House.'

'There in one, Grace,' Brake sighed. 'Lady Ducarn started it. She's been trying to recruit me for months, and while I find her charms quite irresistible—' Brake opened one eye to see if the taunt had achieved its desired effect, to be met with an expression of total disinterest on Grace's face. He watched her for a second, tongue in cheek, while she watched him back, unblinking. Then he closed his eyes and resumed his account. 'She's very persuasive. Hence her constant visits here. She and John, she and Lord Lydiard have concocted this scheme to commission a proper record of this war to end all wars from artists. To have them go to the battlegrounds and show it like it is.'

'So I understand,' Grace said. 'From various conversations recently.'

'I can see the merit in it,' Brake continued. 'I haven't seen one image yet that's stuck in my memory, and I've been to Wellington House. I've seen the stuff the photographers are sending back and it's awful. Not awful in the right way. I mean just plain terrible. Which is why I think their idea is brilliant. But.'

'But they will only allow you to do portraits?' Grace wondered. 'Is that right?'

'How about that?' Brake laughed. 'Just when I've managed to shake the yoke, they want me to step back into

411

harness and go and paint pretty pictures of field-marshals and generals. Not John and her ladyship, I hasten to add. No, the bureaucrats, whose minds run on fixed lines. *Chap's known as a portrait painter, chap can go out and paint portraits.* I've told them. If I go out there, it's not to paint chocolate boxes. It's to paint how and what I'm painting now.'

'What are you painting now, Brake?' Grace asked. 'And how?'

Brake opened his eyes and looked at her again, chewing the top of one of his little fingers. There was a long silence and then he stood up.

'Come on,' he said. 'Come and see.'

It was like coming in from the cold. The moment Brake threw open the door on the room which was his studio and stood aside for Grace, all she could see and feel was warmth. The paintings were all of interiors, mostly Keston but a few of the house in Cadogan Square, coloured in pale reds, oranges, creams, whites and yellows. There were still-lifes of fruit and teacups, of bread loaves, of flowers, there were pictures just of rooms with no one in them, rooms with their windows thrown open on to gardens filled with late summer sunlight, rooms with half-open doors and decorated with the possessions of unseen people, rooms awaiting night, their fires near burned out, the curtains half pulled against moonlit skies, bathrooms with drawn baths and towels draped on chairs awaiting the bather, kitchens where vegetables waited to be chopped on scrubbed wood tables and black pots simmered on yellow-blue flames, and there were pictures of rooms with people in them, the family and their servants, the family and their dogs, the servants going about their tasks, the family sleeping in chairs, or eating their breakfast, the maids carefully sweeping out rooms. And there were pictures of the children, of Henry seen through an open window on the lawns at Keston, lying asleep in the sun with Beanie curled into his back, of Harriet drawing beneath a tree with Grace sewing at her side, of Henry and Harriet playing cards at a window, of John being undressed by Grace, his curly-haired head tucked against Grace's neck and his sturdy body leaning on her as she slipped his nightgown off.

But what made the paintings so distinctive and so original was the technique Brake had now developed. He had always used colour quite arbitrarily, never worrying unduly about its relationship with light, but now he had carried that deliberate carelessness even further, making it perfectly obvious that he preferred the fanciful to the formal and showing a fine perception of the infinite variety of impressions light can have on tone. The result was that the canvases glowed with warmth, because and not in spite of his impulsive use of colour.

More, it appeared to Grace that Brake had decided to disregard true perspective and depth in order to concentrate his compositions, with the result that the paintings were expressive rather than representative, psychological moments captured in sunshine and in shadow, slices of life bathed in a glow of actuality and captured for ever outside time.

'Well?' Brake had been standing patiently by while Grace had walked slowly round the room, stopping to look at every canvas in turn, but now from the nervous tapping of his foot he could obviously contain himself no longer.

'I don't know what to say,' Grace replied.

'Try saying they're marvellous,' Brake suggested, lighting up the stub of a cigar he'd found in an ashtray.

'They're better than marvellous, Brake,' Grace said. 'But I can't think of any better than marvellous words.'

'Phenomenal,' Brake said. 'Amazing, staggering, prodigious, incredible.'

'These deserve a new word,' Grace said, walking round the room again. 'These are worth a word that's never been used before.'

'So let's make one up then,' Brake proposed. '*Super-extramarvelwonderlous*. How's that?'

'Nowhere near.' Grace shook her head, standing once more in front of the picture of herself undressing the infant John. 'These paintings are heavenish.'

'Heavenish.'

'Yes. They're from on high. They're celestial. They're a glimpse of the eternal.'

'You really think so?' Gone was Brake's defensive facetiousness, replaced by genuine uncertainty.

'Doesn't everyone else? What does Lord Lydiard think? And Lady Ducarn?'

'They were very enthusiastic,' Brake replied. 'But somehow it seems to matter more what you think.'

Grace just kept staring at the painting in front of her, now at a total loss for words.

'You've always been so interested in me,' Brake continued. 'In my painting.'

It was bad again, worse perhaps, the ache in her heart. It was worse because he was so brilliant, he was everything she had wanted to be as a painter if she hadn't been denied the chance. On canvas they were twin souls, true minds, they were Gemini. If only she had said yes, what then?

Brake drew on his cigar and picked up the canvas of Henry and Harriet playing cards at the window.

'They're not portraits, as you can see,' he explained. 'They're studies. They're reality interpreted.'

'My only concern,' Grace said, moving to look at a painting of Beanie asleep at Lord Lydiard's feet. Brake had deliberately not included anything more of Lord Lydiard than his legs and feet. 'My only concern,' Grace began again, 'is how you adapt this technique to depict the horror of war. These paintings are the very antithesis, surely.'

'Only a civilian could ask that question!' Brake groaned. 'Only someone who knows nothing about painting!'

'That's not fair,' Grace said hotly.

'For goodness sake, Grace!' Brake protested. 'As if I'd go over there to paint the war in these sorts of tones!'

'I wasn't talking about tones, Brake,' Grace replied, regaining her composure. 'These paintings are – well – they're decorative, the very opposite I imagine to what war is.'

414

'My God, you sound just like Wyndham Lewis and his mob!' Brake ground out his cigar and poured two brandies from a bottle on the paint-strewn table. 'That logic and geometry are at the heart of painting! That that's the only way to express our so-called decadence and superficiality!'

'I simply meant that I couldn't see how you could use this technique to the same effect with such different subject matter,' Grace replied. 'After all, you could hardly have two more different themes.'

'OK,' Brake said, handing her a glass. 'OK, I take your point. OK?'

'So enlighten me, please.' Grace eyed him steadily, determined to make him pay for his impatience. 'I'm interested.'

'Drink your brandy,' Brake ordered.

'I didn't want a brandy.'

'Fine.' Brake took the glass back. 'I'll drink it for you.'

Brake poured the second drink into the first and drank half of it in one. He wiped his mouth with the back of one paint-smudged hand and turned up another canvas. While his back was turned to her, Grace smiled to herself when she realized the reason for his recalcitrance was because Brake hadn't worked this one out.

'I imagine really you won't have to adapt your technique, will you?' Grace asked and then continued to explain before he could interrupt. 'This sort of poetic quality you have now, this sort of detached lyricism—'

'Yes?'

They were both standing staring at a large canvas of the library at Keston empty of all life except a cat in the window.

'If you employ the same style,' Grace continued, 'it will make the point all the better. If you depict the horror of war with this sense of distraction, if you give it all a strange beauty—' Grace fell to silence, as she could see in her own mind a landscape of which she had no proper knowledge, a panorama of skeletal trees, of huge shell holes, of once green fields churned to mud painted as they would both paint the picture, in just the same way as if the battlefield was a place still full of flowers and grasses, of copses full of birds, and hills where the deer ran.

'Yes,' Brake said. 'You're right, Grace. That's how I must do it. That's what I was fighting. I hadn't been able to find a way.'

'What do you mean?' Grace replied. 'What's this?' She pointed to the array of canvases. 'You've found the way,' she said. 'You're there already.'

Initially Grace made Lady Ducarn accountable for Brake's decision to attach himself to her and Lord Lydiard's scheme, a charge she later withdrew in her journal.

In retrospect, in this the twilight, I doubt very much if he would have gone, not then certainly, not at that precise moment. He was determined not to paint any more portraits, particularly specially commissioned portraits of staff officers and major-generals, his much despised 'pretty pictures', not now that he had found such a new and exciting voice. Lady Ducarn was of course at her most persuasive because she knew what a formidable talent B was, and it would be a great feather in her cap to secure him, and secure him she did. But it was me to whom he listened, alas, because we thought as one, which I always think was what infuriated him most. But then what a poorer world this would have been, without his contribution, without his record of the war, the famous war to end all wars. Because of his work, his name will live for ever, so although I blamed myself, perhaps it's time to stop, and instead I should be proud that I was there, that I said what I did. In that way, although in no way do I want to claim any credit for paintings which were so justifiably famous for having somehow distilled an awesome poetry from the very depths of horror, by telling myself the truth I can at least be a small part of them.

Grace could claim no responsibility, however, for the

way Brake chose to answer the call. That was determined by the enemy's decision to use poison gas, particularly late one night during an attack on some unnamed spot on the Ypres salient.

TWENTY-TWO

They brought him back by train, back into the same station he had left seven months before. The train was late by an hour and ten minutes, time which Grace hardly noticed going by as she sat waiting with the other women, waiting for the return of their men from battle.

When the huge grime-stained locomotive steamed in, it seemed to do so more slowly than usual, as if the driver was aware of the infirmity of his cargo. A long row of ambulances and lorries converted into ambulances waited outside in the road, while along the platform groups of nurses and orderlies and charity workers stood around talking and smoking and drinking tea. Two trains had already left for the channel ports, packed with men who looked every bit as weary as they had when they disembarked for leave, their women clinging to them silently or sobbing quietly, their tears falling on the rough serge of the soldiers' uniforms, or being brushed gently away with hands that within hours would be loading guns or twisting bayonets into the guts of the enemy.

And now in came the train bearing those who carried the marks and wounds inflicted by their opposite numbers in the trenches, holes torn by bullets and shrapnel, limbs lost to huge shells, stomachs gouged by sharpened steel, minds unhinged in the thunder of the guns, sight lost in the vapour of gas. Some could only be identified by the labels they wore, on their stretchers or round their necks like stray children. *Smith, Gunner, Royal Artillery. Partridge, Corporal, King's Own Rifles. Naismith, Private, Middlesex Regiment. Rokeham, Lieutenant, 13th London.*

He was brought out on a stretcher, unable to walk due to the injuries to his legs sustained in action, an action which for his part consisted of wiping out an enemy machine gun nest with finally only his sergeant left alive as support, and unable to see due to the canister of mustard gas which had exploded in his dugout when it seemed the battle had finally abated, blinding him at once.

'*Most of the victims of mustard gas aren't incapacitated permanently, however dreadful the initial damage is,*' Lottie had written to Grace from the advanced dressing station in France where she was now nursing, to which they brought the walking wounded. '*But some of the victims of these awful gas attacks, those who get the full force of the poison, often suffer irreversible damage, injuries too serious to be treated out here, which is why we send them home as soon as possible.*'

The canister had landed nearest to Henry, practically asphyxiating him, blistering and scorching all his exposed flesh, burning his tongue, the inside of his mouth, his trachea and lungs, and destroying the retinas of both his eyes.

'Is that you, Nan?' he whispered, as Grace bent over him to tell him she was there. 'Is that really you?'

'The nurse said you mustn't speak, darling,' Grace said, standing to one side as the orderlies arrived to lift his stretcher out on to the platform. 'But don't worry. I'm here by your side.'

His eyes were protected by thick bandages, but the skin on his face and neck was undressed except for an application of some demulcent ointment. The shingle-like blistering was so appallingly painful it had to be left exposed, a great red-raw swathe which ran like a band across the lower half of his face. It was the same on his hands, which lay by his side on deep beds of lint and cotton wool, swollen to twice their normal size and looking agonizingly as though they had been skinned, as if someone had taken a torch to them. *This is what war is,* Grace thought as she stood silently by him on the platform. *This is the truth. It's nothing to do with glory and honour and the nobility of our cause. It's nothing to do with heroism, and victory, and death to the filthy Boche. It's not the Christian crusade they're saying it is, God against the forces of evil, because this boy by my side, wasn't this young man made in the image of God? And so is this God? This war? Because if so then God is mutilation and agony, is blindness and poison and madness. Because see the boy on the lawn, now a man back from war, burned, disfigured and blind. See him and say that this is right.* As the stretchers passed her by, some now with the soldiers' faces covered, the wounded who had failed to survive the rigours of the journey, as she walked by Henry's stretcher down the platform and out to the convoy of waiting ambulances, as they gently loaded up the bits and pieces of men who bore the true testimony of war, men who had found nothing to laugh at when Fritz was strafing them, or little to smile over at a victory which had won them not the day but a few yards of mud, as they lay on the ground wounded or dying, shelled and disembowelled by distant guns, impaled by cold steel or half choked to death by poison gas, as the trucks bore these the victims of the generals' madness away to the hospitals Grace could hear women weeping all over the land.

They took it in turns to be with him, his father, his sister, his father's friend, and his nurse. For a week he lay hovering on the very edge of death, barely breathing, scarcely moving. Grace was with him the night they thought he would die. For an hour she prayed by his bed, until suddenly she realized there was no point in praying because all she had done for the last seven months was pray no harm would come to him yet here he was lying mortally wounded, blind and in agony. So she stopped praying and instead willed him her strength. For four hours she sat by his bed and determined Henry should live. During her long vigil she began to talk quietly to him, to tell him what she was doing, in just the same way that she had encouraged the children to speak to their mother as she had lain unconscious, and then when she had told him what she was doing, she took him back to his childhood, to the moment when Grace had first seen him, a tiny figure on the Keston horizon being walked by old Nanny Lydiard with Harriet and Beanie, and told him how she had taken charge of him, how he was always such a serious boy, and so particular. She told him of the fish they had caught together and the fish they had missed, of the days on the lake and the river, and reminded him of the wondrous salmon he had caught in Ireland. The night became his life story and hers, through his first painful schooldays to her tearful pride when he won at Henley. They had been through so much together, and now during this long and terrible night it seemed they were about to go through everything, although Grace never told him that. Instead she told him what they would do when he got better and how she would look after him, how she would spend her life looking after him, and of how they all loved him.

'I'm not going to let you go, Henry,' she said to him quite firmly as the sun began to rise. 'So don't go getting any ideas.'

Shortly after that a doctor came in on his rounds.

'How is he?' he whispered, bending over his patient. 'Still with us?'

'Of course he's still with us,' Grace said tartly. 'You don't know Henry.'

The doctor felt Henry's pulse and as he did so, Henry jerked his blistered wrist away from his touch.

'Yes, he is still with us,' the doctor said with a frown. 'Very much so.'

Lord Lydiard arrived next, whiter in the face than ever and with eyes like bruises.

'He's a little stronger,' Grace told him as she got up. 'His pulse is stronger, and his breathing is much deeper.'

'What did the doctor say?' Lord Lydiard asked as he took his place at the bedside.

'The doctor said he has a chance,' Grace replied. 'He thinks he might be through the worst.'

In the taxi home Grace reflected on the effects of Henry's terrible injuries. Brake had taken it worst of them all, a reaction which although it had surprised everyone else Grace had half-anticipated. Brake was so volatile and so emotional that Grace had wished there was some way of keeping it from him, but of course there wasn't, not with Brake living with them as if he was a fully fledged member of the family. Of course she could only guess at Lord Lydiard's reaction by the time he had conveyed the news to her he would have pulled himself together, although knowing him as she now did Grace very much doubted that Lord Lydiard had reacted with the same hysteria as displayed by Brake. Certainly Harriet had not. Grace had broken the news to her, and while she had immediately broken down in tears, once Grace had nursed her through her initial shock and told her that they all had to be strong if they were going to pull Henry through, which she assured her they were most certainly going to do, Harriet had been a tower of strength, practical, level-headed and the very opposite of Brake, who had become almost deranged with anger and disbelief.

'What kind of people are they!' he had raged at lunch on the day he had first visited Henry in hospital. 'What kind of a world are we living in anyway that has people like this in it? Who'll fight dirty! Who'll use poison gas! Isn't war vile enough without the Germans making it even viler?'

'I'm afraid to say we use gas as well,' Lord Lydiard had replied.

'Because they used it first!' Brake had retorted.

'I don't think that necessarily follows,' Lord Lydiard had said.

'Of course it does! All's fair in love and war, John! If you're using it, you're only using it because they used it! You can bet your last dollar you wouldn't have used it first!'

'The point is academic, Brake. The point is it is being used. This is a war unlike any other war that has been fought.'

'But you didn't start it! Nor did you start using poison gas! It's a different sort of war because you're fighting a different sort of enemy! An enemy who's prepared to use any dirty trick in the book! You've seen what they did to Henry! To your beautiful son! How can you just sit there!'

'Oh, because they won't have me,' Lord Lydiard had answered sadly, pushing away his plate of untouched food.

'No! But they'll damn well have to have me!' Brake had replied, getting up from the table, draining his full wine glass in one and rushing out of the dining room and out of the house before anyone could stop him.

'What does he mean, Papa?' Harriet had asked. 'Where is he off to?'

'To fight the war single-handed if I know Brake,' Lord Lydiard had replied.

'I'm afraid he's gone to enlist,' Grace had said, standing up as she heard the front door slam. 'Will you excuse me, please?'

That was a week ago, Grace remembered as the taxi turned into Cadogan Square, and Brake had taken himself straight off to enlist in the 1st Artists' Rifles, a volunteer regiment whose ranks were swollen by a large number of painters.

'Even old John Lavery joined, you know,' he'd said to Grace that evening as they took a walk round the square. 'In August nineteen fourteen, soon as war broke out, but he had to bale out with ill-health. Paul Nash – you know who I mean by Paul Nash?'

Grace had answered that she did, having been allowed to take Harriet to London to see his one-man show in 1913 and been greatly impressed by it.

'Nash is out there now,' Brake had continued, 'and Sargeant Jagger, the sculptor. Stanley Spencer's in Macedonia with the Medical Corps, Eric Kennington's in the same regiment as Henry, other guys are in the Royal Fusiliers, the Royal Flying Corps, the Artillery. Who said we daubers were pansies?'

'Not me. I think you're very brave, Brake,' Grace had said, slipping her arm into his proffered one. 'I also happen to think you're mad, but that's my business.'

'Why mad? Except no – yes I am mad. I'm mad what they did to Henry. If I wasn't mad before, that clinched it.'

'It isn't your fight though, Brake. Not even Henry's your fight. You could quite easily have taken the softer option and gone to war with just your palette.'

'And painted generals for the War Office. This way I can make quite sure they don't get any portraits out of me. I'm my own man. Anyway, like I said. Plenty of painters have signed up. It's nothing special.'

'American painters?'

'I'm ashamed of being American. We should be in this war by now. This is a war of principle, Grace, not some regional shooting match. The trouble with my country is that it's a continent. We don't have neighbours the way you do, bullyboys like the Germans. I wasn't going to sit around and wait for Woodrow Wilson to fire the starting gun. He's too damn busy with his new wife.'

'Where will they send you?' she had asked finally. 'Do you have any idea?'

'I've put in for France,' Brake replied. 'I aim to get the sonsofbitches who got Henry, if you'll pardon my American.'

By now the taxi had pulled up in front of the house, and Grace had alighted. Harriet was waiting for her as soon as Clara had opened the front door.

'Henry's come round, Nanny,' she said, clasping Grace's hand. 'They're sure he's going to be all right.'

'He just won't be able to see,' Lord Lydiard said, staring out across the square.

'Not ever?' Grace asked. 'Is that definite?'

'As definite as can be,' Lord Lydiard replied. 'Doctors

424

are after all doctors and not gods, although not all of them would agree.'

Grace sat down on the sofa and began to unbutton John's topcoat. They had just been out for a walk in the park, and although it was June it had been unseasonably cold. On their return they had met Lord Lydiard alighting from his cab, just back from the hospital.

'What about his other injuries?' Grace asked, as John took himself off to stroke Beanie who was fast asleep in front of the fireplace. 'What about his lungs? And his leg? When I was in there at the weekend the doctor said they were going to run some more tests.'

'It seems as far as his leg goes, there should be no permanent damage,' said Lord Lydiard.

'Thank God for that,' Grace said. 'When you remember how close he came to losing it.'

'Yes, I know,' Lord Lydiard agreed. 'Wonderful people. Wonderful place, St George's. It's not quite so good about his lungs, I'm afraid. There'll always be damage there, do you see, and understandably so when you think – well. When you see what the gas did to his face. And his hands.'

'His hands have practically healed,' Grace said. 'Although of course it's quite a different matter with any internal blistering, I should imagine.'

'Yes.' Lord Lydiard slowly raised both his hands and put them on top of his head, still staring out across the square which was now being washed by a heavy shower of rain. 'He'll just never be one hundred per cent physically, athletically really I mean. Which is a great shame when you think how much he loves his games.'

'He can still fish,' Grace said.

'Not really,' Lord Lydiard said. 'Not if he can't see.'

'How foolish of me,' Grace said, closing her eyes. 'How could I be so stupid.'

'You were no more foolish than me,' Lord Lydiard said. 'Talking about how he loves his games.'

'I don't know what I can have been thinking.'

'You're the very last person who should blame herself,

Nanny,' Lord Lydiard said, still with his hands on top of his head. 'Not for anything. Good heavens, you've brought so much to this family. Before I lost Serena, and particularly since. I often think we'd have all fallen to pieces, you know, if it hadn't been for you.'

'What else did they say about Henry?' Grace asked, folding John's coat up carefully on her lap.

Lord Lydiard swung the top half of his body round to stare at her.

'Have I embarrassed you?' he said. 'I'm sorry.'

'I'm not at all embarrassed,' Grace replied. 'I just didn't know what to say. What else did they say about Henry?'

Lord Lydiard returned to staring out of the window, hands on head.

'What else did they say?' he mused. 'Not much. They don't really know the full effects of this wretched stuff, do you see. This mustard gas. Dichlorodiethyl sulphide, to give it its proper name. Smells vaguely like garlic I understand. I think the world's gone mad, you know. I sometimes wonder what we'll think of next.'

'But they don't think he'll get his sight back, do they?'

'No. No, they were quite definite about that, however much or however little they know about the gas. The retinas of both eyes are damaged quite beyond repair.'

'I see.'

'Will you look at that rain,' Lord Lydiard said. 'Just look at it.'

Grace shut her eyes and listened instead, trying to imagine Henry's new world, a world where nothing more would ever be seen, no colours, no landscapes, no sunsets, no people. Just sounds. Just the sound of a world that along with millions of others he had been fighting to save.

When they finally took the bandages off the full extent of the injuries became apparent. Because he had been so close to the exploding canister, the gas had burned the blue from his eyes and left them the colour of frost. It had seared his eyelids so badly that it had shrunk them, turning the bottom of the insides to the outside, and removing all the eyelashes. Henry's eyes had been one of his best features, large and solemn, thickly lashed, with dreamy heavy lids. Now they were half the size they had been, like two holes punched in a sheet of crumpled paper. Grace had been forewarned by the nursing staff who had advised her to look at the patient first through the porthole in his door, and when she had Grace had cried, just as everyone had when they first saw the full extent of his disfigurement. She had resolved not to cry, steeling herself for days against a revelation she knew was going to be dreadful, but nothing could finally quite prepare her for the shock. Henry had been so handsome, almost ridiculously so with his thick curling hair, his wide blue eyes, his aquiline nose and his slightly crooked mouth, that to witness what had been done to him was unbearable, particularly to those who loved him. It was as if his enemy had taken a brush loaded with acid and painted a swash right across his face, scorching the skin incarnadine, turning a flawless face into something with the complexion of orange peel. They had put Apollo to the torch, and all for the sake of a few inches of mud.

'It's all right, Nan,' he whispered to her as she sat beside him, sensing from her silence the depth of her despair. 'It mightn't look like me, but it's still me inside.'

'Of course it is,' Grace said. 'I just didn't realize they were taking the bandages off today. I'm not used to seeing you – I'm just so used to seeing you with your bandages, that's all.'

Grace turned away from him, glad that he couldn't see her expression, that he wasn't able to see the silent stream of tears which she couldn't stop from coursing down her cheeks. She wiped them quickly away with the palm of her gloved hand then set about refilling the bowl by his bed with fresh fruit.

'I brought you in some more apples,' she said, 'and some cherries. Luckily there's no great shortage of fruit still. Not yet anyway. Would you like me to peel you an apple?'

'Thanks,' Henry croaked. 'What are they?'

'Cox's,' Grace replied, cutting into the skin of a shiny apple with a small knife. 'Your favourite.'

Even his voice was wounded, changed from something mellow and golden to a thick husky rasp. Grace stole another look at him and thought her heart would break as she saw him sitting upright in his bed, propped up against his pillows, his hair carefully brushed, the silk scarf Lottie had brought in for him carefully tied around the burns on his neck, staring into a world where now it would always be night.

'There you are,' she said, placing the plate with the perfectly portioned apple on his lap. 'I've taken all the pips out.'

'Is Harriet coming in?' Henry asked, fumbling for the first piece of the fruit.

'I thought I'd bring her in tomorrow, darling,' Grace replied, retrieving an apple slice which had spilt on to the bed and wiping it carefully on a napkin. 'She's off painting somewhere this morning.'

'Victoria or Charing Cross?'

'One of the two I'm sure,' Grace replied. 'She's just finished one of a group of soldiers returning to the front. It's really terribly good, she's got such a sense of composition. Just wait until—'

Grace stopped, knowing it was too late. Henry smiled.

'It's OK, Nan,' he said, stretching a hand out and finding one of hers. 'It's going to happen all the time. You'll get used to it.'

'What about you, Henry dear?' Grace asked quietly, returning the squeeze of his hand. 'Will you get used to it?'

'It's become a sort of running joke,' Henry said. 'With the nurses. The night nurse comes in and pulls the curtains and I tell her to leave them because I prefer to sleep with them open. The first time I caught her out completely because she said why – was I afraid of the dark? Now it's become a standing joke with all the nurses. They come in and say curtains open or shut tonight, Henry? And I say shut I think, because it's a full moon. Or open so that I can count the stars.'

Grace turned her head away again, and took a breath which she held until she was quite sure she had regained control.

'Actually it's a very good way of going to sleep,' Henry said. 'Trying to remember the night sky. You know how clear it used to be at Keston, in the autumn, when we had those wonderful harvest moons?'

'I know. You could practically read by the light,' Grace said. 'And when there was no moon, on a clear night you could see every star in the sky.'

'Andromeda,' Henry recalled, 'the Southern Cross. Hydra, Orion.'

'Noah's Dove,' Grace said, 'Sagittarius and Scorpio, Gemini the Heavenly Twins. The Great Bear.'

'The Big Dipper, the Plough,' Henry said. 'We used to compete to see who could remember the most.'

'And you always won,' Grace said. 'Easily.'

'I can tell you it helps,' Henry said. 'When you're lying here in the dark, trying to get to sleep. I just close my eyes and look at the heavens, and see how many I can count. One of the night nurses, an Irish girl with a rather lovely brogue, she seems to know them all, and we often count them together.'

'I see I'll have to brush up on my astronomy,' Grace said, 'otherwise it'll be no contest when we get you home.'

Henry ate the rest of his apple in silence, staring ahead of him with a half smile on his face. He put a hand out to search for the napkin when he finished and Grace leaned over to wipe his face for him.

'It's all right, Nan,' he said, taking the napkin from her. 'I'd rather do or rather try to do everything for myself. The last thing I want is to be dependent.'

They spent the rest of Grace's visit idly talking about what was happening at Cadogan Square. No mention was made of the war or its consequences, until Grace got up to leave.

'Just before you go, Nan,' Henry said as Grace tidied up his bedside table and upturned a plate over another apple she had left peeled and ready for him. 'I want you to answer me one thing, if you wouldn't mind. Because you always tell the truth.'

Grace knew what was coming but not how to sidestep it.

'I need to know what it's really like,' Henry said, perfectly calmly. 'I need to know just how bad it is.'

'Haven't you spoken to the doctors?' Grace asked, hoping to find a guideline.

'Yes, of course.' Henry felt for the top of his bedsheet and smoothed it flat. By now his hands had returned to almost their normal size, although the skin on both of them was still puckered and discoloured. Grace supposed it always would be. 'Dr Robins who's terribly decent, and really very funny as well, he said I looked a bit like a piece of dried fruit, while Sister said she thought I was much more like a nice well loved old leather glove.'

'I think Sister's nearer the mark,' Grace said carefully. 'The main thing is you're so much better. And will go on getting better.'

A hand found her arm and gripped it firmly.

'That's not up to your usual standard, Nan,' Henry said. 'I'm afraid I expect more from you than that.'

'What exactly do you want to know, darling?' Grace asked. 'And why?'

'I need to know the truth, Nan,' Henry replied. 'Lying here in hospital, among all the other men who've been wounded, people expect to see people like me. They might find it upsetting but they're not surprised by it because although they might not know exactly what they're going to see, they know they're going to see men who have been wounded. But afterwards, when I leave here, when someone meets me who's never met me before, when I walk into a room, when I go down the street, I need to know what people will see. Otherwise I won't make it, Nan. If I think it's nothing, just that I can't see, and I have a few odd scars and it isn't like that at all, then I'll never be able to make sense of any relationship, because everything will be a lie. I don't want people feeling sorry for me, because at least I came back alive. Three quarters of my company were killed at Loos, you know, Nan. Three quarters. That's why I don't want sympathy. But if people are going to be horrified when they see me, I need to know. You have to remember this as well, you see. When you're like this, what you imagine can actually be worse than the actual truth.'

Grace stood there silently, looking at what Henry wanted her to tell him.

'I really need to know, Nan,' Henry said. 'Particularly before Papa comes in.'

'Very well, darling.' Grace said, sitting back down. 'To start with, you have no eyebrows, and no eyelashes.'

'I could feel that when they took the bandages off,' Henry said. 'With my fingertips. Eyebrows and eyelashes grow again. What about my eyes?'

'They're not as blue as they were, darling,' Grace said. 'They've gone pale. Milky blue. And your eyelids are scarred, the left one worse than the right.'

'I could feel that, too.'

'The burns run from your forehead right across your face.'

'And this part of my mouth.' Henry put a hand to the side of his upper lip.

'Yes. And down your neck. As far as I can see.'

'What colour are the scars? Are they bright red?'

'They're still red on your cheek and your forehead. But not bright red, they're not livid any more. They've gone a sort of pink now. The rest of the scar tissue still looks a little blistered—'

'Dr Robins said it always will.'

'Those bits are a pale ochre colour, like parchment.'

'The corner of my mouth, here.' Henry felt his upper lip again. 'It seems to curl up.'

'Just a little,' Grace said. 'It probably feels worse than it looks.'

'So what's the baddest bit?' Henry smiled to where he thought she was, still with his hand on her arm. 'The eyes, I should imagine.'

'I suppose so, yes,' Grace replied.

'Would dark glasses help?'

'Yes. I suppose so.'

'And the overall effect? Is it hideous? Will children run away and hide?'

'No,' Grace said firmly. 'I shouldn't imagine so for a moment.'

'Not if they were children of yours they wouldn't,' Henry told her. 'So what do I look like? Like this? Without glasses.'

'You look like someone very brave who's been badly burned,' Grace said. 'Someone who is bearing scars won bravely with the greatest courage.'

'Good. Thank you, Nan,' Henry said, letting her go and leaning back on his pillows. 'I knew I could count on you.'

Matron walked with Grace down the corridor, past wards and rooms packed with the wounded.

'They all need a medal, with what they've been through,' she said. 'But your young man, Nanny. I'd say he's worth the VC.'

Extracted from Grace Merrill's journal.

Cadogan Square
April 1917

The best and the worst of months. The worst first. On the morning of the ninth Mr Harcross announced at breakfast that Cook had died in her sleep. When she hadn't appeared at her normal hour Becky went up to her room and found her. She had been in worsening health for the past year and Dr Mortimer said the cause of death was heart failure. It was as if I had lost a parent. I suppose that because of the circumstances of my life I was closer to Cook than I was to my own mother. Certainly with perhaps the exception of Lady Lydiard, no one's passing has affected me more. I only have to read back through the pages of this journal to remind myself of the warmth of our relationship, although of course that goes back further than the starting pages of these books. That goes back to when I first began to work at Keston, when Cook was my lode-star.

It might have been heart failure on the death certificate but it would have been more correct to write 'the war'. With the exception of Parker, and Peter Sennett one of the grooms, every member of the household who joined up lies dead, every single one. I think this was too much for Cook to bear, I think it broke her heart. It certainly explained her drinking, because recently all she would talk about when she was in her cups were 'her boys'. The only blessing is she outlived the last of them, so that before they fell, when they came back on leave they still had Cook to call on at Cadogan Square.

Next there was Harriet, rushed to hospital with a burst appendix and half dead when she got there. How they saved her life none of us will ever know and it happened so quickly none of us ever knew how serious it was. She's back home now, but because of her close call her father has forbidden any more talk of her joining the Red Cross. Not only that, but with Henry at home, even though he has taught himself to cope with his disability better than anyone could imagine, Harriet is needed. Henry finds it very difficult if he is left alone for too long.

His father and he are very close. In fact when Lord Lydiard is at home they are inseparable. They talk a lot about the war now and Henry's first-hand accounts gave Lord Lydiard all the inspiration he needed to win the necessary approvals for his war artists scheme, which is now under way. Rumour has it that Muirhead Bone is to be the first official artist sent to France. (This immediately inspired Harriet who while she has been convalescing has been trying to hatch a plot whereby she disguises herself as a boy and gets sent to France to record the war!)

Then there was Lord Lydiard's brother, killed in a Zeppelin raid on Norfolk where he and his wife had retired to their country estate deliberately in order to remove themselves from the dangers of an air raid on London. His wife escaped without injury. Apparently she wasn't with him during the bombing but other than that I know not. Lord Lydiard seemed more puzzled than anything by his brother's demise and all I ever heard him say about it was 'typical'. Typical of what, again I know not. Mr Harcross on the other hand had somewhat surprisingly let it be known downstairs that he wished it had been Mrs Rokeham and not her husband, which is understandable I suppose when one considers the constant chiding and scolding Mrs Rokeham used to give Mr Harcross and his staff whenever she visited Keston.

Finally there was Beanie. We all knew he was getting on, but no one seemed to be certain of his age, due to the fact that when Lady Lydiard had brought him home as a present for the children he was already a grown dog. He died on Henry's knee. He'd been very poorly before Henry got out of hospital, sleeping a lot and with very little interest in his food. Then when Henry came home he recovered completely, and rarely left his young master's side. Dogs really are astonishing. It was as if he knew Henry had lost his sight and decided to be his eyes for him, and you would swear his new responsibility was the reason for his recovery. Certainly there were no more indications of his being a sick dog, right up until the moment Little John (as he's now affectionately nicknamed) found him unable to move under the sideboard in the dining room. Harriet and I gave him some spoonfuls of sugar and brandy and put him on a blanket in a box by the fire in the library, where he slept for an hour or so very peacefully. Then when he woke up he wagged his tail, looked up at Henry, and barked, as if he wanted to be on his knee. So Harriet lifted him up and he settled down on Henry's lap with a big sigh and went back to sleep with his head in the crook of Henry's arm. He must have stayed that way for well over an hour while we all sat and talked, and it was only when Henry went to get up that he realized his beloved dog was dead. I thought his heart would break he cried so much. Try as I would I couldn't console him. At first he just sat there with Beanie still on his lap, while the tears fell silently from his poor sweet eyes, Harriet beside him, holding his hand. He wouldn't let the dog go, but just sat there with him held in his other arm, hugging Beanie to him. Then he began to sob, putting his head back on the chair and crying with an anguish that was unbearable. Finally Harriet and I took the dog from him and I carried him down to the garden for Mr Harcross to bury, leaving Henry with his sister, leaving him to cry alone because I thought he must, that he needed to. He has been so brave and so resolute since his appalling injury that I thought he wasn't just crying for Beanie, greatly though he loved him. I think he was crying for the other flowers, for the poppies that grow between the crosses in Flanders, for the hell where all that youth and laughter went.

The only bright spot in the month was Brake being invalided home from the front, to recuperate from a broken collarbone which it appears he sustained during some horseplay back in his billet. Henry found it typical of him, that Brake should survive nearly nine months in action, a great deal of it in the front line, and come home with an injury sustained off duty! Everyone welcomed him back with open arms. Everyone.

TWENTY-THREE

Brake was a changed man, however. After his first night home when he got deliriously drunk and regaled them all with an electrifying mix of horrific and hilarious stories from the battle lines, he put the top back on the bottle and never took it off again until the evening of his departure, four months later.

'I have work to do,' he told Grace as she met him going up to his studio the morning following his return home. 'See that no one disturbs me, Grace.'

He had come home with everything in his head. Working only from memory he set about trying to portray the images of war, and to use his newly developed technique to find the best and most potent way he could to express them. At first he would come down not for lunch, but only for dinner, where bleary-eyed but oddly elated he would talk with Lord Lydiard and with Henry about the detail of the war and its import, while because of his sling Grace cut up his food.

'What baffles me,' he said one night, 'is how people here just won't listen. We know what this war is like, guys like Henry and me, and you, John, with the information at your disposal, but what the heck?'

'This is precisely why it's so important to get the impressions of artists,' Lord Lydiard replied. 'For once 'words aren't doing it. It's not entirely Buchan's fault, although the official line is that it is—'

'Harriet's just finished reading *The Thirty-Nine Steps* to me,' Henry interrupted. 'Mr Buchan may not be much of a civil servant, Papa, but he's a quite splendid writer.'

'I rather enjoyed it too, Henry,' Lord Lydiard agreed. 'Anyway, the thing is if we were just to fight this propaganda thing with just words, I'd say we'd lose. If people are to see what this war really is and get it into their heads, we need pictures.'

'That's not the official line, John,' Brake said. 'That's the Lydiard line. The government wants a record, not a deterrent. The very last thing they want is for Tommy Atkins to think twice about enlisting, or even once about deserting.'

'Nobody wants that, Brake,' Lord Lydiard sighed.

'Mr Merrowby's only teasing, Papa,' Harriet said.

'Mr Merrowby wasn't teasing when he said that people won't listen. That they won't listen to what war's really like, and he's right. They see it in the sort of terms they hear in the music halls, with columns of cheery soldiers marching off to war all whistling and singing the latest popular songs. All they see is glory. They don't see mud and rats and trench foot—'

'And death,' Brake said. 'They don't see anyone dying, not ever. Only the enemy.'

'There was this letter in the *Morning Post*,' Lord Lydiard said. 'Someone showed it to me. It was from someone who described herself as a "Little Mother", though I should imagine it was written in the editorial office. Even so, it reflects what an awful lot of people feel, particularly, I'm sorry to say, a lot of women. It talked of mothers passing their sons on as sacred ammunition, only sons to fill up the gaps, and that if the common soldier looked over his shoulder before going over the top, all he'd see would be the women of this country at his heels, backing him all the way. It said women are made to give life and men to take it, and if the men fail, Tommy Atkins, it said, the women won't.'

'OK,' Brake said, standing up. 'Then someone had better show these women where their sons really are, dead in the bloodstained snow, dead drowned in mud, beside horses who drowned along with them, hanging dead over barbed wire entanglements like washing hung out to dry, shot dead in trenches filled with filth. Sacred ammunition indeed,' he said. 'Cannon fodder.'

From then on he didn't even appear for dinner, requesting instead that his food be sent up to him. Grace collected it for him from the kitchen, breakfast, lunch and dinner, and took it up to his studio where he was working in a white heat. His arm was out of a sling by now, and with his shoulder just heavily bandaged, he could work freely without too much discomfort. Not that Brake would have noticed any, such was the speed and fervour with which he worked. He never went outside the house during the whole summer. Grace was deputized to organize his supplies and either she or Harriet or both of them would purchase and collect anything he needed in the way of materials: his paints, his oils and spirits, his brushes, and his canvas. He slept in his studio on a day bed, often during the day and sometimes for a whole day, unshaven and with his hair left to grow. He would only talk to say what he wanted, never in conversation, idle or otherwise. From the beginning Grace knew that this was how it was going to be, that not a moment's physical or mental energy was to be used up on anything other than his work, so she never questioned him once, or passed one remark on his enterprise. She simply looked after him, and saw to his needs, and Brake trusted her entirely and without question, also from the beginning, so much so that he allowed her to clean his brushes and refill his paint jars, to stretch his canvases and prime them, and finally even to mix him his colours.

The last decision was instinctive.

'I need a different brown,' he said one evening as he was working on a picture of three men resting up in a billet behind the lines. 'It's not bronze but it has to have warmth. These guys are out of the firing line, back

438

in the comparative safety of their billet, and they've lit their cigarettes and they're cooking something. They're warming something up on their primus. A can of beans, some coffee, what the heck. It's the only source of light, this glow from the tiny little stove, so the whole picture is in it, in just this one colour. A sort of red brown but it must be light.'

Grace was already mixing it, unnoticed by Brake who had collapsed flat on his back on his day bed and was staring at the ceiling.

'*A Cushy Billet,*' he said, 'that's what I'll call it. That's what I love about the guys in the trenches, they have this great good humour. And you have to say it – camaraderie. They have this camaraderie and it breaks your goddamn heart. This painting is these three guys below ground, waiting for whatever it is to boil, not saying anything, handing round the smokes. The next morning the two in the foreground are going to be dead, blown to eternity by a direct hit. Only the guy in the background gets to survive.'

'You,' Grace said, showing him the colour she had mixed on his palette.

'That's right,' Brake replied. 'The other two had only been sent up the day before.'

'Try this,' she said. 'Try it on the corner here, on this old canvas. It's almost terracotta, but if you float it on with a lot of turpentine—'

Brake looked slowly round at her.

'Are you trying to tell me that after all this time—' he said. 'That's cheating. That's like listening to a conversation while pretending you don't speak the language.'

'No one else knows,' Grace said. 'Except Harriet. And no one else is to know.'

'Why's the secret so guilty?'

'I don't know really.'

'You were afraid that if people knew you could paint, they mightn't take you seriously as a nanny?' Brake asked the question with deliberate disbelief, trying to tease the truth from her.

'In a way, I suppose,' Grace replied. 'I thought I might be a bit like a ballerina who sang.'

'I like that.' Brake laughed. 'You're very funny.'

'Then there was you.' Grace carefully brushed some of the freshly mixed paint on to an unpainted corner of an old canvas Brake used to experiment on. 'You were a painter. You are a painter. The last thing you'd have wanted was some ridiculously keen amateur snapping round your heels, asking you to look at this, or try it this way, or whatever.'

Brake narrowed his eyes at her.

'Don't you realize what a difference this would have made?' he asked. 'For God's sake, Grace, don't you realize the difference it would have made?'

'You mean if you'd known I painted, you'd have looked at me entirely differently?' Grace asked coolly, giving him a smile. 'You would have treated me as an equal, and not as a "civilian"?'

'Jeez—' Brake rolled on to his back again. 'You've made a complete lemon out of me,' he groaned.

'If anyone's a lemon, Brake, it's me,' Grace replied. 'Now sit up and tell me what you think of this colour.'

Brake sat up and stared at Grace. Then he stared at the colour, held it up in the evening light, held it away from him at arm's length and then looked back at Grace.

'Grace,' he said. 'That's it.'

She sat and watched him paint the picture from start to finish. It was oil on a canvas twenty-four inches by twenty. Two soldiers sat foreground, the one on the right with his knees up staring at the tiny stove which cast its glow throughout the billet, the one on the left half on his side, and staring with a smile directly out of the painting. Behind, seen only vaguely through the smoke and heat from the stove, the third soldier lies smoking a cigarette, his head propped up on one arm. Brake painted the whole of the scene in the dugout in the colour Grace had mixed, a light terracotta which he did indeed float on with turpentine, mixing

440

only a darker brown into it for the line and the shading.

When it was finished, Brake stood back and Grace stood up to look at it properly. While she was looking, Brake stood behind her, and when she had finished he turned her to him and made to kiss her.

'No,' Grace said gently but firmly, holding him at arm's length. 'No.'

'No? It can't still be the children, surely?'

Grace shook her head.

'It isn't because of the children,' she said. 'It's because of you.'

'Me?' Brake sounded amazed as he looked. 'You don't want me to make love to you because of *me*?'

'Because of your work,' Grace corrected him. 'Nothing must get between you and your work at this time. Look, Brake. Look what you're doing. You're producing work of sheer genius. You can't start embarking on a love affair now. That sort of distraction is the very last thing you need.'

Brake turned around and slowly surveyed his studio full of paintings. In two months he had already painted a dozen and a half canvases.

'What you're saying is that it would be like Delilah cutting off Samson's hair,' he said. 'I'd lose it.'

'Without a doubt,' Grace said.

'But otherwise—' Brake turned back to her. 'If I wasn't working like this, if the circumstances were different—'

'If the circumstances were different,' Grace replied, 'this would never have happened.'

'Ever the pragmatist,' Brake grinned.

'If what you want to know is whether I want you to make love to me, that's a different matter altogether,' Grace said.

'And what's the answer?'

'The answer is yes of course I do.'

'In that case I'd better hurry and finish my appointed task,' Brake said.

'Yes,' Grace agreed. 'I'd say you had.'

'OK,' Brake said, dropping his paintbrush in a jar of turpentine. 'So let's go. We have work to do.'

From then on Grace divided her time between little John, Henry and Brake. Since John now had lessons every morning, and Grace had Dora to help her take him to the park in the afternoons, and because Harriet spent the second half of most afternoons and the whole of every evening with Henry, during the next six weeks Grace managed to spend at least half a dozen hours a day helping Brake, particularly once she had persuaded him to allow Henry to come up to his studio in the mornings.

'He's to help me concentrate, I guess,' Brake had teased when Grace had first proposed the notion, but he allowed Henry up quite willingly, and used him to bounce ideas off, and to check incidental detail.

Within days they were a team, although both Grace and Henry were careful never to make an unprompted suggestion and never to talk between themselves. Grace was now not only allowed to stretch and prepare the canvases, but since the painting of *A Cushy Billet* permitted to mix colours and once Brake had drawn in the initial compositions in pencil to block in the primary background shapes with coats of thin paint, and finally to do detail work, copying the way Brake had painted the husks of the disfigured trees, or floating in a covering of snow on a landscape of mud, or even painting in a whole strange light primrose sky behind a line of wounded soldiers.

There was no difficulty in duplicating Brake's style. Grace had watched and studied him for so long and so closely that his method of painting was second nature to her now. Besides, they seemed to share a vision of things, developing as they worked together a knack of pre-guessing each other, of anticipating each other's needs. They were a surgeon and a nurse, Brake putting his hand out not for a scalpel but for a brush of gunmetal or *feuille-morte*, and Grace handing it to him ready, almost before he had even reached out.

Henry was the official adviser, his memory for detail

honed by his blindness to astonishing accuracy.

'The inside of a German trench,' Brake would ask. 'I can't remember the difference.'

'They're revetted,' Henry would reply immediately. 'Faced with planking, sometimes even concrete. They're much more solid than ours.'

'Down the side of the road from Arras.'

'Posts. Sawn off posts, like small tree trunks. About three foot high.'

'I've got these fusiliers resting here, they're exhausted and I need detail. Their rifles are covered—'

'Our fellows used anything. Bits of old groundsheet, strips of mackintosh, even old pullovers.'

'I've got all that. There's this detail that's missing, something that when I first saw it, brought it all home. A detail of reality.'

'The eating irons in the men's puttees.'

'You are brilliant, Henry. How in heck did you know?'

'It was something that struck me as well. It's the sort of thing you couldn't possibly imagine unless you'd seen it. Carrying your knife and fork stuck in the top of your puttees.'

'Where else?'

They were, according to Brake, the Three Musketeers, with the painter as d'Artagnan, and the days were heady and happy, in strange contrast with the times Brake was depicting.

'Do you think it odd, Grace?' Brake asked her one evening, 'that we should all be fiddling like this at a time when our particular Rome is burning?'

'No,' Grace replied. 'For a start I don't think we're fiddling. You're certainly not. Your pictures will open a window on to this world, this terrible war-torn world of grief and suffering, and unimaginable heroism. Furthermore, if what we're all doing also helps to restore Henry to his right mind then no, it's not the slightest bit odd. For myself, I can't say how proud I am that you've let me be part of it. Until you did I was just a helpless bystander.'

'In another life you'd like to have been out there yourself, painting. Right?'

'They wouldn't let a woman go out there. Not as an artist.'

'I said in another life, Grace.'

'Yes. Yes of course I would.'

'But what you're doing isn't futile.'

'I didn't say it was. I'm not unhappy with my lot. How could I possibly be? Look at the people who surround me. Look at my—'

'At our children.'

'At my family. I don't regret one moment.'

'Not even one?' The way Brake asked the question Grace knew the moment to which he was referring.

'No,' she said. 'I don't regret saying no. There would have been certain gains, but look at the losses.'

'Good girl.' Brake poured them some more coffee and sat beside her on the day bed.

'Anyway, sweetheart,' he said. 'The thing is it's not too late. It's never too late really, is it?'

'Yes,' Grace replied. 'It often is. But in this case, I'd like to think it wasn't.'

He had taken her hand then and held it, while they sat for a long time in silence with the evening sun slanting across the room that was his studio, its warm rays falling on pictures of men asleep on their feet in cold trenches, of men standing-to before the dawn, huddled in greatcoats awaiting attack, of men blinded by poison being led single file, of men and their horses lying dead in huge craters, of men with their lives blown away in the mud, of men resting in billets beneath the cold ground. They had sat hand in hand and stared at Brake's pictures, thirty-six canvases done in less than five months.

'I'm to report back tomorrow,' he said finally, when the sun had all but set.

'Tomorrow?' Grace couldn't keep the horror from her voice. Brake had given her absolutely no warning.

'There was no point in telling you sooner,' Brake

said, still holding her hand. 'It might have upset you for a week rather than a day.'

'You knew last week?'

'I knew the week before last week.'

'Where are you going?'

'Back to France. At least I missed what's been going on at Passchendaele.'

'I heard you and Lord Lydiard talking about it the other evening,' Grace said. 'They say it's the worst battle that's ever been fought.'

'It's still going on. It started just where I left it. On the Ypres salient.'

'Won't they send you back there, Brake?'

'If they do, there'll be words.'

Brake smiled, kissed her hand, and then got up, going to an old school desk he used for drawing and taking out a full bottle of brandy.

'He who aspires to be a hero,' he said, unstopping it. 'Last night of the holidays, so we might as well get drunk.'

This time Grace accepted the offer of a drink and clinked her glass against Brake's.

'To the new world they say we're making,' Brake said. 'May we live to see it.'

Grace sat with him while he drank, listening to his stories, his confessions, his admissions, and his regrets. Sometimes she laughed at what he told her, sometimes she wondered, and sometimes she fell silent, but not once did she argue with him. That wasn't the tenor of the dialogue. Even when he had drunk several brandies for once Brake was not seeking contention, and Grace sensed this was so from the moment he sat back down beside her. As he leaned against the wall behind him with a full glass Grace knew this was to be a recapitulation, a review of the sums and the substances of life to this date, the story so far. It was the last part of the process of going back to war, a war with which he was now familiar, a war he had fought first-hand, a war whose horrors he now part owned.

'And so that just leaves you and me,' he said, as

445

below them far away down in the hall Grace could hear the grandfather clock chiming midnight.

'I shan't be going anywhere, Brake,' Grace said. 'I shall be exactly where you expect to find me.'

'And when I do,' Brake said, staring into the bottom of his glass, 'I shall ask you to marry me.'

'I should think so, too,' Grace said.

'Does that mean this time you'll say yes?' Brake asked.

'Yes,' Grace replied. 'I'm afraid it does.'

'Dammit,' Brake sighed. 'And here was I hoping I could go on asking because you would go on refusing.'

'That's your problem, Mr Merrowby,' Grace said. 'You always overplay your hand.'

Brake grinned and got up only to sit down again.

'Whoops,' he said. 'The legs have gone.'

Grace reached for the bottle of brandy and handed it to him.

'What about you?' he asked. 'One for the road? One for the Menin road?'

'I'm fine,' Grace replied. 'You help yourself. I'm quite happy.'

Brake poured himself half a tumbler full and dropped the stoppered bottle down on the bed beside him. He took a drink, and sat back against the wall.

'When this lousy war is over,' he sang softly, in a fine tenor voice, *'oh how happy I shall be! I shall go back home to Blighty – no more soldiering for me!'*

A minute later he was asleep, slipped across the wall, his head falling on Grace's shoulder. She waited until she was sure he was completely out, then gently she rose and gently she put him to bed, undoing his collar, slipping off his shoes and socks, and tucking the blankets round him.

Before she doused his light and left him, she bent over and kissed his forehead and stroked his dark hair.

'Good night, my darling,' she whispered. 'I love you.'

The only thing he had deceived her about was the time of his train. In the afternoon when Grace returned from the park with John, having left herself a good hour before she thought she had to leave for Victoria, she found his luggage gone from the hall.

'Brake?' she called downstairs, and then up. 'Brake?'

Henry called her from the library, just as she was about to go upstairs.

'Brake's gone, Nan,' he said. 'He left just after you went out.'

'Yes, but only to the barracks,' Grace said. 'His train doesn't leave until five.'

'His train leaves at half past three, Nan. He said he got the time wrong.'

'He can't have done.'

'You know Brake. It's a wonder he got the day right actually.'

It was now twenty-five past three, leaving Grace no time at all to get to the station.

'There's a note on the fireplace apparently,' Henry said. 'And he said to tell you he was terribly sorry.'

Grace opened the envelope. In it was a card with a painting on one side, a self-portrait in watercolour which according to the date and time written underneath he must have done only that morning. Brake had painted himself looking sideways in the mirror, in front of which was a table with his shaving things on it, the nearly empty bottle of brandy, a yellow pack of cigarettes, a box of matches and a jar full of paintbrushes. *Goodbye my darling*, he had written on the back. *I love you, too*.

'What does it say, Nan?' Henry asked from his chair.

'Nothing, Henry dear,' Grace said. 'Just that he's sorry. Except I don't think he's the one who should be sorry. I think I am.'

According to the first letter Grace got they didn't send him to Passchendaele. Instead the 1st Artists' Rifles were posted to a support line somewhere to the north-east of Paris.

'He should be safe enough there,' Henry said. 'He's

probably somewhere in the south Somme, probably somewhere around St Quentin, Cambrai, that sort of thing. Well away from the firing line, according to Papa.'

Brake's second letter confirmed that his regiment was not seeing action and that oddly enough he was rather bored. Grace wrote back and wondered how on earth could he be bored when he could be drawing or painting, only for Brake to reply that he had found he was unable to work once he was back in uniform. He said he found he could only be one thing or the other, either a soldier or an artist but not both. As a sergeant he had responsibilities towards his men and he imagined that the last thing they wanted to see was him sitting around sketching them while they went about their duties. Not that Grace need worry, he wrote. On his last tour of duty he hadn't made one single sketch and yet had managed to reproduce everything he had seen and more once he got home. He signed off having assured her he had enough for another twenty canvases.

In December he wrote to say the regiment was on the move and that by the time his letter was received they might well be back in action. Lord Lydiard privately confirmed this to Grace, although shortly before Christmas he was happy to convey the news that the 1st Artists' Rifles were still only in support and not in the front line.

Christmas passed very quietly. By now the shortages of food had become so serious that rationing had been introduced, and with the Germans intensifying their air raids over England the country was in no mood to celebrate. The war on land was also going badly. Throughout the year there had been much unrest in the French army, a dissatisfaction which boiled over into two major mutinies, so that it was thought unwise to use French troops in the front line. So the British had to bear the brunt on the Western Front, and even though America had finally entered the war the two sides still seemed to be deadlocked, the final victory at Passchendaele proving a Pyrrhic one, a territorial gain of four miles being won at the cost of four hundred thousand casualties, many of whom after the wettest autumn for years had quite literally drowned in the terrible mud.

The best part of Christmas was that Lottie, on leave from her nursing duties and on her way home to see their mother, stopped off at Cadogan Square to visit Grace. She arrived on the morning of the twenty-third, still in her nurse's uniform and totally exhausted. Grace put her to bed at once where she remained until late afternoon, when on Harriet's insistence Henry, Harriet, Grace and Lottie took tea together in the library.

Lottie knew of Henry's disfigurement from Grace's letters. Also, having spent the best part of the last two and a half years nursing at advanced dressing stations she was well accustomed to witnessing the injuries of war. None the less when two people who have met before encounter each other again when one of them has been blinded and dreadfully scarred some degree of dismay or consternation on the part of the unaffected party and some apprehension on the part of the victim is only to be expected. Not so with Lottie Merrill and Henry Rokeham. They simply picked up from where they had left off the day they had first met at Keston. It was as if they had been waiting for each other, and the wait hadn't been longer than a matter of days.

At once they slipped into an easy informality, finding things in common immediately and not necessarily to do with the war. In fact very little of their conversation had to do with their experiences. Most of it concerned their mutual love of nature and the natural world. Henry told her of his plans to coarse fish with a pram-bell attached to his line which would ring when a fish took the bait, and how as soon as he was back home at Keston he intended to buy a sensible sort of dog, like a retriever, and train it to be his eyes. Then Lottie enchanted him with her stories about all the wildlife she and Grace used to tame when they were children, particularly the story about the whole family of foxes who finally trusted the two sisters enough to eat out of their hands.

'Did you know that if you feed a fox it won't kill

449

anything of yours?' Lottie said. 'I mean not anything on your patch as it were. On your territory.'

'No I didn't,' Henry replied. 'Mama, much as she admired Mr Reynard, always told us that really he was a quite indiscriminate killer.'

'He's not really,' Lottie said. 'All this business about him getting into a chicken run and just killing for the sake of it isn't true. What he's doing when he does that is making provision. If he was left to his own devices he'd come back and take all the dead chickens away and bury them against the day when he hasn't anything to eat. It really isn't indiscriminate killing at all.'

'How do you know all this?' Henry asked.

'One of my patients told me,' Lottie replied. 'Before the war he was doing a study on foxes.'

'I suppose you get very close to your patients,' Henry said, his hand looking for his teacup.

'I try not to,' Lottie said. 'But sometimes it's very difficult.'

Harriet guided Henry's hand towards his cup and Henry picked it up.

'And this fellow with the foxes.'

'He was somebody very special,' Lottie said. 'We try not to have favourites, but it really is impossible sometimes. His name was Jack Elliott, he was frightfully good-looking with very dark hair and laughing green eyes, and I've never known anyone so brave. He had lost both his legs yet all he worried about was everyone else. Even though he must have been in pain I suppose all the time really, his main aim was to keep everyone entertained, so they wouldn't be frightened, and to try and help them forget their pain. His stories were so good, so funny or so interesting, that the other lads would beg him to tell them the same one over and over again.'

'You say "was",' Henry said. 'What happened to him?'

'I brought him home with me,' Lottie said. 'He was one of the ones who wasn't meant to survive.'

'Good,' Henry said, not yet having lifted up his teacup. 'Well done.'

'Yes,' Lottie said. 'It was quite wonderful. His wife and his two children were there to meet him at the station.'

Grace was watching Henry because she sensed the meaning of his questions. She knew Henry too well not to know what he was really feeling, and although his eyes were no longer capable of registering emotion, and although his face remained expressionless, Grace could sense his feeling of relief when he heard that Jack Elliott was married.

Then it was Harriet's turn. Grace thought that because of the way Henry and Lottie had fallen so quickly into such an easy and warm relationship Harriet would be resentful and jealous. She thought that if she had been a short story writer that is how she would have portrayed Harriet's reaction. After all, since Henry's return from the war, sightless and shocked, she and her brother had become closer than ever, and had developed an almost telepathic sense of communication. But like so many imagined stories nothing could have been further from the truth. Because Henry so obviously liked and felt at his immediate ease with Lottie, then so too did Harriet, so much so that she brought some of her paintings in to show Lottie, a privilege she had accorded to no one else so far except Grace.

While Lottie was admiring Harriet's work with a profound and genuine respect, Grace excused herself and took John off upstairs. Even the youngest member of the family had fallen for Lottie, dragging her away from the others at every conceivable opportunity to make her try to guess what the presents were under the Christmas tree.

'I don't *want* to have my bath now, Nanny!' he protested, pulling back as she led him away. 'It's too *early* for my bath!'

'Behave yourself, John,' Grace said crisply. 'And do as Nanny says.'

'You don't have to take John up yet,' Henry said, looking towards their voices. 'He's perfectly welcome to stay down here with us a little longer. We were just going to play some cards.'

'There you are!' John announced triumphantly, wriggling to get free of Grace's iron grip.

'That's very kind of you, Henry,' Grace said, 'but I don't want John getting overexcited and overtired just before Christmas. Come along, John. Say good night to everybody.'

By the time she got John upstairs he had worked himself into a rage, and as soon as Grace opened his bedroom door and let go his hand he threw himself on the floor, thumping and kicking it with fists and feet.

'I don't blame you, darling,' Grace said sadly as she closed the door and sat down in the nursing chair. 'I don't know what came over me.'

'And I don't know what came over you,' Grace said to Lottie later when her sister was getting herself ready for dinner. Henry and Harriet with their father's permission had suggested that Lottie might like to stay overnight and not to travel to Keston until the morning. Furthermore they were all to have dinner together, Lottie, Grace, Harriet and Henry, Lord Lydiard and John, who was allowed back downstairs to share the first of the Christmas treats. Lottie was standing in Grace's room holding up one of Grace's dresses against herself in only her underthings, freshly bathed, powdered and perfumed, with the light of a new excitement shining in her eyes.

'I don't know what you're talking about, Grace,' Lottie said with perfect truth. 'I could understand your temper if I'd been tactless or insensitive, but not because we all got on so well.'

'You mean you and Henry did,' Grace said, unable to stop herself. 'You *flirted* with him, Lottie!'

'I most certainly did not,' Lottie replied, discarding the dress she had been trying against her and looking into Grace's cupboard. 'Haven't you anything new to wear, Grace?'

'There is a war on, Lottie,' Grace said, picking up the abandoned dress and carefully rehanging it. 'I'd have thought you were well aware of that.'

'I am, thanks.' Lottie took out a green velveteen dress of Grace's which Becky had made her up from a pattern. 'This is nice,' she said, holding it up against herself in front of the mirror.

'I'm wearing that,' Grace said, who until that moment had intended to wear her dark blue serge. 'If you don't like the first one I gave you then I don't know what.'

'Please let me wear this, Grace,' Lottie begged, turning herself around with the pretty green dress held against her. 'It really suits me.'

Much as she was loth to do so Grace had to agree. The particular shade of green suited Lottie even more than it suited her, contrasting so well with her sister's lovely blond hair. But because it suited her so well, Grace was even more reluctant to lend it to her.

'It really isn't fair, Lottie,' she said. 'I really was going to wear that.'

'*Please*, Grace.'

'Oh, very well.'

Lottie rewarded her at once with a deeply grateful kiss.

'But you really mustn't go on flirting with Henry,' Grace added impetuously.

'I was not flirting, Grace!' Lottie retorted. 'But even if I had been, I can't see the wrong. I told you before, I find Henry most engaging.'

'For a start, you're older than he is.'

'A year and a bit, that's all. Not enough to make any difference.'

'Things aren't the same as when you first met, Lottie.'

'No,' Lottie agreed. 'Henry wasn't blind when he met me. So at least he knows what I look like. Remember, he won't know what anyone whom he meets now will look like, so at least that gives us a tremendous advantage.'

'I don't understand.' Grace stopped undressing herself and turned to her sister.

'I think you do, Grace,' Lottie replied, 'or else you wouldn't be so anxious. You're very protective of Henry and quite rightly so.'

'I don't want Henry hurt, Lottie. That's all.'

'When do you give up being a nanny?' Lottie asked, hands on hips.

'Never,' Grace returned, and then continued undressing.

'Why do you think I would hurt Henry?'

'Be sensible, Lottie,' Grace said, stepping out of her uniform. 'It's all right being friends, but you know that's as far as it can go.'

'Because of our social difference, you mean? Don't be so absurd, Grace.'

'You don't for a moment imagine—' Again Grace stopped what she was doing and stared at her sister. 'Lottie, I work for this family. You're my sister.'

'Don't be *absurd*, Grace!'

Lottie was laughing, and looking at Grace as if she was mad. She flopped down, sitting on the edge of the bed, holding her unfastened dress to her bosom.

'Grace, if this war is going to do anything, if it's going to change things at all,' she said, 'then the one thing that's most certainly going to be different is the old order. How can we still think we're different from each other? When whoever we are and wherever we come from, we've seen each other with all our dignity shorn away, without all our pretences, and our vanities? I've been nursing them all, Grace, farm labourers and gentlemen, workmen and aristocrats, and they all look the same. Everyone looks the same with their arm blown off, with half their stomach missing, with gangrene, with burns, with holes in their chests. We all look the same at the end, when we die, when we're taken off with a sheet over what used to be our face, to be buried alongside each other, dead in a common cause, farm labourers alongside gentlemen, workmen alongside aristocrats. War changes all that, believe me, because nursing them I've seen them. I've seen the young officers sharing their last cigarettes with their men, and I've seen the men comforting their dying officers.'

'Did you see the generals doing that?' Grace asked.

'Did the generals and the brigadiers come round the wards and sit with the dying? Did they fight with their dying? Or did they just stay where they were, miles from the front line, eating the best food and drinking the best wines? You think that the war is going to change the way we are. I don't. Not while we still have generals who look on the men as numbers, as numerals to be called up and stuck in the holes in the front line.'

'You're wrong, Grace,' Lottie said. 'If there hadn't been a war, a lot of people think we would have had a revolution, just like the Russians have just had.'

'When this war is over, Lottie,' Grace replied, 'there won't be anybody left who thinks like that, the way you do. They'll all be lying buried in France. All that'll be left here will be the middle-aged, the old, and the mediocre.'

'And the women, Grace,' Lottie said, her eyes flashing. 'Don't forget the women.'

'There won't be any young men, Lottie,' Grace said. 'The best of this country will have been blown away by the guns. And we'll be left with just the generals and the politicians, and so nothing will really change, not really.'

'We'll see,' Lottie said, getting up off the bed, from the sound of doubt now in her voice obviously anxious to curtail the argument. 'But whatever you say, nothing is going to affect my attitude to Henry.'

'I'm not talking about your attitude to Henry, Lottie,' Grace said, beginning to fasten Lottie's dress for her. 'Or his attitude to you. I'm talking about other people's attitudes to both of you.'

'That's all supposition,' Lottie said. 'That's all a maybe in the future. If I fall in love with Henry, and if he falls in love with me, that's something we might or we might not have to face.'

'Supposing Henry falls in love with you,' Grace said, 'which he shows every sign of doing, and you don't fall in love with him? Have you thought about that?'

'Supposing I fall in love with Henry,' Lottie countered, 'and he doesn't fall in love with me. I can be hurt too, you know, Grace. Being able to see doesn't make me immune.'

It seemed that Lottie was right, because no one in the family seemed the slightest bit concerned about the love which was quite obviously blooming right there in front of them. At dinner Henry had made sure that Lottie was sat one side of him and Harriet the other, with his father at the other end of the table next to Grace and John. The war was momentarily forgotten, and only referred to as something which would soon be over and once it was this was what everyone was going to do. Lord Lydiard was going to learn how to fly, Harriet was going to go to Italy to paint, Lottie was going to act on the films, and John was going to go to India and catch a tiger. Only Grace seemed to be uncertain of what she was going to do.

'It doesn't matter, Nan,' Henry said. 'You can say something silly if you'd rather.'

So Grace said something silly, which was what she preferred to do in the circumstances. Instead of saying she hoped to marry Brake Merrowby and spend the rest of her life either loving him or painting with him, she said she was planning to be the first woman to swim the English Channel backwards. This delighted young John, who could barely stop laughing at the idea, while his father took the notion quite seriously.

'I believed you, Nanny,' he said. 'Until John here said you'd said *backwards*. If you'd said you were going to be the first woman to swim the Channel there'd have been no doubt about it.'

After dinner Harriet and her father played duets at the piano, and then Lottie and Grace did. Finally all four pianists played together, one hand each. John recited his new party piece which Grace had been rehearsing him in, *The Dong With the Luminous Nose*, and got slightly irked when he had to stop three times because everyone was laughing so much, and finally Henry silenced everyone by doing a series of impeccable card tricks.

'Let me see the cards,' Harriet demanded after he had finished.

'Why?' Henry said, putting the cards behind his back.

'I don't see why you should see the cards when I can't.'

'You know what I mean,' Harriet sighed. 'Come on. I mean you have to have marked them.'

'I didn't mark them, did I, Nan?' Henry asked.

'No he didn't,' Grace replied absolutely truthfully.

'Then you did,' Harriet said.

'I didn't either,' Grace replied. 'No one did. At least no one in this house did.'

'Oh, they're *Braille*!' Lottie said. 'How brilliant! Do let me see!'

'Nan gave them to me,' Henry said, handing over the pack. 'An early Christmas present.'

'I thought it would be fun if Henry could polish up some of the tricks he used to do before,' Grace said, before turning to Henry. 'But I didn't think you'd have time to learn some new ones,' she added.

'Ah ha,' Henry said with a smile, while he dextrously made a card appear and disappear in and out of Grace's hair. 'Now you see it now you don't. Do you think I can make my fortune as the first blind conjuror?'

'Probably,' Harriet said, examining the cards. 'As long as you don't try any juggling.'

After Grace had put John to bed she rejoined the party who were now playing *vingt-et-un* with Henry's new cards. When everyone finally got up to go to bed around midnight, Lord Lydiard quietly asked Grace to stay behind for a moment.

'Henry's got me smoking,' he said, taking a cigarette from the box. 'Do you mind? Frightful habit.'

He indicated a chair for Grace to sit, and after he had lit his cigarette he sat down opposite her.

'There's no need to worry,' he said. 'I saw you over dinner, and of course I've been watching you with Henry ever since we got him back, and there's no need to worry.'

'About what, Lord Lydiard?' Grace asked, determined there should be no misunderstanding.

'I'm sure you think as I do, Nanny, that if a young man's old enough to fight for his country then he must be old enough to make his mind up about all sorts of things, I'm sure we're agreed on that.'

'That depends what else we're agreed on,' Grace replied.

'I think your sister is perfectly charming,' Lord Lydiard said, drumming one set of fingers against his lower lip and looking at her. 'Which doesn't surprise me in the least.'

'Nursing has changed her,' Grace said, factually, not meaning to imply any criticism. 'It's made her much tougher.'

'By tougher you mean stronger?'

'Probably.'

'That's not such a bad thing. I'd be surprised if it hadn't. No – more than that, she wouldn't be the sort of person she is if it hadn't. An experience like that, anyone kind and loving and sensitive would be changed by the sort of thing your sister's been through. Anyway, if she and Henry are to be friends, then I'd say the stronger the better.'

'Do you mind if I ask you what you mean by friends?'

'I'm not too sure what to call it nowadays,' Lord Lydiard said, now with his glasses on and staring at the ceiling. 'There's probably some new slang. *Koochy-koo* or some other ragtime thing. I don't know. We called it a romance. *Un amour.* A love affair.'

'And if they do?' Grace wondered.

'Oh – I'd say that's for them to sort out, Nanny, wouldn't you?'

'Would you, Lord Lydiard? But if they do, won't there then be other things that will require sorting out? Things outside their reach?'

Lord Lydiard looked down from the ceiling, across at Grace, and took his glasses off.

'No, Grace,' he said finally, with a shake of his head. 'I can assure you there won't.'

'What a wonderful evening,' Lottie said when Grace went in to wish her good night. 'They asked me to stay, you know.'

'No I didn't,' Grace said, but the reproach had gone from her voice.

'Henry and Harriet asked if I could stay for Christmas,' Lottie said, 'and I must say I was tempted.'

'I'm sure you were,' Grace said, sitting down on the bed. 'But what about Mother?'

'She's got her new husband,' Lottie said. 'I'm sure I'm the last person she wants around over Christmas.'

'I keep forgetting she's married again,' Grace said. 'We've been so used to thinking what-about-Mother for so long now, her being all by herself made such a difference to our lives—' Grace suddenly stopped and fell silent.

'What is it, Grace?'

'Oh for heaven's sake, Lottie!' Grace said, as if shedding herself of a great weight. 'Stay if you want to! This life is far too short! And why should we always be so hidebound by conventions? If Henry wants you to stay, and that's what you want, then stay, Lottie. It's not as if you haven't earned a right to your life, and to do what you want to do, rather than what other people want you to do! Telephone Mother first thing in the morning, and don't lie to her, don't make any excuses. Just simply say Lord Lydiard has asked you to stay for Christmas and that's what you're going to do. She's such a terrible snob she'll think it marvellous that you've been invited anyway, and as you say, she's got a husband now, so she won't be alone.'

'I get the feeling, like I always do with her,' Lottie said with a grin, 'that all she wants me for is to be a pair of hands. So she doesn't have to get her own dirty.'

'Sometimes,' Grace said, 'I get the feeling that's all she ever wanted from the both of us.'

So Lottie stayed and in spite of the state of the world, they had one of the nicest Christmases that Grace could remember. The only thing missing was one person, and that person was Brake.

Grace had sent him off his Christmas parcel, his card and a long letter in plenty of time, and on the 28th she got a letter from France which he had also posted in plenty of time but had been delayed somewhere along the route. It was bitterly cold where he was, with two or three inches of snow and more forecast over and after Christmas. At the moment of writing his company was still in support and not in action. He said he missed everyone terribly, that coming home was the worst thing he could have done, that before he had seen everyone again he had found it easier to tolerate the deprivations and the terrors of war. But now he had been back home he wasn't quite sure how much longer he could bear the strain. Several of the men under him had cracked and been sent home deeply shell-shocked. Brake didn't think that would be his fate because he had Grace to think about. But sometimes during the incessant and terrifying nocturnal bombardments he feared that even if he survived he would never be the same again. He had seen many terrible and horrifying things before he had been invalided home, visions and images that he had transferred to his paintings, but since his return he had seen worse, some things so bad that he really believed he wouldn't be able to cope with them even at arm's length and with his longest paintbrush. The only thing that would pull him through this time round was his rediscovered love for Grace. *Although when I say rediscovered*, Brake wrote, *I don't mean as in renewed, as in found again as in oh look! So that's where it was! I don't mean that at all. What I mean is as in redetermined, as in re-resolved, re-established. In fiction people are forever saying to each other that they're so glad they've found each other again blah-blah. Well that's not how I feel, Grace. I feel we were there all the time and knew it. It just didn't fit then, that's all. And now this time, this time we seem at last to have got the pieces to fit. I don't believe in God, not after what I've seen over here, but if He still believes in me then I hope He believes in me enough to bring me back to you and into your arms for ever and ever Amen.*

'Would you marry him if he asked you again?' Lottie asked Grace on the night of the 29th as they sat talking on Grace's bed.

'One thing at a time,' Grace replied, biting through the thread she was using to darn a tear in one of Henry's shirts. 'Let's all get through the war first.'

'I shall marry Henry if he asks,' Lottie said. 'I wouldn't think twice.'

'You won't have to, if you've thought well in advance,' Grace said. 'As long as you've seriously considered what it involves, because that's all you can do, consider it. You can't possibly know.'

'Yes, Nanny,' Lottie sighed happily.

'Don't you yes-Nanny me, Lottie. I'm talking to you as your older sister. If he did ask you to marry him, and if no one opposed your marriage, you must remember that you'll inherit Keston and all its responsibilities. You must remember that you'll be married to a man who is disabled, so that a great deal of that responsibility will fall to you. It might be a wonderfully romantic notion now, but looking at the life you could have ahead of you, it would need a great deal of careful thought. Forethought.'

'Are you jealous?' Lottie rolled off her back on to her side and lay looking at Grace while she sewed, her pretty face propped up by one hand.

'What of?'

'Henry and me.'

'Why on earth should I be jealous?'

'You said that just like somebody who is.'

'Why should I be jealous of Henry and you?'

'You've always loved Henry. He's been one of the biggest things in your life. You said so yourself.'

'So?' Grace glanced up, needle in mid-air. 'So?'

'Wild oats.' Lottie laughed. 'Remember how I used to drive you mad saying that? You were always saying *so?* And I used to cheek you by saying *wild oats* back.'

'It wasn't as bad as when you used to repeat everything I said,' Grace reminded her sister.

'I don't know how you put up with me.'

'I didn't. Not always, if you remember. Once when you wouldn't stop repeating what I said for days, I shut you in the linen cupboard until you promised never to do it again.'

'You shut me in there for hours.'

'I should have left you in there.'

The two women smiled at each other and then Grace resumed her mending and Lottie rolled back on her back.

'So you really aren't jealous of me and Henry,' Lottie said as a fact, rather than a question.

'Not at all,' Grace replied.

'But when I first mentioned it—'

'That was different. It wasn't jealousy, I simply felt possessive. It's hard for you to understand, because you haven't lived my life. You're my sister and it's only natural you should assume that all I want in a situation like this is the best for you, for you to be happy. But my involvement is twofold. You're my sister—'

'And Henry's been like your child,' Lottie guessed.

'No, Lottie,' Grace corrected her. 'I have been his Nanny.'

That night, just after dawn it must have been, at first light they climbed out of the trench. She could see them quite clearly, and she knew how many there were. Less than there should have been, ninety-two, not any more, the numbers of the company reduced by the prevailing circumstances. It had snowed again during the night, she could see that too, because these were the first footfalls, the first impressions on the frozen white surface. It was deathly quiet as they climbed out of the trench, a long gaping brown mouth that ran away from her it seemed as far as the eye could see, a rut from which the men climbed out and up into the snow as if they had been spawned there, leaving others behind them, others she could see who were lying face down on duckboards, their helmets off and on the ground ahead of them, their arms twisted double-jointed against the frozen earth which made up the walls of the trench. They must be dead already, she thought. No one who was alive could bear to have his arms in that position. The men who were alive were wearing their greatcoats, and had webbing straps criss-crossed from their shoulders down to a thick belt from which an oblong pouch hung at the back. On the front half of the belt she could see the double bank of ammo pouches, and each man had a square of blue on the right arm of his greatcoat, below red shoulder flashes. The ones who were still

462

alive were walking forward, not running, they were walking quite slowly and leaning as if into a wind. They carried their rifles in one hand, their right hands, with bayonets fixed, but no one was firing, no one was even aiming at anything. They were just walking forward, as if into a bitter wind.

One of them fell, one of the last out of the trench, he fell on to his knees first as if he was praying, and then down on his face into the snow. Another one followed him and fell as if swimming, his left arm over his head exactly as if he was swimming. No one was shooting, there was absolutely no noise of guns at all, large or small. But still they kept falling, more and more now, with an almost monotonous regularity. Appalled, she began to count them. Forty-eight, fifty-three, sixty-four and all in no time at all, in minutes, or was it seconds? None of them got far, they all fell within a matter of yards from the trench, down into the snow which was now blood red. A few walked on into the wind, never looking round, their rifles slung in their hands, their bayonets fixed.

Then she saw him, only then. He was leading the men and although she couldn't see his face she knew it was him. She could only see his helmet and the movement as he walked, on and on into the silent wind, but she knew at once it was him, even though she could only see his helmet and before she saw the three stripes on his arm. At once she tried to call out to him, she tried at the top of her voice but nothing came out of her mouth, not one sound. She screamed with all her might, opening her mouth as wide as she could, telling him he must look, he must hear. But nothing came out, nothing at all. The man walking beside him fell, but he didn't look, he didn't hesitate, he didn't even flinch, he just kept walking forward until at last he must have heard her because he turned, very slowly and even though he was still marching he turned his head round and looked at her and when he did she saw he had no face just a wound and when she saw the dark hole where his face had been and when he had turned to take his last look of her he fell sideways in the snow, his helmet tumbling off as he hit the red snow, and rolling back down the hill back down into the dark of the rut they had come from which was now filled with blood, and as he fell down, as he fell into the snow she woke up and she sat up in the dark knowing he was dead.

Some time later, she didn't know how long, Grace finally slipped out of bed and went up to his studio. She left her room in the dark and she climbed the stairs in the dark. When she opened the door, through the uncurtained windows she saw dawn was breaking across a cold, grey sky. She turned on the light and soldiers stared at her everywhere, dead and alive, frozen for ever in time on his canvases, the glory of war redefined. Grace wiped a hand across her brow which was still cold with the sweat of terror and searched Brake's desk for the bottle of brandy she knew was there, the bottle they had drunk from the night before he left.

When she found it she fumbled with the top, unable at first to uncork it, and then the cork came out, crumbling in her hand as it did. She found a glass in the desk as well and with shaking hands she poured herself two inches of amber and stood up straight, staring at the painting in front of her, the three men in their cushy billet, warmed by the light of the stove, wreathed in the terracotta smoke of their cigarettes, friends to the death. She drank slowly, sipping the brandy like medicine, feeling the warmth in her throat and then inside her and she put both hands round the glass as if the drink could warm them, too. She took another sip and said to herself for the hundredth time it was only a dream, it was only a nightmare dream, and as everyone knows it's the opposite of dreams that comes true. That brought some reality to the situation, Grace thought as she felt the brandy warming her now all the way through, that brought the perspective back. It was only a dream, and it's the opposite of the dream that comes true, yet just in case she wrote it all down.

She took another longer sip of brandy and moved from the desk, across the room full of his poetry, until she was by the day bed where they had sat together. Opposite the bed was the table with his books and papers on it, below the mirror where he had painted the portrait of himself

464

that morning, except in its glass now was not his image but hers, although when she first saw it, when she saw the woman staring back at her she thought she must still be dreaming so she walked across to the mirror to get a closer look and when she did she saw she had been wrong, that it was in fact her, and when she knew she was wrong and she saw herself staring back at herself she opened her mouth and screamed, and this time she did scream, a scream which would have woken the dead, but instead it woke the whole house, and when the first person got to her they saw why she screamed because all Grace's long beautiful black hair had turned the colour of snow.

'Yes, that happened to someone in our village during the war,' the one called Ben said, all the while tapping the side of one of his cowboy boots with a pencil. 'A flying bomb landed in the field behind his shop, and the next morning when he woke up his hair had gone white.'

'I've never heard of anything like that before,' the Melford boy said. 'I find that astonishing.'

'That's what happened,' Grace said. 'Take it or leave it.'

'It's not that I don't believe it,' the Melford boy replied. 'It's just that I've never heard anything like it.'

'You can see for yourself,' the one called Ben said. 'Hair like that doesn't come out of a bottle.'

'What about the dream?' the Melford boy asked. 'Was it, you know – well, prophetic? Visionary?'

'His company was called up to the front line on the morning of the twenty-ninth of December, and their number had been depleted,' Grace said. 'There were only ninety-two of them, which I understand is some way below full strength.'

'A company's usually at least a hundred and fifty men,' the one called Ben said airily, still tapping his boot with his pencil.

'There had been an attack the night before,' Grace continued. 'His company was ordered to mount a counterattack that night, or rather at first light.'

'On the morning of the thirtieth,' one of them said, underlining the date and time.

'It was a completely ill-conceived stratagem,' Grace said, 'and a totally disastrous one. I don't think they even knew what they were supposed to be attacking. Sixty-four men fell, and apparently Brake was the last.'

'You even got the numbers right?' The Melford boy leaned forward, chewing a match. 'You even got the right number?'

'Or did that come later?' The one called Ben stopped tapping his boot for a moment and smiled, showing uneven yellow teeth. 'With hindsight.'

'I wrote it all down, what I'd dreamed,' Grace said. 'In the back of one of his sketchbooks.'

'I'm only being the devil's advocate,' the one called Ben said, spreading his hands wide. 'But you could have done that later.'

'Hardly,' the Melford boy said, dismissing the notion. 'Someone who's had a shock like that is hardly going to rush upstairs later and write it all down with the intention of fooling posterity.'

Grace smiled at the young man and nodded. He gave her a so-what shrug in reply.

The one called Ben resumed his impatient pencil tapping.

'They buried him in France, I take it,' he said.

'Of course,' Grace replied. 'Along with a thousand others. In a corner of a foreign field.'

'I don't much like Rupert Brooke,' the one called Ben said.

'No, neither do I,' Grace agreed, to his surprise. 'At least I do, I like his other poems, but I always thought in his war poems he was too much the crusader. His heroics were a bit too chauvinistic for me. I preferred the later poets. Wilfred Owen, Gilbert Frankau, and of course Siegfried Sassoon.'

'And e. e. cummings,' the Melford boy said. 'Wasn't it cummings you quoted in your journal? After you'd been to visit the cemetery for the first time?'

'Some years later,' Grace said. 'Yes it was. Mr cummings bought a picture of Brake's some time in the Thirties. They seemed to share a common voice.'

Extracted from Grace Merrill's journal.

In memory of Sergeant Brake Merrowby, of the 1st Artists' Rifles. Killed in action on 30 December 1917 at Welsh Ridge, Cambrai.

> *my sweet old etcetera*
> *aunt lucy during the recent*
>
> *war could and what*
> *is more did tell you just*
> *what everybody was fighting*
>
> *for,*
> *my sister*
>
> *isabel created hundreds*
> *(and*
> *hundreds) of socks not to*
> *mention shirts fleaproof earwarmers*
>
> *etcetera wristers etcetera, my*
>
> *mother hoped that*
>
> *i would die etcetera*
> *bravely of course my father used*
> *to become hoarse talking about how it was*
> *a privilege and if only he*
> *could meanwhile my*
>
> *self etcetera lay quietly*
> *in the deep mud et*
>
> *cetera*
> *(dreaming,*
> *et*
>
>   *cetera of*
> *Your smile*
> *eyes knees and of your Etcetera)*

e. e. cummings, Two XI

Brake was one of eight and a half million men who lost their lives in the war, Henry was one of the twenty-one million who were wounded. Fifteen million tons of shipping were lost, of which nine million were British. Sixty-three million people answered the call to arms, whether voluntarily or by conscription, and worldwide the war cost approximately six million pounds *a day*. Grace however records no such statistics in her journal. Instead she itemizes only the losses incurred by the Lydiard family and by those who served them at Keston, figures which put the misfortunes of war into a certain perspective because these were not numbers but identifiable people. Keston's Roll of Honour spelled out the names of an artist, a valet, two footmen, two gardeners, three grooms, a handyman, and a pot boy. Fourteen fought, and eleven fell, and of the three who came back only one was without any visible injury. Grace imagined there was hardly a household or a family in the land which had not suffered some sort of loss, directly or indirectly, and although there was wild rejoicing in the cities throughout the day of 11 November 1918, when news of the end of hostilities came, and although the nation duly celebrated its victory on a specially designated Peace Day the following July with processions, dances and street parties, Grace knew as she suspected everyone knew that the cost of the war would finally prove unbearable.

But life goes on, and as far as the world of the winners went, it went on in a progressively silly way, so much so that the more serious-minded and those who had suffered the greatest losses were forced to wonder more and more if this was indeed to be the world for which their sons and lovers had sacrificed their lives. *The Jazz Age*, it was called, and while Jazz could in no way be blamed for society's behaviour, that was the music of the time, hot, loud and fast. Hems were hoisted and morals lowered. A natural reaction the apologists called it, a universal expression of relief. But others less enchanted thought it was just an excuse for bad behaviour, because few of those who *flapped* and drank and smoked had been out in the trenches. Besides, there weren't enough of those sorts of people left to make such a significant impression. They were all lying under the Flanders turf.

Grace saw little of this but heard plenty from Lottie and Henry who were now officially engaged, and from Harriet. All three went to parties in the country and to parties in the town, but soon tired of them and returned to Keston, Henry and Lottie to prepare for their wedding and Harriet to await the commencement of her studies at the Slade. Lottie lived at home with her mother and stepfather, but spent practically all of her waking hours at Keston Hall with Henry, planning the life which they would soon share. As for Lord Lydiard, on his return to his country seat he at once set about reconstituting the estate, a large part of which in keeping with his instructions had been turned over to the production of foodstuffs to help the war effort. During the ever increasing shortages he had further authorized the slaughter of half the herd of magnificent red deer which roamed the parkland and venison was put on sale for sixpence a pound which the ultra-conservative labourers in and around Keston resolutely refused to eat.

Half the trees were felled as well, to make butts for rifles, and as far as his beloved Keston went this hurt Lord Lydiard the most. Deer soon reproduced themselves, he said, but not trees. The war made further inroads, into territories felt by many landowners. Higher incomes were subjected to higher taxes, particularly unearned incomes such as Lord Lydiard's, and although agriculture had revived a little during the war, many landowners who had suffered badly in the earlier depression failed to benefit sufficiently from its recovery. Like some other fair-minded landlords, Lord Lydiard had helped his tenants out when times were bad but now, in the aftermath of the war, he was reluctant to raise their rents so that he might once again prosper. The result was that he had to sell off much of his land, not at Keston itself but where he owned it in other parts of the country. In 1919 he was forced to dispose of nearly a third of his inheritance, six thousand acres in Wiltshire which fetched less than one hundred thousand pounds.

But money was not his declared object. His prime intention was that the estate in Wiltshire should not fall into the hands of speculators but that tenants should be given a fair chance to buy their farms, of which over half of them indeed did. Even so, the dispersal of an estate which had been in the Lydiard family for so long upset Lord Lydiard deeply, particularly since the new breed of owner-farmer emerged as people he could not admire, nor they him. While publicly respectful of him, privately they suspected his liberalism and despised what they liked to call his *fancy notions*, while milking his generosity.

Meanwhile Grace grieved. Quietly and privately through the days, the weeks and the months as the trees were replanted and the parkland restored, she mourned the loss of something that was unsupplantable and some-one who was irreplaceable. It seemed to be winter all the time, for while new life grew up around her, nothing but death was on her mind, the death of someone who had been her life.

It was of course a private grief, even though all the family were mourning him, for all the family knew that Grace's loss was the most heartfelt. In her mind and her heart and her soul she vowed never to forget him, until one day, quite suddenly, she realized that in her determination not to forget him she was failing to remember him. He had become the past instead of a presence. He was a ghost and not a spirit. She was putting up a monument to him instead of living in his shrine, and the moment she realized this she walked out of the shadow of death and back into the light where life continued to grow. The tumult and the shouting had long since died and while she must not forget, she knew what she must do more was remember.

Remember Brake as he was and for what he was, and remember him true. Capricious, passionate, infuriating, wild, tender, drunk, sober, loving, petulant, dark and brilliant. He was a bottle of champagne about to be opened, a piano about to be played, a canvas about to be painted, he was life with the top off, and once she knew that, once Grace began to remember him rather than make sure she never forgot him, Brake Merrowby stopped being something she had lost for ever and became the something she would always have.

TWENTY-FOUR

There had been long and plentiful conversations about the eligibility of Henry Rokeham's proposed bride and a great deal of criticism, not on the part of Henry's father, but from relatives and friends of the family, most particularly Lord Lydiard's sister-in-law, the now widowed Cicely Rokeham. Inevitably and finally it all filtered back to Lottie down the grapevine, and the more she was aware of the opposition the more she sought solace and advice from Grace.

According to the Cicely Rokeham faction the marriage would be a disaster because Lottie was going to drown socially, way too far out of her social depth. Ultimately Henry would inherit Keston and since Lottie had received absolutely no training or preparation for running such a house and estate, she would undoubtedly prove inadequate to the task. A girl like Lottie had neither the necessary pedigree nor the social acumen, she was unversed in the subtleties of etiquette, and furthermore she neither hunted nor shot. Worse, her enemies soon discovered that Lottie was quite unequivocally opposed to such sports, a fact which distanced her even further from the Diehards, as Grace and Lottie soon christened them.

To reassure her sister, Grace pointed out that there were no such objections within the immediate family to her or to her marrying Henry. From the outset Lottie had been welcomed unreservedly by Henry's father and sister from the moment they had realized how happy Lottie made Henry and how very much in love the couple were. Furthermore, as far as her abhorrence of blood sports was concerned, she and Henry were of the same mind on this matter. In fact it had been one of the first things they found that they shared in common. As a result of his experiences in the fighting line and in light of the appalling suffering endured by the warhorses, Henry no longer saw any sport to be gained in the taking of life, and had already persuaded his father to close the Keston estates to the local hunts and guns, a move which well and truly indicated where the family stood when it came to blood sports.

'Even so,' Lottie sighed, 'they're still saying that I am an adventuress.'

'Let them,' said Grace. 'Just remember it's sticks and stones that hurt, not words.'

'At least Mother is happy,' Lottie grinned. 'Embarrassingly so. She keeps saying *imagine, Lottie dear. You – the future Lady Lydiard*. And she's bought a book on social etiquette. Stepfather and I have to sit and test her every evening after dinner on all the points from the latest chapter she's read.'

'Typical of Mother,' Grace said. 'She's such a snob, although heaven only knows why. But then as they say, even workhouses have their aristocracy.'

'How do you feel about Mother, Grace?' Lottie asked. 'Do you love her? Because sometimes I'm not sure that I do.'

'I'm not sure either, at least not in the way I should be,' Grace agreed. 'I've thought about it quite a lot over the years. I've examined my conscience inside out, and I've come to the conclusion that I respect her rather than love her. Which Mrs Jenkins once told me was perfectly all right.'

'Dr Granger said he didn't think any two daughters could have been more dutiful,' Lottie said.

'Perhaps not,' Grace replied. 'But what about Father? Did you love Father, Lottie?'

'I think I did when I was small,' Lottie said. 'Before he ran away. I certainly know that I wanted him to love me.'

'That's how I felt,' Grace said. 'I wanted him to love me so much, but he never really took much notice of us, did he? I'm sure if he had, if he'd shown just a little bit of love, we'd feel very differently. I would. But I always got the impression that you and I interrupted their lives.'

'Do you think we were afterthoughts?' Lottie wondered. 'Perhaps they didn't really intend to have us. I don't think perhaps they did.'

'You know, sometimes, when you and I were slaving away in the kitchen, or with the housework, or running errands, or digging the garden,' Grace said, 'at those times I used to think that we were just two extra pairs of hands. That to our parents we were there to show that they could have children, and had indeed had children, so they'd done what the Bible said they should do, but apart from that they really rather wished we'd keep out of sight.'

They were walking round the lake now, on Grace's favourite route, a way she had walked and talked so many times before. Out in the middle of the water a large fish broke the surface, sending out a set of slow and perfect circles.

'I think you'll have a wonderful marriage,' Grace said, stopping to look out across the lake. 'I really do.'

'So do I,' Lottie said. 'I'm determined on it.'

That was not Lady Hythe's opinion when she had tea with Grace and her younger grandson a week later. Since that first Christmas after the death of Lady Lydiard, Lady Hythe had slowly but surely regularized a series of visits to Keston, ostensibly to visit her grandchildren, and a similar series of visits back to her house when Grace was required to bring John across to see her. As John had grown, so the amount of visiting had increased, until now they saw each other once every week, appointments which the older woman never failed to keep and which young John endured with all the stoicism of childhood.

'I met your mother the other day,' Lady Hythe said on her latest visit to Keston. 'A sweet woman, but what a pity your father is no longer with us.'

'Yes,' Grace said. 'I'm sure he would have liked to have seen Lottie married.'

'Perhaps.' Lady Hythe gave a small sniff and held her porcelain teacup up to Grace for some more tea. 'And perhaps if he had been alive a little more consideration would have been brought to bear.'

Grace took Lady Hythe's cup and refilled it from the silver teapot on the table in front of her.

'From what I hear I understand you don't approve of Henry's choice of bride either,' Grace said, returning the teacup. 'I think that's a shame, and I'm surprised, because I thought you liked my sister.'

'I think your sister is charming,' Lady Hythe retorted. 'But that is by the by, and no, I do not *disapprove* of the marriage. Worse, I think it is a blueprint for disaster, and I care far too much for Henry to sit back and allow such a thing to happen without sounding my warnings.'

'Which are?'

Grace took the plate of cake away from John who was quietly trying to smuggle himself an extra slice, and placed it away from him on the far side of the table.

'You can say what you like about class, Nanny,' Lady Hythe said, 'but it exists whether you like it or not. Inasmuch as we do not race half-breeds against thorough-breds, neither should we expect someone from a lower order to be able to marry into a higher. There are considerable differences between the classes, and these differences must be respected.'

'My teacher used to say that in the final analysis class comes down to expecting slugs to despise the worms,' Grace said.

'Be that as it may,' Lady Hythe continued implacably. 'God distinguished his angels by degrees, and so likewise we have kings and dukes, our leaders, our judges and people of other and varying degrees. That is the shape of society.'

'That is the shape society dictates,' Grace replied. '*If the stone falls on the egg, alas for the egg. If the egg falls on the stone, alas for the egg.*'

'That is the shape of society, Nanny, whether you like it or not,' Lady Hythe replied.

'With respect, Lady Hythe, Lord Lydiard doesn't share your concern,' Grace said.

'With respect, Nanny,' Lady Hythe returned, 'my son-in-law doesn't think straight.'

'If I may ask you,' Grace said, 'does this mean you oppose the match?'

'I most certainly do,' Lady Hythe replied. 'And I intend to do everything in my power to make the concerned parties see sense. I am afraid this is all the result of a rush of sentimentality, which in itself is a form of dishonesty.'

But then because no further mention of the matter was made during their subsequent tea parties, and since Lord Lydiard's approval seemed to remain as constant as it always had been, Grace believed that the Diehards' campaign must be foundering. Naturally she never reported any part of her conversation with Lady Hythe to Lottie, simply because she saw no point. Lottie was perfectly well aware the opposition was well entrenched, and was resolutely refusing to be in the slightest bit deterred. Her love for Henry was totally genuine, as was his for her; but it did not cloud their realism. They both knew they would encounter many difficulties, but because they were sensible they genuinely believed that together they would overcome and triumph over them, and since she shared this belief Grace put any further thoughts of the Diehards out of her head and turned her attention to other matters which required her attention, most particularly the raising of little John.

The youngest member of the family was now rising ten and beginning to cause Grace some concern. There was a very large gap between the ages of the youngest and the older Lydiard children, bigger by far than the five and a half years between Grace and Lottie. When John was born Harriet had been nearly eleven and Henry almost thirteen. Below stairs rumour had it that Lady Lydiard had been persuaded by her husband to have a late baby in order to shore up their ailing marriage, a move which had proved successful in so much that after John had been born the Lydiards seemed totally reconciled, at least according once again to the gossip in the servants' hall.

'Not that for a moment he's ever strayed,' Cook had told Grace. 'Least not as far as anyone knows. He's barmy about her, and always has been. It's just that she's had her admirers, as seems to be the fashion nowadays, God alone knows why.' Cook would sigh. 'She's had her admirers for a long time now, and while I'm not sayin' there's been any hanky-panky, to my mind what his lordship's thinking is better safe than sorry.'

Gossip was of little interest to Grace so most of the so-called scandalizing the other members of the staff indulged in passed her by, although she always enjoyed her talks with Cook, and still missed her old friend greatly. But as far as the reasons why John was conceived went Grace had no interest. All she was concerned with were his care and welfare, nor was there any doubt whatsoever in her mind about the Lydiards' attitude to their last-born. He was adored from the moment he arrived on this earth from out of the everywhere, as a delighted Lady Lydiard used to proclaim when she held the tiny child.

'*Where did you come from, baby dear?*' she would ask, her smile creasing the corners of her eyes. '*Out of the everywhere into the here.*'

John was loved by everyone. He was the perfect baby, bright, beautiful and good-humoured. Because of the age gap between him and Harriet and Henry there were never any petty jealousies between them all, nor any discord. Harriet treated him as if he was a living doll, dressing him up as a fairy at every conceivable opportunity when he was a toddler, or having him lead her round and round the lawns harnessed up as a pony. John thought everything his sister did with him was the greatest fun, and Grace got quite used to presiding over nursery tea with John dressed in a variety of guises, from a pixie to a rabbit. Henry on the other hand treated his young brother very seriously and with great respect, never talking down to him and never losing his patience, even when John struggled to try to master some game or puzzle way beyond his years, and in return John hero-worshipped his older brother.

But now the golden boy was causing Grace concern. She had begun to worry when she saw how badly John had taken the fact of his hero-brother's blindness. At first the boy had just been confused, perplexed as to why such a thing could and should happen to someone as kind and good as Henry. Such things might happen to other people, but not to his god. Something had gone very wrong somewhere for such a terrible thing to happen to his phoenix, and he felt betrayed that no one had warned him about this sort of eventuality. He attached himself to the sightless Henry like a pilot fish to a whale, never leaving his side and trying to guide him through waters too deep for them both. Gone was his boyish enjoyment and in its place came solemnity. He would sit for long silent hours with Henry, just waiting to see if there was anything he could do for him, if there was somewhere he could lead him or something he could fetch him. Henry would reach out for John's head and ruffle his hair, telling him he was fine and to run off and play, but John wouldn't go, preferring instead to sit and read to his brother, or just to sit with him.

'I don't need a dog,' Henry would tell Harriet in front of the boy. 'I've got Johnny.'

It was the arrival of Lottie on to the scene which changed everything. All at once John was an aggravation, hanging around when he wasn't wanted, interrupting conversations, making demands, generally getting in the way. Not that Henry ever showed impatience, far from it. He was as loving as ever with John and as kindly. It was just that things had changed. There was somebody else there now, somebody else demanding and receiving Henry's attention, someone else to talk to him, to make him laugh, to interest him, and John wasn't wanted, not as much anyway.

'It's all right, Johnny,' Henry would say, 'we can cope, thanks all the same. You don't have to do that, Lottie can do that, it's perfectly all right, old fellow, so look – why don't you run off and play?'

The trouble was John didn't want to run off and play. He didn't want to be anywhere except by his hero's side, a right that hero was now denying him, a place that was being taken by a stranger, by a girl. Grace saw it happening, she saw it all and all too clearly, but there was nothing she could really do about it. She would try to distract John when Lottie came calling, organizing an outing or a diversion to keep the boy occupied, but she rarely succeeded. John sensed when the enemy was coming to call, and wherever they were and whatever they were doing he would nag Grace to take him home if they were out in the park, or if they were somewhere else in the house invariably find a reason to go and find Henry and interrupt his time with Lottie.

Lottie was too kind to send him away and would tolerate the intrusion with her usual good humour, but her patience was not appreciated by John who became truculent and impertinent in her presence, causing Grace to scold him privately at the end of the day.

'I like you, Nanny,' John told Grace one night as she put him to bed, 'but I hate your sister. I think she's horrid.'

'I like you too, John,' Grace replied, 'except when you're rude like you were today. And you're wrong to hate my sister because she isn't horrid. How can anyone be horrid who loves your brother? If she hated Henry and was as rude to him as you were to her today, then you'd be right to dislike her, but not to hate her. Hate is a horrible thing, you know. It can destroy people, and you're far too nice a boy to be destroyed by hate. Besides, if my sister was as horrid as you say, then she would have been nasty to you today when you were so horrid to her. I really don't like it when you're rude, and I won't have it.'

'Your sister is going to take Henry away,' John said, pulling away from Grace as she went to settle him down.

'Of course she's not,' Grace said. 'Henry's not going anywhere.'

'That's not what Harriet says. Harriet says Henry and your sister are going to live in the Dower House.'

'Harriet's talking nonsense. And even if she wasn't, the Dower House is hardly the far side of the moon, is it? Henry won't ever leave Keston, darling.'

'Harriet's going as well,' John said, turning on his side away from Grace and ignoring what she was saying. 'Harriet's going to art school and I'm going to be left here without anybody.'

'You'll have your father,' Grace said, giving up the unequal struggle and going to hang up John's discarded dressing-gown. 'And you'll still have me, so bad luck.'

'No I won't because you'll soon be going too,' John said. 'Because there won't be anyone left to look after.'

'That's nonsense as well,' Grace said. 'You certainly don't get rid of me that easily.'

Even so, John's remark pulled Grace up in her tracks. Since Brake's death she had been putting off any thought of what she was going to do with the rest of her life. Before that ill-conceived and disastrous counterattack on Welsh Ridge her future had been cut and dried. She and Brake would be married and have children of their own. Even though he hadn't actually proposed marriage to her before he had left, it was an unspoken agreement, for all Brake's letters were full of references to their joint future, as indeed were Grace's back to him, and because of this private pact Grace had (and quite irrationally as she had now come to realize) given up all thought of his being killed. Somehow his life had become too precious for that, he was too special to be shot down in the mud and the snow. Since finding that he loved her she had made him invincible, just as his love seemed to have made her.

But now that he was dead he was gone from her life and from life altogether, taking with him Grace's future, and now that he was gone there was nothing on the horizon except more horizon. So until John's remark Grace had preferred not to think ahead lest once again she should be disappointed. She had painted out the background and just left the foreground, leaving life beyond the moment as a wash, a blur of nondescript blues and greys. While the backdrop remained unpainted anything could happen, and let it, Grace thought. Let someone else paint it in, perhaps another Brake Merrowby coming up the long drive in a bright red car, another man who could both entrance and infuriate her, someone else to love her for what she was rather than what she did. In the meantime she would concentrate on the detail of the foreground, making sure Henry and Harriet had everything they needed, and that John continued to be brought up as well and as properly as his brother and sister. She wouldn't even look up to see what was in the drive. She would throw herself on the mercies of the Fates, and let be what would be.

Which was exactly how she had been proceeding until John had reminded her of her standing. Soon there wouldn't be anyone left for her to look after at Keston, and even if there was, did she now really want to spend the rest of her days looking after other people's babies? Except what was the alternative? She had saved very little money because the post of nanny paid very little, even though Grace's wage had gone up from the thirty pounds a year she had received as nursery maid to the fifty pounds a year she was receiving now, and with little money saved there was not much she could do except continue working. She was also nearly thirty years old, an age by which any pretty and eligible woman should be and in most cases was married. Besides, even if she did finally resign from her post when John was safely away at school, whom would she meet who would appeal to her? As everyone kept saying *ad nauseam*, the flowers had all been cut down and lay dead in the fields. The corn had been harvested. All that was left was the chaff.

There was one thing she could still do. She could at least paint, or so she thought until Lord Lydiard called her into the library one evening in May. Prior to the move back to Keston, Robert Ross from the recently established Imperial War Museum had come round to view Brake's war paintings, as had the representatives of certain other art galleries who were keen to view this collection of so far unexhibited work. Consequently Ross had recommended the purchase of half a dozen of Brake's largest canvases, with first refusal on another half dozen, while William Nevile of Silks of Bond Street had acquired the right to mount a major and posthumous retrospective. As a result, few of Brake's 'new' works found their way back to Keston, but those that did were immediately hung by Lord Lydiard in the very best situations around the house. Since Brake had named Lord Lydiard as his executor, the exhibition and any proposed disposal of his works was handled with the utmost sensitivity.

There was a small crate on the floor by Lord Lydiard's writing desk which contained some more paintings newly arrived from London.

'They arrived this morning,' Lord Lydiard told Grace after handing her a sherry. 'They should have been here last week, but there you are. These things happen.'

'These are the others you didn't want the galleries to have,' Grace reminded herself.

'More or less,' Lord Lydiard said. 'Also some Brake didn't want anyone to have. Except certain people, as it were.'

He bent over the crate and carefully removed a painting wrapped securely in paper and straw.

'This one especially,' he said, handing it to Grace. 'You can see for yourself from the back.'

The back of the painting was uppermost. On the canvas Grace could see some black-inked writing in Brake's hand. It said: *For Grace. If needs be*.

It was *A Cushy Billet*. Grace knew it before she even turned it over. There were the three brave men in their red-lit dugout. And there was Brake.

'Let me give you some more sherry,' Lord Lydiard said, taking up Grace's half-empty glass. 'And here.'

He had noticed her searching hopelessly for a handkerchief and was holding out his white silk one.

'I'm sorry,' Grace said. 'It's always the unexpected things.'

'No, I'm sorry,' Lord Lydiard said. 'I don't really think I quite prepared you for it. That is to say—'

He stopped and cleared his throat, and stared at the wall.

'Anyway,' he continued. 'I was to make sure you got the picture come what may. As needs be, as he said. I think it's marvellous. The best of the smaller works without a doubt.'

Grace dried her eyes and propped the picture up on her knee to look at it. All she could see through the red haze of the paint were Brake's eyes.

'He couldn't find the colour at first,' she said.

'Really?' Lord Lydiard asked, still looking hard at the wall.

'No,' Grace replied. 'And then – then he got the idea of doing it warm, in just this red monochrome.'

'It says everything and a whole lot more,' Lord Lydiard said. 'It never ceases to amaze me what paint does.'

'No, I quite agree,' Grace said, with a final dab at her eyes. 'I'll wash this handkerchief for you.'

'Thank you, Nanny.' Lord Lydiard moved across to the fireplace and now stood staring up at his wife's portrait which he had rehung in the library when he had given the *boudoir* over to Grace and John. Grace put his silk handkerchief up her sleeve and got up to go.

'We must talk about young John some time,' Lord Lydiard said. 'But not now. Perhaps tomorrow.'

'Yes, I think perhaps we should,' Grace agreed, picking up her precious painting.

'Shaw's terribly rude about painters, isn't he?' Lord Lydiard mused, still looking up at the portrait. 'Empty-headed, he calls them, compared of course to authors. And what else is it? Yes. *Dubedats*. Whatever that means. Scoundrels I think. Yes well even so. My word.'

'I'll look in about this time tomorrow, shall I?' Grace asked from the door.

'Hmmmm? Yes yes,' Lord Lydiard said. 'Yes, that will be fine. Just one other thing, though, before you go.'

'Yes?' Grace asked.

'You're not thinking of leaving, are you?'

'No,' Grace replied carefully, once she had recovered her composure.

'Good, that's all right then.' Lord Lydiard flashed her a brief smile and then returned to staring at the portrait. 'As long as you're not thinking of leaving,' he said.

Grace never painted again after that. She still sketched and illustrated her journal, but she never painted another complete picture. She tried to, the very morning after she had received the gift of *A Cushy Billet*. She had hung the painting in her room that evening, above the fireplace where she could see it all the time, wherever she was in the room, moving Harriet's fine study of the lake at dawn to the other pride of place above her bed. The room seemed to take on the glow of the painting, and for the hour before she went to bed Grace sat in front of it, bathing in its warmth and staring into Brake's dark eyes. Then the next morning, when John was at his lessons and Grace had an idle hour she sat at the table in her window and tried to paint a watercolour of the park, a view she knew so well and loved so much. But nothing would come, nothing at all. She found herself fixed, as if frozen, unable even to lay in the basic washes. There just suddenly seemed to be no point, no point at all. Brake had said everything, and now it seemed he had said it for them both. Now that he was gone there was nothing more to add.

So she put away her paints, and her brushes and her pad of cartridge paper, back up on the top shelf of her wardrobe, retaining only her pencils so that she could still illustrate certain passages in her journal. The canvas had become a blank and it appeared that it would

484

remain so, a flatland stretching away monotonously to the horizon, where all that could be seen was what everyone else finally sees, the sunset.

TWENTY-FIVE

'I am afraid you are going to have to send the boy away, John,' Lady Hythe announced. 'He is becoming altogether too wilful. It's absurd that he's not at school already.'

They were all having tea out on the terrace under a large umbrella. It was a very hot July day with thunder in the air, and John had already thrown two temper tantrums and was at present sitting somewhere up the large oak tree at the top of the lawns, refusing all appeals to come down.

'I was as bad at his age,' Henry said, stroking the sleek black head of Max, his new dog.

'No you weren't,' Harriet said. 'You were too good to be true.'

'You don't know what I was feeling inside,' Henry smiled. 'In my head I was always hiding up a tree.'

'What do you say, Nanny?' Lord Lydiard asked, pushing his straw hat back and mopping his forehead with a silk hankie. 'After all, you see more of the boy than any of us I suppose, all told. You think he should go away?'

Grace turned away from the party and looked back at the oak tree, as if to avoid the question. She was sitting on the wall which contained the terrace, idly making a daisy chain.

'I'm not altogether sure,' she finally said, still looking up the lawns. 'It could do him more harm than good. He could see it as yet another rejection.'

'Why?' Lady Hythe wondered. 'What else does he see as "rejections"?'

She pronounced the last word as if it was something indecent. She was dressed all in the palest yellow, including her veil, one gloved hand resting on her unopened parasol.

'I asked you a question, Nanny,' she reminded Grace. 'I'm curious to know what else young John sees as "rejections".'

'I'm so sorry, Lady Hythe,' Grace replied, who had been hoping someone else would jump in and answer the question. 'There are a number of things I think John sees as – repudiations, if you prefer.'

'No I do not prefer, Nanny,' Lady Hythe said with a humourless laugh. 'I simply cannot understand this modern way with slang. Are you saying a child John's age has a judgement sufficiently mature to make these kinds of assessments?'

'John doesn't see them as such, no of course not,' Grace replied.

'Well then,' said Lady Hythe.

'With respect, I was addressing you, not John, Lady Hythe,' said Grace. 'I'm sure the last thing you would want me to do would be to talk down to you.'

'Of course you're absolutely right there, Nanny,' Lord Lydiard said. 'There's nothing you hate more, is there, Diana? Than people who because you're a woman talk to you as if you were a child. Absolutely not. And of course Nanny is quite right about John. He does see everything in terms of some sort of – what is it? Repudiation at the moment. Not that it's anyone's fault, least of all Henry's. No, it's just one of those things.'

'You're saying that he sees Henry's injuries as a *rejection*?' Lady Hythe asked, once more deliberately overemphasizing. 'Come come, John, I can hardly believe my ears.'

'Oh, I think you know quite well what I mean, Diana,' Lord Lydiard replied, carefully opening a cucumber sandwich and removing the cucumber before eating the bread and then the cucumber separately. 'I'm not talking about Henry's injury, am I, Henry?'

'No, Father,' Henry agreed. 'You're talking about my engagement.'

'In that case I quite understand,' Lady Hythe said, 'and I fully sympathize with John. All the more reason for him to go away to school.'

Grace excused herself from the company and wandered off across and up the lawns, ostensibly to try once more to coax John down but in reality to escape from any further conversation on the subject. The very last thing she wanted was to see John sent off to school but she was quickly running out of defences. Every day he was becoming increasingly truculent, defying everyone and trying all their patience, finally even Henry's. In the circumstances Grace had to agree that the company of other boys his age and the authority of people outside his family might indeed be the best thing for him.

'You do know what's going on, don't you?' Grace asked him when she had finally persuaded him to come back down to earth and John was rowing them across the lake. 'There's every chance that if your behaviour doesn't improve and I mean soon, you'll be sent away to school.'

'I don't really care,' John replied, sounding to Grace as if he meant it. 'Nobody likes me here any more.'

'Oh, that's sheer nonsense and you know it,' Grace replied, trailing her hands in the cool water over the side of the rowing boat. 'No one thinks any differently of you. It's you who's changed.'

'No I haven't,' John said. 'Henry's changed, and so has Harriet. So have you.'

'No I haven't.'

'You have. So has Papa.'

'This is all rubbish and you know it,' Grace sighed. 'And look at the size of that dragonfly!'

Grace pointed out the brilliantly coloured insect which was hovering above the water by the boat.

'I hate dragonflies,' John said, and tried to swat it with his oar. Grace stopped him, taking hold of the oar.

'Behave yourself,' she said. 'Or I'll take you back inside this minute.'

'Just you try,' John replied, and before Grace could stop him he had jumped overboard and begun to swim for the shore.

Grace steadied the rocking boat but found she had lost an oar, which was already floating out of reach. She called to John to tell him, but the boy ignored her and just kept swimming, leaving Grace to navigate to safety with just one paddle. By the time she was ashore John had long disappeared.

They searched the entire estate, but no one could find any trace of him. All the available staff turned out and they combed the grounds in a long line, directed by Harriet to search in hiding places kept secret from the grown-ups for generations, but John had disappeared. Late in the evening as dusk began to fall, Lord Lydiard called the search party off and summoned the help of the local police.

'Well there you are,' Lady Hythe said to Grace, pausing by her car as Harriet and Grace wearily trudged back up the drive. 'This is precisely the sort of thing one can expect to happen at times like this.'

Grace remained silent, refusing to be drawn, but Harriet who had never liked her grandmother couldn't resist the challenge.

'Meaning what, Grandmother?' she said. 'Meaning this is all Henry and Lottie's fault?'

'Meaning this is just the tip of the iceberg, Harriet,' Lady Hythe replied. 'Meaning this is precisely the sort of thing you can expect to happen when you cross the line.'

Lady Hythe got into her car, and was driven off by her black-uniformed chauffeur.

'Isn't she just like something from one of Grimms' fairy tales, Nanny?' Harriet said, taking Grace's hand.

'Not even Mama could stand her. She used to call her Lady Grimthought.'

John was still missing at midnight. By this time Grace was nearly out of her mind with worry as she considered his disappearance was entirely due to her.

'Don't be foolish, Nanny,' Lord Lydiard told her. 'Things we're guilty of we never confess to. Besides, this is something circumstantial, not attributable. This is all part of what my father used to call the due process of life.'

'I shouldn't have mentioned school,' Grace insisted.

'It's been mentioned often enough before,' Henry reassured her, 'and John isn't the first boy in the world to be sent away.'

'I still shouldn't have mentioned it,' Grace said. 'It really wasn't my place.'

After another hour's wait, when there was still no sign of the missing child, as she looked round at everyone in the drawing room Grace realized she was the only one who was visibly worried. Lord Lydiard was sitting with his hands on his head at the piano staring at the ceiling, Henry was in his chair by the fireplace, his dogs at his side, and Harriet was quietly playing a game of patience at the card table. There was no conversation and had been none for well over half an hour. *This is the difference,* Grace suddenly realized. *This is what Lady Hythe was talking about. They have an entirely different way of carrying on. What would Lottie do in these circumstances?* Grace wondered. *What would she do if it was her child? Hers and Henry's? She would pace up and down as Grace had done, blaming herself, worrying out loud, she would make a fuss. And Henry would tell her not to, not to worry out loud, to calm down and sit down, and not to blame herself, because this was all part of the due process of life. As her child lay undiscovered somewhere in a ditch, Lottie would have to take out the cards and play patience.*

Then just when Grace thought she could stand no more of the dreadful silence the telephone rang. For a moment no one got up to answer it since this was a task usually executed by Harcross; then when Lord Lydiard realized they were by themselves he got up and took the call himself.

'Yes?' he said into the telephone. 'I see. I see. Yes. Thank you.' Then he replaced the instrument.

Grace was on her feet, waiting for the news. Lord Lydiard smiled at her, cleared his throat and then went and picked up his glass of whisky which he had left unattended for the last half-hour.

'They've found him,' he said at last.

'Thank God,' said Grace.

'A motorist picked him up on the Oxford Road,' Lord Lydiard continued. 'A clergyman fortunately. Vicar of Long Crendon. Seems that young John was intent on joining the navy.'

Fortunately the heavy chill John contracted as a result of his running away in wet clothing and being caught later that evening in a torrential thunderstorm didn't develop into anything more serious. Grace had given him a good bath, a hot drink of lemon and honey and put him to bed in flannel pyjamas under a pile of blankets, changing his bedclothes twice during the night as he sweated it out. By morning he was running a streaming cold but no temperature.

'An old-fashioned remedy, but nevertheless,' Grace said, opening John's bedroom window wider to let in some more fresh air. 'It always used to work on us when we were children. I got as wet as you once when I was caught in a hailstorm and our maid wrapped me from head to toe in red flannel and filled my bed with hot water bottles. I thought I was going to burst with the heat, but it did the trick. Everybody else thought I was sure to get pneumonia.'

'What's newmonia?' John asked idly, past the thermometer Grace had put in his mouth.

'What you haven't got, young man,' Grace replied, 'thank goodness.'

'What's going to happen to me?'

Grace took out the thermometer, looked at it and shook it down.

'You're going to stay in bed until you get better, that's what,' she replied.

'I meant for running away.'

'That's up to your father. I should imagine knowing your father he'll make the punishment fit the crime.'

'What does that mean?'

'It means since you like running away, he'll probably make you stay at home.'

Grace smiled and tucked John in. After a moment, John smiled back at her, the first time for a long while.

'He said if I send him away he'll run away again,' Lord Lydiard said to Grace when John was better and up and about again.

'I should imagine that's very true,' Grace agreed. 'He's got himself in the most frightful stew.'

'Any suggestions?'

'You mean any more suggestions. Harriet tells me you're being bombarded with opinions.'

Lord Lydiard sighed and closed the piano lid, then opened it up again.

'The consensus of opinion is, opinion that is which I have not sought, Nanny, but which none the less has been expressed,' he said, 'is that I should have sent John away when he was seven, or failing that eight, or certainly no later than when he was nine, and if I had done there wouldn't be any problem because a school would have beaten the sense into him.'

'Yes,' Grace said, 'I can imagine it.'

'That's the very reason why I didn't send him away at that age,' Lord Lydiard said, running his fingers over the piano keyboard without depressing any notes. 'Beating a boy only makes him either more cowardly or more obdurate.'

'Particularly if it's done by a third party,' Grace added. 'The only person who should raise a hand against a child is its parent, surely?'

'I could never hit one of my children,' Lord Lydiard said.

'I could never hit one of your children either,' Grace said.

Lord Lydiard stopped running his hands silently over the keys and looked over at Grace for a long time. Finally he turned away and closed the piano lid which he now stared at instead.

'Is that because they're like your own children?' he asked, rubbing the rosewood piano case with the tips of his fingers. 'Because really they're like your children. I mean in a sense you could almost be their mother.'

'That's not quite what I meant,' Grace said, immediately retreating to the defensive. 'That's not why I couldn't hit them.'

'I think it might be really,' Lord Lydiard said. 'Not of course that you'd ever hit or beat a child, you're just not that sort of person. But with Henry, and Harriet. And now John. And in the circumstances. What I said holds though, don't you agree? You could almost be their mother.'

The way he said it this time was different. Grace heard the change in the inflexion and hesitated, uncertain of her response, afraid that her interpretation might be the wrong one.

'Well?' Lord Lydiard now looked up, looking directly at Grace. He was a very beautiful man, not handsome like Brake, not dark-eyed and brooding, but fair and slightly wan, with a creamy skin and an ever-present sense of melancholy which his smile only seemed to embellish.

'I don't know what you mean, Lord Lydiard,' Grace said, not able to break the look.

'Oh, I'm sorry,' Lord Lydiard replied. 'I rather thought you would. But of course if you don't, when you do we could always talk some more.'

Taking this as her cue for dismissal Grace rose and left, even though the discussion concerning John's schooling had hardly begun.

It was resumed after dinner, when John had gone

to bed and Henry and Harriet were sitting discussing Henry's wedding which was now only a matter of weeks away. Lord Lydiard and Grace were playing chess, a game which Grace had only learned of late, her employer being left without an opponent since Henry had lost his sight.

'Can I go there?' she asked, holding her last remaining knight mid-air over the board. 'I'm never quite sure where this piece can go.'

'Two to the front and one to the side, or one to the front and two to the side,' Lord Lydiard replied, 'and yes you can go there.'

'I thought I could,' Grace said. 'Check. I think.'

'You want to be very careful of Nanny, Papa,' Henry said. 'She was just the same when we taught her Halma. *Can I do this? Is this all right, children?* Then she wiped the floor with us.'

'Actually I think that's check-mate,' Grace said, staring at the board. 'Isn't it?'

'Yes,' Lord Lydiard said, removing his glasses from the top of his head and using them like lorgnettes. 'I don't know how that happened.'

'No, neither do I.' Grace laughed, and pushed back her chair. 'Now if you'll excuse me I think I should go to bed.'

'We haven't finished talking about John and this school business,' Lord Lydiard said, setting his chess pieces out again. 'Let's play one last game while we go on talking.'

'Johnny won't go away, Papa,' Henry said.

'He knows that,' Harriet told him. 'In fact by now I should imagine everyone in Keston knows that. The point is, Henry, we've got to do something. He is becoming a bit of a beast.'

'He won't go to Hillgate House, Papa,' Henry continued. 'I don't think he wants to go to Eton either.'

'Everyone's always gone to Eton,' Harriet said. 'I'm sure once he settles in—'

'Sorry, H,' Henry interrupted her. 'But for once you don't know what you're talking about. You didn't go away to school, so you have no idea what it's like.'

'You liked Eton.'

'I hated my first two years. But that's not the point. If Johnny doesn't want to go away to school, I don't think he should, not now. Maybe when he's a bit older and he feels like boarding, then that's a different matter.'

'Not necessarily,' Grace said. 'If a child says he wants to go away to school, I don't think that's necessarily the best reason or even a good enough reason to send him. He won't know what going away to school means, while his parents or certainly his father will. The child will think it's all right because other children do it, but he won't have been through the experience, and it has to be faced, it doesn't suit everyone. In an ideal world, the best place for a child to be brought up is surely with his family.'

'Quite agree,' Lord Lydiard said, turning the chess board round and beginning to set the black pieces out. 'I hated every one of my schooldays, every one. Far better if you can to bring your children up where they belong, like people used to. People always used to bring their children up at home, or send them away to someone else's home for them to be brought up in return for bringing up those people's children in return, if you follow.'

'From a distance,' Harriet said. 'You're thinking of the Middle Ages.'

'Yes, during the Renaissance, and after,' Lord Lydiard said. 'Odd, isn't it? We seem to have gone backwards since then.'

'But you have been bringing John up at home, Papa,' Harriet said, 'and it hasn't worked out.'

'What we really need,' said Grace, 'is what your father said. We need to send him to another family to be brought up. But since that's possibly an impossibility nowadays, what we need to find is a school which is more like a family than a school. In fact I remember someone mentioning a place just outside Bicester.'

Grace had heard about the Old Priory from another nanny during a birthday party to which she had taken John in a neighbouring house. The family for which this particular nanny worked had also been experiencing difficulties with their youngest child and had been recommended to try a new school which had only just opened up in a particularly lovely estate about ten miles outside Oxford.

'To aim a few high, that is what we have in mind,' Mr Lawrence, the headmaster and owner of the school, told Grace while Lord Lydiard stood with his back to them both, tapping both his feet on the polished floor while gazing out of the window at the garden.

'I see,' Grace said, and nodded encouragingly. 'A few high. Yes, well, that seems sensible, don't you think, Lord Lydiard?'

In order to elicit a response Grace had to walk round in front of Lord Lydiard and ask him for the second time what he thought.

'What?' he asked with a frown. 'Oh yes, most certainly. I should say.'

Lord Lydiard then stared at the Lawrences as if noticing them for the first time, although he had already spent a good quarter of an hour in their company. Grace thought it was most likely the couple's all wool Jaeger clothing and their open-toed sandals that were attracting his attention, and noticing the discomfort his stare was causing Grace tried to catch his eye again and distract his attention. Staring at people as if he was invisible was one of her employer's many eccentricities, that and a reluctance to sit down in strange company, coupled with an equal reluctance to look at people when they were directly addressing him. According to Henry it was a thoroughly Norman habit, one which had originated from keeping an eye on the walls of their castles in case some Saxon had decided to try to climb in.

'My husband has taught abroad with great success,' Mrs Lawrence told Grace, 'but we felt the need for this sort of education was greatest here, in England.'

'I don't understand this business of not having rules,' Lord Lydiard suddenly told the garden. 'Some rules, yes, fair enough. But no rules, I'd have thought that would take some doing. I know that in order to be educated up to a point children have to be left to educate themselves, but I'd have thought no rules was stretching it a bit. Particularly with young. Can't really have them roaming around at will, I'd have said, because people even small people have to know quite what's what.'

'It's not that there aren't any rules, Lord Lydiard,' Grace said, with a reassuring smile at the Lawrences. 'They have principles instead of rules, at least I think that's the idea, isn't it, Mr Lawrence?'

Both the Lawrences, their eyes shining bright with idealism, nodded happily, relieved that at least one of their visitors seemed to be getting the hang of the place.

'As I understand it there are two principles,' Grace continued.

'Tenets of behaviour rather than principles,' Mr Lawrence corrected her.

'Doctrine rather than doctrinaire,' his wife added.

'Whatever you like to call them,' Grace said. 'What you impress on the children are basically two things, to honour and respect each other.'

'Yes I see,' Lord Lydiard said, thoughtfully, before turning to look at the two very earnest but quite obviously stout-hearted Fabians who were both perched expectantly on the edges of their straw-seated chairs, two people who were clearly more interested in winning the war against capitalism by better education than by direct confrontation.

'Yes, I see what you're getting at,' Lord Lydiard continued, 'at least I imagine I do, but won't boys always be boys? Do you know? I mean how do you cope, what do you do about the sort of thing boys do? Bows and arrows? Sticks and stones? Fishing hooks, that sort of thing?'

'Fishing hooks?' Grace wondered. 'Fishing hooks are simply used for fishing, surely?'

'A boy I used to know, a cousin, he had other ideas, Nanny,' Lord Lydiard replied. 'Used them for all sorts of things, including putting them in your slippers.'

'We don't have any bullying here, we don't allow it,' the headmaster said.

'But if you don't have rules I don't understand how you stop it?' Lord Lydiard asked. 'How do they know they shouldn't do it?'

'We tell them,' Mrs Lawrence said. 'We tell them it will not be tolerated, and let all the children know it is as big a crime not to tell on a bully as bullying is in itself.'

'Ah,' Lord Lydiard nodded. 'Forewarned et cetera. That sort of thing.'

'How long have you been going now?' Grace asked later as they toured the grounds of the lovely Queen Anne house with young John bringing up the rear.

'We've been here now for two years and it seems to be working,' Mr Lawrence said.

'No one has run away, been taken away, wanted to leave, had to leave,' his wife continued. 'We've had really very little *crime*—'

'And absolutely no *punishment*,' her husband finished. 'A loss of privileges, yes, but no corporal punishment. What makes a man of a boy isn't a beating, but – what was it? Yes – *the lure of things that are worthy to be loved*.'

If Lord Lydiard hadn't been convinced already that alone would have sealed his decision. Grace saw him smile as he folded his hands behind his back.

'Good,' he said. 'Then I'd say it sounds as if you are making a success of it, although rather you than me.'

He smiled at Grace and then nodded towards a group of children who were sitting outside under a tree having a music class. Like all the children in the school they seemed happy and relaxed, and interested in the subject being taught.

'Good,' he said. 'Very good. Wouldn't have minded being sent here myself. In fact wish I had been. What do you say, John? Think you'd like it here?'

'I think so, Papa,' John replied with suitable gravity. 'I like that it isn't only boys.'

'If you do come here and you like it, you can come home at the weekends, you know,' his father added.

'If I do and I don't like it,' John replied, 'I shall come home earlier than that.'

Once it was decided to send John to the Old Priory, the youngest Rokeham seemed to come back to himself. There were no more temper tantrums, no more disappearances, and no more constant demands for attention. John even accepted Lottie and the fact that she and his beloved elder brother were going to be married.

'That means they'll be having babies I suppose,' he said to Grace.

'Yes,' Grace agreed, not altogether sure how John would assess his latest discovery. 'Eventually, yes, I suppose it does.'

'That means I shall be an uncle,' John concluded, and took himself off to play, apparently well satisfied with the prospect.

It was well after midnight when Harriet knocked on Grace's door. There had been a dinner party that evening and Grace had retired to her room long before the arrival of the first guests, whom she had seen alighting from their chauffeur-driven vehicles shortly after half past six. John now had been moved out from the *boudoir* nursery to a larger room opposite, leaving Grace the suite of rooms for her own occupation, a space which she gratefully accepted, as she did the invitation to furnish it how she liked from what was in store in the basement. The result was a sitting room decorated mainly in pinks and primrose, with a small kitchen off which Grace used to cook herself light meals, and a charming bedroom off the other side of the sitting room which Grace had asked to be painted in a cool *eau-de-Nil*.

Everyone liked to come and chat in Grace's room, her sister when she was visiting, often bringing Henry with her, Harriet constantly, and any of the servants whenever they had a question or a problem. Mrs Bennett the new cook, while being an excellent chef, as a mother-figure was no substitute for her much mourned predecessor, so the staff all now turned to Grace for comfort or advice. Grace welcomed her new responsibility, and soon learned the art of counselling, realizing that the way to give the best advice was what she did with children, namely find out what they want and then advise them to do it.

'So what can I do for you this time, Harriet?' Grace asked, wrapping her dressing-gown around her and pulling up two chairs by the fireplace. 'Not another young man to be given his *congé*?'

'No, it's nothing like that, Nanny,' Harriet said thoughtfully. 'I'm a bit worried about the Diehards.'

'Ah,' Grace smiled. 'Lottie told you, did she?'

'It suits them down to the ground, Nanny,' Harriet said. 'They're not going to give up, you know.'

'They can try as hard as they might, Harriet darling,' Grace said, 'and for as long as they like. But as long as your father stands firm, there's no need to worry.'

'You should have heard them after dinner,' Harriet said. 'Lady Hythe and Aunt Cicely in particular. They said they were agreed to make Papa see the folly of his ways as far as Henry and Lottie were concerned, and nothing would stop them. Lady Hythe even threatened to hire a private investigator to see if she could dig up any scandal in your family.'

'There isn't any scandal in our family,' Grace said, feeling as though someone had just walked over her grave. Would the fact that their father had done a bolt with the local schoolteacher amount to a scandal? Grace was rather afraid that it might.

'Someone else, Mrs Sherwell-Cooper I think it was,' Harriet continued, 'said it wouldn't be necessary to go to the expense of hiring an investigator. She said from what she understood of your family all one would have to do was make a few enquiries in the village.'

'Let them,' Grace replied. 'As I just said, there's no scandal attached to our family, at least nothing I'm sure which can't be matched by yours.'

Harriet saw the humour in Grace's eyes and laughed, and so did Grace, although Grace was deadly serious. If it came to it, Grace was perfectly prepared to trade blows. After all, few people are better placed to know a family's true history than its servants.

'Even so,' Harriet sighed, sinking in her chair and stretching out her long legs, 'I do hope you're right, Nanny. Lady Grimthought is pretty formidable. She said that allowing Henry to marry so far beneath him was dragging the whole family down, and that included the memory of Mama.'

'You don't think that, Harriet,' Grace said. 'Neither does Henry, or your father.'

'No of course we don't,' Harriet replied thoughtfully. 'Henry would never think such a thing. He loves Lottie far too much. He's devoted to her. And neither would I ever think such a thing either.'

'And your father?'

'No.' Grace thought Harriet sounded a little less sure, but rather than press her, she waited, fixing Harriet's eyes with hers. 'No.' Harriet shook her head again and frowned even more deeply, biting her bottom lip thoughtfully. 'Papa doesn't think like that either. Not really.'

'But?'

Grace raised her eyebrows expectantly. Harriet smiled when she noticed Grace's expression, remembering how it had been used against her time and time again when she was smaller and Grace wanted to will the truth out of her.

'It's just that – well, I did think Papa would make a bit more ado about it originally,' Harriet confessed. 'He and Mama were determined Henry should marry Sarah Bethell. There were no two ways about it.'

'Sarah and he were childhood sweethearts,' Grace said, recalling the pretty red-haired girl who had been a frequent playmate when Grace had first taken up her duties. 'But parents always say these things. They don't necessarily mean them.'

'Her parents and ours were awfully close friends,'

Harriet explained. 'It was a sort of unspoken agreement really.'

'Then along came Lottie.'

'Yes. Henry says the day he first met her in the library, when he arrived back early from school, you remember.'

'Of course I remember, silly.'

'Henry says when he saw Lottie that day he was determined he was going to marry her.'

'They both looked as though they'd had the wind knocked out of them,' Grace said. 'But tell me, Harriet, do you ever think if Henry hadn't been wounded—'

Harriet stopped her, with a flash of anger showing for a moment in her eyes.

'No,' she said. 'The answer is definitely no. Papa just isn't that sort of person. If he didn't like Lottie, or approve of her, he wouldn't have given his consent in any circumstances, I promise you.'

'I'm sorry, but it had to be asked, just once,' Grace said. 'Your father's such a kind man, it would be perfectly understandable.'

'Perhaps,' Harriet said crisply. 'But that just isn't the case.'

'I can see that,' Grace replied. 'I'm sorry if I upset you.'

'That's all right, Nanny,' Harriet said, and then gave another sigh. 'But even so, we're going to have to do something. Don't you think?'

'Just leave it to me, darling,' Grace said, getting up and opening the door. 'And stop worrying.'

'Yes of course I'm well aware of all this nonsense, Nanny,' Lord Lydiard said. 'And do you want to know what I think? I think they can all go whistle.'

'I'm very glad to hear it, Lord Lydiard,' Grace said, putting down her second glass of sherry on the table beside her.

'They can all go whistle,' Lord Lydiard repeated, one foot tapping fast on the floor. 'Private investigators indeed.'

'People will go to any lengths to protect their families,' Grace said.

'But not these busybodies' families, Nanny!' Lord Lydiard said, getting up from the piano stool and then sitting down again. 'They're only related by marriage – my frightful mother-in-law and my equally frightful sister-in-law! My wife used to implore me not to marry her in case she turned into her mother! Lor', what a couple of – couple of—'

'Jabberwocks?' Grace offered.

'Oh, Jabberwocks, yes absolutely!' Lord Lydiard cried in delight. 'What was it that was used to slay the beast?'

'A vorpal sword, wasn't it?' Grace replied.

'I shall get me one at once. The Jabberwocks, oh yes, that's those two absolutely.'

'Even so,' Grace said carefully.

'Yes?' Lord Lydiard wheeled round on the piano stool and stared at Grace. 'Look, don't worry about your family,' he said. 'If you're worried about your family, don't be. I know all about your family. Your sister told me.'

'When?' Grace asked.

'When I asked her, of course.'

'And when was that?'

Lord Lydiard shrugged, and spun back round on the piano stool.

'Oh, I don't think that matters, do you?' he said, in the manner of someone not expecting an answer.

'Yes I do actually,' Grace said, 'mainly because I'm curious.'

'When Harriet told me what the Jabberwocks were up to, if you must know,' Lord Lydiard replied. 'I thought all those things, you know – those erm things. Those clichés. First come first served, soonest whatever soonest mended, all that sort of thing. Get in there first. Not that whatever I'd have found out would have made any difference because I assure you it wouldn't. I just wanted to know before anyone else did. It doesn't make the slightest difference that your father ran off. Not the slightest. And all the rest of it. Not the slightest bit of difference. That you were left disgraced and with no money. How can it? Least of all to people such as the Jabberwocks whose entire family fortunes – both of them, mind. Their entire family fortunes were made out of the slave trade. Let he who casts the first stone, don't you think. Nanny? Because I most certainly do.'

'Even so,' Grace said after a moment. 'Even so.'

'Now what?' Lord Lydiard frowned. 'Don't tell me you've got some just cause or impediment, Nanny?'

'No,' Grace replied. 'I just think that perhaps a big wedding isn't a good idea.'

'I wasn't thinking of a big wedding, Nanny,' Lord Lydiard said. 'The very opposite in fact. I feel exactly as you do, because I know what you're thinking—'

'How?' Grace wondered, interrupting.

'Because I do, that's why.' Lord Lydiard swung once more round on his piano stool, stared at Grace long and hard and then swung back round away from her. 'Because I do, that's why,' he repeated. 'And you don't think a big wedding is on and neither do I because it's nothing to do with all those people out there.'

'I don't think marriage ever is,' Grace said. 'I've never quite understood why people want enormous weddings. I'm sure the bride and groom don't.'

'Ah, precisely, Nanny!' Lord Lydiard agreed. 'My point precisely, which is why I asked Henry and Lottie. I don't think it's anything to do with that lot out there, particularly not this lot because most of them think it's going to be a social *catastrophe*. So why should they come to jeer behind their fans or hands or whatever? My thoughts entirely – not that I was going to put them into Henry and Lottie's mouths exactly—'

'Or even your words into their heads,' Grace added with a straight face.

'No, precisely.' Lord Lydiard nodded, staring at the wall the other side of the piano. 'Far be it from me. So that's why I asked Henry and your sister. They want just as I thought. As you thought. Just as we thought. They would prefer a sort of party, a family party, with just family and friends, true friends, real friends. And the dogs. Henry insists on his dogs – Henry wants Max to be his best man.'

'Lottie doesn't mind either?' Grace asked. 'Not that I would expect her to.'

'She wants whatever Henry wants,' Lord Lydiard said, 'which in this case is precisely the same thing as she wants. We shall close the park gates and the Jabberwocks can all stay outside.'

He swung round on his stool for the last time and smiled at Grace, one of his quick, shy smiles, before spinning back round and electing to play Bach's Prelude in B flat.

And so it was Henry and Lottie were married. On a gloriously fine late summer afternoon in the private chapel on the estate Henry Rokeham, first son of John, Lord Lydiard and Serena, Lady Lydiard, deceased, heir to the barony and holder of the Military Cross and Bar, married Charlotte Mary Louise Merrill, younger daughter of George Merrill, deceased, and Mrs Herbert Granger at a private ceremony attended only by the immediate family, Miss Merrill's mother and stepfather, and sixteen close friends. The bride was given away by her stepfather Dr Granger, and attended by the Honourable Harriet Rokeham, while the bridegroom was attended by his youngest brother the Honourable John Rokeham acting as page, and Captain William Donat DSO of the 13th London Regiment, otherwise known as the Kensingtons. Besides a wedding dress of silk, the bride wore a garter in blue silk, the buckles from her grandmother's wedding shoes, and a pearl clip under her veil in her hair, three items which her sister Grace, the Lydiard children's nanny, had been intending to wear should the day ever come when she married Brake Merrowby, and at one point the ceremony was interrupted by a large black dog bounding in from the vestry and trying prematurely to guide his master down the aisle.

After the marriage ceremony a small reception was held at Keston Hall, attended only by those who had been invited to the church ceremony. The guests ate a luncheon of freshly poached salmon, chicken, and strawberries and cream, and drank only champagne. After the luncheon everyone danced and sang to music played at the piano by the bridegroom's father, before sending the married couple off on a three-week honeymoon to be spent on the family yacht moored off the south of France.

When they returned, the couple moved straight away into the Dower House on the west side of the estate where a small staff awaited them. The bridegroom's sister Harriet left a week after their return to go to London where she was to begin her studies at the Slade School of Art, moving into the family house in Cadogan Square with an aunt as her chaperon. At the end of the same week the younger son of the family left Keston to begin his first term at the Old Priory, which he found he enjoyed so much that after the first two or three weekends spent back at his home he asked his father if he wouldn't mind terribly if he stayed at school in future because he was rather enjoying it. His father said that he didn't mind and neither did his nanny, although in private they both did. Even the two dogs had gone, gone across the park to the Dower House with Henry and Lottie, leaving the Great House quiet and almost deserted.

Deserted by all except Lord Lydiard, and Grace, his children's nurse.

TWENTY-SIX

It was monotonous, day in day out always the same. There was simply nothing for Grace to do, there was nobody who needed her care, and no one who needed her attention. Sitting up in her small suite of rooms all by herself Grace felt as if she was a guest in a house where she wasn't wanted any more, or a long term resident in a hotel whom the management had all but forgotten about. At first she kept herself occupied with carrying out invented and unnecessary tasks, such as emptying John's wardrobe and sorting out his clothes, emptying the toy cupboard and sorting out the toys, and emptying the games cupboard and sorting out the games, then when she grew bored at emptying out already tidy cupboards and repacking them just for the sake of it she started rearranging furniture, first of all moving it around in her rooms, then in Harriet's, then young John's and the room which had been Henry's and then finally once more in her own.

Once she had exhausted these routines, there was really little else she could do except let each day run its natural course, filling her time sleeping in later than she had ever slept in before, writing letters in the morning, eating lunch alone in her room at midday, writing more letters or reading in the afternoon, going for a walk before tea, having tea up in her room alone, taking a nap, soaking in a bath and washing her hair, dressing herself for dinner by herself up in her room, reading some more or playing patience, and then finally going to bed and reading even more until she would usually fall asleep with the light still on.

'Is that how you're going to spend the rest of your days?' her mother would enquire when Grace called on her. 'Just sitting around in that empty house waiting for someone else to have babies which you will look after? That really is no sort of life for a woman, no sort of life at all.'

When her mother took this tack, Grace was often tempted to agree and say she wouldn't be leading that sort of life if it hadn't been for her, for her making a mess of her marriage and then choosing to take to her bed rather than cope with the aftermath. Had her mother been the unselfish one she would have been the one to go out to work so that her daughters might be able to take their chances in life, but instead she had capitulated and as a result Grace was now sitting in a vast house by herself approaching middle age and wondering what to do.

She knew what she should do. She really should get another position, because for the moment where she was her work was done. John was old enough now to cope without a full-time nanny, and in the holidays one of the maids could always help out when needed. Even if Lord Lydiard wanted her to stay Grace thought she should refuse because it would be better for all concerned if she left, particularly for Lottie. Now that Lottie was married Grace thought the last thing she would want was her sister round her neck. With her experience and her references there would be no difficulty in obtaining another good position, and since Grace had finally decided that she had no life other than that of a children's nurse, then she might as well get as much experience as she could into her working years. *Who knows?* she used to think as she sat sewing in her room, *I might see something of the world. I might even get to America.*

And yet there was always something, something there in the back of her mind which made her feel a good deal less than certain. Grace tried to ignore it, but it wouldn't go away. It wasn't a doubt, it was a fact and Grace knew what it was. She was tied to Keston, both to the place and more important to the family, a bondage which had begun in earnest the day she was promoted to the nursery floor. The Lydiard family was her family, and if she left now it would be like leaving home. In fact it would be worse than leaving home because Grace had never felt about her own home and family the way she did about Keston. Everything interesting that had happened to her so far had happened at Keston, everything that had turned her life from a potential disaster into something extraordinary and memorable. There, up the very drive down which she was now staring, up that drive Brake Merrowby had driven in his red sports car and down that selfsame drive he had driven off with her, carrying her away on the beginning of a memorable adventure. In the beautiful parkland that stretched as far as the eye could see she had sat with the children, she had walked with them, and played with them. There was Harriet by her side under the tree, carefully making her first sketches, Henry tumbling with Beanie down the lawns, and John taking his first steps across the rug she had spread under the chestnut tree. There was Lady Lydiard beating some bewildered male house guest 6-0, 6-0 at tennis, then standing on the terrace like a Greek goddess, swinging her racquet in one hand while drinking lemonade from a crystal glass. There was Cook either roaring with delighted laughter or laying down the law with her tongue firmly in her cheek while preparing mountains of wonderful food, and there finally again in the drive was a line of men and boys going to a war from which most would never come back. As she put her sewing down on her knee she wondered how she could finally ever leave such a place as this. In spite of the terrible reversal of fortunes that had brought her here in the first place, Grace knew she loved Keston and everything about it.

None the less, in her heart of hearts, she felt she should and must go, and so determined to do so, telling herself she would give in her notice just as soon as she found the right moment. *After all*, she said to herself, *when all is really said and done, what is there to keep me here now? Nothing at all.*

'Goodness,' said a voice from the doorway, 'goodness, that really does smell good. What is it?'

Grace looked out from her small kitchen to see Lord Lydiard standing in the doorway of her sitting room.

'It's my lunch,' Grace replied. 'I didn't realize the door was open. I hope the smell of cooking's not going down the corridor.'

'It doesn't matter if it is,' Lord Lydiard replied. 'It's a most delicious smell.'

'I'm making myself some French toast,' Grace told him. 'A nursery favourite.'

'Oh lord, French toast,' Lord Lydiard sighed. 'One just doesn't get French toast anywhere but the nursery. Not that's worth eating anyway.'

'Won't Cook make you some?'

'It's just not the same. It's just one of those dishes.'

He looked like a small boy the way he was standing, hands sunk in his pockets, and with such a look of childish disappointment on his face that Grace couldn't help but smile.

'Would you like Nanny to make you some?' she asked.

'Would you mind?' Lord Lydiard said, not taking up the tease but looking as serious as someone would who had just asked the most exacting favour. 'Isn't it an awful bore?'

'Not in the slightest,' Grace said. 'I've plenty of everything.'

Lord Lydiard sat in silence and ate the dish of thick slices of bread soaked in egg and cooked in butter until golden as if it was the finest and rarest caviare.

'What in heaven's name can't you do?' he wondered, as he finally put down his knife and fork. 'That was perfect.'

'It's not a very difficult recipe, you know,' Grace said, pouring them out some more lemonade. 'Henry can cook this just as well.'

'Only because you taught him,' Lord Lydiard said. 'And I bet it doesn't taste quite like that. Cooking isn't all ingredients, you know, as I'm sure you know.'

'I had to cook a lot at home,' Grace said, sidestepping the compliment. 'We both did, Lottie and I. Henry'll be all right because Lottie makes good French toast as well.'

'Oh, I'm not in the slightest bit worried about Henry, Nanny, I know he's in good hands,' Lord Lydiard said. 'Now. Any chance of a second helping?'

Slowly the visits became a habit, Lord Lydiard managing to appear along the corridor outside Grace's rooms when she had just started cooking her lunch. Before the Great Exodus, as Grace and Lord Lydiard now referred to the children's departure, whenever Grace had eaten in her rooms her meals had been sent up from the kitchen on a tray, but now she needed to occupy her time she generally made her own lunch since it helped to pass a couple of hours both pleasurably and creatively. It soon became apparent to Grace, however, that Lord Lydiard's visits were not just because he wanted to eat her French toast or sample her perfect rice puddings. It seemed to Grace that Lord Lydiard was as lonely as she was.

They both wanted company, although neither of them ever said as much, and not just company but the right sort of company, one that was sympathetic to their needs. At first Grace had tried to find it beyond the green baize door, but there was no one left there now, no one who knew her from the days when she had been just a kitchen maid, just another servant, one of the lowest of the low. They were polite and friendly, and willing to talk or mostly to listen, but there was no real intimacy, even with those who came to seek advice from Grace in her room. It seemed it was a different matter when she went to see them on their territory, that her presence made them feel uncomfortable or self-conscious. So after a while Grace stopped going to the kitchens, and until Lord Lydiard found his way upstairs and into her rooms, whenever she had felt a rush of desperation coming on she would take herself out for a walk in the park or down to the village.

Before he was trapped by the nostalgic aroma of nursery food, Grace had seen very little of her employer. Sometimes when she went out walking she would catch sight of him at a window in the house, in the study or the library, or somewhere upstairs, but their paths rarely crossed. If they did, their exchanges would be brief and to the point, concerning only the matters in hand. Otherwise all she heard of him was his piano-playing. Sometimes he would play for hours, often late into the evening, and Grace would sit in her room with the door open and her lights off, letting the wonderful music wash over her. She could sense his moods from the pieces he played, and became intrigued when she noticed that over the weeks he had begun to drop the more elegiac pieces in favour of the more passionate profundities of Beethoven. She had rarely heard him play much Beethoven before, since it seemed he always preferred instead to attempt Chopin, Debussy and even the fearful complications of Liszt, yet now there were no nocturnes, études or consolations, just Beethoven's magnificent sonatas, which he played with great fluency and deep passion.

'You play the piano so you probably know this already, Nanny,' he said over a lunch of fish pie followed by apple crumble. 'Because while I can't speak for you, I'm fascinated by tempo. Of course a lot of people take metronome markings for gospel and that just isn't so. The great composers used them strictly as an indication, not as some sort of edict. Although of course tempo was a prime concern.'

'Yes it was,' Grace agreed, 'at least if one of the books I read was right. It said that when someone came to report to Beethoven they'd just heard one of his symphonies, his question wasn't how was it played, but what was the tempo.'

'Good,' Lord Lydiard replied with a frown. 'That's absolutely it. Take the opening movement of the Moonlight Sonata for example, probably the most famous piece most often abused by being played not too fast but too slow. But if you play it like this – ' here he demonstrated what he meant by miming his interpretation on the tablecloth and humming the theme '– if you take it at that sort of lick, that much faster,' he said, 'it actually sounds slower.'

She heard him play it later that night, sitting upstairs in her room with the door open while the music floated up from the drawing room. Even though the tempo was as he had described, much quicker in the left hand than normal, there was nothing at all earth-bound about his interpretation. As the notes of the heavenly music drifted up from the room below, Grace closed her eyes and yet could see every tree in the park and the waters of the lake bathed in the moon's pale glow, below a clear sky full of the light in which she and Henry used to spot their stars.

The days grew shorter, from October into November, and as they did the time Lord Lydiard spent with Grace grew longer. Lord Lydiard would attend to all his business in the mornings, and then after they had lunched together, three or four times a week, he would sit and talk while Grace sewed or did her *petit-point*. Sometimes as the fire reddened he would fall comfortably asleep in the armchair, one long arm draped over the side, and one long leg hooked up on the fender. As the weather worsened and the October winds and rains were followed by the first November frosts, since he didn't hunt there was little reason for him to venture outside, so after lunch he would set out one of the children's more advanced jigsaw puzzles which he generally completed in about the time it took him to sort out the pieces. When he had exhausted all the best puzzles, he then invited Grace to play some chess, an invitation Grace was happy to accept because she had now become enthralled with the game. As the light faded outside and the winter wind rattled the windows on those cold November afternoons, the two of them could be found locked together in a series of long and silent battles.

As November grew older, Henry and Lottie began

to come to dinner regularly, at least once or generally twice a week. They were very much a couple now, no longer the two shy people who had walked down the aisle less than three months ago, Lottie loving and attentive to Henry's needs without ever fussing him, and Henry teasing her the way lovers do, while searching for her hand to hold under the table. The conversation usually centred around the history of the house and the family, instigated and prompted by Grace who had found that the more she learned about the house the more she understood the occupants. As they all talked, Lottie and Grace asking the questions and Henry and his father supplying the answers, it seemed a very natural thing for all four of them to be doing, sitting round a dining table discussing the chronology of a family of which they were all part, the four of them, two couples, Henry and Lottie and Lord Lydiard and Grace.

'My great-grandfather was so reclusive he built a warren of tunnels under Keston so that he could avoid seeing anyone, particularly the servants,' Henry told them. 'Haven't you ever been down there, Nan? If you haven't, you must get Papa to show you.'

'My father wasn't much better,' Lord Lydiard added. 'He used to dismiss any servant who as much as dared to show his or her face to him.'

'I remember standing pressed to the wall once when he caught two of us upstairs, when I was first working here,' Grace said. 'I remember being terrified.'

'We were all terrified,' Lord Lydiard continued. 'You know, he wouldn't have anyone precede him into the library before dinner in case there'd be any footmarks on the hall carpet which weren't his.'

'I'd forgotten that,' Henry said. 'Didn't he also use to make the maids rebrush the carpets after you'd all gone in to dine?'

'Every evening.' Lord Lydiard sighed. 'Made them repolish all the door handles as well, in case there were any fingermarks.'

The more they talked the more Grace realized how

spartan life had been at Keston not only downstairs but upstairs. It seemed her predecessor in the nursery had been such a stickler for fresh air that once he had grown up Lord Lydiard's father had spent the rest of his days sleeping in his overcoat, summer and winter, so determined was he never to wake up cold again.

'It didn't matter how many fires were lit in winter, when there was a heavy frost even the water beside your bed would freeze,' Henry said.

'I'm glad there's central heating now,' Lottie sighed. 'I hate being cold.'

'So I notice,' Henry replied. 'You know your sister sleeps with the window shut, Nan, don't you?'

'So do I,' said Grace quickly.

'No point in opening a window in this place,' Lord Lydiard said. 'So many draughts you'd be blown out of bed.'

Sometimes the talk would go back to the Lydiards' respective childhoods at Keston, and while Henry confessed to enjoying practically all of his, it seemed to Grace his father had been a very lonely child, despite the fact he had a younger brother.

'Trouble was no one seemed to have the remotest interest in us as children other than teaching us to kill things,' Lord Lydiard related. 'My brother didn't mind because he couldn't wait to go hunting and or out shooting but I wasn't at all keen.'

'Papa got beaten by his uncle once,' Henry told Grace. 'When he was eight he was sent home in disgrace because he got in a rage when a hare was shot in front of him.'

'Absolutely right, Henry,' his father agreed. 'And being beaten didn't change my mind about killing things, even though they still made me hunt and shoot. Out hunting I used to ride the foxes off when everyone was coffee-housing and with a gun it was even easier. I just used to fire into the ground or just deliberately miss everything.'

'But you were ready to go to war,' Grace said. 'If you remember you were very keen to join up as soon as the war broke out.'

515

'Touch and go, Nanny,' Lord Lydiard replied. 'Very much touch and go. Thing was I was like everyone else at the time, we were all caught up in the outrage over Belgium. But then you see if I'd known then – if we'd all known then what we know now, what a lot of well informed people were saying – no. No, I don't think I'd have had quite such a mad rush to the head. I'd say that goes for a lot of people.'

Lord Lydiard seemed to think quite differently from most of his contemporaries. From what Grace learned during those comfortable discussions it appeared that most people with grand houses and large estates were bent on returning to the style of living they had enjoyed in the days before 1914. Lord Lydiard considered that those days had gone for ever, and he for one was glad of it.

'You understand that before the war, Nanny,' he explained over one of their nursery lunches while a day of icy rain swept over the leafless parkland, 'life in these big houses was to all intents and purposes inviolate. But then along came the war and things changed. At least I think they have. In fact I'm sure of it. It would be a nonsense if they hadn't. Take the men who were in service before the war, the ones who survived. Last thing they want to do is to go back into service. There were all these duties before, do you see. People were brought up on them, serving your lord and master, your elders and betters, your king and country. The word *service*, well – well, it was like an unalienable right. Something a sort of person did which of course is a complete nonsense. The men who came through the war, they have to have been fighting for something, and I don't think it was the Treaty of Versailles, not a bit of it. Perhaps at the back of it what they were really fighting for was a better country, a better life. They won't like it if it's denied them, if things don't improve from where they were before the war. The changes are being rung and if we're to survive, any of us, we have to listen.'

'You could create employment here,' Grace said. 'Not just domestic employment.'

516

'Such as?' Lord Lydiard wondered. 'Any bright ideas? Because all this taxation's taking its toll.'

'The other night Henry said something about using itinerant sawmen,' Grace said, 'to cut up the fallen timber, and also to do the thinning out.'

'Absolutely right,' Lord Lydiard agreed. 'The way it's always been done, although that's not to say it's the best way. In fact because that's the way it's always been done it's bound to be the opposite.'

'So why don't you have a sawmill instead?' Grace asked. 'When I took young John over to the birthday party at Gilford House, Nanny Gilford told me they'd found employment for a lot of men who'd have been laid off otherwise by starting a sawmill, and making furniture.'

'Go on, Nanny,' Lord Lydiard said, visibly intrigued.

'The point seems to be that as far as timber goes someone else cuts it and takes it away. You're only selling it on for someone else to use. You could do the same thing here as they've done at Gilford House. The men you were thinking you'd have to lay off could work the sawmill, you could employ a master joiner to apprentice people, and you could start making furniture.'

'Good thinking, Nanny,' Lord Lydiard said. 'Blow it, why couldn't I have thought of that? That is really very bright, very bright indeed.'

'Good,' Grace said. 'And let me have that jumper you're wearing some time; it needs a darn.'

Grace's idea was put to the dining room committee that night where it was immediately sanctioned by Henry who recommended putting the plan into action as soon as possible.

'That's just the sort of direction in which we should be heading, Papa,' he said. 'If we have to rely on just the agricultural rents I'm afraid we'd find it a bit of a struggle.'

'If you're looking for things to do here, I can think of some,' Lottie said, determined not to be outdone. 'You could start a stud and breed horses, like your friends the Mainwarings at Nylands, Henry.'

'Not crossbreds, surely,' Henry frowned. 'There's not the demand for remounts now, not now the army's getting mechanized.'

'I wasn't thinking of the army, Henry,' Lottie said. 'Why not thoroughbreds? Who knows, you might even breed a Derby winner.'

'We might, you mean,' Henry said. 'Being married to me makes you one of us, Lottie.'

'What about that idea you always had for a motor racing circuit, Henry?' Grace asked. 'You had even ear-marked that land on the north side of Keston which you said had been fallow for years, do you remember?'

'Yes of course I do, Nan,' Henry replied. 'But frankly since the war, since losing my sight, I'd sort of put that to one side really.'

'Why?' Lottie asked her husband. 'You've got a perfectly good pair of eyes now you've got me.'

'All right,' Henry decided after some thought. 'Why not? What do you think, Papa? They say motor racing's going to be quite a thing. Could produce some useful income.'

'You – sorry, we –' Lottie smiled, correcting herself '– we could also have a racecourse on that side of the estate. Down at the bottom of Hanker's Valley. You could put the motor circuit in the middle and run a racetrack outside.'

'Fiendish,' Henry said with a laugh. 'What would we do without Nan and her sister, Papa?'

'You tell me, Henry,' Lord Lydiard said. 'We'd probably be up a what-do-you-call-it tree.'

'A gum tree?'

'Precisely. We'd be well and truly up it.'

Lord Lydiard looked at Grace then, and kept looking at her, something which he rarely did with anyone, even with members of his family. It wasn't like the absent-minded stare she had seen him give before. To Grace it was as if he was seeing her properly for the first time, as someone other perhaps than his children's nanny.

*   *   *

Or had she imagined it, Grace wondered as she lay in bed that night, unable to sleep. Perhaps it was just wishful thinking on her part, fuelled by her desire to find a reason not to leave Keston. If Lord Lydiard had seen her as herself, as Grace Merrill rather than as Nanny Lydiard, if he had suddenly found himself attracted to her as a woman, then anything was possible. After all, his son and heir had fallen in love with and married her sister, so surely it wasn't altogether out of the question to imagine that in turn the father could fall in love with Grace? He had been spending a lot of time in her company, time which he had chosen to spend with her of his own volition, not by any invitation extended by Grace, and he had begun to include her more and more within the family circle where she found herself relaxed and at her ease. *Just suppose,* Grace thought as she tossed and turned in bed, *just for one moment suppose it were true, suppose Lord Lydiard was attracted by her, suppose she was to take that look to mean that he was falling in love with her, just suppose. And suppose that she was falling in love with him? It was perfectly possible. He intrigued and fascinated her, he was highly intelligent and sensitive, and he was attractive, very much so, with his sad serious face, his perpetual look of bewildered fascination, his natural elegance and his little-boy-lost quality, the absolute opposite to the raffish, passionate and mercurial Brake, which was why Grace thought she well could love him, because there would be no conflict with Brake's memory, and no comparison with him as a man.*

There would be difficulties, of course. Most important there was Lottie to consider. If this was true, if what Grace was imagining came true, it would mean stepping in front of Lottie, stepping over her and taking her place as the next Lady Lydiard. Grace turned over in her bed again, pulling the covers up around her pillows and down around her head so that she was practically buried in her bedclothes. *What would Lottie do?* Grace wondered. *What would she say? Lottie wouldn't mind, of course not. Lottie would welcome Grace into the family because that was the sort of person Lottie was, mindful not of her own position but only of the*

*happiness of others. Lottie would understand, she'd probably
even think it was Grace's just reward for all the hardship she
had endured because of the reversal of their family's fortunes,
for the sacrifice Grace had been forced to make, the sacrifice of
her life as an artist. In fact if there were any doubts in any of
the family's minds, it would be Lottie who would dispel them.*

By the time she shook herself back to sense, Grace
had seen herself married to Lord Lydiard and bringing
up her own children at Keston, two boys and a beautiful
little girl who looked half like her and half like the former
Lady Lydiard. The boys were like their father and their
uncle, they were tall and graceful and became very famous
in their lifetimes, one as a philanthropist and the other
as the prime minister of England, while their daughter,
also tall like her father but with Grace's gift and Grace's
determination, became the most famous woman landscape
artist in the nineteen forties before marrying the son of an
American senator. Between them the Lydiards had turned
Keston into a model estate run on cooperative lines, as well
as a house famous for its gatherings of the intelligentsia. As
she stood wrapped up in her warm dressing-gown waiting
for the milk to heat in her little kitchen, Grace smiled at
the absurdity of her fantasy and put any further thoughts
of such things from her head. Lord Lydiard had simply
looked at her over dinner, once, probably because he
had never before really considered the possibility of a
woman's having a constructive idea, but instead Grace
had allowed herself to believe there was a possibility that
the look meant her employer was falling in love with her.
If it wasn't so pathetic it would be funny, Grace thought
as she made herself a mug of hot milk and honey which
she carried back to drink sitting by the embers of that
evening's fire. She smiled again when she remembered
she had even recalled Lord Lydiard's saying that she might
as well be his children's mother, again taking the statement
not at its face value but to mean that Grace might *as well*
be his children's mother. In other words, he had intended
it as a hint, as a half-hidden proposal, as the precursor of
the look he had given her over dinner.

Now she was up and fully awake Grace could see quite how ludicrous her fantasy had been. Lottie marrying Henry was one thing, but Lord Lydiard marrying his children's nanny was another thing altogether. She had imagined it all, and she had done so because that is what she wanted to imagine, she decided as she prepared to go back to bed. She had allowed herself to fantasize in order to put off the moment of decision regarding her future. Seduced by the warmth of the family dinners, and by Lord Lydiard's apparently sympathetic attention, Grace decided she had allowed herself to lose the one thing she had always been so proud of, her sense of reality, of what was possible, practical and true, allowing herself to take one odd look and one chance remark to mean that Lord Lydiard had fallen in love with her, so that with one absurdly envisioned bound she was free.

Of course he hadn't, Grace told herself, making sure the fireguard was in place before she turned off the sitting room light. Without a wife and now that his children had gone, her employer was lonely, and what better way to ease the pain of loneliness than to wander upstairs and talk to Nanny? In fact what better way to escape from reality than to regress back into one's own childhood, sitting eating the comforting food you used to eat and idly playing the games you used to play and solving the puzzles you used to solve. *There there, let Nanny see it, show it to Nanny and Nanny will kiss it all better.*

When I am old enough, Henry had told her, *when I'm grown up, Nanny, I'm going to marry you.*

Just as so many little boys told their mothers and their nannies, just as Lord Lydiard had probably told his mother and his old nanny, Grace thought, as she went to turn off the light. Everything she had thought as she had lain in bed, everything she had imagined in that twilight zone between sleep and consciousness was nonsense, and Grace found herself blushing when she realized quite what a nonsense it was. The hot milk and honey would make her sleep now, and when she woke up after a good night's rest all such thoughts would have gone from her tired head.

521

Then she heard him. At first she thought it was just a floorboard on the landing creaking the way they did at night-time, but then as she stood by the door she distinctly heard footfalls coming along the corridor from his bedroom at the end. Grace held her breath, realizing too late that her light was on, and that if she turned it off now it would draw attention to the fact she was up and awake. The steps got nearer, then when they reached her door they stopped. He was there, the other side of her door, probably no more than a foot away from where Grace was standing. Her heart was thumping in her chest now, louder and louder it seemed the longer she held her breath, loud enough surely for him to hear, and had he? Grace heard another floorboard creak, nearer her door, and now she could sense exactly how close he was, he was right by the door and she knew his hand was there by the handle. And still she held her breath. All she had to do was open the door, that was all she had to do. She could put her hand down to the handle, turn it, open the door, and once the door was open she would know once and for all.

'Oh, it's you! It's you, Lord Lydiard. You gave me such a fright.'

'I'm sorry. I saw your light on, and I wondered if you were all right.'

'I couldn't sleep.'

'No. No, neither could I.'

'I had to get up and make myself something. A hot milk and honey.'

'I was just on my way downstairs, for the same sort of thing. Except I was going to have a glass of brandy.'

'Would you like me to make you what I had? Hot milk and honey instead? Brandy won't be very good for you at this time of night.'

'I'd like that very much.'

She had her hair down, her long white hair which had been so black and shiny was down below her shoulders held back by a blue ribbon. She had grown used to her hair being white and thought that in some ways it looked even better. Lottie said it did, and so did Harriet, but no man had remarked on it yet, not even Lord Lydiard.

Now he did.

'I've never seen you with your hair down before. It looks wonderful. It looks even more beautiful like that, it's such a wonderful pure snow white, if you don't mind me saying. In an odd way it makes you look quite absurdly young.'

'I used to think about dyeing it, after it happened. I was so appalled I thought I'd have to dye it.'

'Like you did mine, remember?'

'Yes of course I remember. You were like a small boy again. You were just like Henry.'

'I wish I was a small boy again sometimes. Particularly at times like this.'

'Why times like this?'

'Times one has to make decisions. Children have everything decided for them, and while sometimes it can be frustrating, always being so dependent on grown-ups, at other times there can be no greater freedom.'

'Drink your milk up before it gets cold.'

'I don't think this is going to make me sleep any better, Nanny.'

'Drink it and see. What else do you suggest?'

'I think perhaps the only thing that might make us both sleep again is if I tell you what's on my mind. What's been on my mind now for some time. Ever since – well, I'm not quite sure when. Do you remember I said to you once that you might as well be the children's mother?'

'Yes. As a matter of fact I was thinking about that when I couldn't sleep.'

'Did you think about anything else?'

'I thought about how you looked at me tonight.'

'I'm sorry about that. It was very rude. I couldn't help it.'

'It seemed to me you were looking at me for the very first time.'

'I was. I was seeing you for the very first time. You

won't remember, but when you first started I used to find myself staring at you.'

'I remember.'

'You do? Do you know why? I used to say you reminded me of someone. But it isn't that. It wasn't that. You see, this depends on whether you believe in the possibility of love at first sight.'

'I don't know what that means.'

'Neither do I. But they say, people do, that what it is is we've all been here before, do you see. And we come back again and again, this is what they say, until you meet the one person you truly love, because that person is the other half of the couple you both once were. This is the theory. And when you find each other, each half of the couple finally reunited do you see, that is love at first sight, that explains the *coup de foudre*. And once you are both found that is it. You never come back again.'

'What about Brake?'

'Brake died. You didn't marry Brake. You were in love, but you weren't the two sides of a whole.'

'It seemed as though we were.'

'It doesn't mean you didn't love each other, it just means you were two people still travelling.'

'But not any more.'

'No. Well no not for me, certainly. But you must tell me what you feel. Although you mustn't think that because it didn't happen the first time we saw each other that it isn't true. *First sight* doesn't have to be the first time two people see each other. It's the first time they see each other properly.'

'Like tonight.'

'Yes.'

'Then I think perhaps I shan't come back again.'

'I know I shan't.'

He kissed her then. She hardly knew it was happening. Or how it happened. Or that it was in fact a kiss. All she knew was it was dark and it was soft and this was love. There seemed to be sounds of the ocean, whispers in the dark night, like tall grass being gently blown and the sea breaking somewhere on a distant shore, and in the darkness she felt madness and joy, terror and delight, strength and kindness, the dark and the light. Then she saw his eyes, his eyes gazing into hers and his mouth on her mouth, his hands on her and her arms round him, sweet love and passion, his body and hers, a sigh, a long gasping sigh and a roll down long soft green lawns, down and down to where the water was, down into the sunshine where they both lay. And then came the tears.

She didn't feel the tears, she didn't sense them arrive, she just saw them fall as if from someone else's eyes. They fell on her hand which was just there above the handle of the unopened door. For a moment she just watched the tears fall and wondered *why, why am I crying when it was so beautiful, why should I cry?* until she realized why she was crying and it wasn't because it was so beautiful, it was because the door had stayed closed, the door had never been opened, he hadn't opened it and neither had she and she was crying now because of that and because she could hear his feet going away down the corridor, away from her room with the unopened door.

She stood away from the door, staring at it and wondering, wondering why she hadn't turned the handle and why he hadn't when they had both been standing there not a foot from each other, when they had both had the same thought because she knew they had, she was certain of it, quite and utterly certain, just the way she had been the night she had seen Brake's death. And then as she stood looking there was a knock on the door, two knocks, he was there outside and he was knocking on the door to come in.

Grace opened it and saw him, standing back from the door now, dressed in a dark red quilted dressing-gown, his hair for once unbrushed and tousled, making him look little-boy-lost even more.

'It's you,' she said. 'You gave me a bit of a fright.'

'I'm sorry,' he replied, frowning and staring past her. 'I saw your light on, and so I thought you were up.

I didn't mean to frighten you.'

'It's just that I couldn't sleep.'

'Really? No. No, neither could I. It was probably something we ate at dinner.'

'I got up to make myself something. A hot milk and honey.'

'I was just on my way downstairs, for the same sort of thing. Except I was going to have a brandy. Except what I'd actually like is exactly that. A hot milk and honey. Just like old nanny used to make.'

Grace hesitated then smiled.

'Would you like this nanny to make you one?' she asked.

'I'd like that very much,' he replied.

She stood aside and he came in, going and standing at once by the last of the fire, facing it, back to Grace, who left the door half open, even though there was no one else in the main part of the house.

He said nothing while he stood by the fire, while she heated up the milk in a nursery mug and spooned in the honey. She took it to him by the fire and he took it from her, still staring down into the dying glow of the coals.

'Do you want to sit down?' Grace asked.

'No,' he replied. 'No I'm really fine, thank you. And this is lovely, Nanny. Just what I wanted.'

He stood sipping his hot drink, both hands on the mug, staring into the fire, then up at Brake's painting. He said nothing, he just looked at it for a long long time, then he turned round and finished his drink facing the half-open door. While he did, Grace stood where and how she used to stand when young John crawled out of his bed and demanded a nightcap, by the kitchen door with her hands folded in front of her.

'That was very nice, Nanny, thank you,' Lord Lydiard said, putting his mug behind him on the mantelpiece. 'That was exactly what I needed.'

'You'll sleep like a top now,' Grace replied. 'I always do.'

'Absolutely,' Lord Lydiard agreed. 'Good night.'

He went to the door, hands behind his back, never

once looking at her. Then just before he left he turned and faced her.

'By the way,' he said. 'I like your hair like that. Down. I always liked Nanny's hair like that.'

When he was gone, Grace didn't go back to bed. Instead she sat down by the fire where first she thought, then she smiled, and finally she laughed. And when she had stopped laughing she went to her desk and took out some cuttings she had taken from various magazines and newspapers. She took them out and spread them on the table beside her because she had now made her mind up, and because her mind had been made up for her. If she was to have any sort of life she must leave Keston and she must go now, and where she would go would be determined by which of the cuttings she was spreading out before her she chose.

They were all of places abroad, places to travel to, places particularly for painters. She would take down her paints and her pencils, her pens, her charcoal sticks, her inks, her pastels and her brushes, and once she was away from Keston, once she was out of its shadows and the shadow of Brake, she would paint again because she knew she would be able to do so because she would be herself again and not Nanny Lydiard. She would set her easel up here, in this place in Italy, in the countryside that was called Tuscany. She would take the little money she had saved and she would find somewhere cheap to live, just as it said you could in the article she was reading, because the article said Italy was so cheap you could live there for next to nothing. She wouldn't make any plans, since there was absolutely no need to make any plans. With a companion, or perhaps even by herself she would travel to this part of Italy where the light was so wonderful and where life was so cheap and she would live there and paint there. Then if she couldn't make her living and it would only be a simple living selling her paintings then and only then might she think of coming back to England and if she did, then and only then would she look for another position as a nanny.

She would go to the hills outside Florence, somewhere in the foot of the Apennines, where the sun would be warm on her back, and the breezes from the hills would be cool on her face. As she fell asleep her box of paints was already open, her easel was set up and she was already painting.

TWENTY-SEVEN

The next morning the four of them were driven in the Rolls into Aylesbury to do their Christmas shopping, Henry and Lottie, Lord Lydiard and Grace.

'Since it's our first Christmas together, Grace,' Lottie said, as they drove through a landscape where the frost had now disappeared under a blanket of rain, 'and since both Harriet and John have been away from home for the first time, we all decided that it's going to be a family-only Christmas.'

'Just the family,' Henry said. 'No one else.'

'I think that's very sensible,' Grace replied, reminding herself to telephone her mother when they got back to see if the invitation she had half-heartedly extended to Grace was still open. Her mother had obviously been hoping for a summons to Keston which was now not going to be forthcoming.

'We're having people in on Christmas Eve,' Lottie continued, 'and I gather there's to be the usual drinks party at the Hall on Boxing Day morning—'

'Smaller than usual,' Henry said. 'No Jabberwocks.'

Lottie laughed delightedly and took Henry's hand.

'But Christmas Day is going to be just family,' she said. 'Only us. And all the girls are to wear red. Do you have a red dress?'

'No I don't as a matter of fact,' Grace said after a moment, before she had thought of the best and politest way of refusing the invitation. 'Not one that's smart enough anyway.'

'Don't worry,' Lottie told her. 'We'll buy you something in Aylesbury.'

'If anyone's buying anything that person will be me,' Grace corrected her sister, back-pedalling and still looking for the best way out. Being included in the family Christmas lunch would only make it even harder to wrench herself away. Making a decision at night-time as you're tucking yourself back up in bed is one thing, Grace was discovering, while finding the courage in the cool light of day and with the people she loved all around was quite another. 'Let's discuss it when we get into town,' she said to Lottie. 'I wasn't quite prepared for this.'

'I don't see what the difficulty is,' Lottie said as they walked together down the High Street, Henry having taken his father to help him find a present for his wife. 'You can't really want to go to Mother's and she certainly won't really want to have you.'

'Who's going to do the washing up otherwise?' Grace asked, poker-faced. 'Who's going to make sure the vegetables don't boil over?'

'But you're one of the family, Grace,' Lottie insisted. 'We all want you here, all of us. Me particularly.'

'Why you particularly?'

'I'll tell if you come to the party.'

'And if I don't?'

'I won't tell you.'

'Not ever?'

'Probably not.' Lottie smiled at Grace, and then took her arm confidentially. 'Besides,' she said, 'it's not only me who wants you there.'

That was enough for Grace, enough to rouse the curiosity she hoped she had put to bed the night before, so she allowed her sister to take her shopping for a dress, and finally she allowed Lottie to pay for it, not just to forestall

Lottie's insistences, but more because the dress they both liked best would have made too big a hole in the monies Grace now intended to spend on her prospective Italian adventure. It was an evening gown made from the now fashionable georgette, a semi-transparent crepe made in this instance of twisted silk in a colour described by the salesgirl as Nivelle red, a colour which Grace had never seen on a palette anywhere. The dress was cut with an almost horizontal *décolletage*, with the bodice held in place by simple shoulder straps which gave a soft appearance to the upper part while below the skirt was cut much more severely, almost like a uniform.

'It's too boyish,' Grace said, turning round in front of the mirror, only for Lottie immediately to pooh-pooh her.

'On the contrary, Grace,' she said, 'it makes you look even more feminine and even younger.'

Grace turned herself round one last time in front of the mirror and then stood back. Lottie was right, the dress was very flattering and the colour was rich and deep against Grace's pale and still flawless complexion.

'You look wonderful, Grace,' her sister said again. 'Looking like that, you could be just anybody.'

The rain had stopped and Christmas Day was fine and bright. After glasses of champagne in the library the family went in to lunch. Henry sat opposite his father, Lottie next to her father-in-law, Harriet next to her elder brother, John the other side next to Lottie, and Grace between Harriet and Lord Lydiard. They ate Christmas goose with potato stuffing and drank claret so old it had gone red-brown.

'I think this year we should all make a wish,' Lord Lydiard said when the Christmas pudding was produced. 'And not John who always gets all the luck because he somehow always gets all the threepences.'

Everyone put their hands on the knife, closed their eyes and wished in silence. For a moment Grace almost found herself wishing the unwishable and then instead she wished for everyone to be happy.

531

When the port was passed, Henry tapped on the table with the handle of a knife.

'Speech,' he said. 'Let's make Father make a speech.'

'I have nothing to say,' Lord Lydiard said. 'When everyone's as happy as this, there's nothing really left to say.'

'That's an extremely good speech,' his younger son said. 'That's exactly what a speech should be. That short.'

'Somebody else then,' Henry insisted. 'Unlike my brother I happen to like speeches.'

'I have something to say,' Grace said, 'although I'm not sure this is the time to say it.'

'I have something to say as well,' Lottie announced immediately her sister had finished. 'The difference being I'm sure this is the time to say it.'

'In that case, after you,' Grace said. 'Sail before steam.'

Young John found this particularly funny and laughed uproariously. He had such an infectious laugh, and because everyone was in such a festive mood, they were all soon laughing at absolutely nothing in particular. Henry tapped his knife on the table again to bring the party to order.

'Do listen everyone,' he said, 'seriously. Lottie does have something to say.'

'This is a special Christmas present for everybody, I hope,' Lottie said, looking round the assembled company. 'For Henry, for you Lord Lydiard, except you both already know, but Harriet doesn't, and neither does young John here, and nor does my sister. I'm going to have a baby.'

For a moment no one said anything. They all looked at Lottie in their various ways, Lord Lydiard with a happily bewildered frown, Harriet wide-eyed, young John with an intense stare, and Grace with a smile which at present was firmly fixed.

'Hooray!' young John cried. 'Three cheers! Hip hip hooray!'

'I knew of course,' Henry said. 'Obviously.'

'Oh, congratulations, Lottie,' Harriet said, kissing her

sister-in-law and then getting up to hug her brother. 'And you, Henry darling. Congratulations. Except oh heck! This means I'm going to be an aunt!'

Harriet fell back on to her chair in peals of laughter.

'And I'm going to be an uncle!' John carolled, joining in the merriment.

'And you're going to be an aunt as well, Nanny,' Lottie said to Grace with a smile. 'I'll bet you never thought of that.'

'No, as a matter of fact, Lottie, you know I didn't?' Grace replied. 'That's one thing that I left out of my considerations.'

'What was that?' Lottie asked. 'I missed that.'

'Well, well, well,' Lord Lydiard said, putting down his glass. 'Well, well, well.'

'It doesn't matter,' Grace replied to her sister, wishing all the while her smile would unfix. 'This is absolutely so, is it?'

'According to Dr Granger,' Lottie said, 'and he should know if anyone should. Babies are his speciality.'

'Well, well, well,' Lord Lydiard said again, pushing his glasses back on to the bridge of his nose while he slowly shook his head. 'This is quite a thing really. The first grandchild. What about that, Nanny?'

'Yes, what about that, Nanny?' Lottie smiled, looking again at Grace who at last had managed to turn her smile into something more convincing. 'Isn't it wonderful?'

'I don't know what to think,' Grace replied with complete truth. 'Except that I'm thrilled and delighted for you.'

'Typical.' Lottie sighed. 'You're always thinking of everyone else and never of yourself. I want you to be thrilled and delighted as well, because this also involves you, silly! I can't tell you how afraid I was that I mightn't have a baby for ages and it would be too late. That you'd leave here and go somewhere else because there wasn't anything to do.'

'Oh absolutely,' Lord Lydiard agreed. 'That goes for all of us.'

'Absolutely,' Harriet said.

'Gosh yes,' added young John.

'Really,' Lottie said, as Grace continued to stare at her, 'honestly I was convinced you'd take another position with another family, and I nearly drove Henry mad. I just had this feeling. You know how often we used to be practically able to tell each other what we were doing in advance before we'd done it? It was just like that. I even saw you abroad somewhere, living by yourself and painting. I was absolutely convinced we'd lose you.'

'She was,' Henry added. 'As soon as Dr Granger told her she was anticipating, all that really concerned her was that you'd go. I told her it was nonsense. I told her you'd never leave Keston.'

'Well of course she wouldn't,' Lord Lydiard said. 'I wouldn't have heard of it.'

'You should have said something before, Lottie,' Grace murmured, still trying to order her thoughts. 'Talk about a surprise.'

'You know what the oracle says,' Lord Lydiard said. 'Someone surprised is a man half beaten. Or in this case, a nanny.'

'I was only absolutely certain the day before we all went shopping,' Lottie said, laughing. 'The last time I saw Dr Granger. So I thought by then I should wait until Christmas.'

'Happy Christmas, Nanny,' Henry said, finding his glass and raising it. 'To Nanny.'

'To Nanny,' they all agreed, turning to Grace and raising their glasses. 'Nanny Lydiard.'

'Nanny Lydiard,' young John echoed. 'Three cheers for Nanny Lydiard!'

'Hip hip hip hooray,' said his father. 'And three cheers for Nanny's sister.'

'It's no good,' said Lottie. 'You know we couldn't do without you.'

There they all were, all the people that she loved, all except Brake. Yet it was Brake who answered the question for her, it was Brake who showed Grace the way. *Love is many things*, he had told her the night before he finally left for France. *It's all sorts of things, but most of all the love you give is the love you get to keep.*

Before Henry and she returned to the Dower House, Lottie insisted Grace take her up to the empty nursery. It was almost midnight, and there was a full moon which shone so brightly there was no need for any artificial light.

'It's extraordinary,' Lottie said, 'this whole place. It feels like home, like your room did at home.'

'It feels as if everyone is still up here,' Grace said, looking round the deserted suite of rooms. 'I can hear all their voices, Henry, Harriet and John.'

'Soon there'll be another voice,' Lottie said. 'Another brand new voice.'

'I think it's a very good thing you're coming back to live here,' Grace said. 'I think this is a wonderful place to bring up children.'

'I wonder how many,' Lottie mused, walking through from the main nursery into what had been John's room, and Harriet's before John, and Henry's before Harriet, the little room on the south side which was where the babies slept, where they'd always slept, ever since there had first been a nursery. 'How many,' Lottie wondered again, in a whisper, 'and who first? A little boy or a little girl?'

'*Where do you come from, baby dear*,' Grace said, picking up the patchwork blanket she had made for John's cradle and redoubling it, although it was already perfectly folded. '*Out of the everywhere into the here. Where did you get your eyes so blue? Out of the sky as I came through.*'

'I think that's sweet,' Lottie said. 'Absolutely charming. What is it?'

'It's something Lady Lydiard always used to say to John,' Grace replied as she replaced the little blanket at the foot of the cot, and then smiled. 'The last Lady Lydiard.'

'This is such a lovely room,' Lottie said, looking round. 'I just love it. It's a happy room. And when my baby is born—'

'God willing,' Grace said.

'When my baby is born, God willing,' Lottie agreed, walking to the cot, 'I think we shall have the cot over here, in this corner.'

'Oh no,' Grace said at once. 'Where it is is much the best place for it, Lottie. Over there in the summer the baby will be in far too much sun.'

'Yes, Nanny.'

'Where it is is much the best place,' Grace assured her again. 'And besides, from where I sit out there –' Grace turned back and looked out into the main nursery which was filled with moonlight. 'From where I sit out there,' she said, 'if you move the cradle I won't be able to see the baby, and more important, the baby won't be able to see me.'

I am writing this in my usual state of anxiety, a state I always get myself into whenever the family is travelling. I try not to, but it is difficult. We both find it difficult. His lordship pretends he doesn't, but he never finishes up when they're travelling and spends most of his time outside, usually in his hothouses, pretending to see to his orchids. He always ends up here, ostensibly to see that I'm all right, but of course it's to stare out of my sitting room window because I have the best view of the drive. From my window you can see right down to the gatehouse and on to the road beyond. So that's where we stand, the two of us, at my window idly chatting, while really what we're doing is praying for everyone's safe arrival.

Ever since B was killed I've always known that of course prayer can only do so much and not everything. Perhaps prayer's for the people who pray rather than the people we pray for. I prayed for B and all to no avail, although history tells me otherwise. Thank heavens I have his wonderful painting still, although nowadays I have to put on my specs to look at him, to see him in the background through all that wonderful haze of red-brown smoke (how did he paint it?). There he is and his eyes follow me everywhere, just as they did when he was alive and we were together, eyes still so full of life. That was the strange thing. In spite of all the horror he saw, his eyes don't despair, which helps me not to either.

His lordship spends more time up here with me than he does downstairs nowadays. He loves to sit and look at all the photographs. We both do. We can sit here for hours going through the albums over and over again and we always find something fresh to say. He'll be up any minute now, and of course they'll be late which he can never understand, never accounting for the fact that where there was no traffic when we were young there's plenty of it now. Then when he's decided they're going to be late, down he'll go again, out on to the front steps with his fob-watch in his hand, just the way the old housekeepers used to do, waiting to greet everyone, although the moment they arrive he'll disappear off inside again as soon as he sees them.

I shall wait up here where I always wait. While I wait I sometimes talk to B as I sit in front of his painting at which I never tire of looking. I know I'm getting eccentric, but I don't care. Despite everything I've had a very happy life. I probably shouldn't say it, but what married woman could have had so many wonderful children and still be in possession of her senses? Yet there they all are, there are all my children on the table by the fireside in their silver picture frames. Their past is my present, and when I look at them I can hear their voices quite clearly, just the way they were, every one of them, every single one. I love the sound of children's voices, especially in the early morning, the sound of their half-whispered chatter and their secret laughter.

Now I must go down because I know they are here. Even without going to the window I know the first car has turned into the gate. That's an old nanny for you, we know things before they happen. It's a sixth sense we have. It's an instinct that grows with the job. So now I shall stop. His lordship will be on the steps and when they arrive the grown-ups will follow him through the double doors into the hall if he hasn't disappeared inside already.

But the children won't. The children will dash to the side of the house, to Nanny's Door. It's still called that. Then I shall hear their feet on the stairs, just like the old days, and the sound of them running then dashing down my corridor. The youngest ones will stay and have nursery lunch and then we'll all go for a walk around the lake. So much in this world of ours is changing, so many things, but not, thank heavens, children.

THE END

THE NIGHTINGALE SINGS

'A racy tale of love and heartbreak . . . This is a novel
rich in dramatic surprises, with a large cast of vivid
characters whose antics will have you frantically turning
the pages'
Daily Mail

When Cassie Rosse becomes the first woman to train an
English Derby winner with her home-bred horse *The
Nightingale*, she knows that she shares this success with her
dead love, Tyrone. For it was to his Irish family home of
Claremore that he brought Cassie as a young bride, and it is
from Claremore that Cassie has at last stormed home to win
a place in the history books.

But life will never be simple for Cassie, a woman who
stands alone in what is essentially a man's world. Unable to
escape from the long shadows cast by the early death of her
husband, yet torn between two extraordinary but very
different men, Cassie's integrity and her indomitable will to
win trigger a set of circumstances which quickly turn a
brilliant triumph into a nightmare. Suddenly it seems that
nothing can reverse the downward spiral of events
surrounding her famous horse and its future and Cassie is
forced to battle hard to keep Claremore, and with it her past
with Tyrone and everything that makes her life worthwhile.

Charlotte Bingham

Available in Bantam Paperback
0 553 40895 X

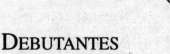

DEBUTANTES

A century ago marriage, and marriage alone, offered a
nicely brought-up girl escape from the domination of her
parents. Indeed it was the only path to freedom. That path
led her to a Season in London and, the ultimate goal,
Coming Out as a debutante. But along the way she had to
survive a terrifying few months, a make-or-break time in
which her family's hopes for her could only be fulfilled
through a proposal of marriage.

For Lady Emily Persse, Coming Out means leaving her
beloved Ireland, and its informalities, for England and its
stricter codes. For Portia Tradescant, released from the
boredom of life in the English countryside, it means trying
to get through the Season despite the best efforts of her
eccentric Aunt Tattie. For beautiful May Danby the Season
is an entree to a whole other life, worlds away from her
strict convent upbringing in Yorkshire.

Debutantes, Charlotte Bingham's delightful and stylish
new saga, centres around a single London Season in the
eighteen-nineties. But it is not just about the debutantes
themselves. It is as much about the women who launch
them, and the Society which supports their way of life. It is
also about the battle for power, privilege and money, fought,
not in the male tradition upon the battlefield, but in the
female tradition . . . in the ballroom.

Charlotte Bingham

Now available in Doubleday hardcover
0 385 40605 3

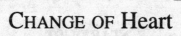

CHANGE OF Heart

When the parents of Fleur Fisher-Dilke discover that
their daughter is a musical prodigy they are dismayed
rather than elated. Richard Fisher-Dilke is set on
becoming a famous heart surgeon, so there is certainly
no time for him to develop anyone else's talent. As
for his wife, Amelia, the sum total of her ambition for
their offspring is to see her grow up quite normally,
imbued with all the usual social graces. So Richard
and Amelia do nothing to encourage Fleur's
outstanding musical abilities.

Even as they are congratulating themselves on having
successfully coped with the cuckoo in their nest by
forbidding Fleur the piano in favour of riding ponies, they
find she has merely taken to playing the violin, and with
even greater precocity. Little wonder that they finally
have to give way and allow their daughter's genius to
flourish.

But Richard and Amelia find their lives are changed for
ever as Fleur becomes famous beyond their imaginings.
Choices are made, but not forgiven, and it is only when
Fleur's own life takes a sudden, tragic turn and she meets
Frederick Jourdan, a fascinating and irreverent character
with a talent equal to her own, that Fleur has to face a
change of heart.

In her romantic new saga, Charlotte Bingham
exposes the reality that surrounds the lives of the truly
prodigious and explores the effect a child can have
on the adult world.

Charlotte Bingham

Available in Bantam Paperback
0 553 40497 0

STARDUST

Elizabeth Laurence is astoundingly beautiful. So beautiful she has never known what it is to have even a plain day. Used to the admiration of all, it seems that she will always be in charge of her own destiny. A star from the first minute she appears on celluloid, her future is certain, until she is cast opposite Jerome Didier in a hit play. Staggeringly handsome and tipped to become the leading actor of his generation, Jerome would appear to be made for Elizabeth.

But Jerome has fallen in love with the tousle-haired and carefree Pippa Nicholls, who is neither conventionally beautiful nor an actress and, much to Elizabeth's fury, he marries her. All is set for them to live happily ever after until the playwright, Oscar Greene, creates a part for Elizabeth which she intuitively recognizes is based on the character of Pippa - and Jerome is tragically deceived by the duplicity of his art.

Set against the glamorous world of theatre in the 1950s, **Stardust** is full of sharp insight into the destructive power of beauty: the stars who possess it, and those who live in their starlight. In Elizabeth, Jerome and Pippa, Charlotte Bingham has created three unforgettable characters, and **Stardust** is the triumphant achievement of a novelist at the height of her storytelling powers.

Charlotte Bingham

Available in Bantam Paperback
0 553 40171 8

TO HEAR
A NIGHTINGALE

'A delightful novel pulsating with vitality and deeply felt
emotions'
Sunday Express

Brought up in smalltown America, Cassie McGann's
childhood is one of misery and rejection. Fleeing to New
York she falls in love with handsome Irish racehorse
trainer, Tyrone Rosse, and when he marries her and takes
her back to his tumbledown mansion in Ireland, it looks
as if she has found happiness at last.

Passionately in love as she is, Cassie finds the all-male
world of horses and racing rather lonely. There is much
for her to learn, not least about the man she has married.
And when tragedy strikes, it seems that Cassie must once
again face rejection and lose her hard-won security.

THE BUSINESS

'The ideal beach read' *Homes and Gardens*

Meredith Browne came up the hard way, starting at the
bottom as a child actress. Max Kassov has always had
everything. Despite their different backgrounds the two
are very alike, and a mutual attraction deepens into a
passionate love affair. But Max betrays Meredith; a
vicious betrayal that leaves her humiliated and
determined to rise to even greater heights than he - if
only to exact retribution . . .

Set in the glittering world of showbusiness. **The Business**
is a powerful tale of romance and sex, of money and
corruption, and of brilliant talent used and abused.

Charlotte Bingham

Available in Bantam Paperback

A SELECTION OF FINE NOVELS
AVAILABLE FROM BANTAM BOOKS

THE PRICES SHOWN BELOW WERE CORRECT AT THE TIME OF GOING TO PRESS. HOWEVER TRANSWORLD PUBLISHERS RESERVE THE RIGHT TO SHOW NEW RETAIL PRICES ON COVERS WHICH MAY DIFFER FROM THOSE PREVIOUSLY ADVERTISED IN THE TEXT OR ELSEWHERE.

☐	50630 7	**DARK ANGEL**	*Sally Beauman*	£5.99
☐	17352 9	**DESTINY**	*Sally Beauman*	£5.99
☐	40727 9	**LOVERS AND LIARS**	*Sally Beauman*	£5.99
☐	40803 8	**SACRED AND PROFANE**	*Marcelle Bernstein*	£5.99
☐	40429 6	**AT HOME**	*Charlotte Bingham*	£3.99
☐	40427 X	**BELGRAVIA**	*Charlotte Bingham*	£3.99
☐	40432 6	**BY INVITATION**	*Charlotte Bingham*	£3.99
☐	40497 0	**CHANGE OF HEART**	*Charlotte Bingham*	£5.99
☐	40296 X	**IN SUNSHINE OR IN SHADOW**	*Charlotte Bingham*	£5.99
☐	40496 2	**NANNY**	*Charlotte Bingham*	£5.99
☐	40171 8	**STARDUST**	*Charlotte Bingham*	£4.99
☐	40163 7	**THE BUSINESS**	*Charlotte Bingham*	£5.99
☐	40895 X	**THE NIGHTINGALE SINGS**	*Charlotte Bingham*	£5.99
☐	17635 8	**TO HEAR A NIGHTINGALE**	*Charlotte Bingham*	£5.99
☐	40820 8	**LILY'S WAR**	*June Francis*	£4.99
☐	40996 4	**GOING HOME TO LIVERPOOL**	*June Francis*	£4.99
☐	40817 8	**A DISTANT DREAM**	*Margaret Graham*	£5.99
☐	17504 1	**DAZZLE**	*Judith Krantz*	£5.99
☐	17242 5	**I'LL TAKE MANHATTAN**	*Judith Krantz*	£5.99
☐	40730 9	**LOVERS**	*Judith Krantz*	£5.99
☐	17174 7	**MISTRAL'S DAUGHTER**	*Judith Krantz*	£5.99
☐	17389 8	**PRINCESS DAISY**	*Judith Krantz*	£5.99
☐	17505 X	**SCRUPLES TWO**	*Judith Krantz*	£4.99
☐	17503 3	**TILL WE MEET AGAIN**	*Judith Krantz*	£5.99
☐	40206 4	**FAST FRIENDS**	*Jill Mansell*	£4.99
☐	40938 7	**TWO'S COMPANY**	*Jill Mansell*	£5.99
☐	40947 6	**FOREIGN AFFAIRS**	*Patricia Scanlan*	£4.99
☐	40945 X	**FINISHING TOUCHES**	*Patricia Scanlan*	£5.99
☐	40483 0	**SINS OF THE MOTHER**	*Arabella Seymour*	£4.99

All Transworld titles are available by post from:

Book Service By Post, P.O. Box 29, Douglas, Isle of Man IM99 1BQ

Credit cards accepted. Please telephone 01624 675137, fax 01624 670923, Internet http://www.bookpost.co.uk or e-mail: bookshop@enterprise.net for details.

Free postage and packing in the UK. Overseas customers allow £1 per book (paperbacks) and £3 per book (hardbacks).